BOOK 1 *of the* UTOPIA FALLING SAGA

UTOPIA FALLING

A DARKNESS RISES

AWARD-WINNING AUTHOR

R.C. VIELEE

Cover designed by Miblart

Map by Inkarnate

eBook ISBN: 979-8-9881090-2-0

Hard Cover ISBN: 979-8-9881090-0-6

Trade ISBN: 979-8-9881090-1-3

Audiobook ISBN 979-8-9881090-3-7

Library of Congress Control Number: 2023914926

For rights and permissions, please contact:

Bobalou Publishing

C/O Robert Vielee

PO Box 127

Clarks Summit, PA 18411

r.c.vielee@outlook.com

For Louise, love always.

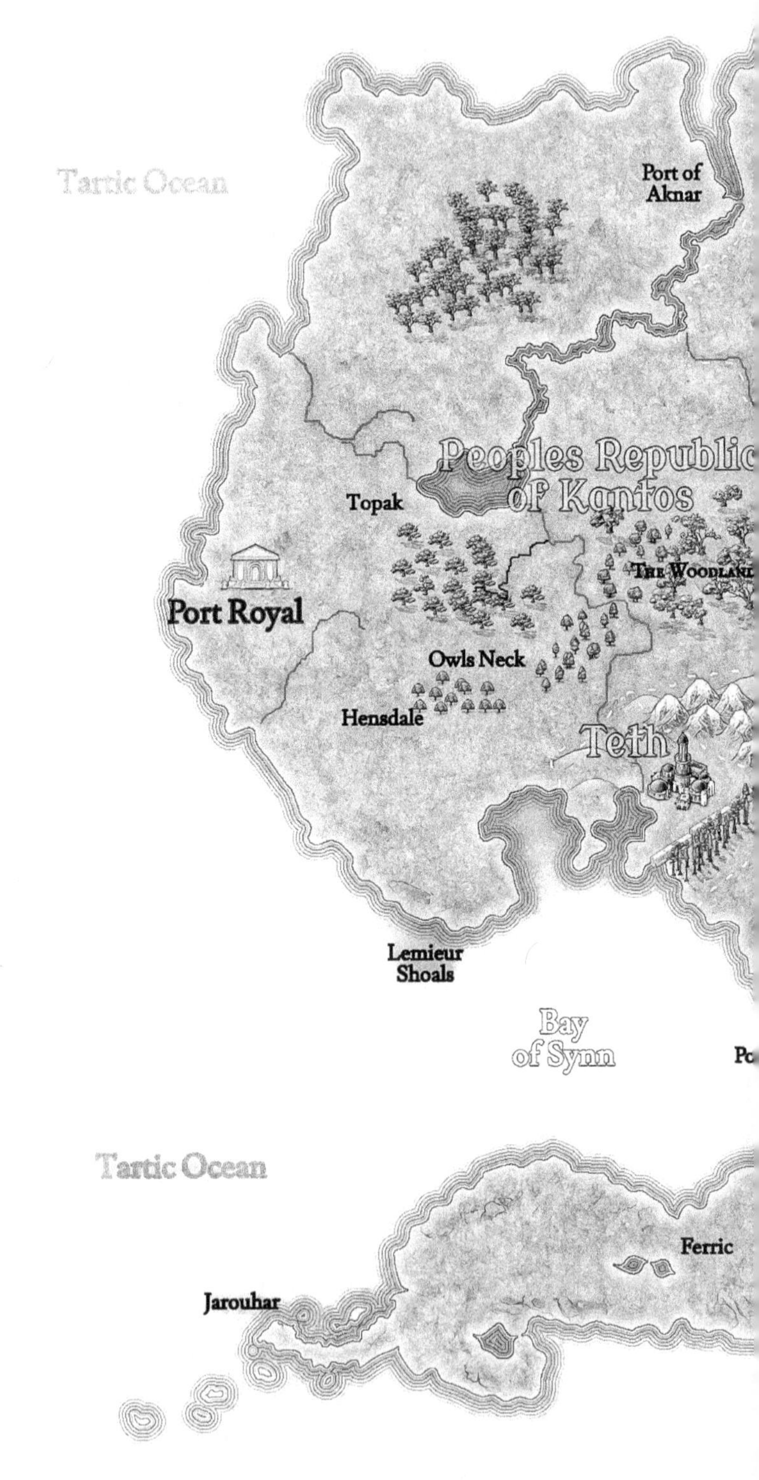

Tartic Ocean
Port of
Aknar
Peoples Republic
of Kantos
Topak
The Woodland
Port Royal
Owls Neck
Hensdale
Teth
Lemieur
Shoals
Bay
of Synn
Tartic Ocean
Ferric
Jarouhar

Tartic Ocean
Greenlin
Lake Louise
New Condordia
Dead Crow
Ciara Desert
Ishtar
Pfister Bay
Mehrlich
Hunters Point
Tandure
Penique Plains
Kingdom of Adelle
TARTICA

All I Ever Wanted

Hensdale: 27th Day of the Salmon Moon

Reyne

Reyne Brenton surveyed the husks of several calorie-rich alphen nuts. A light fog concealed much of the orchard from his view, but the young proprietor gave it little notice. He brushed his hand over a nut he'd knocked off a nearby branch. His nose captured the bitter aroma of the inner shell escaping the newly formed split in the outer casement. With the Salmon Moon waning, and the emergence of splitting husks, the crop would be ready to harvest in a few weeks—right on schedule. The processing center of his brain glossed over all of it. He operated by rote while thinking about his upcoming marriage.

"Hey! Rey, you out there?" Daedyn called out from the porch of the childhood home the brothers shared.

Reyne, appearing as a ghostly apparition in the fog, emerged through a row of veiled trees.

"Little brother, is that you?" Daedyn stopped on the top step, anticipating a reply.

Reyne hated being called little brother.

Still imprisoned inside his thoughts, Reyne barely registered his brother's efforts to get his attention. He'd looked forward to the wedding, eager to begin his new life with Mithany. It wouldn't really be all that new since she'd practically been living with Reyne for the past year in a cozy family unit of Reyne, Mithany, and, of course, Daedyn.

"Don't be a dick. Answer me."

"Yeah, yeah, it's me," Reyne yelled back. "The husks are starting to split. Nothin' yesterday. Just barely splittin' today. I checked out a bunch of trees. All the same. Right on schedule. Looks like we're gonna get lucky. You timed the labor contracts with the harvest perfect this year. Nice job, Bro." His feet, doing the thinking, steered him towards the house.

Daedyn stepped off the bottom of the stairs. He headed towards the orchard where his brother was emerging from the shrouded grove and called out, "Someone had to do it. You got your head up your ass ever since you two announced the wedding date. As though that's gonna change anything."

"Can't wait. It's all I've ever wanted. You're still mad she picked me. Besides, you love the fact the house is clean, and she makes that stew you like. Beats the shit outta the slop you make."

Daedyn shrugged. "Picked you? You can have her. I pick a new one almost every other night. It's *all* I've ever wanted. I just love the Gift of Flesh. You, I see you more as a devotee of the Gift of Love. I'll take flesh over love every day of the week. You follow your heart. I'll follow my dick." He arrived to stand shoulder to shoulder with Reyne.

Daedyn put his arm around his brother. "I'm happy for you, Bro. Really, I am. You two are perfect for each other. Not my cup of tea. And I'm not gonna complain if she picks up the mess every day or cooks now and then. I'm not goin' anywhere. It's the three of us. Like it's been. Married or not, no difference. My life's not gonna change. Neither is yours. I'm happy for you."

Reyne was the younger of the two brothers, if only by a few minutes, as their mother told the story of birthing fraternal twins. Both were a little bigger and a bit more muscular than average. Almost twenty-two years old, the siblings were of an age some might consider them men. But if you were to ask anyone in the small village of Hensdale, they'd probably tell you Daedyn still had some growing up to do.

Reyne's face showed a firm jawline with friendly, heart-melting, easy green eyes able to charm anyone he cared to. Daedyn was similar in every way, with one exception: he had the propensity to be less than friendly to those he didn't care for.

Reyne's jet-black hair, cropped traditionally like most young men in the rural community, hung a few inches above his shoulders and loosely combed back. The same style as his brother Daedyn. Though not identical twins, the brothers looked a lot alike. If it wasn't for the unique coat Reyne wore throughout fall, winter, and spring, and on exceptionally cool summer evenings, it would be impossible to tell them apart from a distance.

Reyne dumped an alphen nut, husk and all, into Daedyn's waiting palm. Daedyn looked it over and nodded his concurrence with Reyne's assessment of the ripening stage the nut had achieved. "Yep, perfect." He turned his palm down, allowing the shell to fall to the ground. "The dehusking operation is gonna cost us a little more than last year, but it looks like it's gonna be one helluva harvest. We'll make it up in volume."

Nature packed each alphen with more energy than a full meal. Alphens were sometimes called the Jewel of Nuts and coveted all over the continent. The prized nuts grew in a narrow band that included the region around Hensdale. The trees were prolific, and under just the right conditions, produced two harvests in a single year. Each tree begot many barrels per harvest, and the hardy trees required only a small staff to be properly maintained. Harvesting, on the other hand, took a considerable labor force.

"That's what I love about you. You got a good head for business. Means you're not always an asshole." Reyne laughed and punched Daedyn's arm.

Daedyn pulled his younger brother into a headlock. "Not always. Where is she, anyway?"

Reyne broke free, pushing off from Daedyn. "Her and her brother headed out to Owls Neck late yesterday afternoon. They set up a meeting with some merchant to offload excess inventory from their shoppe. You didn't notice she's been gone?"

"I barely notice if you're here half the time." He returned a solid punch to Reyne's arm.

"Ouch! I take it back. You're an asshole all the time."

Daedyn's face spoke in place of words; he was pleased with himself.

"What would you do if you weren't gettin' married to her?"

Reyne's brow scrunched, and his eyes narrowed. "Come on, enough of that shit."

"No really, what would you do?"

"You're a dick most of the time, and you know I still love you, but I can't live without her. You, on the other hand, I can live without." They both knew it wasn't true. Reyne needed both Mithany and his brother by his side. Reyne shoved Daedyn, pushing him back a few steps.

Daedyn's feet scraped the dirt path, keeping him on balance. He took the nudge in the spirit it was intended. "I'm bein' serious. We've talked about it before. Ever since Mom passed, you're different. Used to come out with me on the hunt for the ladies. I miss having you with me like we used to do. Remember the time we met those Ranber girls at the Forest Maiden? That one had those sexy, exotic yellow eyes." Daedyn paused. "Ah, to be forever known as the Night of the Three Sisters."

"Of course. A memorable night. A great night. Can't ever forget those eyes. And when she aimed them at me, she made me believe I was her entire world. At least until she rolled over in your direction and her sisters found their way back to me. Best night of my life up to that point. That's all behind me. You understand why I gave it all up.

"When Mom died, Dad was already gone. Both died too young. Made me realize what's important. Family. I want what Mom and Dad had. Here at the orchard. Married. A bunch of kids runnin' 'round. It's what I want. It can all be taken away too soon. Why wait? Do it now. I love this place, my life, Mithany, and even you. Even though you can be a pain in the ass sometimes—well, let's be honest, most of the time."

"Think she'll join us runnin' the operation we got goin' here? She already helps with the books."

"Nah, she loves her shoppe on Hensdale's square too much. She told me she and Arek are gonna keep it goin' after we get married. Oh, I almost forgot, she asked me to stop by while they're gone to check up on Ilyn—she's holding down their shoppe all alone. Told Mithany I would see if Ilyn needs anything. Come on. Why don't you take a walk with me into town? These nuts don't need us. They'll split open on their own. Besides, Santander is around here somewhere. I seen him earlier, workin' on one of the drying barns."

"Like I got nothin' better to do. But sure, why not?"

Ten Days Earlier

Jarouhar: 17th Day of the Salmon Moon

Dylla | Jirek

Across the street from Lorique's apartment, a team of assassins shared a carafe of coffee at an outdoor café while reviewing their plan to kill her later that morning. The twilight of dawn had given way to the rising sun and passersby from the quaint seaside village of Jarouhar shuffled past the deadly foursome, affording them little notice.

The unit's leader, Dylla Weisner, pointed at Selundra Quith, a well-built middle-aged man with a full head of white hair. She shifted her gaze to a fellow operative sitting next to Quith to include him in her orders. "You two will be on her. We've surveilled the pair for days. She leaves for her job shortly after her husband. That's our window of opportunity, gentlemen. Quick and clean. No mistakes."

Quith offered a casual nod; they'd been over their assigned roles many times.

Dylla faced the fourth member of the team seated at the small wrought-iron table. "You'll be tracking the husband. Remain on him after he leaves. Make sure he stays out of the way."

While sipping his coffee, he gave her a thumbs-up.

Dylla nodded. "Good. You will all report to me when it's done. You know your assignments and what I expect from each of you. There're only two of them left, and one of them is in that room. We've been successful in dealing with the others who might transport into our reality. These last two will never know what they were capable of. Better they never did, for our sake."

Lorique was one of the few individuals in the Third Age who the assassins suspected of possessing the rare ability to transport between two starkly different versions of Earth. Lorique knew nothing of moving between dimensions or that another reality even existed.

The only other person to have the same potential as Lorique and who hadn't yet been eliminated by the team was a young businessman running a nut orchard, Reyne Brenton. Neither Lorique nor Reyne, strangers to each other, had ever guessed at what they were capable of. The ignorance of their unrealized talents meant little to the wetworks team. Death was required of them both.

Dylla continued. "After this, we're headed for Hensdale. That little shithole up north out in the middle of fucking nowhere. The nut grower will be the last suspected Tweener after today. One more associate from our world will join us in Hensdale, if she makes it there in time. I'll brief her in Owls Neck first, one of the little villages near Reyne Brenton. I'll set up there to coordinate our final op."

Quith asked, "You need us in Owls Neck too, or should we just head straight for Hensdale and get rid of Reyne Brenton?"

"Get going as soon as we're finished here. Make it to Hensdale as fast as you can. I want to do it without the new woman we've been told to take on. I don't think we need her, but I've been directed to add her to our crew, just in case. She's supposed to be some young hotshot, and they want to see if she's for real or all hype. This isn't the time to test a new operator, but I have my orders. So, after we get this done today, we're out of here immediately. Are we clear? I want you three to finish off Reyne Brenton even before I meet up with this prodigy to brief her."

Inside the apartment, Lorique's husband Jirek had done a quick rinse off. He carried the scent of lovemaking with a lingering hint of salty ocean air wafting in from the ocean through their second-floor window. He hadn't left himself enough time to shower, but watching Lorique sleep was worth the sacrifice. He dressed and was ready to head off to work.

He called out, "Honey, I'm leaving. Need my goodbye kiss."

Lorique appeared out of nowhere and hadn't bothered to dress. She stood in the doorframe between the bedchamber and the hallway. Reaching high above her head, one hand came to rest against the top of the doorway arch. Tilting her hips, she taunted him with her other hand. Long, thin, delicate fingers glided over flawless skin and commanded his full attention.

Was there anything in all of creation more beautiful, he wondered. Soft, round powder-blue eyes. Long, chestnut-brown hair. A gentle face. Full breasts and rounded hips. All that perfection in one woman proved almost too much for his brain to handle. Even the birthmark on her inner thigh he thought beautiful. She was stunning, at least to him. It mattered little if anyone else thought so.

A notion crossed his mind: he was dreaming. How did he ever get so lucky? How did he ever convince such an intelligent, witty, thoughtful, kind, and loving woman to marry him? As he looked at her standing there, the hyperactive thumping in his chest told him it was real. And he was the luckiest man in the world. He couldn't take his eyes off her or those roaming fingers, which had stopped wandering and found a home.

Waking up next to her every day for the past five years held him captivated by the love she showered on him. He hoped she would continue to do so for all the years to come. At the very least, until the day he died.

Lorique teased, "Okay, put your tongue back in your mouth and pull up your jaw. This is just a little incentive to make sure you get home on time. None of that working late nonsense."

"Oh, by the Goddess Teth, you are stunning," he said, as though seeing her for the first time. His look spoke to her with an aching want in his heart and intense desire in his eyes. It was the fuel that fed the fires of their passion. She often told him he was all the "handsome" she ever wanted.

Lorique ran to him and jumped into his welcoming arms. Her thighs clung to his waist. She squeezed them tight, holding her body off the floor. Her legs wrapped around his back, crisscrossing just above his firm derriere. He held her off the ground, gripping each cheek of her buttocks in the palms of his powerful hands. He squeezed hard.

Her flesh felt good in his grip.

Lorique giggled, telling him she thought so too.

With her calves, she pulled herself in even tighter, ever closer, pressing every inch of her body snug against his. She looked down at him as he held her tight. Their eyes met, and she locked intertwining fingers behind his head. Pulling his face close to hers, they kissed. He poured everything he held in his heart into that single kiss. He always did.

He mustered every bit of willpower to leave Lorique behind and prepared to set out for work.

As he extracted himself from her affections, walking towards the door, he extended his arms out the bedroom window, grabbed both opposing shutters, and pulled them closed.

Lorique's husband could not have known their life together had ended with that kiss. It was the last time he would ever see her.

Across the street, Quith, still seated at the café facing Lorique's apartment, observed two arms reach out the second-floor window. The white-haired assassin didn't speak, but signaled to Dylla, it's time.

Dylla addressed her team. "Okay. Get ready. Her husband will be leaving in a few moments. Leave no trace. And make sure you get rid of her body."

Open Your Eyes

Hensdale: 27th day of the Salmon Moon

Daedyn | Reyne

The brothers had made it from their shared homestead to the outskirts of Hensdale's market square. Hensdale was a small community of less than five hundred, made up mostly of farmers, ranchers, and assorted agricultural laborers and supporting trades. An inconsequential village but for alphen nut production, in a lightly populated area of the Peoples Republic of Kantos.

Daedyn, confused at the state of their discussion, called to Reyne as they walked apart on opposite sides of the road, "When did this conversation go wrong? I'm just saying, Mithany doesn't get me goin'. But, hey, great that she does it for you."

Reyne shot back, "Fuck you. She wouldn't have you, anyway." He didn't intend his words to be mean or hurtful, but a competitive streak ran deep into their unbreakable bond.

The sound of horses and wooden wheels attacking the gravel surface grabbed Daedyn's attention. A cart pulled by horses shot past, and when it was gone, Reyne was lying on the ground, and much to Daedyn's consternation, Reyne wasn't moving.

Daedyn dashed across the familiar roadway to his brother's aid. His immediate efforts proved ineffective in bringing Reyne back to the conscious world. One knee on the ground alongside Reyne's limp body, Daedyn's frantic mind searched his brother for any sign of movement. Although blood was absent, none of the usual telling signs of life appeared to Daedyn during his desperate and rushed visual inspection. He lowered his ear to Reyne's mouth to realize shallow breaths escaped his brother. Yet the discovery did little to bring relief to Daedyn, who continued to coax more determinative signs of life from his brother's motionless body.

Only seconds passed when Daedyn caught movement out of the corner of his eye. He tore his attention from Reyne, and to his surprise, several of the townsfolk were racing towards him. Villagers from the nearby market square who'd caught sight of the wagon veer into Reyne came running. Some offered help. Others were there for the excitement. Daedyn dismissed them all from his thoughts and remained attentive to his unconscious sibling.

Others, curious at the rushed activity, couldn't resist the draw, and it didn't take long for the wave of voyeurs to stake their territorial claims just beyond Daedyn and Reyne.

A woman named Dorana tried to peek between the shoulders of the gathered onlookers. Known throughout the small village for her ability to find her way into everyone's business, she said to her wife standing next to her, "Can you see who it is?"

Without turning around, another onlooker spoke up. "It's those two guys over at the alphen grove. You know them. The brothers. The nut farmers. One of 'em's down. Hurt bad."

"I think it's the nice one," Valillia, Dorana's wife, replied. "Not that other one. You know the one I'm talkin' about. He should be the one lying there. Not the nice one."

"Oh, I don't like the older one. He's such a smarty-pants," Dorana said.

"Ladies," one onlooker cut in, "how about a little compassion here? The guy's brother's lying there unconscious."

Dorana shot back, "Well, is he breathing? Is he?"

"Yeah, but he's still unconscious, you old bitties."

"I don't like you," Dorana said, poking her head through the crowd to show him her stern, scrunched-up face.

"Come on, Dorana, let's go home. He's so rude," Valillia offered.

The two women joined arms and walked away from the scene of the brothers: one lying motionless, the other frightened, imploring, trying to coax a reply out from unconsciousness.

Daedyn pleaded, "Come on, Rey, open your eyes."

Muffled voices seeped into his consciousness, starting Reyne's return to the world around him. He pried open one eye, but his sight didn't perform as expected. Forms, the shape of people, were scampering about, yet without enough definition for him to be certain of who they were. A blinding white haze filled his vision as it hung over the silhouetted human shapes.

Reyne pondered what had happened but stopped mid-thought. Pain interrupted, hammering hot spikes through each eye, reaching deep into his brain, wiping every other thought from his awareness.

The silvery glare permeating his vision proved painful. Closing his eyes to escape the searing pain, he strained to listen to the din of voices.

His mind, in a fog, battled two fronts: blazing light thrashed at his eyes, and disjointed speech attacked his ears. All he could put together was his ass was on the ground; his head hurt like hell; and there were lots of people around. He was missing the details of how he got himself into this predicament. Through sheer willpower, he did his best to focus, yet shadows moved against the backdrop of the overwhelming whiteness and silhouettes danced across his vision.

The haze in his head was giving way in small measures, but with increments of awareness came magnitudes of pain. Gradually, more sounds took the form of words. With both eyelids locked down, he concentrated on what he could recall.

Reyne shook his head—a mistake. *Fuck!*

He tried to get up but couldn't. A sharp, needle-point ache at the back of his neck kept his mind focused inward, ignoring the people around him.

He reached around the back of his neck. Feeling around, he probed the spot with his fingers, searching for anything akin to wetness or even something crusted, like dried blood. Reyne brought his hand around from the back of his head. He propped open both eyes and looked down. Empty fingers announced no blood.

Nausea and a cold sweat swept over him. Still on his ass yet sitting up, Reyne grabbed his stomach with both arms, leaned to one side, and retched. It was a dry heave; nothing came up, save more pain. He retched again and again. Agony was the only thing escaping the pit in his stomach.

Reyne took in a few deep breaths to calm himself through the anguish and nausea, but calmness didn't answer the call as a series of hammer-like blows pounded the back of his head. *What the hell!*

To distract himself, Reyne turned his focus to the shapes and faces all around. They were looking down at him. He didn't like it. He wasn't comfortable with all the attention. Never had been.

It was the Feast of Teth, and more people were in the square than normal, although the holiday didn't include any village-wide celebration.

He struggled to get up. Hushed silence overtook the small gathering as though waiting for some pronouncement of life or death.

The young businessman rubbed the back of his neck. "What the hell happened?" He wasn't certain he was speaking the words aloud, and he saw his brother Daedyn standing in front of him. Reyne watched his sibling raise one arm to silence the onlookers. Daedyn squatted down on his haunches and rested his hands on Reyne's knees.

"Rey—Rey—can you hear me?"

"Daedyn?" Reyne blurted, not fully trusting either his ears or his eyes. "What happened?"

"You dumb fuck. You stepped into a moving wagon. How could you miss it? It's the size of a small barn. The horses pulling the damned thing passed between us, and I guess you never saw it because even after the horses passed inches from your back, I'm guessing you turned and stepped right into it."

"A wagon… huh," he cut his brother off mid-sentence. "Guess I never saw the thing coming."

"Anyway, I couldn't see exactly. The horses and wagon blocked my view. I'm guessing you stumbled after being hit, then fell ass-backwards. The wagon was from the Temple, but they just drove on. Like nothing happened. Probably that asshole Fegmin. Then again, maybe he didn't know he hit you. Nobody could be stupid enough to step into a moving wagon, huh? We'll take a walk over there later, after you're up and about, and see if we can find him." He paused and followed with, "How could you not see a fuckin' wagon?"

Reyne could see the relief on his brother's face.

"Well, that's one way of escaping those greedy bastards," he said, half-laughing before realizing some of the crowd was still there. Speaking ill of the Temple wasn't just a slight to the Temple of Life but a slap in the face of the religious folks of Hensdale.

Even though most of the onlookers had been neighbors and friends for years, folks didn't take kindly to open criticism of the Temple of Life. The Temple was the positive guiding force for so many throughout civilization.

The good folks of Hensdale, like most in the region, were religious followers to one degree or another. There were the true believers, and there were the believers in name only. The fervent devotees wouldn't take kindly to Daedyn's comment.

Daedyn leaned in for only Reyne to hear. "Fuck 'em, if they don't like it."

Reyne scanned the faces of those still hanging around and realized he knew everyone there. Reyne put one hand on his knee and planted the other hand on the tree behind him. He tentatively rose, yet didn't get far. Vertigo seized him and he fell back.

While falling back, time drifted. He fell at a lumbering pace, if only in his mind. Thistles dancing in the wind appeared frozen before his eyes. Seconds became minutes. Reyne watched the crowd mull about as though passing through molasses.

Among the usual coats, dresses, pants, and other apparel worn by the gathered onlookers, the shabby, filthy, torn, and tattered clothes of one person grabbed

Reyne's attention. In his slow-motion world, he caught sight of an old vagrant. Even in his current state, the old vagabond looked familiar. Reyne spied him slinking about in the background. He might have asked Daedyn, "When was the last time you saw the old coot around here?" Yet, the words never came out.

Reyne watched himself from outside his body, falling back while the beggar held his gaze. He wasn't sure who looked away first—himself or the shabbily dressed old man.

All at once and without warning, time snapped back to normal and pulled Reyne's mind into his body. He tried to put his hands down underneath himself to soften the plunge, but he wasn't quick enough.

He tumbled back. Hard. Right on his ass.

"Damn, that hurts." Reyne grimaced, leaned to the side, and rubbed his butt.

"Take a minute. Just relax. We're in no hurry," Daedyn said and took a seat beside him on the hard, gravelly surface. "We'll sit here as long as you'd like or until my ass can't take these rocks anymore. Whichever comes first." Daedyn paused. "Cause that's just the kinda guy I am."

"Screw you, asshole. It hurts." Reyne pushed his brother, not quite knocking him over. Daedyn laughed. Things were getting back to normal, and it didn't take long for Reyne to think he'd caused no actual harm by his stupid mistake.

The two brothers sat there for another few minutes, talking. Daedyn, by chance, noticed a strange mark on Reyne's neck. It was a small, light-brown circle with a single raised bump in the center. Tiny. It was ever so faint and ever so small; hard to notice. But it was there. Daedyn had seen something like it before. Without drawing attention to it, Daedyn figured he'd get a better look after they both stood up.

Daedyn rose, brushed his hands on his pants, and stuck out an arm. "Let me give you a hand," Daedyn said and pulled Reyne up. "You're lookin' a little better."

Reyne brushed the dirt off his butt.

Daedyn put his arm around Reyne's shoulder, leaning in close. "I'm glad you're okay, little brother."

Reyne frowned. "Shit, we were born only minutes apart. Good thing too, since Mom saved all the good-looking genes for me, the cute one."

"Says the man who looks a lot like me."

Not giving Daedyn time to enjoy his observation, Reyne doubled over, shaking, retching, and coughing up blood.

Brothers in Arms

Hensdale: 27th Day of the Salmon Moon

Daedyn

Reyne's vomiting continued. Throaty grunts rasped rhythmically before giving way to intentional coughs. Daedyn looked helpless while Reyne wrestled back control over his body. Another minute passed with Reyne doubled over before the incessant hacking stopped.

"What the fuck was that?" Daedyn asked in a tone somewhere between a question and a demand.

"I don't know. Couldn't stop puking." Reyne rubbed the back of his neck. "Throat's a bit sore, and I'm a little tired, but I'll be fine."

Despite Reyne's affirmation, Daedyn didn't buy the I'm-okay act. "You sound a little hoarse." Daedyn moved in close, hoping to glimpse the mark on Reyne's neck.

"What, d'you wanna kiss me or somethin'? Back off," Reyne demanded.

"Kiss you! I'd rather smell the beer farts of a hundred drunks than kiss your ugly face." Obvious to Daedyn, Reyne wasn't fine, despite his declarations to the contrary.

Before Daedyn moved away, he leaned in for a closer inspection. He wanted a better look at the tiny mark on Reyne's neck. Daedyn wondered if the mark had something to do with the shaking and vomiting. A covert inspection confirmed his suspicions. The mark looked like an insect bite. Not just any bite, but one, Daedyn suspected, from the venomous spiderworm.

The creature was either a worm-like spider or a spider-like worm. Daedyn didn't remember which. What he did remember was that spiderworm venom was nasty stuff. Venom from the strange-looking, short-bodied worm—or was it a long-bodied-spider, with eight long legs and two short piercing fangs—heralded death in rare cases. To be safe, Daedyn knew to seek treatment as soon as possible. Lucky for Reyne, Daedyn recalled just enough of his schoolboy lessons.

Spiderworm bites were rare but not unheard of in and around Hensdale. Folks took extra care to keep an eye out for the creatures and avoided their known habitat. The *Arachnid Annelidan* hybrids were underground dwellers, rarely seen above ground, and the spiderworm rarely bothered above-ground dwellers unless threatened.

Daedyn considered either Reyne had a concussion, or venom from the bite triggered Reyne's puking spell.

With a bite to the neck, so close to a major artery, who's to say how fast-acting it might be? Daedyn didn't want to alarm Reyne, but he wanted the village's longtime doctor to examine him sooner rather than later. Daedyn counted on Doc Hollid Brenal having the anti-venom serum to treat Reyne. If not treated in the next few hours, the poison might well seep from the site of the bite on his neck and into his bloodstream and begin its trek to Reyne's heart, where it would do its worst.

"Hey, Bro, what do you think? Maybe we have Doc Brenal check you out."

"I'm a little tired, but I'm fine," Reyne said in a gravelly rasp.

Daedyn didn't want to get Reyne upset, so he didn't share his suspicions. Fortunately for the village of Hensdale and fortunately for Reyne, Doc Hollid Brenal, while the only doctor in Hensdale, was the best in the entire region.

Daedyn had time. "Not to worry, you'll be fine. But just to be sure, the Doc should check you out."

Daedyn called out to the gathered onlookers, "Anyone see Doc Brenal today?"

Hushed silence filled the air.

We Have a Problem

Evidar

Lesni

The door to the underground dwelling was set in a structure that looked like a cairn. Gray skylight the color of charcoal did little to illuminate Evidar's dismal landscape—a world forever in darkness. Mister Lesni, Dylla Weisner's liaison, was late for an appointment he'd been summoned to. He hoped to walk away with his life from the hastily requested meeting.

Mister Lesni didn't know why he'd been summoned. He'd done as he was asked—or did he miss something? He was running late, and that didn't make his chances any better. The lack of a specific unit of measure and the absence of even the hint of a shadow left time a less certain construct in Evidar's reality. Instinct told him morning was slipping away, and in the dimension of Earth's dark twin, time was measured by instinct. It may have been morning, yet it looked much the same as midnight. But that too was normal in the world from which Mister Lesni, Dylla Weisner, and her team of assassins hailed.

He stayed behind while the others transfigured to the utopian version of Earth, Tartica, in order to complete their task aimed at saving Evidar's future by killing those who threatened it—before they ever got the chance.

Several similar bunkers serving the purpose of housing littered the burg, if it could even be classified as such, given the utter absence of cohesion amongst the occupiers. The struggle for survival, was all the small group of homelings held in common. Though they approached its demands separately.

Mister Lesni surveyed the half dozen rock-pile-door structures that were strewn about haphazardly over the span of a hundred yards. Like all creatures of the night, his Evidarian-born eyes were more than a match for the ever-present darkness. Smoke escaped a flue rising from the only barrow with a yellow door. He'd been given instructions to enter the one matching that color.

He gulped down fear and reached for the latch.

He told himself he had nothing to worry about. He'd done his job, but even so, he was summoned to this meeting. *This can't be good.*

Minimal luminance the dark gray light afforded gave way to black tones as the man stepped through the yellow door and began his journey down the long, narrow stairway entrance to the underground bunker.

Reaching the bottom, he heard his chest thumping against eardrums surrounded by burning hot lobes. A single sip of water would have allowed a reprieve against the cotton balls that had accumulated in his mouth.

Near pitch-black darkness welcomed Mister Lesni inside the dwelling, but that too was normal in Evidar. His Evidarian sight could clearly make out the person occupying the subterranean home and recognized him immediately. His ears grew hotter and his mouth became even drier.

The target of his fear was comfortably seated on a couch along the northern wall. The Devil's Blacksmith, with deep-set, malevolent eyes darker than a black hole, glared back at him.

Mister Lesni took another gulp upon discovering who he was meeting with and remained standing. He fidgeted, fearing his knees would buckle in anticipation of judgement for something he wasn't sure he did. The two men, one sitting, one struggling to remain upright, continued to look at each other through the gloom.

Mister Lesni broke the threatening silence. "Hello, sir. I apologize for being late. I was attacked on my way—"

"Shhhh." The Devil's Blacksmith cut him off. The silence continued for a few dozen heartbeats before the seated man spoke. "We have a problem with your operation, Mister Lesni."

"I did as you asked. I've been working through Dylla Weisner, and her team has eliminated the woman Tweener they call Lorique."

"Yes, thank you, Mister Lesni," the Devil's Blacksmith spoke in soft, deep, resonant tones, with commanding confidence in his words. "But I am concerned with our two other problems. The Chancellor fellow and the nut farmer. Both have the potential to change the trajectory of the two timelines. The Chancellor, their timeline, and this Reyne Brenton fellow could affect ours. I do not need to tell you how devastating either would be to our plans.

"My contact in their world assures me it is under control, but they both yet live. My Damus calculates the opportunity to remove them from influencing her probability equations predicting how our future unfolds, the very foundation of our plan, is growing short. The nut farmer poses the greatest danger should he make it to our world. Yet, they both need to be removed before either can do irreparable damage to one or the other timeline. I need them dead if we are to successfully collapse the two Probability Wave Functions into one reality—ours. Mister Lesni, do you appreciate the implications of their ongoing existence?"

Standing, Lesni fully grasped the omneity. He gulped hard.

"Sir, I am not worthy to intercede in what you've planned out, and I don't fully understand things like Probability Wave Functions, yet I believe I can help you with this problem." Mister Lesni chose every word carefully. The Devil's Blacksmith was not one to suffer insolence, intended or otherwise.

"Yes, Mister Lesni, I do believe you can help me. You are quite talented concerning the vagaries of moving between realities. You prepared and assisted Dylla and her team in getting to that other version of Earth. That is why I've asked you to join me here this morning. And I would advise you to never be late again." The seated man folded one leg over the other across his knee. He rested both hands on top. "Mister Lesni, I need you to ensure a new agent gets to her appointed meeting place over in the other reality. She is exceptionally good at what she does, and I have tolerated her behavioral issues because of her talents. Her handlers are having a challenging time managing her."

The man standing took a deep breath, relieved at the opportunity to continue living. "Is she the new addition promised to Dylla?"

"Yes."

"And how soon do you want it done, sir?"

"Immediately. Before morning completely slips away. Mister Lesni, the other-worlders use a phrase that observes time somewhat differently than we do. They say, 'within the hour,' and as it is what I intend, it doesn't leave you with much of it. And yes, I want her to join Dylla Weisner's unit for the next stage of their operation 'taking out the nut farmer.' She is the most capable archer to come along in some time."

"I understand, sir." Mister Lesni forced the words through his throat, which threatened to expose his panic, fighting the effects of adrenaline washing over him. "Has the girl ever transfigured between realities before?"

"No."

Fuck! This is not going to be easy. "Yes, sir, I will get it done. May I ask where she is at this moment?"

"You may ask."

Mister Lesni was at a loss. Did he just get permission to ask, or was that a signal he wouldn't like the answer? "Sir, where can I find her?"

"I do not know, and neither does anyone else. You have your job, Mister Lesni. Get it done. That will be all."

Well, that seals it. I'm a dead man walking. "I won't let you down, sir." He said the words, but had no clue how he was going to live through the assignment. The Devil's Blacksmith did not accept failure.

Unknown to Mister Lesni, or anyone else, the agent in question had done something thought impossible for a first-timer on her own: she had already transfigured from the world of Evidar to Tartica earlier that morning. As mid-day approached, with his subject nowhere to be found, it would no longer matter to Mister Lesni. Before the end of the day, nothing, ever again, would matter to Mister Lesni.

Appearance Is Everything

Teth: 26th Day of the Salmon Moon

Derr

In the afternoon on the day before the Feast of Teth, Chancellor Tomelai, a tall, middle-aged leader with a rugged confidence in his steel-gray eyes, decamped with his entourage in tow. They set up about two miles outside the city of Teth. Everything had gone as planned. The three-day trek from the Kingdom of Adelle to The Gate of Teth proved uneventful.

The Adelleian delegation accompanying the Chancellor on the state visit to Teth included more than a dozen senior members of the current administration. Tomelai held his position as Chancellor for life; however, his administration's senior personnel turned over every four or five years. The nation's leader kept no one in a position of authority long enough to get used to power. Except for Druin Derr.

Security arrangements for the Chancellor were always problematic anytime he strayed outside the safety of the capital city of Tandure. Even in Tandure, the leader of the hundreds-strong Kingdom's Chancellor's Guard, Captain Druin Derr, faced security challenges caused by Tomelai's own disregard for security measures. The Chancellor cared more about appearing to be a man of the people than he did for following Derr's safety protocols.

"Appearances form the foundation of perception, Drew," was Tomelai's off-the-shelf reply to Derr's just-as-frequent protestations. Both men were certain Chancellor Tomelai was not a man of the people. But the people didn't know that, and it didn't stop him from doing all he could to portray himself as an average person who just happened to be a Head of State. Behind closed doors, he was as ruthless as any Head of State had to be, perhaps even more so.

The position, along with the title of Chancellor, he had inherited from his father in the long line of Tomelai men and women who ruled Adelle.

Druin Derr was an average-looking man who might otherwise go unnoticed in a crowd, of average height with an average build and short-cropped, sandy-colored hair, along with sky-blue piercing eyes and a stern face whose muscles rarely formed a smile. He was a serious man with serious responsibilities whose visage reflected both. He embodied the rare quality of being both an educated thinker and a man of action.

"That's your job to worry about me, Drew," the Chancellor would observe, dismissing Derr's concerns for security issues. "You worry about it. Do whatever you need to secure the situation. Eliminate the threats. Since I know you will, I am free to do whatever I need to do. To go wherever I need to go, and do it whenever I want to. If I did not have you leading your team, things might be different. But I do. So, I will not give security a second thought. I trust you will do your job, my friend, because I've seen you in action. You are even more heartless than I can be."

Derr had heard the same speech a thousand times. Tomelai may have even spoken those exact words when Derr outlined his concerns for the trek from the Kingdom of Adelle to the city-state of Teth. Derr might have saved his breath if he told the Chancellor, "You don't make it easy for me to keep you in power," but he didn't. Not because Madrotti Tomelai was sensitive to the comparison of himself to a monarch, holding absolute power, but because it wouldn't make any difference. Instead, he told the Chancellor, "Don't trust me so much, Rotti. There are smarter people than me out there." Only one person addressed the Chancellor as "Rotti," and Druin Derr inherited that honor from the childhood nicknames they held on to.

For Druin Derr, pushing harder wouldn't change anything. Any follow-up challenge would face another pat Tomelai response: "We have been friends since we were kids. You were the only one I ever trusted growing up, and now even more so. I do not trust any of these bastards. You have free rein to do whatever you need to do. My approval is implied in any action you take. Take whatever compensation you feel is fair without limits. If you cannot do the job, nobody can, and I am lost."

Both men could play out the conversation to its conclusion without ever speaking the words. A look from either of them said all that needed to be said.

Whether anyone else in Tomelai's entourage was safe held little concern to Derr, unless it somehow affected his ability to maintain security for his friend, his Chancellor. Derr couldn't care any less if anyone else lived or died unless it affected Tomelai's ability to rule. His mission was to protect the Chancellor. Nothing else mattered.

Derr had at his disposal several hundred men and women of the Kingdom's Chancellor's Guard, a clandestine, intel-gathering unit that also functioned as a paramilitary security force dedicated to the Chancellor's security. Fifty of them accompanied Derr on this particular state visit.

It was the eve of the Feast of Teth, and men and women were about setting up camp. The Kingdom's Chancellor's Guard, known as the KCG, pre-selected the site weeks in advance. For the Chancellor, his duty in setting up entailed walking about and talking with his people. For Derr, it meant he had to keep his eyes open, and his ears piqued while his leader pretended to be a man of the people. Derr would be watching. He was always watching.

Everyone feared the KCG. As its leader, they feared no one more than Druin Derr. The KCG had free rein to operate outside the laws of Adelle, but no one across all Tartica had the authority to violate the Covenant of Absolute Human Obligations. The Covenant stood above the laws of every nation. It was the underpinning of the rebuilt human race all these centuries later, on the last remaining habitable spot on Earth in the aftermath of the Great Destruction, the continent of Tartica. Yet, even the Covenant didn't stop Derr in carrying out his duty.

The encampment had been painstakingly prepared and secured. Derr didn't like the location, but it was the best choice amongst a host of less desirable options. Derr chose not to avail Adelle's elites of the housing in the nearby town of Mehrlich because of security blind spots he could not eliminate.

The KCG set up the Chancellor's series of yurts, which he shared with his First Lady, at the center of the encampment. It was more of a complex than a series of tents. Several elaborate temporary structures set around a single central yurt made up the Chancellor's traveling pavilion. Within the stately enclosure were subdivisions for dining, bathing, and the First Lady's private bathroom.

There were separate spaces for attendants, for dressing, the sovereign's bedroom, even a special tent housing the Chancellor's steeds. Walls, layered with thick fabric and adorned with art, prevented voices from carrying. Furniture, meeting the taste and preferences of the First Lady, Kaythlin Tomelai, rounded out the look inside. The ruler would want for nothing while Derr made certain the two remained safely secured.

Higher-ranking officials in Tomelai's administration enjoyed a placement closer to the center. Prudents from the Temple of Life, assigned to the Kingdom of Adelle, enjoyed the privilege of being placed closest. Among all the dignitaries of Tomelai's entourage, Prudent Garragent Serco of the Temple of Life received the most coveted location. Garragent Serco was the highest-ranking Prudent serving in Adelle, with open access to the Chancellor. He was pleased to be placed closer than any other functionary. Faith, in the service of the Temple of Life, was no match for human frailties such as vanity. Tomelai counted on it as he cultivated Serco's loyalty.

Prudent Serco and Chancellor Tomelai had developed a strong bond over the past several years. A bond methodically nurtured by Tomelai. On its face, it served both the interests of the Temple of Life, led by the First Lord Jerithan Cree, and the Kingdom of Adelle. Below the surface, it served Tomelai's interests more.

"You've found something in Serco First Lord Jerithan's ignored," Derr said.

The Chancellor replied, "Serco welcomes the chance to return to Teth, holy ground. It is a homecoming for all the Prudents scattered about the continent. Those assigned outside of Teth have only a fleeting time to make their individual impressions with others of the conclave. A short time to move up or down the pecking order of power. I give Serco a little more juice. He thinks I am unaware of how he uses it."

Derr nodded in agreement.

"Serco has more earthly concerns than most of his fellow Prudents. I have helped him reach a few goals during his stay in our capital. He sees me as his ticket to the dance. He thinks he has carefully manipulated me. It is always so much easier when they think it is their idea."

Derr laughed. "He doesn't have a clue how you're playing him, Rotti. It's a shame. Electrics would've done so much to advance all of us. We've talked about it. How better the lives of everyone would be. Easier. More productive. Safety. Increased food supplies. But the Council's going to protest, saying electrics aren't natural. They'll say it's a man-made creation. Unleashing it on the world as an anathema to their religion. That fucking Covenant gets in the way all the time," Although, the Covenant never impeded Derr or the KCG carrying out its stated mission.

Tomelai confessed, "The Council is afraid of the slippery slope electrics introduces and the unforeseen impact on their power. They are afraid it will diminish the demands of living a life grounded in nature, or more precisely, the masses might drift out from under the Council's hold over the faithful."

Derr added, "And all their opposition carefully maneuvered behind the scenes by that sneaky fuck, First Lord Jerithan Cree. He'll do anything to keep the Temple of Life at the center of all things."

Tomelai frowned. "Concerning Serco, I gave it to him, Drew. Let him run back to his Temple masters. We were not going to win the vote. So, I gave him the inside scoop on our plans for electrics. You and I both agree the votes are not there. President Dimenk and Prime Minister Larsed are posturing for what their nations can extract from Jerithan in concessions to secure their votes against my proposal. They will both vote against it, along with Jerithan. The proposal to permit electrics across Tartica is dead on arrival. Giving Serco our plans was a throwaway for us, but the info I gave away was a big win for him. Puts him in a stronger position in Temple politics that we can use later. He owes me."

“Serco’s going to run home to Mommy with all the confidential info you supplied to make himself look good in the view of the First Lord and his fellow Prudents. Exactly as expected, he’ll betray your confidence for his own sake, even though he hates Jerithan. He’ll make sure the other Prudents know it was his doing that propped up the First Lord’s successful defeat of your proposal to permit electrics. At this point, it’s a foregone conclusion at the Council’s annual meeting.”

The Chancellor reflected, “Sure. At least we will get something out of it. We tried. Electrics would have moved civilization forward. The lot of them are too single-minded to see it. Someone will pull a quote from the Covenant of Absolute Human Obligations. These fucking people cannot see what is best, and they think the Council will hold Adelle back from doing what we have to do. I do not give a shit what the other nations do. We will find a way to bring electrics to Adelle.”

Derr prolonged the probe. “As I told you the other day, Jerithan thinks you have a chance. Sources inside the Temple Palace say he’s worried. He doesn’t realize Dimenk and Larsed are playing him.”

“Negotiations must not be going well, or he hasn’t been willing to give up the goods to Larsed or Dimenk. But he will. He is firmly against electrics and will do anything to stop me.”

“We’ll get there. When have you ever failed to get what you wanted?” Derr said.

“You know me too well, Drew. We, and by *we,* I mean you, me, and Kaythlin, since we cannot bring in anyone else given the proclivity of leakers, are going to figure out and execute a plan to get around the Council vote, First Lord Jerithan Cree, and that fucking Covenant.”

The KCG gathered later that same day, on the eve of the Feast, in Derr’s tent. Together they reviewed and revised the security protocols in place to provide for the Chancellor's safety during his ceremonial entrance into Teth early the next morning: just like the leaders of the other two nations, Prime Minister Larsed from the Republic of Kantos and President Dimenk from Greenlin.

While a basic tenant of the Covenant forbade taking a life, any life, Druin Derr knew its protections did not prevent an adventurous assassin from disregarding everything the Covenant stood for and attempt to remove Chancellor Tomelai from the political arena. Derr had taken similar actions many times himself, eliminating threats to Adelle's Chancellor in defiance of the Covenant's dictates concerning the sanctity of life.

What-if scenarios bounced back and forth between the men and women of the KCG in rapid fire, one after another. Even if the scenarios were highly unlikely, yet possible, Derr wanted a plan to deal with them if one wasn't already in place. The KCG had done the same exercise several times while planning for the trip back in Tandure, Adelle's capital.

Captain Derr prepared for just about anything. The facts on the ground presented Derr with a considerable challenge. He had sent scouts to walk every inch of the planned route, back and forth, several times evaluating blind spots, threats, or covering locations for a possible attack. By the time the KCG finished, they'd been well prepared and knew every inch of the Chancellor's course. And still Derr wondered if it would be enough. Something wasn't right. It still felt wrong.

A young lieutenant, Jerith, yelled out, "Okay. What if those monkey men, the Anatese, scampering about the treetops along The Stand drop down on us without warning?"

Lieutenant Jerith stopped and looked around, as if waiting for approval. When Derr gave a thoughtful look in reply, he witnessed pride written across Jerith's face. He was watching the young man just as he'd been watching every one of the KCG closely that night. He was always watching.

Derr didn't expect the Anatese to attack. A defensive role and nothing more had always been their function. War never raised its ugly head in all the years of the Third Age, but in spite of the Covenant, assassinations, though rare, stained it.

The Anatese always appeared above it all, both politically and as tree-top dwellers, loyal to the defense of Teth, the city itself, never to its stewards, only to the First Lord. The Anatese had never been pawns in any assassination in Teth's storied history. But, Derr considered, *best to be prepared*. Anything is possible.

Derr watched his lieutenants closely. Unknown to anyone in the KCG, Derr had them followed throughout their tenure in the unit—families too. As far as Derr could tell through secret reports on his KCG personnel, none of them gave cause for concern.

Throughout the meeting, he watched them all, looking for the slightest sign, a twitch, a raised eye, a hidden swallow. But he didn't see any of those signs or any other giving him cause to dig deeper. Least of which, he saw nothing in this young Lieutenant Jerith, who now seemed so proud to have received the slightest bit of affirmation from Derr.

Derr recognized the look on the man's face. It was clear he was proud. His chin rose ever so slightly. Most of the other men wouldn't have recognized, but Derr did. He always did. He was waiting for that or any other reaction that might give him answers.

Planning continued into the night until Derr and the KCG planned for every contingency. But still, he worried. If he got it wrong, his Chancellor would die.

A Thin Veil of Pretense

Hensdale: 27th Day of the Salmon Moon

Reyne | Daedyn

Foot traffic at Hensdale's market square rebounded within minutes of Reyne's recovery as the crowd, brought together over the excitement of an accident, returned to their typical day. Looking about the departing host, Reyne once again noticed the familiar vagabond's intense stare aimed at him. It pissed him off. He returned his own offensive scowl at the man.

The old beggar whirled around then darted away.

Reyne shifted his attention when he thought he heard his brother say "... alright," answering to a question he imagined Daedyn asked. "A little tired, but I think I'll be fine," Reyne replied. He rubbed the back of his neck. Constant throbbing, although weaker, still demanded his attention. Reyne pulled his hand back and gave it a quick inspection. "At least there isn't any blood," he said with a hint of satisfaction.

The last few stragglers in the crowd drifted away, leaving Daedyn and Reyne there alone. Then, as they walked along the gravel-covered roadway to the unmarked and unofficial entrance to the market square, the brothers came to a stop. Still a few miles from the farm and business they ran, Reyne said, "Turn here. Let's head home."

Unaware of the spiderworm threat, Reyne's thoughts drifted. The sun's position let him know morning had slipped by with little notice. A typical warm, sunny day for the waning Salmon Moon of summer's end. Reyne looked up and imagined the beautiful deep orange and brilliant reds would be on the leaves soon.

He hoped for another warm autumn. Experience told him it wasn't likely, given how unseasonably cold the nights had been these past few weeks. The last warm fall occurred almost five years ago, when his mother was still alive. The last one she lived to see. He was almost seventeen then. The warmer weather extended the growing season, and he remembered how happy it made his mother, with the additional money the family made with the double harvest that year.

Reyne gazed at the view of the trees lining the square. Their small market space wasn't much, yet this view held a special meaning for Reyne. It represented the beauty he saw in the quiet life he desired. He paused at that spot every time to admire the view and to appreciate the effect it had on him.

Daedyn said, "Hey, what say you? We head for the Maiden instead of heading home. You know, for a quick one." Daedyn made a course correction, and Reyne continued alongside his brother. Reyne wondered if Daedyn had an ulterior motive of searching out Doc Brenal at the Maiden but didn't care either way. A lack of energy tugged at his body and his mind as he let slide all extraneous efforts of thought.

The marketplace of Hensdale, if it could even be called a marketplace, was small. Hensdale's market square totaled only sixteen separate buildings, half facing the others from opposite sides. The wide gravel road passed along the main street before breaking off into two perpendicular branches before turning back again to flow along the storefronts on each side of the square. The Communal Temple of Life structure stood apart at the far end, facing it all. In the middle of the square, a park-like grass median outlined by tall, thin trees provided a canopy of shade. Although small, the shared place of commerce served the community of Hensdale well.

While Reyne enjoyed the serenity of the picturesque village square, he considered Daedyn's favorite spot in the small collection of storefronts, the Forest Maiden Inn. The largish tavern had a good-sized room. It filled the role as the village's unofficial meeting place.

The two brothers continued talking as they walked along the gravel road. Daedyn scrolled what-if scenarios in his mind. He hoped to find the doctor at the Forest Maiden or somewhere else in or around the marketplace. He still had some time before the venom would spread if it was a spiderworm. From what he thought he remembered about the thick, gooey venom, it usually pooled at the injection point for several hours before gradually leaching out into the bloodstream. He played along with Reyne's idle chatter, thinking he didn't need to worry him with what might be at stake.

Reyne questioned Daedyn. "I thought I saw the beggar staring at me back there. Did you notice?"

"Yeah. He didn't take his eyes off you while you were out of it. He got close once, but I shooed him away. You figure he remembers the time we left a pile of dog shit near his face when he was sleeping? Remember, he was under that bench over there?"

Reyne laughed. "Yeah, I remember it was your idea. You did that. We were just kids. Didn't know any better."

"The old bastard probably hates us. But everyone there couldn't take their eyes off you lying there on the ground. Don't give it any worry. Besides, look at him. Look at you. Even after being knocked out for five or ten minutes, you'd be able to kick his ass. If not, I'd be seriously disappointed in you, my brother."

"Shit. I was out that long?!" Reyne rubbed the back of his neck again. "Feelin' a little nauseous. I gotta sit down, feelin' weak."

"Alright, just a few minutes. You're gonna be okay. Nothing to worry about," Daedyn lied in a calming, deceitful sort of way. He offered Reyne a wide grin.

"That's not a good look for you."

With his hands on knees, Reyne doubled over and dry heaved yet again. He lifted his head to face Daedyn. "I feel like shit."

"You look like shit, too. Is it the stomach again?" Daedyn asked, knowing damn well it wasn't. *It's possibly the spiderworm's venom making its first efforts to spread past the bite. Shit!*

Daedyn hadn't shared his thoughts with Reyne. *What's the point of bringing it up now? Just get 'em worried and anxious. Not worth it. He still has time.*

Daedyn looked around the small village square. It wasn't too hard to find a place to sit. He'd been through the marketplace almost every day since he was a child. He was looking for a place in the shade given the time of day and looking for a bench not occupied. Trees lined the small marketplace, providing shade here and there amongst the rustic-styled wooden benches liberally placed along the grass median.

"Look at 'em all," Reyne said. "These people find time every day to sit here, discussing rumors about anyone and everyone who walks by. The favorite pastime of just about everyone who lives here."

"I know. Not much escapes the spying eyes of friends or neighbors. Everyone in Hensdale has an opinion about everyone else," Daedyn added, playing along to distract Reyne's mind from his recurring nausea. "Can only imagine what they say about us."

"I probably fare a wee bit better than you."

Even as Daedyn looked around, eyes from lingering onlookers fell across them both. He helped Reyne to the bench nearest the Cobbler's Shoppe. With his shoulder under Reyne's arm, Daedyn made his way over to the bench under the shopkeeper's sign, which read, "Cobbler's Knob." He lowered Reyne to the bench.

"Here, sit here for a while. I'm goin' for Doc. You need anything before I go?"

"Nah, I'm just gonna sit here. You go."

"It'll be five, ten minutes there and back. I'm gonna look around the square. See if anyone knows where the Doc is. I'll be quick."

Reyne put his head back, resting it on the top rail of the bench, and closed his eyes.

"In no time, you'll appreciate the cool shade I found. You'll feel better."

Daedyn watched Reyne drift off, his head resting against the top rail of the bench, and then left to search for Doc Brenal.

He had a few hours before the venom, if it *was* venom, would put Reyne in any real danger. Yet he didn't like the body shakes or all the retching. *No time to waste. Now where the hell would the Doc be at this time of day? Might be on a patient visit. If that's the case, he could be anywhere. He could be home as well. What to do?* Daedyn contemplated his next move, looking around the square.

At the far end of the market square was the Communal Temple of Life building—a structure symbolizing the celebration of Nature, and the core of Temple doctrine. A tight grouping of trees with unbroken space between their trunks made up its walls while a rich, thick canopy of large green leaves enveloped the ceiling like a roof protecting the visitors within. The leaves, while they would change with the seasons, never fell at the end of fall, as did all the other trees. Inside was like a gentle glade with sunlight streaming down on the green grasses covering the Temple's floor. The canopied ceiling of tree branches reaching across the top of the structure in a delicate dance of interlocking leaves would take it upon themselves to part, letting the sunlight stream in on clear days.

It was a wonder to behold, and the good people of Hensdale had lost the story of how it came to be. Although the local Temple of Life's Communal Leader continued to recite to anyone who would listen to her how the Hensdale Communal Temple was gifted to their community by Teth herself. Anyone who bothered to do the math would conclude the story, while comforting, not possible.

Daedyn cared little at the moment about the Communal Temple or whether the leaves fell off. But he did care about Reyne and finding Doc Brenal. He stood contemplating whether to check at the Communal Temple only a moment before concluding, *Nah, the Doc's not a religious guy.* Turning his attention away from the Temple, his thoughts settled on the Forest Maiden Inn. *That's my best bet.*

Entering the Forest Maiden Inn, Daedyn noted it was sparsely populated and, as usual, poorly lit. Day or night, the Forest Maiden was always poorly lit. Several tables dotted the main gathering space. The room seemed larger with so few people inside. But then again, whenever he visited the Maiden, it was always after a hard day's work in the orchard when more people were there.

The carved reliefs on the walls of the town's only watering hole always garnered attention. An unnamed artisan from long ago had carved hunting scenes into the smoke-stained treestone walls. One large scene, taking up most of the open northern wall from floor to ceiling, depicted the fabled killing of a Great Yetgnal.

The story, if it was to be believed, recalled how eight men died in the effort. The Great Yetgnal stood twice as tall as any man alive. With nothing but spears, the remaining six men depicted in the carving took down the beast. It was a myth amongst the villagers from a time lost to history, but it held powerful emotions for the people of Hensdale.

Every now and then, someone would claim to run across a Great Yetgnal in the nearby forest. Not that such tales were accepted as truthful, yet each telling of a Great Yetgnal encounter fueled the fires of the Hensdale rumor mill. The excitement of each new reported sighting, real or not, provided the townsfolk something to mull about for weeks.

When the large hearth held fire, the flames flickered from its gaping mouth, and both warmed and lifted the room. The flickering fire shifted the angle of light coming from the flames and made the men of the frieze appear to move within the carving. To any first-time visitor, the unique effect made the relief appear to come alive.

To the people of Hensdale who frequented the Forest Maiden, the impressive scene no longer brought awe as when first viewed, but it still held everyone's attention. Daedyn enjoyed every time he witnessed the hunters of the carved relief dancing in the firelight. But this wasn't the time to admire anything. He had to find Doc Brenal, and soon.

Daedyn spotted a group sitting in the far corner of the room. He heard one of them telling the end of what must've been a bad joke. It was Spetzer. *It has to be Spetzer Bilseck. I hate that fucker. But it's for Rey. Suck it up.*

"Rabbit ate mashed potatoes. Squirrel ate mashed potatoes. Bear ate mashed potatoes. Get it! Hah hah hah," Spetzer roared in laughter.

Nobody appeared to get the joke, but it didn't stop the storyteller from laughing himself into a stupor. But within a few seconds, everyone joined in the laughter, except Daedyn.

Uh, I gotta deal with this bunch of douchebags today, Daedyn thought. "Hey everyone." He paused. "Spetzer." Daedyn nodded toward the leader and self-appreciated joker of this rabble. "How you guys doin' today?" Not really giving two shits what the answer might be, and before anyone answered, Daedyn continued. "Has anyone seen Doc Brenal today?"

"Not in here," one of the four replied. It was Trell. Daedyn knew Trell and cared for him about as much as he cared for Spetzer. Both Trell and Spetzer were first-class assholes, if they were first-class anything.

"Well then, Reiger, how've you been? And what about the rest of you mopes? How are you all doin'?" *What a bunch of fuckups these guys are.* He and Reyne grew up with them all. Life had turned out much different for this crowd than it had for the brothers.

Daedyn ignored the tension in the room. His presence caused it, but whether any of this crowd liked him held no sway. Life and poor decisions put this bunch on a path much different from his own. Aware each of them resented his success, it still bugged the hell out of Daedyn that they didn't consider the years of hard work and all it cost him. No, all they ever cared about were the things he had without a thought of what it had taken to earn it. Daedyn looked hard at Spetzer, knowing Mithany had always been the head fuckup's object of desire.

Reiger broke Daedyn's chain of thought. "Heard your brother got run over."

Daedyn saw the intensity in the way Reiger looked at him. Resentment dripped from every word he spat.

Putting down the half-full mug of beer he was nursing, Reiger said, "News travels fast. Speaking only for myself, I hope Reyne's okay, but I haven't seen hide nor hair of the old coot Brenal."

The face Reiger offered as he spoke the words, Daedyn interpreted as: "And fuck you and your asshole brother besides."

Another one at the table spoke up, "Hey, I hope everything is okay. And, no, I haven't any idea where the Doc is either."

Obvious to Daedyn, the underlying, unspoken meaning included the phrase, "And why would I tell you if I did, you dickhead?"

"Anybody?" Daedyn said as he looked around the room. They had nothing to offer, and even if they knew, they weren't talking.

Turning to walk out, Daedyn heard Crip gurgle out a noise coming from his nose via a snot bubble taking shape. Crip, also sitting at the table, obviously drunk, blurted out sounds resembling something akin to slurred speech before his face fell hard into his plate of half-eaten lunch.

Spetzer, Reiger, and Trell all broke into hysterics at the site. Beer squeezed out through Spetzer's nose while Trell involuntarily spat out masticated pieces of potato in every direction. After a momentary pause, seeing the sputum all over the table and reflecting on the cause, the small, gathered band of losers laughed even louder.

Daedyn wouldn't be getting anything else from this crew. "Screw yourselves. You deserve each other," he offered, intending it to be perceived as a lighthearted jest, but everyone in the room knew better.

Besides, he spoke drunk well enough and understood everything Crip had said before face diving into his plate. Apparent to Daedyn, Crip gave him a clue to the doctor's whereabouts. "The north groves it is. Enjoy the rest of the day, gentlemen." Daedyn smiled back at them and left the Forest Maiden.

It had only been five minutes since he left Reyne on the bench near the Cobbler's Knob storefront. He didn't want to waste any more time with that gaggle of knuckleheads. He'd wasted several precious minutes and questioned why he'd even bothered with Spetzer. But he did gain valuable information if what Crip drunkenly provided proved to be useful. He stepped outside the Maiden, closed his eyes, and sucked in a breath of the warm, early afternoon air.

Adjusting his eyes to the light of day, from the vantage point atop the Forest Maiden's doorway steps, he expected to see his brother resting quietly on the shaded bench where he'd left him just minutes ago.

Reyne was gone.

He's Always Watching

Teth: 27th Day of the Salmon Moon

Derr

Two miles outside the city of Teth, Druin Derr, Captain of the KCG, rose just before dawn. Stars glimmered against the muted colors of the dawn sky. Chilly air bit at his cheeks.

"Damn, it's cold this morning," Derr told his Senior Lieutenant, Wilem Ferpratt. "Tomelai's Chief of Staff had better get this bunch of prissy hangers-on moving if we are going to enter the city as planned."

With hands cupped to his mouth, Ferpratt fiercely blew hot breath into his stiff, cold fingers. "It will be light out soon. We got lots to do."

"You have a lot to do. I have one job. He's in the tent," Derr said, nodding over his shoulder to Chancellor Tomelai's pavilion.

The makeshift encampment comprised an amalgam of state officials, guards, horses, sheep, hogs, and servants. That being the pecking order as well. Derr looked over the scene of ornately decorated canvas structures huddled closely in the middle of the camp to the patchwork of shabby, small, flimsy tents scattered about the outskirts.

The Senior Lieutenant said to his Captain, "These pretentious high society folks consider themselves lucky Tomelai picked them to join him on this silly trip. I don't know about you, but I'd much rather be fast asleep back in my bed right now."

Derr ignored Ferpratt's insights. "Get the rest of the KCG moving. Break down and pack up. You're moving out ahead of the procession. We need fresh recon. We're bringing our Chancellor into Teth this morning, and I need to know what awaits us once we get there. Our intel is stale already. It's from last night. We've got to know if anything's changed, so go scout ahead. Talk to your contacts. Take Milvoe and Jamine with you. I'll lead the KCG riding with Tomelai and will be about an hour after you. He doesn't want too many others around him when he comes out the other side. He wants to stand out. You know, the center of attention."

Derr's loyalty to his Chancellor was beyond question. His disdain for those who made up Tomelai's entourage, also beyond question. The elite class's collective contempt for him never concerned the Captain. He had the full support of his friend the Chancellor and, while only titled "Captain," he held a higher position than any of them. The courtiers feared Derr more than they despised him. But not by much.

Derr looked on as the small KCG unit roused the camp. The lesser attendants prepared breakfast and attended to their respective charges as they scampered about.

Ferpratt said, "This'll be a big day. Everyone wants to look their best. Every day is a big day for members of the entourage, and every day they want to look their best. Why should today be any different?"

Derr ignored the comment.

Temporary stables required cleaning from horse droppings while maids and cooks rustled about, doing their chores. With the sun climbing a little higher in the morning sky, warmth slogged its way into Derr's cold cheeks.

From his spot overlooking the camp, Derr followed the dance of laborers moving about. Each played their part without regard for what anybody else was doing. Cooks darted here and there, grooms led horses away, and maidens shadowed officials through the labyrinth that was the encampment. All the while, Derr scrutinized their comings and goings with an eye towards the Chancellor's complex. Derr was watching. He was always watching.

The rest of the morning went off about as well as anyone involved with the planning would have expected, which is to say it went according to plan. To some, pulling off a plan as outlined would be a compliment. Derr expected as much.

Derr's thoughts focused on the Chancellor, specifically his elaborate tent arrangement. He spied servants rushing about, packing up belongings, preparing them for others to whisk away later when the entourage moved out. He randomly marked a young girl taking a tray from the Chancellor's cook, and he followed her in his sights as she moved towards the Chancellor's personal dining tent.

Derr grabbed the arm of the young servant girl. "What have you got there under the cloth on the tray?" Derr knew the answer but used unannounced inspections as a tool to instill fear.

The young woman stiffened at the deep sound of Derr's cold, confident voice. Derr expected his voice to frighten her more than his grip on her arm. He intended to plant in her the fear that he spied what she hid in her thoughts.

Her voice crackled. "It's the Chancellor's breakfast, sir." She bowed her head for Derr while carefully pulling back the white linen on the platter. "Please, sir." Still looking down, she said, "The Chancellor's own cook asked that I bring him the meal he prepared for the Chancellor and the First Lady."

Derr sensed her fear. He wanted that exact reaction. *Keep them on edge all the time. Good, she's scared. They should never suspect when I might stick my nose in their lives.*

He waited a moment before replying, reaching onto the plate, picking off a piece of one of the sweetmeats. Tasting it, he said, "Tell the cook it's overdone. I expect better." It wasn't, but Derr cared little for hog's bladder, and besides, he also wanted to remind the cook everything he made is subject to his inspection.

"I'm sorry, sir," she said, shaking. The young woman appeared reluctant to raise her head and stood trembling. Derr let her tremble. He wanted her to be afraid; any act against the Chancellor would cost her life.

Derr thought she might piss herself if he held on to her a second longer, so he released his grip on her arm. "Go. Put the cover back on the dish and bring it to the Chancellor, quick. You're letting his breakfast get cold." It wasn't fair to blame the helpless woman for the meal getting cooler by the minute, but that was Derr.

The servant girl never looked up, and Derr noted she didn't even offer a defense for the now cooling meal. He stood silently as she covered the platter and moved off. Druin Derr scrutinized her as she walked away, still visibly shaken. He watched her go. He was always watching.

Lieutenant Ferpratt sidled up to Captain Derr. "Why do you do that to all the new ones?"

Turning his face toward Ferpratt, Derr said, "She's shitless right now. She'll think twice about this moment before ever doing anything. I suppose having her think of me as a miserable prick is okay by me just so long as she is afraid. Terrified. For the sake of our Chancellor."

"I suppose," Ferpratt said while patting Derr on the shoulder. Derr ignored Ferpratt. The Lieutenant walked off.

The camp looked like a small ant colony with people scurrying about, moving this, packing that, while members of the ruling class barked orders to anyone on their support staff who was nearby. Derr watched. He was always evaluating, always calculating, always watching.

The efforts of the elites breaking camp proved to be the opposite of the KCG's well-choreographed oversight of those who constructed it. Derr didn't care, though. The lesser officials meant nothing to him. As close to the Chancellor as any of them thought they were, they still feared Druin Derr.

Not pretty, nor well organized as it should have been, yet Derr assessed the camp would be ready to move out shortly. He had beheld the same dance each day on their journey from Adelle's capital, Tandure, to Teth.

Derr espied one of his trusted KCG approaching. He had seen him speaking with a hooded man moments ago. The Captain of the KCG expected the hooded visitor. "Captain Derr," the trusted officer called out, "one of your agents has requested an audience."

Druin Derr nodded to acknowledge the request but never stopped looking about the camp. It wasn't unusual for the leader of the KCG to continue his constant scrutiny while engaged in conversation. Eerie, though, often giving cause for others to suspect he'd not been listening. But listen he did, to every word. He was just watching while he was listening, on rare occasions breaking his concentration to look directly at whomever he was listening to. Those who knew him came to accept it and didn't think Derr rude. If they did, no one ever said so. It was just his way. Those not familiar with Derr struggled, often stopping mid-sentence at being so unnerved. "Are you listening?" was a common phrase spoken to Derr. He didn't care. "Yeah," was his usual reply. Just "Yeah." Sometimes he'd offer more words, adding, "Keep going."

With a hand now raised, Derr motioned with his index finger to Milvoe, as if to say, "Come here."

Milvoe and his guest approached Derr, who had picked up on something disturbing near the tent of Prudent Serco. Derr observed an older servant look around as though scanning to determine if anyone was aware he'd slipped something under his coat. The unfortunate servant hadn't detected Derr watching him.

Both the hooded man and Milvoe approached together. Agents of Derr dressed in charcoal gray, with a loose-fitting, hooded cape over all-gray clothing. Gray silk mesh covered the man's face, or was it a woman's face underneath it all? Nobody but Derr would ever see any of them unmasked. It would have been hard to determine who or what was beneath the mysterious attire—loose fitting with the purpose of leaving what was underneath to the imagination. Exactly what Derr wanted. They were his eyes and ears throughout Tartica. He had agents everywhere, or so it was presumed. The Agents of Derr reported to him and him alone. Good intel was the backbone of keeping the Chancellor safe.

Anonymous, faceless specters proved difficult to corrupt. Agents of Derr held out the possibility of being anyone from any walk of life: a barmaid, a homemaker, a thug, a thief, a doctor, a prudent, or even a foreign minister. How many there were or who they were, Derr kept only to himself; not even his only friend, the Chancellor, nor trusted members of the KCG, were privy to the identities of the agents of Derr.

Derr raised his right hand to signal to the hooded specter to stop where he or she stood. Derr turned his head to Milvoe and leaned in to speak privately. "There, near Serco's camp, the older servant in the brown coat. He slipped something under his clothes. Check it out and take whatever action you deem appropriate."

The KCG leader expected nothing serious. He was a realist, yet he left nothing to chance. He understood everyone in the underclass was a thief at one time or another. For that matter, so were the members of the ruling elite; he'd dealt with enough of them over the years. For Derr, however, it was an issue of trust.

Perhaps the old man was just trying to steal away a small trinket he could sell or a piece of leftover food. By the Goddess Teth, they were always hungry. The plight of the underclass suffered all the more in Serco's employ, a frugal man towards his servants and with everyone else. Derr could accept it, but he needed the KCG to measure the old servant. *Just how untrustworthy was he?* He nodded to Milvoe, and Milvoe moved towards the old man as Derr looked on.

"Excuse me. You there, I would like a word," Milvoe said to the man in the shabby, brown coat.

Derr scrutinized the servant, looking about, deciding if he could run to get away or if he should just face the KCG knowing they'd caught him. Obvious to

Derr, it took little time for the old man to decide he couldn't get away, and he dropped his head in submission. The man put his hand on a young girl's shoulder who had been sitting near to him.

"It'll be okay, Daughter. It's just a small piece of bread I was saving for you."

The young girl looked up at her father. Milvoe took him by the arm. With her eyes growing larger, Derr knew the question she would be asking herself: would she ever see him again? She was young, yet not so young not to realize what the KCG was capable of. Her eyes welled up, and her lower lip quivered. There wasn't anything she could do.

Anyone other than Derr who might have taken in the event would have seen it broke the old man's heart to see the fear in his daughter's eyes. Even Derr could see the old man tried to do his best, as any decent father would, to relieve her anxiety. But Derr didn't care.

The old man said, "I'm going with this nice man for a little while. You'll be alright. Will see ya later. I love ya, Kell. Stay with your mum."

Milvoe said nothing as he led the man away.

"I love you too, Daddy. Don't be long," she yelled out, her voice squeaking with uncertainty.

Milvoe will handle the situation, thought Derr. *A broken finger, at least, death at worst.* Milvoe had served the KCG well since being selected by Derr some ten years ago. Derr turned his attention back to the person in the hooded cloak.

The hooded agent stood silently, waiting for Derr's attention. "Alright then. What do you have for me?" Derr said. Pleasantries weren't his style.

"Sir, it's quiet. Nothing out of the ordinary to report. I'm concerned that in Teth, where shit happens every hour of every day, there's nothing to report."

Leaning in close, Derr said, "How can that be? With leaders, Heads of State, others already assembled in the city, and that sneaky bastard Jerithan orchestrating the celebration. He wouldn't pass up such a golden opportunity. Give me every detail of your report."

The two spoke for some time, but Derr never took his eyes off the doings in the camp.

With no warning, the conversation concluded. The hooded person turned from Derr, mounted a nearby horse and rode away, heading back to the city. Derr watched him ride away. He was always watching.

Derr switched gears in need of his Senior Lieutenant.

"Ferpratt!" the Captain commanded. As if out of thin air, Ferpratt appeared before Derr. Ferpratt was tall and well-proportioned for a big man. Intelligence was evident in his eyes yet accompanied with a bit of constant levity Derr both appreciated and hated. He stood half a head taller than Derr. A protruding jaw complimented his otherwise unattractive face. His nose was too big, and having been broken more than once, it visibly angled to the left. Ugly or not, he served the KCG, which meant he served Derr. He was Derr's most trusted officer, only by degrees, as Derr demanded trust from every member of the KCG.

"Yes, Captain?" Ferpratt replied.

The title "Captain" could have been Sergeant or General. It didn't matter to Derr. Druin Derr was the most powerful man in the Kingdom of Adelle after the Chancellor. Titles meant nothing to him. It was just as easy for him not to have one, but Tomelai insisted.

For appearances if nothing else, Tomelai told him years ago, "You need to take a rank." Appearances were important to Chancellor Tomelai, and he wanted Derr to take on the title of general, but Derr declined, as it was too military. The KCG wasn't a military unit. Besides, he disliked every general he ever met. Thought them all too pretentious, too self-important, and often too stubborn. Derr considered himself close to the men and women of the KCG, yet high enough in rank to command. He looked out for every member of the KCG. The whole of Tartica hated him, but not the men and women of the KCG. He judged himself more as a leader than as an entitled officer. He did as his Chancellor requested all those years ago. Captain it was.

"I'm sending you, and take Milvoe and Jamine with you. Do as we planned. Scope out the setting we'll face once we exit The Gate and stand before the entrance to Teth. Determine if anything looks different from what we've negotiated. You have the details of what I want you to look for.

"Like we discussed, you'll be about an hour ahead of us. Send Jamine in plain clothes into the city with the others already there and have her hang around just inside. She should keep her eyes out for anything that doesn't feel right. Anything—and I mean anything—out of place, you send Milvoe back here immediately. Milvoe should've finished dealing with the old man by now. I don't trust that prick Jerithan or his lackey Razoal. The holy Temple of Life, my ass. The holy Temple of Power is more like it. I can't imagine a less holy pair. I'm aware you don't need me to tell you your job. You know what to look for. You've never failed me before. I trust you won't today."

Ferpratt received all the same orders before. The two went over them several times. He didn't interrupt when Derr restated them again. It was Derr being Derr.

Ferpratt had his orders and didn't need to hear them again but would never say so to his Captain. "I live to serve," he offered with a smirk instead. Derr wasn't laughing. He looked Ferpratt square in the eyes. The smirk didn't last long.

"Enough of that shit. Do your job," Derr replied with understanding yet steel in his voice. Not a condemnation of Ferpratt but a matter-of-fact statement Ferpratt and everyone else in the KCG understood about Derr. He'd received a troubling report from one of his agents. It wasn't the only report he received. Not one to put all his trust in a single recognizance effort, Druin Derr had many sources. He kept them separated and unknown to each other. It was his way of ensuring both accurate information and honest agents.

Druin Derr was worried.

Teth was too quiet.

Dirty Deeds of Holy Men

Teth: 27th Day of the Salmon Moon

Razoal | Jerithan

First Lord Jerithan Cree woke early, as was customary for the leader of the Temple of Life faith. First Lord Jerithan's most trusted ally, Razoal Baswun, slipped into his bedchamber to ensure Jerithan would be up early enough to prepare for the first of many events on the Feast of Teth, in the city that bore the goddess's name.

The First Lord's designs for the Feast of Teth went beyond the traditional, perfunctory religious events. If all went as expected on this day, the First Lord's plan to deal with Reyne Brenton and Madrotti Tomelai would come to fruition, the first steps in his scheme to grasp even greater glory—uniting all four nations under his banner in creating the Empire of Tartica.

First Lord Jerithan Cree was a short man, slightly overweight, with salt-and-pepper hair hugging his temples just below the baldness, which took up a large piece of territory on his head. Jerithan Cree looked older than most at fifty-one and burned with more ambition than his frumpy frame suggested.

Second Lord of the Temple of Life, Razoal Baswun, greeted his leader, his friend and his co-conspirator with an emotionless, "It's a good day to serve God and those devoted to the Temple, my lord. We've got a lot to do. Time to get up."

Jerithan was already awake, as was obvious to Razoal, who pulled the cover off the lume crystal jar set in the alcove near the bedchamber's door. The soft green light reached out from the alcove to fill the First Lord's sleeping quarters as best it could. Razoal continued to glide across the cavernous space in his flowing green ceremonial robe. He moved effortlessly as he made his way to the room's east window.

It's such a large room, more than any one man needs, Razoal thought, just as he did every morning when waking the First Lord. He shared many private thoughts with his leader, but never that one.

Razoal stopped momentarily to reflect. *Why haven't I ever said that to my friend?*

Razoal guessed Jerithan might not understand or approve of his Second Lord passing judgment of him. Though not really judgment of Jerithan but on the trappings of the Office he held. In the end, Razoal didn't think Jerithan would care much for whatever reason. It was one thing he resolved never to share. They were allies and friends, sure enough, yet it was Jerithan and not Razoal who held the position as First Lord of the Temple of Life. It wasn't Razoal's place, friend or not, to judge traditions of the Temple or to judge his friend's desire.

Razoal, walking towards the window, looked around at the enormous circular room just as he did every morning. He was in awe, just as he was every morning. *This will be an eventful day. How fitting it should start in this magnificent room.*

One could not help but admire the fine artistry that went into it. The domed ceiling by itself was a marvel. What inspired Razoal more than any other feature was the feeling of being outdoors, being one with nature, the compelling mural created. And that respect for nature was at the heart of the Temple's faith. A faith Second Lord Razoal was devoted to. His decision to join with his First Lord to take control of the continent grew out of his devotion, and in his belief, it would best serve the remains of humanity that populated Tartica. The room reinforced his commitment to both.

The First Lord's room followed one continuous mural and afforded no transition, flowing from floor to wall to ceiling. Nature emerged as though standing in a forest: the painted walls of trees, undergrowth, nurse logs and leaves, hundreds of thousands of green leaves, green of every shade and leaves of every shape on the endless branches on the hundreds of trees of every kind found in the natural world, all lined endlessly along the walls and appeared to recede off into the forest. Branches reached the dome and flowed from the walls to form the ceiling; a woodland came to life painted on the walls.

Looking up enhanced the feeling of standing in a glade. Along the dome, the branches gave way to a bright blue sky on a sunny day with clouds drifting overhead. The skilled hands of artisans left not an inch of the First Lord's bedchamber untouched. Painted on the floor were millions of individual blades of grass that looked as natural as the genuine gift of nature Mother Earth offered in the world outside the room. Only a wash basin, privy pot, desk, conference table and a large four-poster bed distracted one from the feeling of being joined with nature. A special room Razoal understood provided strength to Jerithan as he had contemplated many important decisions since the Council of Prudents chose him First Lord.

Razoal assumed the room gave his friend strength each night as he lay down to sleep and each morning as he rose. Strength to lead the followers of the congregation, from commoners with their petty problems to the bullshit politics of the ruling classes. The room was a cathedral. A representation of the glorious gift Mother Earth presented to humankind, one of many found in nature so graciously depicted in the room.

Razoal pulled back the heavy green curtain embroidered with scenery to fit seamlessly into the mural scene. He unlatched the upper and lower hooks of the tightly fitting shutters of the eastern window. He swung open the left shutter, as tall as three men, followed by the right. Morning light flooded into the bedchamber. Turning his head towards the large four-poster bed, he said, "We've been together a long time, my lord, and today will be the start of even grander heights."

"Yes, we have, and yes, it will," Jerithan replied, while propping himself to a sitting position against the headboard. "And I wouldn't be here, in the First Lord's bedchamber, without that strategic mind of yours."

"You give me too much credit, as usual. I haven't been the one to hold on to it these past three years or the one who consolidated your support amongst the

Council of Prudents. No, my lord, I only serve." Razoal bowed respectfully. He was as close to the First Lord as anyone, but even he knew his place, friendship notwithstanding. Razoal knew the true nature of his friend. Jerithan Cree demanded respect due the Office, and in Jerithan's mind, he and the Office were the same. It conferred the title and position of First Lord upon him and him alone, an unbroken line of legitimate leadership over not only the religious world but it conferred de facto influence into the secular realm as well. Nobody but Jerithan himself, as he saw it, was responsible for his own rise to power. Razoal was grateful for the compliment, yet smart enough not to accept it.

With his hands clasped at his waist, Razoal stood just a few steps from the window he had just opened. "You know, I can wake you each morning for the next fifty years, and I will never lose this feeling. The feeling I get from the scenes on the walls, from the branches reaching up to the sky. It is a testament to the gifts He has bestowed on you. You're a lucky man, my friend, to sleep here each night." Razoal let his hands drop to his side and slowly moved them behind his back as he brought them together again.

"I know the feeling well," Jerithan replied, even though he didn't. He was a believer, but Jerithan Cree believed in Jerithan Cree more than anything else. Committed to doing good for the followers of the Temple of Life, he believed he could make a difference in their lives. It was just that they were secondary to his own well-being. He hid it well, even from his good friend Razoal. He suspected Razoal had him figured out, yet Jerithan understood the man well enough to realize Razoal would never allow himself to speak aloud the shortcomings of his leader.

Jerithan counted on Second Lord Razoal's deep faith more than his own in leading the faithful. "We've got a lot to do today. That means you and me both." Still sitting up in bed, he offered a big, knowing grin. Behind the look on his face was knowledge of the plans they had set in motion. Plans that promised far-reaching consequences.

"We both have our parts to play, just as we planned, Second Lord." Jerithan purposely used Razoal's title as a reminder of who was in charge.

"Let's get you dressed. We have Firstmeal Ceremony with the Council of Prudents in a little while. You know what that's going to be like."

"You know why I enjoy the Firstmeal Ceremony?"

"You ask me that same question every year," Razoal replied, reaching for the green silk comforter covering Jerithan's ornate bed. As the bedsheets flittered over the plush mattress, Jerithan swung both legs around to hang them over the side.

"I know, but you know why, right?" he asked, slipping both feet into his slippers, palms pressed against the mattress as he stood.

"Let's just say I get your position has evolved, grown deeper, since the first time we did this. I faithfully support you in your view that this day begins with the Temple of Life leadership gathering to symbolize the Temple's being unified under your leadership for the secular Heads of State to see."

"Good!" He laughed. Jerithan let his sleeping gown drop to the floor, stepping forward into the bathrobe Razoal held out for him. His naked form held little attention for either man. Leaving his belt unsecured around his expansive waist, he walked to the privy pot to relieve himself of his water. Jerithan stood and reflected on the plans they made for Firstmeal as the prelude for what was to come later in the day. While watching his water begin its brief journey into the basin in front of him, he turned to look over his shoulder at Razoal. "Everything set for today?"

"I've completed all the preparations you've asked of me." He picked up a towel that was draped over the handle of the nearby washbasin and handed it to Jerithan. "I'm certain Firstmeal with the prudents will go off as expected, just as I am certain that what we arranged for the Chancellor inside The Stand will as well. He will not exit it alive. How many twists and turns did we have to take to get this far?"

Jerithan wiped his hands and tossed the small towel back to Razoal.

Standing before the washbasin the First Lord splashed cool water on his face and ran his fingers through his hair. Razoal handed the towel back.

Jerithan took hold of the fabric and rubbed it over his face. Returning the cloth to his faithful Second, he said, "We've done our best to plan for Tomelai's demise. Remind me, did you involve the Anatese in our plans?"

"I did not. They would not engage with me. Only you. Involving you in such a base act of assassination is beneath your Office and something we dare not expose you to with the Anatese. Plans are in place, but the Anatese are not involved. Even though we won't have them aid us, I'm all but certain they'll stay out of it. When have they ever intervened in any goings-on inside The Stand? They'll stay out of it."

Jerithan looked around the room, thinking about what it represented to the followers of the Temple of Life when he heard the Voice in his head whisper to him, "*Every man is alone, especially here.*"

Jerithan never knew when the Voice would speak or where it came from. He had a hunch but couldn't be certain.

He stopped to think about what he just heard responding in his own thoughts. *What do you mean, here?* He stood silently, waiting for a reply. The two had many conversations even before Jerithan Cree ascended to the position of First Lord.

No reply came from the Voice.

Jerithan asked of the Voice in his thoughts, *Do you mean here in this room? Here in this place? Or is your meaning deeper? Alone as First Lord?* Again, nothing but silence. *Alright, my silent friend, I'll bite. What's your point?* He waited for an answer, oblivious of Razoal moving about the room. The Voice, the source of whispers in his head, had been insightful before, always offering something worth considering whenever it spoke.

And then it came, laughing at him, mocking him, challenging him. "*You figure it out.*"

Jerithan always thought divine providence had a hand in him becoming First Lord. To Jerithan, the Voice was proof. He suspected God spoke to him, and to no one else. The one God was guiding him again, just as it guided him through the politics of being selected First Lord. The Voice helped him throughout his tenure.

So why now are you laughing? You're right, though. I am alone, here, now, in what I must do. It is for the good of the Temple. It must be this way. You helped me plan all of this, so why are you laughing now? I await your insights.

No reply from the Voice was forthcoming.

"First Lord." Razoal was standing in front of him. He called out again, "Jerithan!"

"What? What? What's so damned important?" the First Lord spat out.

"You're doing it again. You've been standing there staring blankly at what I cannot guess. We cannot do that at the ceremony with the prudents this morning."

The Voice joined in. "*Razoal is treading on dangerous ground. Friend or not, it does not grant him the liberty to question your competency. He should be grateful it happened while you're both alone. Razoal has seen you do this too many times. It would be a problem if your enemies observed such behavior.*"

Annoyed at Razoal, the First Lord waved his hand at the man as a dismissive exclamation point. "I'm fine, just reflecting on what comes after we rid ourselves of Tomelai."

Razoal took the reprimand with little fuss, pleased it wasn't anything more. He let it go at that. Razoal and Jerithan would face several powerful prudents on the Council who were not supporters of the way the First Lord had led the Temple these past three years. As First Lord, Jerithan had the authority to lead the Council of Prudents, yet he served at the Council's pleasure.

Jerithan was their equal before his ascension, one of thirty-two on the Council of Prudents, not more than three years ago. Razoal could imagine what Prudent Serco would do if Jerithan froze like he just did in front of the Council. Serco would waste little time undermining Jerithan to the point of removal from Office, rallying support for a vote of revocation. Serco thought the First Lord position should have been his.

Bowing to his leader, Razoal took another approach to remind Jerithan of what was at stake. "Serco, our dear fellow prudent, has been busy behind the scenes. He speaks of you in glowing terms in public, and he provided important information about Chancellor Tomelai's arguments supporting electrics due to come up in the Council of Nations meeting. The final factor in our decision to move against Tomelai this morning. But we both recognize what Serco's been covertly doing amongst the other prudents." Razoal had his spies everywhere. *A holy man, Prudent Serco might be,* Razoal thought, *but only a man just the same.*

"It can be dirty work trying to lead a group of holy men and women down the right path," Jerithan offered as an obvious conclusion to Razoal's concerns for the Firstmeal Ceremony. "We are sentinels. As leaders, we hold the basic tenants of the Temple of Life to our hearts, dedicated to the natural way of life. If there is any truth in the scriptures, any truth at all, it was the reliance on machines that led to the Great Destruction. The raping of the world's limited natural resources and the struggles between greedy city-states that contributed to the Second Age coming to an end," Jerithan said, and Razoal heard the passion in his voice.

"It's been the Temple that has held back the forces inching humanity to return to the machine world," Razoal proffered, sucking up to his leader and friend while reciting the vague history of Earth's past leading to its demise as taught to all in childhood. Whether any of it was true, nobody in the Third Age knew, but the story was what they all believed—as a matter of faith.

"We've come this far, my friend," First Lord Jerithan observed, "but we've come as far as this way of life can take us. They will remember you and me for centuries to come when we lead the Temple of Life and what remains of God's special creatures into a new era. I will change everything. I will unite all under my leadership. No nation-state leaders will remain for us to deal with. If we succeed in this, and we will, history will honor me for millennia to come."

Continuing to ingratiate his First Lord, Razoal chimed in, "Who else but the Temple itself, the defender of natural-based technologies as the only acceptable path ahead?" Razoal didn't want to steal any thunder from Jerithan, and so he offered only enough to keep his friend on the path from which he could not be moved.

"Well said, Razoal. Who else but us? You and me. But there are a few on the Council of Prudents that stand between us and greatness, between the children of Teth and better lives. We must pave the way and let the bodies drop in the wake of our success!" Jerithan slapped Razoal hard on his back in confirmation of their shared bond.

Razoal gauged how worked up Jerithan was. He appreciated how his friend reacted every time the two of them talked about pulling the Temple of Life out of the shadows of secular power. The Temple could be more than religious authority. Only the Temple of Life could rule over all of Tartica. But everything could come down on them if they got it wrong, and that didn't leave any opportunity for even one mistake.

Razoal put in, "Serco will be a most powerful foe."

"*He's right, you know,*" came the soft whisper of the Voice into Jerithan's mind. "*You need this. The world needs this. You can help humanity to become great again, all under your leadership. They will hail you for millennia for what we do now... and the nut farmer from that little, inconsequential village. He must be eliminated as well. He can't get in our way.*"

Jerithan offered to the Voice, *Plans are underway for this morning's events and yes, "we" are hopeful both the nut farmer and the Chancellor will be behind us before this day is over.*

The First Lord quieted his mind and waited for a reply. No reply came forward.

Jerithan searched his mind and discovered only silence. "Razoal, it's just you and me. Let me know as soon as you hear that it's done."

Digging at Secrets

Owls Neck: 27th day of the Salmon Moon

Mithany

Morning of the Feast of Teth continued to roll across Tartica in Owls Neck. Mithany, Reyne's fiancée, wearing one of her own designs of a brown leather travel ensemble, was a powerhouse in a small package. A petite, dark-haired young woman of otherwise average proportions with large round eyes set in a triangular face possessed an uncanny ability to read people. It often made those who knew her uncomfortable.

She'd been waiting for her brother, Arek, to meet their leather goods counterpart in Owls Neck, and as usual, he was late.

Seated alone at one of the smaller tables at the tiny village's only outdoor café, she forced down her meal. She didn't wait for him to eat, being too eager to conclude business and get back to Hensdale before nightfall. She missed Reyne.

Mithany wanted Arek with her for a late breakfast. They'd come to Owls Neck hoping to wholesale some of their excess inventory. Anxiety crept into her frame of mind at the prospect she might have to do the meeting without him. At the foot of her chair rested a travel case with her samples.

She and Arek had arrived at dusk the day before. They each took separate rooms. She stayed in a small room with only a bed, a dresser, and a small fireplace—a simple and inexpensive auberge. Mithany turned in soon after they arrived, but Arek chose a different path. He'd left her and set out to explore the village. She loved him dearly, yet long ago she had accepted his wild ways. Both had been to Owls Neck many times, and his words didn't fool her. It wouldn't be the village he'd be exploring.

Mithany loved her brother for many of the same qualities so many young women found appealing about him. Arek always seemed to have fun at whatever he did. Life's concerns never proved too serious for him. He made everyone around him think they were special. She accepted that others saw her much taller brother a more charming person than herself. Mithany not only accepted it, she counted on it. Arek attracted many young ladies to their small leather-goods shoppe in Hensdale, a boon to the business they operated together.

With morning slipping away, it was growing closer to brunch-time. "Where are you?" she muttered under her breath. Mithany loved her brother, but sitting alone, waiting, she was angry with him.

Mithany looked around at the few tables set up outside on the deck and said aloud to herself, "A table for two, and I'm here all alone. I should've known better." However, Mithany noted a woman take a seat with her back to her.

The deck stood above street level by several feet. It wrapped around the front of the quaint little inn. Mithany and the empty streets of Owls Neck welcomed the orange glow of the sun rising over the trees lining the street. The rays warmed her skin. The surrounding air had forsaken its morning chill and contributed a refreshing clean aroma to the idyllic setting. Too bad Arek ruined another lovely morning.

Mithany's view exposed her to most of the shops lining the narrow street. As she looked about, she spotted the leather goods store she was hoping to visit later with Arek, if he ever showed up. She wondered little what he had been up to; she didn't need to guess.

Birds sang their songs of love in the growing warmth of the quiet day. An occasional breeze interrupted the stillness, causing leaves to rustle loudly against the solitude. Idyllic as any of recent memory, the peacefulness she was trying to enjoy ended as a man sauntered onto the deck and settled down to join the other lonely woman.

She heard him offer his greetings to the woman. He tried to speak in hushed tones, but voices carried in the placid setting. The woman told the man she had already ordered meals for them both.

"A planned meeting? A lovers' escape?" Mithany said under her breath.

She didn't mean to eavesdrop, but it was impossible to ignore the only other voices breaking through the serenity of the morning. She tried not to listen in, thinking to herself, *Come on, Arek. We have things to do.*

As soon as the man sat down, the elderly innkeeper appeared at their table—an older woman Mithany had become acquainted with on past visits.

"Excuse me," the innkeeper said to the other couple and placed the preordered meals before them. "And how are you enjoying yourselves on this beautiful day?"

"Just fine," said the seated woman.

"Tell me. Where are you from? I haven't seen you here before," the innkeeper asked the man while reaching for a hand towel hanging limp over her shoulder.

"I'm up from the south near Jarouhar," replied the gentleman. "Well, let's see. I expect there is much I could share about life in the south, but that might tie us both up all day. I can say the weather was just lovely. Jarouhar's a wonderful little seaside village."

The innkeeper continued to stand at the table, wiping her hands on the dirty shoulder-towel. "The young woman at that table over there is from Hensdale. She had little to say about it. Boring, I guess. Half the fun of this job is hearing about what goes on in the big wide world. I never get away to see other places and we get so few visitors here. Any news you might share with me? We get so little news in these parts."

Mithany laughed to herself. It was the same conversation she exchanged with the same innkeeper only minutes ago. *Did she call me boring or Hensdale?*

"You said the girl's from Hensdale. I was there much earlier this morning," the man said.

The innkeeper's face lit up. "Oh, tell me some news from Hensdale. Make an old lady happy."

The man said, "Well, I just sat down and haven't even had time to chat with my lady friend. Give me a few minutes to catch up, eat this great-looking meal you've brought us, and then maybe I can sit with you and tell you some news."

Dropping her head, the older woman spoke without looking up. Her disappointment leaked through her every word. "It's alright. I understand. You're busy and don't have time for folks like me. Hensdale is only several miles from here, but it seems like we're separated by an ocean."

He looked down at his meal, sighed, and said, "Alright, but if I do, you have to promise to let me finish my breakfast. I'll stop inside a little later and give you all the details."

"Yes, yes," the innkeeper replied.

"Just the headline. I have your word?"

"Of course."

"Okay, here's something about Hensdale. I didn't even have a chance to share this story with my friend here. It was going to be the first thing I told her. Anyway, I was passing out of town I saw a young guy, twenty-ish, lying on the ground just off the square. A horse or a wagon hit him. I'm not really sure. I think one local called him Reim, or Rean, or Rai. Something like that. Do you know him?"

The innkeeper's face transformed in an instant, but before she responded, Mithany jumped out of her chair and was on her feet.

"Excuse me, sir!" Mithany blurted out while pushing her chair out from underneath. Her slight frame turned towards the couple. She caught the hint of a name. *Was it Reyne? Was he hurt? Was he okay?* Her thoughts raced.

Her chest exploded in fear before she ever got to the nearby table. Not normally bold enough to approach a table of strangers, Mithany wasn't like her brother in that way. But when she needed to, she could be more determined than him. She had to find out if it was Reyne she heard spoken of.

Adrenaline swept over her as she turned to see the bearer of the bad news. Fear gripped her. All she comprehended was someone was unconscious back in Hensdale, and it could be Reyne. Stumbling from her table, the chair fell forward. She paid it no mind. She glared at the prematurely white-haired man seated with a middle-aged woman.

The dumbfounded innkeeper, stringy gray strands of hair haphazardly scattered about her face, turned, facing Mithany. Warmth was not the emotion projected from the older woman's scowl. Mithany's brow crunched, and her eyelids drew close together.

Mithany stepped between the tables and separated them swiftly as she passed. It was a small seating area, only a few steps for Mithany. Long strides with short legs swept her across the deck. She introduced herself. "My name is Mithany. I'm from Hensdale," she announced.

The innkeeper turned and walked away, leaving Mithany with the two patrons.

Unable to keep from shaking, Mithany stopped for another moment and said, "Sorry to interrupt you. I'm not normally moved to poor manners or to listening in to someone else's conversation, but I couldn't help overhearing you. Please excuse me. But"—she paused—"you said something about a young man named Reyne."

"Yes," the white-haired man said. Though his stern facial expression said much more. Mithany looked at his face and his furrowed eyebrows. Her read of the stranger told her he wasn't too happy with the interruption. She didn't care.

Manners be damned, Reyne, I have to know. She pulled over a chair from a nearby table and sat down.

"What I told our innkeeper is about all the news I really have for you."

"What do you remember seeing?" She tried to hide her crackling voice and her heavy breathing.

Annoyance poured through the words of his reply. "What I told you already is about all I got. I passed through on my way here. I was in a hurry. Sorry, that's everything."

Without regard to the stranger's irritation, Mithany was determined to extract more information. She asked, "Did he get up and move about before you left? Did you notice what he looked like? Can you help me with anything like that?" The questions shot out at him one after the other, with no time offered for a reply. She stopped short, eager for his response.

His eyes narrowed with a determined pause, and he folded his arms across his chest. "I picked up on a name but can't be sure. It might have been Reim, Rain, Reggel... I don't know, Reh something. As for the rest, I never saw his face. On my horse, I passed along the road where a group of people had gathered. I caught a few words, only there for a few seconds as I rode past. I'm not able to say how bad the man was hurt or anything else. That's it." He picked up his fork to attend to his meal.

She tasted the anger in her soul yet needed to gain control of herself to get what she wanted out of this man: more information. Her ears grew hot, hotter, then red with fire. She did her best to control herself, yet her outrage gave her away. Of all the emotions she practiced controlling, impatience had been the hardest for her to master. As much as she desired to push the wrath down, her body reacted to the intense emotions. She had to cool down.

Mind and body are one. Mind and body are one. Where one goes, the other follows. She tried to slow her breathing while repeating in her mind the calming internal message she had learned. *Mind and body are one. Where one goes, the other follows.*

Battling her inner turmoil, she tried desperately to control her behavior, but fear was winning. Mithany reasserted her inner strength as she struggled to take back control.

His eyes.The eyes always give something away, and his are telling me he's hiding something.

She grew proficient as a child at reading her mother's every expression. When Mithany discerned the signs of frustration building in her mother, it signaled to her the time had come to find a place to hide. A skill borne of necessity. Failure meant pain, beatings.

Mister Whitetop—a name she decided fit him perfectly given the distinguished look of his white hair—was a man she needed to figure out quickly. She needed information, and a sweet young woman persona usually worked better than a screeching banshee. She determined she'd move the tone of the conversation in a different direction.

She lowered her voice, softened her eyes, slowed down her speech, and softly pleaded, "If it is Reyne who was hurt, if he's the man you saw lying on the ground, I need to know. Please, I've gotta know. Please, he's the love of my life."

Mister Whitetop spoke slowly, and Mithany thought he was intentionally condescending, "Again, if I had anything, I'd tell you. Now, please. Yes, it's my turn to say please. Please, we just want to enjoy our breakfast. For your sake I hope it's not your young man."

A tear welled up in Mithany. *He's lying.* She saw it written across his face, and not knowing what he was hiding frightened her. It didn't seem she was going to get the answer she craved. He was obviously hiding something. It was in his eyes.

Her heart ached for answers.

Her dream of marrying Reyne, just days away, was threatened. A future they both wanted more than anything hung on the words of Mister Whitetop.

She thought of Reyne, who told her many times that she was such a unique, smart, confident woman, of how he appreciated her gentle and loving way with him, but he confessed to her that sometimes she could be cold towards those she didn't like. She heard Reyne in her head telling her that underneath it all, she was a complicated woman, calculating when she needed to be and loving when she wanted to be. It all depended on who she wanted to be at any given time. Towards Reyne, all she ever wanted was to be his wife and the mother of their children.

She determined to show Mister Whitetop her cold, calculating side. She still had another card to play, even though all her raw emotions were real. She would use them to advance her cause. *The middle-aged woman sitting with him might respond to another female in need.* She sniffled, a genuine sniffle, and another tear, a real tear, rolled down her face.

She was operating of two minds: one a frightened woman, the other a manipulative, calculating hellion. Out of the corner of her eye, she watched for a reaction from the middle-aged, red-headed woman. The woman looked toward Mister Whitetop, raised her eyebrows while giving him soft puppy eyes as if to say, "Do something." At least, it's how Mithany read it.

He sighed, rolling his eye at hers in return.

"Dylla, what do you want me to tell her?"

Apparent to Mithany, Dylla's approval appeared to be all he cared about. Mithany looked on; another glance from Dylla was all it took. Evidently, Dylla was interested and wanted to unearth more of his story.

Mithany watched it all transpire in seconds. She didn't experience guilt for manipulating Dylla. Manipulation wasn't a bad thing in her mind. Everyone wants to get their own way. Mithany did it with purpose.

Mister Whitetop turned away from Dylla, facing Mithany, annoyed. She forced him to say more. He tried to hide his frustration, but Mithany peered through his deception.

"I was riding by on my horse. I was in a hurry to get to Owls Neck to meet this lovely woman," he said in measured, choppy sentences. "There were about twenty or thirty people mulling about. From where I sat on my horse, I tried to look through the crowd of people gathered in a half-circle. It was too difficult to see anything. I heard one of them talking to another. He said something about a guy. I made out the name Reim, perhaps, getting knocked out by the tithe-wagon. The guy said he guessed this Reim fellow, or whatever name it was, just walked directly into a horse or the wagon. Then, splat, the guy was on his back, knocked out. Someone said he was still breathing. I rode on. Seemed nothing I could do. I wanted to get here as fast as I could. That's all I got. Sorry if it isn't enough."

He raised his arms off the table, turned his palms upward, shrugged his shoulder as if to say, "That's it, sorry. Are you satisfied now?"

Mithany, while not satisfied, didn't think there was anything else she was going to get out of him.

Before she could consider what to do next, still seated at the table with the two travelers, she recognized Arek's voice calling out to her.

"Hey, Sis, sorry I'm late," was Arek's attempt at an offering of goodwill. He strode across the outdoor café deck, waving one hand high in the air while clinching the hand of a red-haired young woman he dragged along behind.

Maybe more of a girl than a woman, Mithany reckoned, watching the pair approach. The girl's red eyes stole Mithany's attention. A wide variety of eye colors was common. While most common were blue, brown, gray, and green, it was not unheard of for the occasional yellow, pink, copper, or violet-colored eyes. Golden coloring was rarer still. But red was never seen. Red pupils were spoken of, yet few ever claimed to have known someone with that rarest of affectations.

Almost pulling the red-eyed girl behind him, he weaved through the tables. Grinning from ear to ear with so much life and happiness on his face, he approached the table where Mithany now sat.

He cared little about being timely. For Mithany's older brother, time was something everyone else got hung up about.

"Oh, Arek," was all she said with disappointment under her breath. Speaking up, she added, "Arek, we have to rush back to Hensdale. It's Reyne. He may have been hurt, bad. We gotta go."

"Oh shit. I'm right there with you. Before we go, Sis, wait," he said, coaxing his newfound partner to stand beside him. "This is Neladith. Isn't she just lovely? Who're these folk, new friends? When did you meet these people?" He jumped around. His thoughts spilled out of his mouth rapidly. One flowed after another with little consideration given to anything he was saying.

Neladith, the young redhead, waved to everyone and said, "Hi," with a big grin just like Arek's.

Arek lived for the moment. Armed only with looks to blend into a crowd unnoticed, the tall and thin young man increased his appeal and improved his connection rate with an overabundance of charm. A quality he seemed unable to turn off. His thick black hair looked as though he had just rolled out of bed, which was most likely the case.

A frequent observation Mithany made of her brother: *He can charm the pants off anyone. And often does.*

Arek wore an affable smile, tan pants, and a powder-blue, long-sleeved shirt opened from his neck to his chest. His smile matched well with the ever-present, childlike excitement in his voice. He rarely failed to take life up on whatever it offered.

"I made a new friend. Isn't she so cute? We met last night." Arek, speaking rapidly, turned toward Neladith, offering her a warm, welcoming look. He leaned in to kiss his new friend, pulling her body close to his. When their lips moved apart, Neladith looked down, embarrassed. Mithany spied conflict on the girl's face, and the fact she tried to hide it from everyone at the table. Something her oaf of a brother didn't realize.

Mithany thought Neladith looked to be sixteen or seventeen. *She can't be that young. She's gotta be older than she looks.* Neladith was a wiry, thin, buxom youth slightly taller than average. Her plaid skirt was short, highlighting her long legs, and her white top was tied off above her waist, exposing her youthful torso.

"This is Dylla," Mithany told her brother and his new partner. "Sorry, but I don't know this gentleman's name. My brain's been calling him Mister Whitetop."

"I never introduced myself. I'm Selundra Quith. I'm up from Jarouhar in the south. No offense taken," Mister Whitetop stated flatly.

Mithany sensed something unsettling in Neladith's body language. Specifically in the way her eyebrows reacted to the introduction of Selundra Quith. Mithany caught the way Neladith focused on Mister Whitetop while paying little or no attention to Dylla.

Arek jumped in, pretending to care who they were. He was good at faking interest and discovered early in life feigned interest works just as well as sincere interest for those skilled enough to pull it off. To help Mithany with her deficiency in social skills, he tried to teach her how. He often told her, "Sincerity is tough to fake. But if you can, the world is yours." He was good at pretending, but not so good at staying focused. Pointing at both Neladith and himself with his finger wagging back and forth, he said, "We met last night. She was standing on the bridge overlooking the square. She looked lonely. We talked all night. Well, talked most of the night." With a guilty look on his face, he offered a one-eyed wink aimed directly at Mithany.

Oh, big brother, was all Mithany could muster in her thoughts.

Out of the corner of her eye, Mithany noticed Mister Whitetop give Neladith a quick visual once-over while still clasping Dylla's hand.

Mister Whitetop, she's too young for you. And with Dylla right there... Not important. Mithany refocused her mind.

The distraction offered by Arek and Neladith annoyed her. Mad at herself for allowing the diversion to command her attention, she forced such thoughts to recede from her awareness. "Arek, we have to get back right away." Her emotions seeped into her tone, and her voice cracked when she spoke. She knew it and she couldn't stop it. Admitting to herself she wasn't in control, fear leaked through her voice. She didn't care, which was unusual for Mithany.

"Reyne may've been in an accident, and he might be seriously hurt. I know little more than that, so we need to return to Hensdale right now."

The disruption of only moments ago out of her mind, tears dripped down her cheeks again. She raised both hands to wipe them away with her palms. "I'm so sorry, Neladith, but I need my brother right now." Turning to Arek, ignoring Dylla, Mister Whitetop, and Neladith, she said, "Arek, we have to leave, now."

Arek failed to let go of Neladith's hand. Mithany gave it little attention as the three of them walked away.

The two travelers remained at their table. With no one left to hear her, Dylla Weisner turned to Selundra Quith, Mister Whitetop, and said, "So, I gather Reyne Brenton isn't dead?"

"There's still a chance. Depends on how much venom I put into him. I put a lot on the tip. Used a dart shaped like a spiderworm, so even if anyone sees it, it wouldn't raise any suspicions."

"Why didn't you stay and finish it? You could've sent word. I don't mind breakfast alone."

"Meratoruc was about, disguised as a grungy old man, but I saw through it. I had to evade him. It was the only clear shot he left to me all morning. Just as I took it, Reyne Brenton stepped into a passing wagon and then, out of nowhere, I saw Meratoruc approaching. I got out of there."

"Meratoruc frightens you?"

"I thought I had killed the slippery bastard more than once, but he just keeps coming back. The last time, I was certain he was dead. No, not frightened, just cautious when it comes to Meratoruc. Didn't want to mess up the op by being detected. So, I got out of there quick. But Reyne Brenton still might die. I tipped it with a lot of poison. We'll see."

"If he's still alive at dusk, implement the backup op. I sent the shooter to meet you at the designated location. Told her to be ready in case she's needed. You met her. Agent Arrow. I briefed her yesterday afternoon. She'll be ready. If Reyne Brenton is still alive by the time it gets dark, finish the job tonight. Now get back to Hensdale and stay out of sight. And don't let me down again. The next time I hear from you, it better be the words, Reyne Brenton's dead."

A Sacrifice Made

Hensdale: 27th Day of the Salmon Moon

Daedyn

Daedyn faced a conundrum. Reyne was missing, and he desperately needed to find Doc Brenal. But one without the other was useless. Finding Reyne gone changed everything.

Daedyn didn't know how much time he had. He was in a hurry but not yet frantic.

Daedyn hurried past the shops that lined Hensdale's market square. Mithany and Arek's leather goods shoppe sat two doors down from the Forest Maiden Inn. Mithany's shoppe was smaller than most of the other stores lining the street. It was quaint, framed with bay windows on each side to allow displays of the various goods they offered. A sign hung over the door, *"Leather Goods and Services"* carved into an oval-shaped wooden plaque with leather inlays outlining each letter.

This sucks. If only Mithany were here. It would be easy. I find her... I find Reyne. Arek, that fucker's worthless, anyway. So much for help from either of 'em.

Passing the dry goods store where Daedyn sold a small amount of alphens to Hangus, the owner of the dry goods store, he thought, *Worth the chance. If I can get Hangus to help look. Hangus, now there's a decent guy. I suppose he'll help me search for Reyne.*

He couldn't afford to be wrong.

Daedyn swung open the door and looked around for Hangus. He saw Y'vay standing behind the counter, and in front of her was the store's last full wooden barrel of his own alphens left over from the last harvest. She smiled from behind the long wooden counter. Behind her were familiar shelves stocked with assorted items in large glass jars. Oil lamps and lume crystals lit the small shoppe. On another shelf were candles, lume crystals, dried bacon, along with soaps and various dried roots. Large canvas sacks lined the floors with corn, wheat, and flour.
"Hi, Y'vay, is Hangus in?" he said in a hurried voice.

"Hello, Daedyn," Y'vay said, flirtatiously brushing her long, cinnamon-colored hair away from her face with the flick of her hand. She offered him a slight head tilt. Her big, welcoming smile drew Daedyn in. "He's not here. I'm here all alone," she said, raising one eyebrow.

Any other time... but not now. No time. Shit. What a waste... damn you, Rey.
"Y'vay, you are looking lovely as usual. How is it you're not taken yet? But I've got no time today. I'm in a hurry to find Doc Brenal. Have you seen him?"

"Who says I haven't been taken? And, no, sorry, ain't seen him." She laughed. Her eyes sparkled. An average young woman by Hensdale's standards with a thin face, small, almost tan eyes, mixed with a personality that shouted fun. She rarely put any limits on her desire to experience all of life's offerings.

Daedyn had not known the boundless limits of Y'vay's pursuit of fun by firsthand experience; it was just what others had said. Who knew if any of it was true? Besides, his own reputation fit within the same parameters. Under different circumstances Daedyn fancied the opportunity to get closer to Y'vay and to honor the Gift of Flesh in the ways of Temple teachings for both men and women alike. Just not this day.

I don't have time for this. Ahh, my loss. You owe me big time, little brother.

"Y'vay, unfortunately I have to go find both Rey and Doc Brenal, and I was hoping Hangus might help," he said, gesturing with both arms with upturned palms while shrugging as if to say, "No choice." He was sure she sensed his desire to accept her invitation.

"Your loss," she exclaimed. "Anyway, my dad ain't here. He left a while ago. Something about the tithe master. I don't know. Who listens?" She paused and finished with, "Perhaps we can pick this up again next time... Maybe."

Daedyn thought the last "maybe" made it sound like she teased him with a change of mind whenever "next time" might be. Nothing to be done about it at the moment, Daedyn had greater concerns, and he was wasting time exchanging banter with Y'vay.

He wanted to ask her to help, but he understood Hangus well enough to know he'd be pissed if Y'vay closed the shop early for any reason. Impetuous as she was, all Daedyn had to do was ask. But Hangus ran a tight ship, and firing his own daughter wasn't outside the realm of possibility. If he was in, Daedyn was sure Hangus would close the store, but he wouldn't let Y'vay or Daedyn make such a decision for him.

He's a control freak. I can't ask Y'vay to put her job at risk. I'm done here.

"Thanks anyway, Y'vay. Have a good one." He turned and strutted out the door, confident in the knowledge Y'vay would watch him walk away.

She watched him, of course, and without him seeing, she gently blew him a quiet kiss and whispered to nobody there, "Next time. We'll see."

The door closed behind him. Stepping off the storefront decking onto the street, Daedyn looked around, finding only a few people passing by. He lost valuable time gambling on Hangus. Back on the gravel roadway, Daedyn picked up his pace and started running.

It Matters Not

Evidar

Emosh

In a conference room off the main reception area of the Devil's Blacksmith's underground compound, the recently declared Damus shared her calculations for their planet's future, their version of Earth—a world forever in darkness.

With the salvation of his dying planet the Devil's Blacksmith's obsessive purpose, only one path pointed the way towards its deliverance. The convergence of two independently existing versions of Earth from different dimensions, at the expense of—and the ruination of—one of those dimensions, an idyllic, utopian Earth: Tartica in the Third Age. The total devastation Tartica faced, the immeasurable suffering that would be forced upon its populace, and the massive loss of life a convergence promised mattered not to the Devil's Blacksmith, nor to any who followed him, including Damus Synja Emosh. Saving Evidar was all that mattered.

"It's a complicated thing I do," Emosh said, fidgeting.

The Devil's Blacksmith, a man with empty eyes darker than a black hole, replied with a hint of annoyance, "I am aware of the complexities."

The youthful Damus swallowed hard and ran her hand over her long, silver hair while pacing back and forth. "I'll try to explain it, but honestly, people just don't get what a Probability Wave is. How it might or might not collapse because of phase-shifting interference patterns. And those phase shifts, when there's two or more waves, well, then they are either in a state of Coherence or Decoherence.

It's just so beautiful, well, for me. But for everyone else, seems this stuff makes their brains go numb."

Synja Emosh, honored as the first to be declared a Damus in over twenty years, took pride in her peerless mathematical abilities. Not that Evidar's inhabitants measured time in years, days, or hours. They didn't, though only for the lack of sunlight or shadows. They couldn't. However, the Devil's Blacksmith did—as did his Damus. The death of the last Damus at the hands of a Tartican assassin named Edruk set the Devil's Blacksmith in search of a replacement. A quest that consumed two decades and dealt a serious blow to the single-minded objective from which the effort was now only beginning to recover.

He offered her a rare smile. "Other ambitious pretenders tried to fill the shoes of my last Damus but proved incapable of converting their experiences in the Void to accurate numeric formulations. Still others failed at the impossibly complicated mathematical equations required of the job. The marriage of physics, calculus, and interpreting Void-driven experiences to quantify the future of an entire reality as a single equation-defining-probability-outcome proved an impossible task, beyond their skills. Until I found you."

Through the darkness, a flush of pride danced across Emosh's face.

He continued, "Synja Emosh, yours is the rarest of minds amongst all men and women."

"Thank you, sir. I'll make you proud."

The man called himself the Architect, the one who wrote the blueprint his minions followed to create a better future for the world he lived in. However, the name most associated with the man, the Devil's Blacksmith, was a moniker earned by one who raged to forge a new reality out of the fires of a dying planet. No life proved too precious to avoid ruination if it stood in his way. No quarter given to anyone who failed him. No false hope or praise toward any. The Devil's Blacksmith, a name invoked by others, and only when out of range from the man to hear it spoken, is how Synja Emosh and everyone else thought of him. His utter disregard for others left her to wonder if his quest to save their Earth held hidden, more personal motivations.

"Miss Emosh, you brought me findings not long ago about a handful of Shifters from Tartica, each capable of disrupting our plans. Based on that, I have taken steps to eliminate them. All those who have been eliminated can no longer disrupt our purpose. As for the one who remains, agents I've dispatched to Tartica will terminate him in short order. Have you completed your calculations to remove the threat of the Tartican Shifters from the equation, as I have requested?"

Her pale skin, ubiquitous on Evidar, matched her silvery-white hair and stood out against her wide-set, upturned, brown eyes. Youthful in appearance—having never been assigned an age like all who existed in the environs of Evidar—yet her figure more than adequately confirmed her womanhood. She knew her appearance mattered little to the Devil's Blacksmith: he prized her for her beautiful mind.

Her lips smacked as she opened them to speak. Synja Emosh's voice was intoned with a hint of anxiety, as though engaged in public speaking before a hostile crowd. Her tongue searched her dry mouth for relief while her brain forced out the words, "Yes. But."

The blackness of his eyes couldn't begin to match that of his soul, invoking a gut-twisting hesitation in her response. He needed information, and scared people make mistakes, she thought.

"You have not caused these ripples in time. Tell me what concerns you, Miss Emosh. Speak freely." The Devil's Blacksmith tried to ease her fears, not out of compassion; she knew he lacked for any.

With her hands clenched together behind her back, her eyes gazed down at her feet parading around the room as she spoke words in rapid succession. "There's one potential Random Phase Offset that could bring about Decoherence to the wavefunctions of the two worlds, destroying everything you've mapped out and forever cutting the cord between the two dimensions. That Random Phase Offset variable is one man... Reyne Brenton. The Void has not shown me how he achieves it, but I know this, based on my calculations, if he steps foot on our world—"

Synja Emosh stopped. She forced her head up to face the Devil's Blacksmith.

Sounds lacking any emotions dripped from him. "This is the man I spoke of who my operatives are currently dealing with. Go on."

She spoke in a brisk tempo, pushing out words to keep pace with rapid-fire thoughts racing across synapses, with little forethought or consideration afforded as to whether the Devil's Blacksmith could keep up with the meaning they carried before the next thought queued up for release. "There may be another like Reyne. I'm still refining the data and need to explore the Void for other Probability Waves. The picture's unclear on this second Random Phase Offset: a Tartican, but not a Shifter like Reyne Brenton. Yet, like Reyne Brenton, this person who I haven't identified is the cause of a fourteen percent chance to mess up our plans. It could be the actions of two Tarticans. I wasn't able to get a fix on the exact Probability Waves causing the disruption. I need more time in the Void to search for these two other influences."

"You need not worry about delivering me this news. I understand the vagaries of nailing down the highest probable outcome amongst all the untold possible futures the Void shows you. Yet, time we do not have."

She swallowed again. "I know."

The Devil's Blacksmith prodded her along. "Let us continue, Miss Emosh. I have had many years to study these ideas and have been through these theories and physics concepts with all your predecessors. You have thrown out a lot of technical jargon, so let us agree to eliminate the fancy words. Speak plainly, and settle yourself. Take a few deep breaths."

"Yes, sir. I can do that. I'm just nervous." Although, nerves or not, Synja Emosh spoke to everyone the same way—fast. A blemish on her beautiful mind; she understood better than anyone how to commune with numbers, not so much with people.

"Good. Now slow down when you speak."

"Yes, sir." Her chest rose and fell. "This is all theoretical. Using quantum mechanics, I can explain what's going on, but that's just it." Uncertain he would accept her explanation, she paused. "It applies at the tiniest levels of existence. In the laws of physics that govern any object with qualified mass, especially big things like planets, General Relativity applies, not quantum mechanics. Two entwined dimensions of Earth behaving like quantum particles is scientifically impossible. In the world of quantum mechanics, all this is possible, but only for tiny electron, photons, and quarks."

"Lions and tigers and bears... electrons and photons and quarks, oh my."

Emosh shifted her head sideways, "I'm sorry, sir, I don't understand."

"A reference from long before your time Miss Emosh." He folded his hands in his lap and looked up at his Damus, who had stopped pacing. He continued, "Are you starting from the point of divergence I specified? At the instant the asteroid struck Earth—the Great Destruction—a second Earth inexplicably became unmoored from its dimensional tether as the Many-Worlds Interpretation of the universe postulates is possible. This second Earth popped into existence before the asteroid-induced devastation sped across the planet. This other pristine version of Earth burst into existence, with some differences... minus the people and the footprint of destruction left to us... and given this second Earth is real, sharing information across separate dimensions should not exist, even in the Many-Worlds scenario. But it does."

"That's the working model I've been using, sir. It's what accounts for both Earths and the ability of Shifters to move between them."

The Devil's Blacksmith's encouraging tone helped Emosh settle down, but her hurried vocalizations proved a stubborn affectation to master in the moment. "As best I can figure, the Earth, the sun, and our entire solar system rises and falls against the galactic plane—you know, the Milky Way—while circling around the galaxy at more than a half-a-million miles an hour. And if you consider the work of scientists from the nineteenth and twentieth centuries who established the velocity of the Milky Way, when you add it all together, Earth is racing through space at almost two million miles an hour."

"You are doing fine. Continue."

"Again, based on my research from the ancient books and journals in your library, sometimes Earth is above the galactic plane. Millions of years later, it's below it. Earth moves up and down, up and down as the millennia roll on, and measured over light-years, over eons of time, it follows that our planet has a wave pattern just like a photon's wave frequency, only much bigger. Oddly enough, Earth behaves like a photon particle of light moving through space. Earth has a wave pattern, a frequency, and a quantifiable amplitude. Just on a cosmic scale."

He offered her a hint of excitement in his reply. "Rare books indeed, Miss Emosh. You, and all my previous Damus, possess the rare ability to experience the Probability Wavefunctions of Earth's two dimensions in the Void as one might experience the same for an individual such as Reyne Brenton. Until now, its genesis has eluded us. This is brilliant work; the basis of our planet's, and Tartica's, individual Probability Wavefunctions that will prove crucial to even greater accuracy in your future calculations."

Her face lit up in the gloom of the dark room. "I am so proud to be a part of this, sir. Two versions of Earth, rising and falling in their respective galactic planes at the same rate, traveling at the same speed, until our two planetary wavelengths, in sync from different dimensions, line up at a single point in space and time where these two dimensions will converge."

The Devil's Blacksmith smiled. She'd never seen such a full smile from him before. Although, she thought something malevolent hid behind it.

"I'm committed one hundred percent. You know that, sir. It's just... none of this should be happening. The splitting of spacetime as though each version of Earth is a single photon in an oversized Double Slit Experiment is an impossible state of being. Two Earths in two separate dimensions, behaving like quantum particles. Physics doesn't allow for it. I deal in hard facts, numbers, equations... what is real. This is abracadabra stuff on a planetary level, and it's hard for me to accept... scientifically. But I know this, only one of these two states of reality can be true, either we exist in a multiverse where the laws of physics have broken down or that asteroid—fifteen hundred years ago—slammed into Earth and opened a door to a mystical realm. It can only be one or the other."

"What is real Miss Emosh?" He spread his arms open in a sweeping gesture. "The 'why' of it does not lead us out of darkness. The 'how' of it does not deliver us a better future. The supernatural and physics need not be mutually exclusive.

The very existence of the Void should open your mind to accept there is more to the universe than human thought is capable of understanding. We must simply play the cards we have been dealt."

Shaking her head in disbelief, Synja Emosh confessed, "I just don't know anymore if I'm dealing with science or magic."

"It matters not, Miss Emosh."

Forbidden Is Just a Word

Teth: 27th day of the Salmon Moon

Derr

The morning of the Feast of Teth rolled on two miles outside the city named for the goddess the fete so honored. Chancellor Tomelai finished the breakfast he shared with his wife, First Lady Kaythlin. The pair were running late, having stolen time from the schedule for a passionate session of shared intimacy. An appropriate start to a day that would shower Tomelai in adulation—if all went according to plan.

Outside the sovereign's pavilion, servants all about camp packed up the travel belongings of their respective patrons.

Adelle's entourage prepared to move out.

The support staff would follow later.

Chancellor Tomelai and First Lady Kaythlin were the last to appear at their appointed station. The Tomelais' delay resulted in getting started later than expected. It irked Derr, but as it was Tomelai's doing, Derr held back from voicing his frustration. He would do it in private when he had the Chancellor alone.

The sun was fully over the horizon on its path across the sky. Chancellor Tomelai looked across to his glowing wife. The two locked gazes and smiled back at each other. In his overactive sex drive, he had found the perfect mate. Other aspects of life between them weren't perfect. When it came to sex, however, they were great together. It helped make everything else between them work.

Derr was watching. He'd seen the look between them many times before. He understood the cause of their tardiness. Irritated at the delay, yet it didn't stop the smirk he gave his Chancellor as the pair approached. Tomelai gave a discreet nod to Derr, as if to confirm the reason for their late arrival. The Tomelais' early morning dalliance kept over one hundred people waiting.

Atop his horse, Tomelai sidled up alongside Derr, telling the Captain for no one else to hear, "If a Chancellor can't spend a morning with his lovely and naked First Lady, what good is it being Chancellor?"

A stoic face from Derr followed in reply.

The procession moved at a steady pace, and it wasn't long before they could see the city of Teth before them. Up and over the last small rise along the rolling green Hills of Rathia, they approached the city-state of Teth. From a mile away, the city remained partially hidden behind the stunning magnificence of The Stand.

The KCG were the first to catch sight of The Stand from their position at the front of the procession. Unique in the known world, The Stand, a narrow strip of forest, was more spectacular and more formidable than any man-made creation. The Captain of the KCG looked up at the two-hundred-foot-tall giant sequoias standing in a tight line as if they were guards in a well-drilled unit. Immovable against any force man or nature could throw at it, the conifers grew so close together they looked like huge fence posts put there by forces only gods could muster.

No matter how many times a traveler came upon the site, a sense of awe and deep respect for nature swelled in every heart. Those in the ruling class in the Kingdom of Adelle, lucky enough to be part of the entourage, were no different.

The Stand grew larger and more commanding the closer one approached the colossus. Imperceptible from a distance, The Stand granted passage through one large break in the otherwise impenetrable barrier, simply known as The Gate. The Gate, an opening in the seemingly never-ending line of the giant trees, granted entry into a tunnel-like passageway through the dense yet narrow grove that made up The Stand.

The Captain of the KCG scanned the overwhelming scene before him. The extensive line of trees went off for several miles on either side of The Gate. To his left, The Stand ended when it reached the Bay of Synn. The site impressed even Captain Druin Derr, and Derr wasn't a man easily impressed by anything. It wasn't his first visit to the city nor the first time he had seen The Stand, but it didn't diminish the awe he felt for the impressive natural formation.

He admired the protection it provided for all who stood behind it, even though the Covenant took war off the table in all the years of the Third Age. It was just how Derr's mind worked.

"It's a magnificent sight, isn't it?" Derr said in what sounded more like an observation than a question.

Tomelai looked less impressed. His face gave nothing away. Being Chancellor, Tomelai mastered the art of giving nothing away. Unless, of course, he wanted to. "Yes, it is, Drew. It surely is," Tomelai replied with just enough well-practiced warmth in his tone to let Derr know everything was proceeding to his satisfaction.

Druin Derr had ridden side by side with the Chancellor and First Lady since meeting up. He barely spoke to either of them. It wasn't unusual. Derr always had a lot to think about, and it afforded Tomelai to attend to the First Lady. Derr didn't feel slighted at the silence.

Teth had no real need for such a defense. There hadn't been war in the history of the Third Age. Most weapons from the Second Age—those they knew of—were banned, as were standing armies. Accounting for all the false posturing of friendship and professed cooperation between nations as demanded by the Covenant, Teth was de facto, neutral ground.

Alongside Tomelai at the head of the procession, upon glimpsing The Stand, Derr thought, *I can almost believe all the Temple of Life's bullshit looking at this.*

Derr had seen too much killing, too much blood, too much of what humanity could do to each other to believe in a benevolent and loving god. He had done a great deal of the killing himself. He had done it all in defiance of the Covenant, which precluded the taking of life for any reason. Killing or even causing harm to another was forbidden given the demands of humanity's repopulation.

Meaningless to Derr.

Maybe wars weren't hanging over his Chancellor's head, but threats, real or imagined, to Tomelai's life needed to be eliminated. The Covenant's dictates were universal and absolute and that should have been enough to protect his Chancellor—but that was just on paper. Derr wasn't the only one to disregard its demands. Other forces were as proficient as Derr in ways forbidden by the Covenant.

To Derr's way of thinking, "forbidden" was just a word—noise one could make. A modulating wave passing through air held no inherent power over Derr. With no actual physical energy, speech was weak. Words themselves couldn't kill with the force of the sound they make, and, therefore, words couldn't stop Derr. Power was in the deeds of the man and women who acted. Letters written on paper couldn't exert any physical restrictions on him, either. The word, any word, spoken or written, held no power over him. Only when either came from Chancellor Tomelai did words matter.

The people of Tartica surrendered to words by their own choice, by their own actions, by their own acquiescence. Derr didn't acquiesce to anyone or anything. Nothing stopped Captain Derr from protecting Chancellor Tomelai. Ancient signatures, scribbles from long-dead people on a dried-up old piece of paper never entered the equation as Derr put into practice his one and only mission: to protect his Chancellor at all costs. Chancellor Tomelai, the man he called Rotti, was his only real friend, and he'd do anything to safeguard him.

Looking up as he approached The Gate, Derr took a map out from under his formal dress coat. The map in his hands and the scene before him showed trees lined up so closely together barely a man could slip between them. Trunks of thirty feet or more in diameter, tightly positioned together, stood not only side by side but one behind the other. The Stand was at least fifty massive trees deep, spanning a width of miles all along its entire length.

Most troubling for the Captain came after passing through The Gate. It was not a straight path through The Stand. The map showed the passage made two sharp turns, like the path winding up a steep mountain. Derr had studied the map many times to prepare for Tomelai's visit to Teth, and with one last review, he searched for anything he might have missed, hoping to quell his concerns for the dangers lurking in the darkness of the sunless passage. His search found nothing.

He rolled up the map and placed it back under his coat. He didn't like what The Stand offered to his side of the equation.

Teth guards stood at the entrance of The Gate while people from all around lined up to pass through. Derr watched, scanning the rabble for any sign of anything out of the ordinary. Others of the KCG were doing the same. Derr nodded to the Teth guards to suggest Tomelai's procession was ready to begin their trek through The Gate into The Stand. Derr intently observed the Teth guards move everyone away to permit the Chancellor from the Kingdom of Adelle with his KCG protectors to pass.

"Rotti, this is the part I like least," Derr offered, while gripping tightly on the reins of his mount. "May I suggest we stay close together?" He paused. "As we agreed and as we planned." Derr had experienced his Chancellor's disregard for his security measures too many times before.

"Drew, you worry too much, but you have been right before. Too many times."

"As we planned, Muroy, Richelle, and Jerith will ride in front of you with another three KCG directly in front of them and another three behind you for the entire trip through The Stand," Derr said. Then added, "I'll be on your left and Dillip on your right."

"My safety is in your hands, Drew. Let us keep moving with all the pageantry the situation will allow us." Tomelai wanted to ensure Derr's preparation for his safety didn't interfere with appearances. For Chancellor Tomelai, appearances were more important than anything. Appearances led to perceptions, and perception seeded reality. Tomelai couldn't afford to give the appearance of anything less than commanding or regal.

As per Derr's plan, Tomelai would move to the front just before they exited The Gate on Teth's side of The Stand. Kaythlin and the rest of the entourage would follow.

"How The Stand came to be, a mystery of the ages," Tomelai said as he pulled up alongside Derr, "but the Temple lords have weaved their stories to humble the faithful about the power of their god, or is it gods? I should know it by now. The Book of Teth or the Temple of Life scripture say something about how this came to be. Something about how it was created is used to support their deeply rooted belief in Mother Earth, the great unifying power of nature."

Derr knew his friend Rotti didn't believe all of what the Temple was selling, but he was respectful of The Stand, however it got there. "You know, each tree is at least thirty feet thick. Close enough to each other that a squirrel's ass might struggle to squeeze through. And row after row of the giant trees would hold off even the most well-trained forces. It's quite remarkable. Can't see how Mother Earth came up with that military calculation, since nobody is supposed to be killing anybody else."

Derr was even a little jealous. How easy it might be to defend Adelle behind an impenetrable wall. Derr wasn't so lucky. His ability to protect his Chancellor would have to rely on the skill of his guards and Adelle's well-trained police force under General Kiple's command. *Kiple, now there's an asshole if ever there was one,* Derr considered.

The thought of Kiple brought Derr back to reality. "As impressive as The Stand might be, once inside the city, The Stand will not keep an archer off a stray balcony or an assassin from a shadow."

"You will not let that happen, Drew. Besides, what reason would someone ever want to assassinate a beloved Head of State such as me?" Tomelai said confidently. Although, he knew there were a thousand reasons and a lengthy list of people who would like to see him dead.

Derr saw risk everywhere. In his mind, everyone was a threat. He didn't give a shit whether the KCG considered them a friend of Adelle or not. To Druin Derr, everyone, at all times, presented a potential threat. It was the single-minded approach that made him so valuable to his friend, Rotti.

The Feast of Teth, what better irony than for some asshole to kill a sovereign in celebration?

Derr was determined not to let his Chancellor die today.

Still, something didn't feel right. In all his years at Tomelai's side, Teth had never been so quiet. Every report claimed nothing of note was happening inside the city. Even the pimps weren't pressing their girls or guys for ever more coin, as they did on any other day. Absent were the beatings pushing them into service, regardless of whether buyers were buying, demanding more in return than any purveyor of the Gift of Flesh could ever deliver. *This level of quiet inside Teth is unnatural.*

Teth, a holy city in name, but like any other place where large numbers of people gathered, was also a cesspool of corruption.

With the Feast of Teth upon them, more pikers were in the city to be taken advantage of by the thieves and pickpockets. The runners for the wards' drug business, constantly at each other over ever-expanding locations from which to sell the addictive drug called dust, appeared to be at peace. An impossibility, as the wards were always at odds over clientele or vying for more product by any means possible. A lucrative business to be certain, dealing dust was a most deadly occupation as well. Like so much of the illegal activity in and around Teth, the Thuggery had its hands all over the dust trade. It wasn't what they called themselves, not at first anyway. But everyone else did. Over time, as decades passed, the name just settled in. Factions within the Thuggery were often at war over the inveterate drug business. Never in all the years Derr monitored Teth had the factions of the Thuggery been this utterly silent, if the reports being delivered to Derr were to be believed.

Then there was always some irrelevant, lowly-yet-ambitious criminal out to make a name for themselves, setting off a chain of events no one could predict. If it wasn't a one-off event, factions were forever pushing farther into another's territory. Worst yet, factions within the Thuggery were always vying for a larger share of the control despite Thuggery-imposed territorial limits to the contrary.

And now, no drug squabbles, no ambitious young dealers, no blind ambition, no pimps, no pickpockets. Just silence from the Thuggery. *Not possible,* Derr considered.

Reports about the city Derr commissioned to prepare for Tomelai's travels all came back the same. Nothing. It was wrong, not natural for Teth. Druin Derr knew better. *They overplayed their hand*. It told him someone was keeping the players in check—someone powerful enough to scare off anyone who might fuck things up, or someone rich enough to buy off someone powerful enough to do their bidding. To keep Teth this bottled up would take an awful lot of muscle and an awful lot of money. It worried him.

What they planned and who planned it, Derr desperately needed to know what or who was the target. If it was Tomelai, he was ready. But were his preparations enough? He didn't like the question. The answer had to be, "Yes." Failure wasn't an option. In the game of death, it never was.

Druin Derr, along with Tomelai and a small unit of KCG approached the cavernous tunnel, hoping to enter The Gate and pass through The Stand without incident. Passage through it was the only way into Teth for such a large procession. Tomelai dismissed a proposal to travel downriver from Tandure to Port Lucy and on into Teth by way of ship. Teth's docks, while well-kept, were chaotic. The setting did not afford Tomelai the grandiose pageantry of an entrance into the welcoming arms of Teth's citizenry as did the spectacle of his emergence from The Stand—a resplendent heroic figure emerging into the light from the all-consuming dark background of the sunless passage. Derr knew the symbolism of it was much too compelling for his friend the Chancellor to pass up.

Derr looked upon The Gate. The opening between two massive sequoias on either side of the foreboding entrance gave off the appearance of stoic sentries, silent at their posts for at least a thousand years.

Derr watched as Tomelai bid adieu to the First Lady, assuring her they'd meet up after, but he needed to go through alone with his KCG protectors—for her safety. Derr knew it for the lie it was. This was Tomelai's moment, and he wasn't interested in sharing it, even with his wife.

The sentry-like sequoias stood only far enough apart to permit barely seven or eight people to pass shoulder to shoulder. After only a few strides into The Gate, all natural light faded away. High overhead, the branches and needles of the lordly canopy blocked out the sun. If not for the oil-fed, glass-covered lanterns resting in sconces positioned on trees every few feet, the KCG would have been in total darkness. *Strange,* Derr thought, *so much fire, so many trees. It seems so careless. Lume would've been the better choice. But then again, giant sequoias do not burn or catch fire easily.*

Not too far from the entrance, the trail turned quickly into a musty, dank burrow, dark as night but for the lighted sconces. Thick granite tiles provided a semi-even and gentle walkway for the first twenty yards, then turned into a dirt forest floor the rest of the way. The only natural light came courtesy of what snuck through the entrance or the exit. Neither reached in very far.

Druin imagined the tip of an arrow or the point of a spear suddenly appearing from the shadows. The bark was rough, dark, and gave the appearance of shifting colors as light from the lanterns danced this way and that. It was a natural distraction to the eyes. An assassin's quiver, dart, or spear in amongst the shifting pattern of the endless bark could be impossible to spot in time. Anxious, his eyes darted in every direction.

With the efforts of the last evening planning session, Derr hoped to pull through this threat without the loss of Chancellor Tomelai.

"Quickly, with haste!" he called out to the squad.

It was already too late. In the span between heartbeats, the impossible happened.

The tunnel went completely dark.

To Kill a Chancellor

Teth: 27th Day of the Salmon Moon

Derr

"Lume!" Derr's shouted command spoke volumes to the KCG.

Derr's world froze in an instant. It always did when shit hit the fan. Some unknown quality he possessed took control of his mind. His brain processed everything at once, causing his perception of the world to slow down as he consumed every detail in his field of vision. Although events didn't move in the slow-world timeframe his mind created, his ability to grasp it quickly gave him the advantage.

The scene before him flowed through into his mind, where synapse connections raced to construct a complete picture of what was happening. Faster than humanly possible he understood, and his mind jumped from option to option, searching for a path to steer Tomelai away from imminent death to the possibility of life.

The question of the disappearing light Derr let go in the moment because the *why* didn't matter. *Why* was a question for Derr only if he survived. The uncertain chances of living through charging men hung on the KCG's contingency planning and on skills of his unit.

Each member of the security team pulled the fist-sized lume crystals from under their hon-silk, armor-like dress suits and yanked back the black cloth coverings, exposing the warm green glow of lume. Men with spears appeared before Derr just yards ahead, stopped in time, if only in his mind.

Several rows of attackers stood between Chancellor Tomelai and the city of Teth. A charge through the human obstruction was not an option as men angled long pikes, anchored into the hard dirt, positioned chest high to a horse, preventing the KCG's forward movement.

Men came through the space between the piked warriors and rushed toward his sovereign.

A lot of men.

A lot of spears.

Men with purpose.

To kill.

He calculated myriad responses in a blink of an eye. Derr's world moved again, snapping forward. The attackers moved fast, as did Derr's thought process. The two-word command from Derr, "Form 8!" resonated in the confined zone of conflict. The two words held detailed orders for each one of his team.

Men and women of the KCG, set atop their steeds, four in total, closed in around Tomelai. A dense mass of horseflesh and well-trained personnel now shielded the Chancellor. The remaining KCG protectors prepared to dismount and ready themselves against the imminent charge.

Light from the lume crystals showed Derr there were too many of them. Not enough KCG. Realization came quick. They all weren't going to get out of this unscathed or even alive.

Horseflesh from the front and sides pressed close against Tomelai's own steed. Moving forward wasn't an option. Derr's team needed to remove the piked formation. He and the KCG would have to get through the men closing in on them. Warriors with spears were only steps away. Derr shouted above the cries of the approaching force, "Dismount! Swords!"

The proud young Lieutenant Jerith was a fraction of a second too slow. He dropped from his horse. His feet hit the ground. He reached for his sword. A spearman pushed steel through his chest. The young Lieutenant's eyes opened wide. Surprised, he looked down at the lance buried in his body. The young Lieutenant fell forward on his face.

Dead.

Derr blocked a thrust, spun, and struck his assailant across the cheek. The deep cut separated the man's jaw from his face. The man dropped his spear. Reached out in agony. Tried to catch pieces of his face flying away from him. Derr didn't hesitate. He swung down hard, severing the man's outstretched arm. Blood spurted. The man screamed. He grabbed for the stub of his arm with his other hand, giving up on recovering the missing pieces of his face. It didn't matter. Derr swung again and lopped off his head.

"Line up!" Derr shouted loud enough to cut through the din of battle.

Four of the remaining six KCG in front of Tomelai had dismounted as part of the battle plan response. Derr's order of "Form 8″ required four of the KCG to remain mounted close to Tomelai to keep the horses in tight formation. Derr used the horses to block access to Tomelai, and the four troops still mounted remained as a last defense as human shields. One KCG officer on each side of Tomelai, with another directly in front and the fourth directly behind.

The well-trained riders, being prepared, drew their bows, nocked arrows, and let fly the KCG's response. Despite the tight and dark conditions, the KCG arrows brought down three assassins manning the piked barricade.

Almost there, Derr calculated.

Two of the three KCG troops stationed at Tomelai's rear dismounted, passed around the side of the small herd, and joined the rest of the KCG out in front.

Barely a heartbeat in time, the KCG line formed. Assailants, with the numbers on their side, changed tactics, throwing their spears in Tomelai's direction and drawing swords.

A spear hurled through the air headed directly towards the Chancellor. He turned his head to the side, evading death by a fraction of a second and a fraction of an inch. The near-death projectile swooshed by Tomelai. The mounted rear-guard KCG protector never saw it coming. It entered through his eye and sliced deep into his brain. Death was instant. Tomelai's rear protection was gone, but it mattered little given the entire attack came from directly in front of him. Unless another surprise from the rear was in store.

Derr couldn't pinpoint who among the assailants was leading the charge. He wanted to take out their leader. They were well prepared, well trained, and the attackers were executing a well-choreographed assault.

Another spear flew at Tomelai. Off course, it instead sliced open the neck of Lieutenant Dillip, one of Tomelai's human KCG shields mounted on the Chancellor's right. Blood gushed from the wound. To the woman's credit, she died in formation protecting her ruler. None but Tomelai noticed the woman slump forward.

Another KCG officer dead.

The human-shield formation Derr set up as a perimeter around the Chancellor was being methodically stripped away.

The full force of the assailants crashed into Derr and his team. A mistake, Derr thought, seeing his assailants give up their weapons advantage to engage in swordplay with the KCG.

The width inside the passage didn't allow the assailants to take full advantage of their numbers. Only five or six could stand shoulder to shoulder. Perfect for the KCG. The KCG could stand toe to toe and fight with anyone. But they couldn't do it forever. The enemy would wear them down, and when the KCG showed signs of fatigue, fresh attackers from the assailants' ranks would finish them.

Two more heartbeats and another man was down. The assault was just seconds old. Several of the assault force were dead.

Too many of the KCG were dead.

Derr's team had no way to retreat with the horses at their rear facing forward, and no way to turn them around. They couldn't move forward and couldn't go back.

They were trapped.

As good as the KCG were, they couldn't hold out indefinitely. A heavy sword drained one's strength. Derr's demanding training sessions to the point of exhaustion prepared his unit to battle through fatigue. Fatigue wouldn't be a factor for Derr's team today. They would all die before exhaustion set in.

The clang of metal resounded within the confines of the tight passage. Another assailant thrust forward at Derr, catching the coattail of his hon-silk dress uniform. Derr saw an opening and drove his weapon into the man's thigh. The thrust struck deep, and the man fell to one knee. Before Derr could take the death blow, a fresh opponent jumped out from behind and brought his axe down, aimed directly at Derr's head. Inches from death, Derr brought his sword up with both hands and blocked the strike. His hands were numb from the strength of the man's blow.

Horses? Derr heard them. Everyone heard them growing wildly scared. The battle pause lasted only half a heartbeat. Not long enough for the killing to stop.

The assailant grabbed his leg where Derr stabbed him. Derr looked away at the immediate threat from the axeman. The injured assailant saw his opportunity. He reached for a knife hidden in his boot.

It came out quickly.

As the axe man brought down another fatal blow, Derr rolled from the wounded man holding the knife just in time. The axe, intended for Derr's head, came down on the knife-wielding assailant's neck. Blood shot out in every direction. With the axe buried deep in the assailant, Derr, still on the ground, thrust his sword upward through the axe man's chest.

Derr's unit was struggling. From his vantage point, he couldn't see how many were still alive. He could only assume the worst.

His human-shield formation mostly dismantled by the enemy, Tomelai pushed the dead KCG officer still mounted off to the side and jumped down to join the fight.

Derr saw Tomelai move out of the corner of his eye. "No!"

Tomelai, sword drawn, squeezed alongside Lieutenant Ting's horse, intent on joining the men and women giving their lives to protect him. Chancellor or not, he would not die with his ass plastered to his saddle, sitting on the sidelines.

Without regard for his own life, Derr jumped up and turned his back to his opponents to race to Tomelai's side. Planning meant shit if everyone didn't execute exactly as directed. It was the single most difficult element of a battle plan to account for: someone who doesn't carry out orders. Chancellors were no exception to the rule.

Tomelai ended up pressed between a massive tree trunk and a horse—in immediate danger of being crushed to death. It was Derr's immediate concern.

Outnumbered, two to one, the KCG response was falling apart.

Derr needed to come up with a new plan quickly. There were too many attackers. They were good—too good. Everything was falling to shit.

Fuck!

Derr raced to his Chancellor's side while his thoughts raced for a solution.

A woman of the KCG jumped in to block an assailant chasing Derr from behind.

A quick thrust into his back ended the invader's pursuit.

The KCG's horses, even though trained under assault conditions, were growing visibly anxious, trying to move in any direction the confined space allowed. Penned in on all sides, the path forward for the beasts remained blocked. Fewer staked pikes stood in their way, yet enough to prevent the horses from entering the melee as the tactical advantage they offered.

The assault force had not only taken away the advantage of cavalry from Derr but transformed it into another threat to deal with: Tomelai was being crushed against a giant sequoia by sixteen-hundred pounds of frightened tribian pure breed. There was no controlling the magnificent steed and no way out for Tomelai.

Tomelai's death was imminent.

Derr jumped onto the horse in front of Tomelai's and on to the next. Reaching the horse compressing Tomelai into the trunk of the tree, unable to get it to budge, Derr jumped down. He was at Tomelai's side in an instant. With every ounce of his remaining strength, Derr inched Tomelai free. Once freed, Derr pulled his Chancellor to the rear of the formation.

Other men intent on killing them both followed, but weren't able to press through the wall of horse meat. One attacker jumped up to traverse across the backs as he moved towards Derr and Tomelai.

An arrow punched through the horse-jumper's eye.

He fell hard under the restless stomping hooves of frightened steeds.

Derr's first responsibility was to his Chancellor, even if it meant sacrificing his own life or the lives of the people of the KCG.

Derr's world stopped again.

He measured the attack.

The number of assailants.

Counted his remaining forces.

The outcome looked bleak.

He searched myriad options for a way out in milliseconds, as experience, training, intellect, and the fear of failure, as well as the threat of death, pushed his mind to the extreme.

Arrows flew as if out of thin air and the remaining pike brigade fell. It didn't take Derr any time to assess the impact and the opportunity it presented. In the instant the long instruments of death blocking the forward movement of the horses dropped to the ground, a plan formed.

It might work.

The world jumped back in real time.

Derr knew what had to be done.

It was the only way.

But it might not work.

He had to try.

He didn't hesitate.

With a slap to the backside of horseflesh with the broad side of his sword, the horses reared up, legs flailing as they struck an approaching assailant. Attackers, along with Lieutenant Fritz of the KCG, disappeared under wildly thrashing hooves. Derr assumed both the assailants and Fritz faced death by hoof.

Derr slapped every horse within reach with the side of his sword. Over and over, steel attacked their hindquarters. The steeds pushed and pushed, whinnying, snorting, startled and fearful, and they all stamped forward.

It took only half a dozen heartbeats for the stampede to start.

Derr had no way to judge who'd survive. He had no choice. Forty-eight powerful legs and forty-eight dangerous hooves trampled over everything in their path.

Assailants went down.

KCG went down.

Everything went down.

The unstoppable force of more than twenty thousand pounds of crazed horseflesh would not be denied. The stampede thundered over everyone in their path.

Screams from men.

Screams from women.

Terrified horses.

The harrowing sounds of anguish filled the narrow passage as death reverberated inside The Stand.

The Comforts of Home

Hensdale: 27th Day of the Salmon Moon

Reyne

Reyne looked about his bedchamber, unsure how long he had been out or how he got there. The front door to the dwelling appeared ajar, as seen through his own open bedroom door. Sunlight crawled along the walls, giving off enough light for Reyne to guess afternoon in Hensdale on the Feast of Teth had arrived.

His thoughts were interrupted. His head was ready to explode. Reyne lowered both hands to the sides of his temples and let out a tremendous groan. Nausea overtook him and he heaved. With nothing in his stomach, save a few alphen nuts, nothing came up except pain. With determination, he pushed through the miasma.

He wasn't certain if he was alone. *How the hell did I get here? Where's Daedyn? Anybody?*

He reached for the compulsory lume crystal jar set atop the sturdy yet petite side table. Reyne spotted the washbasin with the promise of cool water on the wood dresser. He glanced at his reflection in the small mirror propped against the treestone wall. A single maple-wood dresser, made by his father, stood in the corner.

Reyne looked at the washbasin. *The cool water might be refreshing. Anything to get rid of this pain.*

He swung his feet over the side of the bed. Looking down, his boots were still on. His feet were hot in the calf-high leather coverings. He pulled them off, one at a time, followed by his thin wool socks in need of a good washing. He planted both feet on the coolness of the treestone floor.

Ahhhh, that is good. He wiggled his toes.

Standing slowly and continuing to let the cold surface soothe his hot soles, he moved from the bed and stumbled across the spartan room to the small washbasin. He plunged both hands, palms up, into the water. Reyne's hands delighted in the coolness. He raised them, cupped together, and slapped the liquid prize on his face. Silvery wetness caressed his skin. Refreshed, his face reacted, almost as well as his feet, at the relief. Water splashed over the back of his neck and he rubbed. There, he found it. A tiny bump on the back of his neck.

His hand stopped moving.

Pressing his index finger over the small pimple-like bump he just now discovered. *Bug bite?*

Reyne strode through the short hallway between his room and the front door. Daedyn and Reyne both grew up in the house they once shared with their parents. Since their deaths, the brothers now called it their own.

He stepped through the heavy open door, reaching his hands to the lintel above. He stopped there. His hands caressed the bottom of the lintel. As was customary for inside walls, artisans stripped treestone timbers of bark and smoothed the surface once set in place. The hue treestone treated timbers gave off, in the light of day, resembled the natural tan color of untreated ironwood, though a shade darker. Reyne's hand rode each upright timber, jumping from one to the next until his hand landed on the front door. The sensual habit spoke to his soul, comforting him. It told him, you're home, you're safe.

Reyne looked about. Daedyn was nowhere to be seen. Nobody was anywhere to be seen, but why was the door open?

He looked out over the alphen orchard, scanning for a sign, any sign of anyone. He still didn't know how he ended up in his bed. The last thing he recalled was resting on the bench back at the market square.

How long ago was that?

A shadow or something out of the corner of his vision grabbed his attention. Someone was there. But the pain didn't let go of its firm grip on him, making it hard for him to give attention to the moving object. With every bit of concentration, with every bit of strength, he raised his head long enough to see the old beggar from the market square coming through the last line of trees along the edge of the grove. Moving fast with purpose and...

Heading straight for him.

Sovereigns Always Get Their Way

Teth: 27th Day of the Salmon Moon

Derr

Sounds of the stampede faded from Derr as the horses thundered further away with each passing moment. How far down the forested passageway the outcry of death would carry, Derr was uncertain, but relatively sure not far enough to reach either end.

Dead men.

Dead women.

Shattered lume crystals.

Fallen swords.

Broken spears.

All of it scattered everywhere across the landscape of death. By the faint glow from crushed lume, Derr, alone with his friend Rotti, looked over the carnage.

They were the only ones who remained standing. They stood in silence, looking over the horrific carnage of what were once human bodies.

With cold dispatch, Derr studied every detail. He always studied every detail. It was only death. Some were the men and woman of the KCG, which gave him pause.

Hanging from his neck, the green, soft-toned light from the lume crystal provided enough support for their eyes to make out the extent of the slaughter.

His entire unit, every one of them, dead.

Skulls crushed. Legs exhibited more qualities of pounded steaks than human body parts. Faces rendered flat, appearing two dimensional against the gray mass of scattered brain tissue sprawled about The Stand's passage floor. Tattered remains of KCG uniforms clung to, or driven into, raw flesh provided the only discernable way to identify which side the dead gave their lives.

The dark soil on the forest floor obscured the blood that splashed everywhere. In a small way and without the perforce ritual of the Temple of Life, the Cycle of Return took what it was owed.

Derr spoke first. "Rotti, look at the clothing on the dead bodies of the assailants. It's common. They all appear to be commoners, or they hid their origins by trading for standard garb off street scum. These faces are too badly mangled to make out any identifiable features."

Derr kicked away a detached arm. "Looks more like a club than an arm. No detectable markings to help identify these broken bodies. Can't tell most apart. Can't make out man or woman. I got nothing," Derr confessed to Tomelai. "Yet."

"Among the broken, bloody bodies, the nondescript clothing, and the shattered weapons, it's going to be tough figuring out who these people were," Tomelai said.

"The KCG will find out who was responsible. We'll take every step necessary to piece it together. My team'll study this mess of dead bodies for answers."

The two survivors walked through the dead, inspecting each carefully. Derr stopped. "Quiet, I heard something."

Tomelai froze in place.

"Listen, over there. Someone's still alive."

Derr and Tomelai walked over to the survivor, who was from their own KCG. Her body was badly broken, much of her flesh pounded into raw meat. A wonder she remained alive given the looks of her. The flesh of the woman's face was half torn away, from a hoof that came down and scraped skin and muscle away from her skull. One eye hung loosely from its socket, still attached by a tangle of nerves anchored somewhere inside her head. Her legs were both crushed at the thighs, and blood was freely flowing where her crotch had once been. A barely perceptible sound gurgled from somewhere in the remains of her throat.

Derr looked up at Tomelai and pursed his lips. "That, I'm guessing, was once Lieutenant Richelle."

Turning to the dying KCG compatriot, Derr said, "You served well and with honor, Lieutenant Richelle. May the Community of Life welcome your life force into His world for you to join the Circle of Life." He didn't believe in the Temple of Life's faith, but somewhere back in his mind, he remembered Richelle did. For her, he said the words.

Owing to Derr's sense of duty, he slipped his sword into what remained of Richelle's chest. It was a rare moment of heartfelt compassion from Derr. The woman didn't deserve to die in slow agony. Even if she couldn't speak, her misery was obvious, as was her relief at being released from pain. His blade eased through her heart. Derr owed at least that much to Richelle.

"Goodbye, my friend."

Tomelai said nothing.

The two continued their walking inspection.

Tomelai noticed movement off to his right. He pointed. "Look over there; something moved."

Derr walked over to the man and, looking down at him, said, "He's one of theirs."

As for the lone assailant still alive, Richelle had fared much better. The man was writhing in agony. With what could have been hands, he grasped at his crushed windpipe; the man was shallowly gulping for air from the hole in his throat with every breath. His mouth didn't move. Derr considered the once human-looking chest and suspected the assassin's right lung hung loosely from what remained of his rib cage. A small wonder breathing was possible, even with great difficulty. Less of a wonder was the obvious intense agony the exposed lung delivered at the cost of its continued use.

Tomelai looked at what was once a man and said, "Well, at least I think he still has hands."

The unknown assailant's shin had been crushed. His foot connected only by a thin strip of skin stretched from his pulverized ankle. But just barely.

Derr was content to let him die slowly. He deserved to writhe in pain forever if left to Druin Derr. It wasn't. Tomelai's sword came down hard on the man's neck, biting deep. Blood pulsed from the dying man's neck and throat. His neck spit blood for several moments. His throat gurgled, then stopped.

Derr looked up at Tomelai, puzzled. Tomelai just shrugged. Derr was furious, but he didn't let it show. He was sure Tomelai cared little if he was livid. Calming his tone, Derr said, "We should've let him wither in pain, Rotti. He'd be dead soon enough."

"We are the only two survivors once again, Drew," Tomelai said in a cold, emotionless tone. The Chancellor showed little concern for the dead men and women. Even his own, who'd been sacrificed by Derr for the Chancellor's benefit. "What do you suggest now?"

Derr knew his friend all too well. Tomelai's concern for others, outside those he let in, was nonexistent. In public, he was good at hiding it. They weren't in public.

"I can't just walk into Teth with the Captain of the KCG by my side." Appearances were always important to the Chancellor.

"Men died for you, and all you can fucking think about is how it's going to look if you just walk into Teth with one man at your side!" was what Derr wanted to say. What he wanted to shout. What he did say, however, "A second unit of KCG will be the first to arrive. The main body of your processions should be through a little while after that."

"I'd like to change the plan," Tomelai stated. Derr understood it as an order.

"What do you suggest, Rotti?"

"We meet up with the second KCG unit. Get this mess cleared out. Bag whatever you want to take, and then I'll wait on the far side just before we exit. I'll wait there for the rest of our procession to catch up. We all exit The Stand together."

"The KCG I sent ahead this morning to clear everyone from that side of the passage will be, or should be, at the other end, holding off all traffic. No one is getting into the passage from the city's side. Unless these bodies here dispatched our advance team somehow."

Tomelai just looked at him.

Sovereigns always get their way. He'd get what he wanted. As Chancellor, he always got what he wanted in the end. Derr stayed silent for a moment, just short enough to avoid pissing off Tomelai. "I'll make it work." Druin Derr couldn't have said anything else to satisfy his friend.

"Our men will get this cleaned up before the main body of your entourage gets here. We placed a rear-guard protection unit just inside The Gate where we entered. Didn't want anyone following us from behind. They'll be along in a few minutes. All part of the plan. The KCG is experienced at cleaning and removal in situations like these. Something we both appreciate all too well. It's not our first rodeo."

They both stood in silence before Derr spoke up again. "And our people at the other end should be able to round up the horses before they show up riderless." Derr kept his eyes looking down.

The Chancellor offered a concern, "But I'm going to guess the Teth guards will not want The Gate to stay closed for too long."

"We paid them well," Derr said before continuing. "I made sure no one will get through The Gate on either side until I give the order for the Teth guards to release the crowds. Shouldn't take too long. Our men will be along soon. In the meantime, we can press into the shadows and wait. Safely."

Derr and Tomelai backed up against the massive trunks of two nearby sequoias. Derr placed the dark cloth over the lume crystal hanging around his neck. The two men faded into the darkness, consumed by the surrounding trees.

Chancellor Tomelai and Captain Derr had survived. His people, all dead, but his Chancellor remained alive. He did his job. Among the dead were loyal men and women of the KCG, who'd followed his orders without regard for their own safety because they trusted Derr and because they were dedicated to their sworn duty to protect Chancellor Tomelai.

Derr said, "A second attack in the aftermath of the first is a possibility. But it makes no sense. They expected to succeed here. They sent their entire force inside. Somehow, they bypassed the city-side of The Gate. Found a way to bypass our advance team. Found a way to kill the lights. I don't get how they did it, how they pulled it off, but they did."

Saddened at the loss of his comrades, yet proud they'd sacrificed themselves to save the Chancellor, Derr didn't feel guilt at the decision he'd made in the heat of battle, killing everyone on both sides except himself and Tomelai.

"Rotti, there wasn't time to remount. Our team had to keep them engaged. If we broke off to gain the horses, everyone would've been cut down. It had to be that way."

"You do not owe me any explanation, Drew. You did what had to be done."

"I know. Just wanted you to know I sacrificed everyone because it was the only option."

"I never gave it a second's thought."

"You'll see their families are taken care of." Derr's words came out more of a demand than as a question.

Without speaking, the Chancellor offered a slight nod in reply to Derr. His friend would do the right thing. The intimate trust Derr and Tomelai shared demanded nothing less.

Tomelai walked to one of the lightless sconces. Derr followed him with his eyes and spoke, "Rotti, let's not relight any of the lanterns. I preferred to keep you in the shadows. We're hard to see in the dark, and if I'm wrong and there are trailing assassins out there, better you stay in the dark while we wait for the second KCG unit to arrive. I'm aware you don't always pay close attention when you and I review our plans. Trust me. They'll be along soon."

Tomelai didn't reply but backed away from the sconce. The two returned to waiting in silence. Chancellor Tomelai trusted Derr. His men would be along soon.

In the faint light, Derr studied Tomelai. Perplexed at first by the look on the

Chancellor's face, his apparent lack of interest at his own dead, along with the Chancellor's far-off stare, made Derr wonder about the man beside him. Derr wanted to give him the benefit of the doubt, having faced certain death moments ago. And it hit him. *Fuck me. Does he know something about this? And why did he kill the only one of them left alive?*

Minimal light radiated from the small, broken shards of lume scattered among the broken bodies pierced the pervasive darkness. A tomb for the dead lumps of meat once human, the passage seemed more like a crypt than a tunnel. In near darkness, the two men quietly waited for the next wave of KCG to arrive. Dead bodies didn't concern either man much. They had seen it all too many times. This wasn't the first assassination attempt against Chancellor Tomelai in spite of what the Covenant demanded.

Derr thought he had heard horses but couldn't be sure.

Where did this assault start from? Had they hidden amongst the sequoias all night waiting? How did they snuff all the passage lanterns at the same time? He had a lot of questions and no answers. Yet.

"They should be along shortly," he said to his Chancellor with a hint of suspicion taking shape in his mind.

Derr recalled discussing the KCG's plans with Tomelai. Out of concern for his wife, Tomelai moved her to the head of the Adelle procession scheduled to follow shortly behind Tomelai's group. He told Derr it served two purposes, her safety, and it put her out in front of the Adelle entourage.

But did it? Derr pondered. *I should have seen it sooner.*

When had he ever agreed to make a grand entrance without the First Lady on his arm? Shit, she was usually the main attraction. Everyone loves her. Him, not so much. The people of Teth tolerate him. Unless, of course, he experienced sincere concern for her safety. Fuck me! Derr had a lot to think about. He always had a lot to think about.

But why didn't the other end of the passage stop the band of assailants from entering? They had to enter some other way. Could they have hidden their weapons along the passage in between the giant trees?

He turned his thoughts to the stampeding horses. He had confidence in his team on the other end. *The agents placed at the opposite end of The Stand would certainly recognize the Chancellor's horse and gather all of them before they enter the city riderless*. Of course, Derr considered his team might not be there any longer. *Compromised? Dead?* He didn't expect so. He would have the answer soon enough.

Derr crossed his arms over his chest, bent one knee back and rested the sole of his boot against a trunk, and returned to watching. With his arms crossed, he was thinking. He had a lot to think about. He was always thinking when he was watching.

"Guess we learned why everything has been so quiet and buttoned-up in Teth. Someone wanted us feeling safe enough to let our guard down," Tomelai said while staring straight ahead.

"Well, that didn't work out too well for them now, did it?" Derr replied.

A long moment passed. "Thank you, Drew," Tomelai said to his friend in a quiet voice.

The two returned to unspoken contemplation looking over the dead.

Several long minutes passed when Tomelai spoke. "Drew, this changes everything. There's no going back. For all the reasons this failed assassination was attempted, my best guess is that someone is pushing back hard on our proposal to introduce electrics. Either they are going to be stopped, whoever they are, or I am. And you and I are going to make damn sure it is not me. I am not going to let this go unanswered. People are going to die. And we are going to have to find a way to get around the Council. I was willing to let the vote go against me before this and find another way, but not now. They just made a big mistake. I am still alive, and that is going to be a big problem for them."

Derr considered. *His words a thoughtful diversion... perhaps? But if not, he's right. This changes everything*. Gears were grinding through Derr's thoughts.

"I'll get answers, Rotti."

A staged assassination planned to fail—gone wrong—or a real assassination attempt will be the first question I answer.

No Time to Dally

Owls Neck: 27th day of the Salmon Moon

Mithany | Arek

Observance of the Feast of Teth no longer held meaning to Mithany. She and Arek, along with Neladith, had been walking back to Hensdale for more than two hours since leaving Mister Whitetop and Dylla in Owls Neck. Mithany remained deep in thought. She couldn't think of anything but Reyne. One notion consumed her: was he the one injured and *if* it was him, would he be alright? She cursed her short legs—they couldn't get her back to Hensdale fast enough.

Turning her head to look over her shoulder, she was painfully reminded that Arek, her flamboyant older brother, had insisted Neladith accompany them on the return to Hensdale. Why Neladith agreed, Mithany didn't understand, never asked, and didn't care. It was Arek she was mad at.

"Insensitive clod," she protested under her breath.

She watched the two of them walking hand in hand as though it was just another day in the park. Though too far back for Arek to hear, she told him, "I was hoping to have you all to myself. Someone to talk to, to distract my thoughts. Instead, I feel like the only adult in the room babysitting two horny, mischievous teenagers. You're acting like a child, brother. Don't you care what I'm going through?"

She needed him, and he chose Neladith instead. His new bauble. It infuriated her. It ate at her because, more than anything, she realized she was jealous.

Mithany loved her brother, but hated how selfish he could be. The troubling news that Reyne might have been seriously injured made her an emotional wreck. She needed her brother to shore her up. Obvious to Mithany and much to her displeasure, Arek, instead, engaged in pursuing other, more prurient needs of his own.

Arek was preoccupied, playfully enjoying his time with Neladith, much to Mithany's growing anger. It would be a few more hours, if all went well, before they'd be back in Hensdale. A horse would have been welcome or even a coach, but neither was to be had from the small village. Occasional traffic between the two hamlets kept the small communities connected, but not enough to justify an enterprising person establishing transportation services between them.

The time-worn dirt road between Owls Neck and Hensdale was littered with weeds from underuse, as though Mother Earth herself held the path open through sheer force of will, pushing back against the relentless onslaught of aggressive vegetation to claim new ground. The gangly greenery, biting along the edges of the road, attacked the open terrain of the light-brown earth roadway. An army of weeds fought to capture fresh territory daily. Mother Earth teased the unsightly trail with hope, sprinkling white and yellow petals of late-blooming meadowsweet here and there. The thin forest formed an outline along each side of the trail-like roadway.

Passing through a lightly wooded area, the road was wide enough for the occasional private coach. The road was safe for travelers, mostly because of its infrequent use. Not enough commerce to keep an enterprising bandit properly fed.

In a foul mood, kicking at loose stones as she walked, Mithany continued talking to herself. "There... my only sibling, playing puppy love with his newfound toy. As much as I love you, I hate you sometimes. I need your support but that red-eyed child-woman is sucking up all your attention."

There was no way of knowing how Reyne was doing until she got back to the village. With every step, one foot after the other, wondering about Reyne, distracted by Arek's behavior, she fumed. It gnawed at her. She imagined Reyne lying on a wooden cart, bleeding in agony, calling out her name. She loved Reyne so much, and she couldn't be there for him when he needed her most.

Her heart ached.

She imagined the worst, *What if he dies*?

Her eyes welled up. She wiped away the pooling tears. "No! I won't let myself think like that. He's gonna be fine," she said, a little louder than she wanted to.

"Hey, Sis," Arek blurted out.

She turned to face him.

Mithany didn't hide the sadness in her eyes, the pain in her furled brow, or her quivering, pouting lips. If she was being honest with herself, she wanted Arek to see how much he'd hurt her. Plastered across her face, a message easily deciphered by their years of reading each other with just a gaze, she told him: *I know you don't mean to be insensitive, but what did you think would happen when you brought Neladith along on this trip?*

Arek replied to her facial accusation, "Just one more person to share conversation with over the long trip, Sis."

Unfortunately, bringing Neladith along didn't turn out as he planned.

He noticed from the start Mithany was sulking. Reyne often said he was the only one who understood her. Not so in Arek's assessment. Nobody understood his sister better than he did.

She wasn't like this often. It wasn't in her nature. But when it did happen, she acted like a completely different person. He'd given her some time to adjust to Neladith's presence, but it was obvious Mithany wasn't warming up to the idea of sharing him. He needed to do something, or the remainder of this trek was going to be about as much fun as a colony of fire ants in his skivvies.

There were two problems, as Arek saw things. He'd neglected Mithany when she needed his support, and he had to keep Neladith in a pleasant mood if he was going to get laid later that night. The key to both was getting Mithany to change out of her dark mood and bringing the threesome together as one happy band of travelers.

"Come on, Sis, talk to me. Who's the one who used to find you, wherever you hid, after a beating from Mom?"

Their mother hadn't been kind to them as children. She might have intended it for their own good, but they were just kids. Who could hit such a little person with so much anger?

Arek was certain that making Mithany remember what their mother did to them would bring them together. He hoped she would turn to the one person in the entire world who understood what she'd gone through, what they'd gone through together—him.

The innocence of childhood for Arek, much like Mithany, had been overshadowed by the outlet of their mother's irrational, angry episodes. He lived through them, endured it as much as her, even more so. He offered himself up to protect Mithany from the fevered and wild beatings by taking the blame for whatever upset the crazed woman in the moment. More often than not, he took the whippings meant for Mithany. It's what a big brother did for a little sister—at least whenever he could.

Arek knowingly played on her emotions, bringing her back to a childhood they both wanted to put behind them. To forever forget—as if they ever could. A woeful childhood they both shared.

Something that enjoined them forever.

Something intimate and secret.

Something Mithany or Arek rarely spoke of to anyone other than to each other.

How a mother's anger at what life had dealt her found its answer, its outlet, in the pain it inflicted on the two of them as little children, he nor Mithany could ever understand.

He counted on Mithany recalling their special bond. A bond forged in ways anyone who had not lived through it could ever understand. A special bond that conditioned them to rely on each other when there was no one else to trust.

Their special bond caused many in Hensdale to look at the two of them in a "funny" way, wondering out loud for either of them to overhear, "Just how close are those two?"

He plastered a big, broad grin across his face. His eyes conveyed more information to Mithany than all his words ever could.

She always tells me it's in the eyes; it's always in the eyes. What are my eyes telling you right now, Sis?

Arek watched his sister's expression fade from a scowl. She closed her eyes, and upon opening them Mithany looked up at him. When he saw her lips purse in a tight pucker, he knew he'd won her back.

"There's my girl!" Arek said with open arms. An emotion far greater than joy swept over him. A unique reaction he always experienced when his sister responded—born not in a prideful way because of his efforts to comfort her had succeeded—but simply because she was happy once again.

Running up to her, the sister with whom he shared so much, so much love, so much pain, he said, "You can't ever stay mad at me." He gloated as he hugged her in a tight embrace.

Mithany bowed her head to hide her joy. She wanted to rebuff him. To withhold from him the knowledge he had the power to manipulate her so easily.

She couldn't deny him anything.

She never had.

She knew it.

And she was certain he knew it, too.

Arek wrapped Mithany in an ever-tightening, python-like hug.

She pressed her palms to his chest and nudged him but then relinquished into the comfort of his strong arms.

"You make me so mad sometimes," she said as she lifted her head to let their eyes meet.

"I know. I don't mean to. I'm just a guy. We aren't so good at all that stuff that goes on inside your heads." He leaned down and kissed his sister on the forehead. "But you know I will always love you, Sis." He released her, stepping back, circling her as he pranced about.

She followed his antics, partly mad at herself that he'd disarmed her so easily. She wanted to be irate with him, wanted to hold on to her anger. Unlike her mother, she couldn't. She was lucky that way.

Watching Arek foolishly skipping about made her happy. He always found a way to make her joyful. It was the very thing she wanted from him on the trip back to Hensdale. She almost forgot all about the red-eyed seductress, but then Neladith spoke, and the moment between Mithany and Arek was lost.

"Arek. It's lonely back here," Neladith coyly offered, twisting her head sideways while opening her eyes wide like a puppy confused by its master. She might have looked innocent, but Neladith was challenging Mithany for Arek's attention. Mithany knew it for what it was, and, she guessed, so did Neladith.

Is it fair to call her a seductress? We love our Gift of Flesh, free love, naked bodies everywhere and all that. Faith puts a premium on procreation, and you gotta get down and nasty to procreate as much as the Temple wants us to. What's Arek if she's a tart? A man-tart? Oh, screw all of it. I just don't like her.

Mithany's eyes narrowed looking in Neladith's direction, and lines formed across her forehead.

"Oh, this can't be good," Arek let slip out. His visage offered Mithany, in the bond they shared, an insight into the confusion of seeing Neladith's gambit for what it was, a potential all-out war for him over the next few hours.

Arek, although charming, had not been graced by the Goddess Teth with a deep, abiding love for the Gift of Knowledge. Arek understood women very well, but in other ways. Mithany was smarter than him. She saw he was trapped. Neladith was forcing him to make a choice. The question she had to answer was whether she would let him off the hook.

"You put yourself into this mess. You figure it out," she pouted to Arek.

He looked to her for release from his self-imposed prison. His obvious facial expression said, "Please help me, Sis!"

When Mithany looked back, she made it clear it wouldn't be that easy. She offered nothing to allow Arek to read it as a pardon. Mithany turned away so he wouldn't see her laughing at his predicament.

Neladith's intentions toward Arek weren't clear just yet to Mithany, as she didn't know her well enough. Those red eyes of hers were distracting enough to blunt Mithany's attempt to read her properly.

With both hands together as if in prayer, Arek turned his back to Neladith and offered his sister a non-verbal plea: "Please, I'll owe you big time. Let me off the hook here."

Mithany closed her eyes and subtly nodded. She capped it off with a smile for his eyes only.

Before turning back to Neladith, he mouthed words to Mithany, "I love you, Sis."

Mithany responded aloud, "Of course you do."

She couldn't deny him.

She never could.

Mithany observed Arek return to Neladith's side. The pit in her stomach reached up to take hold of her once again. The entertainment value of Arek's dilemma afforded Mithany a small measure of relief from the unrelenting anxiety hijacking her thoughts. A result of the brief interaction, via her acquiescence to Arek's pleas, was releasing him from the burden of distracting her along the journey back to Hensdale. The consequential gloom of her decision crept back in to consume her. Urgency pushed away the momentary joy Arek released from her heart, as though it never happened. She determined she would bear the weight of her fears on her own for the remainder of the trip.

Nothing else mattered to her but getting back to Reyne.

Lust, Not Easily Dispatched

Teth: 27th Day of the Salmon Moon

Jerithan | Beezup

All thirty-two on the Council of Prudents, including Second Lord Razoal and First Lord Jerithan, gathered at the Temple Palace for Firstmeal. On the morning of the Feast held in honor of the Goddess Teth, Firstmeal was just a fancy name for breakfast. On any other day, it would have been called as much but for the symbolism it held and, of course, tradition. It wasn't even held at a time of day to give meaning to the word—it was more like Firstbrunch.

Firstmeal with the Council of Prudents was a tangle of unavoidable traditions. With the Prudents already gathered in the main dining area, Razoal and Jerithan huddled in an antechamber just off the main room.

Second Lord Razoal reflected, "There is so much more we can achieve outside these antiquated formal strictures."

First Lord Jerithan wasn't in agreement. "Razoal, do not make a single alteration. You know how change encourages distrust in the unruly Council of Prudents. Change is coming. We cannot upset them just yet. We need more time."

"There just isn't any. Always petty bullshit with this bunch," Razoal complained. "The event is moments away from starting, and I've got last-minute seating change requests to deal with."

"Give them what they want, Razoal," First Lord Jerithan suggested. "Change is coming. No sense in making it harder by denying the Council the comforts and the little pleasantries they desire. It brings us closer with less resistance."

"The longest-serving Prudents originally placed nearest to you at the head of the table will have to be moved to make way for the highest-ranking Prudents: Serco, Hansel, Marvo, and Aquila," The Second Lord of the Temple of Life outlined.

Reassuring himself, the First Lord inquired, "The seat to my right remains unchanged?"

"Of course. I will be at your side throughout the event."

"I wonder, Razoal, why there is no news yet from our people inside The Stand? Did they get done what we asked them to do this morning? Well, we will find out soon enough. Either Tomelai's gone, and it will mean his quest for electrics is dead and big changes to Prudent assignments. If we failed, Tomelai will have his day at the Council of Nations. If he makes it out the other side alive, we will have to figure out another way to defeat his proposal."

The Voice offered First Lord Jerithan his own insights, *"Change is coming, but not electrics. That would be a big problem for us while consolidating secular authority under the Temple banner. Electrics will usher in too much change. Not sure we could muster popular support for what we have planned under those circumstances."* Jerithan Cree listened to every word the Voice fused into his thoughts while looking out over the Prudents mulling about.

From one of the side rooms, Razoal continued to prepare the First Lord for the ceremonial entrance.

Thirty-two Prudents, all dressed in flowing green vestments and fortunate enough to be elected by their fellow Prudents to sit on the Council, had assembled. They congregated around the large table set in the Life Temple's formal dining hall, awaiting their chosen First Lord.

"The ceremonial dining hall is so ornate," Prudent Hansel said as he and Prudent S'Leen walked the grand space. Hansel had been in the hall many times since first elevated to Prudent over twenty years ago. He was round in his middle, which didn't carry well on a short man, but he was a much-respected member of the Council. When he spoke, others listened.

Prudent S'Leen jumped in. "I love the huge mural celebrating each member of the Holy Family covering every inch of wall space." She was so excited to be part of the event. This was her first time at Firstmeal, being the newest member to sit on the Council of Prudents. "Teth's honorific stands out. It is so compelling," S'Leen gushed.

Unlike the forest scene in First Lord Jerithan's bedchamber, the dining hall emoted images of scripture telling the central story of the joining of Father Sun and Mother Earth when all life began. Encircling the great room, at least two hundred feet in circumference, long-forgotten artists fashioned a continuous, unbroken fresco.

Prudent S'Leen's eyes followed the image of Teth rising from the floor as it curved up to the domed roof. "Just look at that Prudent Hansel, her arms open across an entire section of the room. Her head looks down at the room. And her eyes," she exclaimed. "Her eyes follow you everywhere. She's connecting with me." The middle-aged Prudent could feel the warmth, the serenity, the peaceful contemplation flow into her, as would anyone who met Teth's gaze in that room for the first time.

"Yes," Prudent Hansel noted. "They depict her much as she is sculpted atop the city entrance. You've probably already noticed. Few can look away from the breathtaking beauty of the Goddess Teth in her naked form. You know, I find her eyes to be the most captivating feature of this painting."

Hansel continued, "This depiction is a testament to how deeply she is loved as the founder of the city. Did you know she originally named this place New Phoenix? Humanity rising from the ashes after the Great Destruction. It wasn't until after she left to find other survivors that the people changed the name of the city to honor her."

"You are a devotee of the Gift of Knowledge, I assume. And thank you, I love that story."

"Father Sun and Mother Earth can't stand up to the love bestowed upon this human woman who is also a goddess. She stands at the center of Temple of Life doctrine. Through sheer will, overcoming impossible obstacles, she led the refuge of humanity following the Great Destruction to settle here in this place. By lore, the first settlement was established here, at the very spot of the great dining hall." He sounded more like he was speaking to the flock than to another Prudent.

"We're all intimately aware of Teth's story," Prudent O'Hurn politely offered, hoping to put an end to Hansel's pontificating to Prudent S'Leen.

"Maybe," Prudent Serco joined in, "to those few Prudents, holy men and women all, who choose instead to look upon her form, worshiping her differently, diminishes all of us. We may celebrate the Six Gifts: Love, Knowledge, Flesh, Life, Nature, and Renewal as Teth guides us, yet in telling of her story this day, she sets her example for us to follow, but it does not give freedom to lust in our hearts." He didn't give Hansel a moment to reply. "Lust is one of the Six Torments, remember? Prudent S'Leen, you are our newest member to join the Council. I am Prudent Serco. I believe we've met before," he said upon the conclusion of his condemnation of his fellow Prudents.

Leaning in so only she could hear, Prudent Hansel whispered, "You'll get used to him."

Stationed in a nearby anteroom of the great dining hall, waiting for Firstmeal to begin, Jerithan watched the gaggle of Prudents prance about. He followed their movements, one by one, gauging each of them: evaluating them, judging them, adding new insights into every Prudent in the room.

The Voice offered, *"Do they seek her eyes and feel the connection with her, or do they seek other parts unspoken? It is not all that hard to figure out. Watch O'Hurn, follow his gaze as he looks upon your savior."*

Jerithan replied, *Free love, a consequence inherent in the demands of aggressive repopulation, as the Covenant requires, is ingrained in our culture. The human body in all its glory is everywhere. Temple of Life doctrine promotes The Six Gifts. A favorite among the faithful is the Gift of Flesh.*

"The Gift of Flesh's underpinning focuses on the physicality of the human body as a host to Communal Life forces. Free love and the celebration of the human form, as delivered at birth in all its glory, cuts deep into the entirety of your civilization. Everyone everywhere, in all nations, is committed to the Covenant, yet lust is a powerful human trait not easily dispatched."

Given how pervasive the human form is throughout society in its depiction of both men and women, it does not surprise me how lasciviously several of my colleagues look upon the Goddess Teth.

Jerithan reflected on the stolen glances he often enjoyed and thought, *We are only human. Lest we not judge ourselves too harshly.*

Wasting no opportunity while still waiting for Firstmeal to begin, Prudent Serco continued to foment opposition amongst his fellow Prudents to First Lord Jerithan's rule. Prudent Beezup was the current recipient of Prudent Serco's observations. "It is no secret to you, my friend, I detested both Razoal and the First Lord. They've done nothing to advance the standing of the faithful in the outlying Kingdom of Adelle. Tandure is in my charge. It's because I opposed Jerithan's ascendance to First Lord and voted for Marvo that he's holding back favors for Tandure to punish me. It's going to bite him in the ass one day. Sooner than later if Tomelai ever decides to do something about it." Prudent Serco did not hold back on his displeasure with Jerithan's leadership.

Prudent Beezup asked, "Why then, if you despise him so much, did you give him all that info on Tomelai's plans for electrics?"

"I had to—the right thing to do. I might not think much of our First Lord, but he has the connections with the other national leaders to kill the proposal. Electrics are wrong. Not natural. Electrics directly opposes the Gift of Nature. I serve only what's right for the Temple. Even if someone undeserving sits at the head of the table," Serco explained.

"You aren't concerned Tomelai will find out you gave his plans to Jerithan?"

"No. He'll never find out."

Unlike fellow Prudent Beezup, who gave the appearance of accepting the vote of the Council to raise up Jerithan, Serco chose a different path.

Prudent Beezup bent his head forward, close to Serco's ear, and replied, "You are my friend. I mean this only in the sincerest way. You only have yourself to blame. You are too obvious. Play along, give them their due. They are our leaders. But not forever. Bide your time. An opportunity will come."

Serco couldn't let it go. Animus roiled to the surface. "What's right is right. Razoal and Jerithan aren't 'what's right' for the good of the Order. The First Lord is the face of the Temple. I'm not convinced our current First Lord has our sacred way of life as his guiding principle. He's going to lead us down the wrong path. All of us. You wait and see."

He continued to whisper his rants for only Prudent Beezup to hear. Or so he thought. The sum of all his conspiratorial ranting would find their way to First Lord Jerithan before the day was through.

Beezup didn't reply. He concluded there wasn't any comfort to offer his friend to dissuade him from the destructive path he was on. Beezup watched from a distance in the hope his friend would come around. He would not be part of a groundswell against the Order's most powerful member, First Lord Jerithan. If such a groundswell were to take hold, like the coward he was, he would be ready to join the cause—then and only then.

Razoal gave the signal to start the proceedings, letting Beezup off the hook from Serco's belligerence. Beezup and Serco turned their attention away from their private conversation to dutifully face Second Lord Razoal, who was taking his first steps into the main dining hall.

Barriers Are Not Enough

Teth: 27th Day of the Salmon Moon

Derr

Replacement KCG protectors, along with Captain Derr and the entire Kingdom of Adelle entourage, having met up with Tomelai and Derr, finally exited The Stand in what remained of the morning. Derr's eyes darted in every direction as he rode out from Teth's side of The Stand. He looked about, assessing every threat. Adjusting to the light of day, squinting made him look even more formidable, if that was possible.

"Hold here," Derr commanded his team, giving them time for their eyes to adjust. The KCG, the Chancellor, and himself were all seated on the same steeds that had turned flesh into raw meat. The KCG advance unit had rounded up the horses while still inside the passage, wiped them free of blood and pieces of brain tissue. The band of horses rode in perfect formation, in perfect unison, and not even a trained equestrian could see anything in the behavior of the remounted steeds to suggest they had been in battle. Horses kept better secrets than any man or woman alive.

Lady Kaythlin and members of the Adelle entourage were right behind Tomelai. The entire procession would parade through down Teth's Protisium, its principal thoroughfare, later in the day.

Shadows fell across the gap between The Stand and the stone wall standing before them.

Specialist Nardel of the KCG rode up alongside Captain Derr. “It’s my first trip to Teth,” she offered.

“Keep your eyes open. The city looks welcoming, but we know better.” Derr trailed off, catching sight of an older man slip something under his coat.

Nardel continued speaking. “Why this wall? Seems to me, The Stand did its job.”

Not looking in her direction, Derr continued to focus on the old man. “They need a dedicated space to queue up travelers and merchants looking to get into Teth. Can’t have lines of people inside The Stand. The Stand doesn’t afford city officials much opportunity to properly manage incoming visitors, incoming commerce, or keep out the unwanted. This second wall structure is all about money and collecting duties, fees, and taxes efficiently. It’s not intended as a defensive structure if you don’t consider squeezing every ounce of revenue out of every potential source defensive.”

Derr stopped.

An old man reached under his coat. Derr tensed, ready to pounce. A small writing pad appeared in the old man’s hand.

Derr eased and turned his attention away from the man back to Nardel.

“So, the second stone wall was a means to properly administer entry into the city,” Specialist Nardel said. “I see.”

Two barriers separated Teth from the rest of the world. One of stone and the other, now behind them, of wood. Each of the two barriers served a different purpose and stood separated by some fifty yards.

Dwarfed by the sequoias casting long shadows upon the open space, the stone structure rose from the ground a mere thirty feet. Unlike its taller sister, the inner wall offered a large opening, wide enough for the many incoming and outgoing travelers city officials processed each day.

Nardel’s jaw hung open. Rather than scolding the young woman for allowing herself to be distracted, in a moment of understanding, Derr offered an explanation. “Hanging over the entrance is more than a large wooden door positioned to drop across the opening if ever needed. It’s made up of several intact thirty-foot-thick sequoia trunks. The city practices the opening and closing of the inner wall at least once a year to ensure it's in working order. You should see them try to get the huge trunks back up in the ready position."

Eyes wide, she replied, "That must be quite a sight."

"I've seen it myself," Tomelai offered, jumping in the middle of the conversation. "They wanted to impress me on some state visit I can't recall much about. But I remember seeing that thing come down," he said, pointing to the massive wooden emergency door.

Although one of the younger members of the KCG contingent, Nardel was one of its brightest. She showed herself when she responded, "Something, my lord Chancellor, you would surely not forget. Perhaps you do recall Teth's objectives for your state visit."

The Chancellor laughed and gave her a practiced smile. "Drew, keep your eyes on this one. She might take your job one day. I remember thinking that same thing when it was added to the itinerary at the last minute."

Specialist Nardel blushed at the praise from her ruler. "Thank you, my lord Chancellor." Then she turned her attention, but not her face, to Captain Derr. "But please forgive me, Chancellor. You know so much more than me, yet I fear there's no one alive today who can replace our Captain."

"Oh, Drew, I'm going to keep my eye on her." A chuckle escaped Tomelai.

"Drew?" Nardle asked.

"Captain Derr to you," Derr replied.

Never threatened by insecurities, Derr gave her patronizing compliment little thought. He was assessing everything and everyone between The Stand and the wall. He kept on watching. He was always watching.

Lieutenant Ferpratt was waiting there too, between The Stand and the inner wall. He rode up to Derr. "We were here the entire time. Nothing went in," he said, offering a short, direct explanation.

"If that's all you have to report." Derr trailed off. He would have none of it.

"My unit has already begun gathering intel, and they'll inspect the remains. We'll get you answers," Ferpratt offered his Captain.

Derr, always clear about where one stood, made it obvious to the Lieutenant that he just stepped foot in Derr's shithouse. Derr sent Ferpratt away with a stern look and a dismissive wave of his hand.

There would be hell to pay, and Ferpratt was likely to take the full brunt of Derr's fury. The delay would offer Ferpratt time to organize his analysis and give Derr time to cool off. All things considered, it could have been worse for Ferpratt.

"Form up," Derr gave the command to the entire Adelleian contingent. They moved in unison to take up their assigned placement. The Chancellor rode out in front.

Peddlers yelled out as the cortege passed. Chickens squawked, ducks quacked, and flesh merchants offering both men and women discreetly showed off their private pleasures to anyone who looked like they might be a paying customer. Derr made out pickpockets working the gathering of onlookers.

Derr studied every one of them as he approached the entrance to Teth's second passage. He thought an attack here would have had the second-best chance to succeed. He wasn't letting his guard down just because they survived the first attempt.

He had trained himself over the years to never get angry or allow any of his emotions to take hold of him uncontrolled. Anger, as much as any emotion, clouded one's judgement. Any normal man would have been angry with Ferpratt and Milvoe. In their defense, he wasn't sure how the assailants got through the posted KCG agents. It gave him little comfort as he looked ahead to see Tomelai riding out in front without protection, surrounded by no one and in the knowledge one assault on the Chancellor's life had already been attempted.

A middle-class merchant approached from one side, holding a chicken upside down by its legs. Before the man could reach them, Ferpratt lifted his foot out of its stirrup, pushed his boot hard against the man's chest.

"Get back!" Ferpratt commanded. The man flinched and fell back, losing his grip on the squawking bird, which took off running mindlessly in every direction. The crowd laughed at the guy lifting himself from a pile of dung, shaking it off his hands while trying to stand, only to slip and fall back again.

Fucking idiot, Derr thought. *Ferpratt should know better. We don't need the commotion.* It put Derr on edge, surveilling as many of the merchants as he could. He saw danger everywhere. Even when the laughter died down, Derr's senses heightened, his fingers tingled, and he squeezed them into fists.

Teth's honor guards stood ceremonially, blocking the entrance to the inner wall. The two guards loomed in the center of the passage with scythes crossed.

By mutual consent, the two nations' delegates agreed the official greeting was to take place at the main entrance to the city at the wall. Tomelai preferred a more grandiose setting. His delegation gained other concessions from Teth's delegation for the low-key greeting.

Several wagon carts could pass through the entrance side by side. The wall was also much shorter than The Stand. At thirty feet tall, the builders made it of granite quarried close to the city. An arch decorated the top of the main entrance. Sculptured forms of the Holy Family stood looking down on all who approached. Over the years, other First Lords of the Temple of Life were added in sculptured form lining the top of the structure on both sides of the Holy Family: Father Sun, Mother Earth and their four offspring deities. Efros, the moon god, Malthus, god of night, Satrin, god of water, fire and wind, and their beloved city namesake, Teth, savior of humanity and the patron goddess of all the children of the world.

Father Sun and Mother Earth stood at the center atop the grand arch draped in sculptured robes, as were all the First Lords flanking the Holy Family. All the godly offspring stood sans clothing. Teth stood to Mother Earth's left, garnering the lion's share of attention.

Depicted as a young woman, naked like her brothers, with her arms spread wide, welcoming the children of Earth to her city. Representing a scene from the Book of Teth, she stood looking down on all who, symbolically, wished to enter her and her namesake city.

"Teth welcomes the honorable Lord Chancellor of the great Kingdom of Adelle, and all the good citizens he represents." The words spoken by Provost Kwuinan were short, as per the agreed language. He was a tall man approaching middle age. A well-groomed full head of rich brown hair quaffed to perfection.

An heir of competency and even confidence rolled off him as he stood in silence awaiting the Chancellor's scripted reply. As the First Lord's Chief Secular representative and selected by Jerithan himself, Kwuinan ran the day-to-day functions of Teth's quasi-secular government. Other Teth dignitaries stood a few steps behind the guards posted at the entrance. The responsibility of welcoming high-ranking visitors was one duty Provost Kwuinan most enjoyed. He was a true politician at heart.

"Thank you for your First Lord's gracious invitation to attend the Festival of Teth. I am Chancellor Tomelai of the Kingdom of Adelle, and these are my people. We formally request your First Lord's permission to enter the great city of Teth."

It irritated Derr his sovereign had to make such a pronouncement, as though he was someone subservient to First Lord Jerithan or his lackey, Provost Kwuinan. It was all diplomatic bullshit. *The First Lord ought to be the one bending over.*

Tomelai did his stately duty with grace and ease. Derr looked on as Kwuinan gave a signal to the guards to uncross their scythes, stepped apart, and permitted the Adelle retinue to enter. The entire Teth contingency bowed in unison as Chancellor Tomelai passed.

Provost declared, "It is our nation's great honor that the Chancellor of Adelle blesses us with his attendance."

The Chancellor graciously smiled as his official reply. Chancellor Tomelai welcomed the opportunity to interact with those of the lower classes, especially since it was only a few words and took so little effort on his part.

"Look, the city came out to greet the Chancellor. There's a heck of a lot of them," Nardel said.

It was the Feast of Teth. These were the moments that brought Derr to great consternation. Having heard Nadel's thoughts, Derr added his own. "Too many people. Too few of us in the Guard. Too many possibilities to account for. Keep your eyes open."

Ferpratt joined in, trying to soften up Derr. "But not today. Not after the incident in the tunnel. The assault on Tomelai failed thanks to your quick thinking."

Derr listened but said nothing. He often said nothing.

Ferpratt went on, "There won't be another attempt, at least not this morning. They shot their load. They failed. Might be regrouping. But not this quickly."

Derr replied, "Hope you're right."

It should have put Derr at ease. Druin Derr at ease was much like Druin Derr at any other time, day or night—always on high alert. That was exactly what he expected from every man and woman of the KCG.

Derr watched the crowd closely. He watched faces. He looked at clothing. He evaluated groups. He followed arm movements, hand gestures, and took in all he could. But mostly, he examined faces. Druin Derr watched everything. He was always watching.

The reassuring words he offered were a lie. He equivocated to put the Chancellor at ease, but Derr didn't let his guard down for even a second. Danger was everywhere. Someone wanted Tomelai dead, and one failed attempt wouldn't put an end to it. Whoever arranged Tomelai's assassination already knew the plot failed.

The hit men were dead.

Tomelai lived.

The threat of a second attempt hung in the air. Derr had to be ready when it came.

A Rock and a Hard Place

Owls Neck: 27th Day of the Salmon Moon

Mithany | Arek

Midday had arrived for Mithany and her fellow travelers making their way back to Hensdale. Frantic to find out what had become of Reyne, the day wore on her. She rubbed her chest, attempting to relieve the ache that had settled there, longing to see Reyne safe and unharmed.

She was oblivious to the sound of birds, oblivious to the fields of wildflowers along the roadside and oblivious to Arek's boundless energy. She had given up waiting for Arek's comfort, forsaken to be imprisoned in her own misery the rest of the way home.

One thought kept all others at bay. *Is he alright?* It replayed over and over in her mind. *Is he alright? Is he alright? Is he alright?*

"You okay, Sis?"

No reply.

"Sis?"

Nothing.

Arek expected a reply from Mithany. When he failed to get one, he blurted out, "Time to take action." For Arek, "taking action" meant anything was possible.

Turning to Neladith, he said, “Be right back, Nel.” Pecked her on the cheek, then ran up behind Mithany, who was shuffling along. He lowered himself to walk on bended knees with outstretched arms and open palms. With each foot carefully placed on the dirt roadway so as not to alert her to his approach, his arms shot forward. He grabbed her ass and squeezed hard.

Reacting with a loud squeal that echoed throughout the forest, Mithany jumped several paces ahead.

Laughing at the site, Arek got a few words out, “That leap would’ve set the long jump record back in Hensdale.”

She landed safely with her hands coming to rest on her knees. Looking down at the dirt beneath her feet, Mithany yelled back at her brother, “You’re a dick!” followed by a long and loud, second pronouncement, “DICK!!!”

Laughing hard at his sister’s reaction, a cramp took hold along his rib cage. “Oh, it hurts. I gotta stop laughing.” But he kept laughing anyway.

Arek’s cackling filled the air. Mithany took her hands off her knees, spun around to observe her brother holding his side in delightful agony, and also saw Neladith’s shit-eating grin at her expense. Anger flared and she wanted to scream, “Why did you even come on this trip? Another roll in the hay?” But for Arek’s sake, the words only rattled around in her head.

Mithany wanted to embrace her fury. She wanted to be mad at them both. Mostly, she wanted to hold Reyne in her arms. Her shoulders slumped and she released an audible sigh. She didn’t have the strength to fight it. Worrying about Reyne drained her, and he was all that really mattered.

With exhaustion in her eyes, Mithany patiently walked over to Arek, still bent over in pure glee. She raised one leg, rested it on his hunched shoulder, and used her foot to topple him over. His body didn’t seem to change position when he hit the ground, nor did he stop laughing.

Mithany turned to see Neladith's look locked on Arek now rolling about delightfully on the ground. Mithany stood over her brother and was amazed at the full measure of joy Arek took at her expense. Resentment proved impossible to embrace watching his childlike innocence, and Mithany seemed to change with each passing moment.

She let out a little smirk. "You're still a dick."

Before Arek responded, a piercing, deep, fearsome roar, louder than anything Mithany ever experienced, nailed her in place, to the identical effect on both Arek and Neladith.

"What the fuck was that?" Arek whispered from his position on the ground.

"Shhhh," Mithany said, bringing her index finger to her lips as she scanned the area.

Arek opened his mouth to speak when Neladith quietly jumped in, "Arek, would you shut the fuck up? You want whatever made that sound finding us?"

Not one of them moved a muscle for the next few minutes. They waited silently, motionless, listening to every noise the forest threw at them, hoping for any signal telling them what it was and hoping like hell they would hear nothing like it again.

Despite her fears, Mithany reflected on Neladith's admonition of Arek. She liked that Neladith told Arek to "shut the fuck up." *He deserved it. She might be one of those gals who stands up for herself. I can respect that, especially in a young girl, woman, whatever. Good for you, Neladith.*

Arek was the first to speak. "Okay, so nothing. It's gone. Let's move on. Or in your case, Sis, let's hop along further down the road." He started laughing again.

"Oh, wipe that grin off your face," Mithany said with little to no conviction. She never stayed mad at Arek for too long.

"I guess it's safe to continue on," Neladith said, and to Mithany's surprise, Neladith directed the words at her.

Reyne was still foremost on her mind. "I agree."

"Hey, anyone gonna ask me what I think?" Arek asked in what Mithany recognized as a pretend hurt voice.

In unison, both women replied, “No!”

Which surprised Mithany again. *Huh, I can get to like this one if he keeps her around long enough.*

“Can we cut out the nonsense and pick up the pace?” Mithany said, returning her attention to her fears of what had become of Reyne.

Reyne, my love, I’m coming.

A Goddess Incarnate

Teth: 27th day of the Salmon Moon

Jerithan

The Feast of Teth's Firstmeal celebratory processional made its way into the great hall. The Prudents rose as one and graciously bowed to the procession led by the maiden chosen to represent Teth's incarnation, Lilly Marvo.

Each year, the Order of Teth selected a maiden from the city to represent their namesake goddess. Considered a great honor to be chosen, whomever the Order selected as the ceremonial maiden brought respect to herself and her family. Families could parlay their good fortune to last the year and beyond. The ceremonial maiden remained in demand throughout the year at events and private functions until the inevitable, when a new maiden would be chosen the following year. A lucky few captured the love of the city and remained in favor for many years after their initial tenure ended.

The Order of Teth's selection process was not without its inducements from those who would seek advantage. Having one's daughter considered for the honor required duly proffered payments to both the official channels of the Temple and to the unofficial channels within the Order. The Order of Teth comprised prelates appointed by high ranking Prudents of the Temple and included secular officials from the ranks of the city's administrative community. Bribes were part of the process and known to all who cared a whit.

Lilly Marvo, a blossoming young woman of eighteen years chosen as the current maiden Teth, held her head high while stepping out as the lead. Proud as any grandfather would be, Prudent Marvo beamed at the sight.

The selection of Lilly Marvo had been unexpected. Although the usual secret payoffs were exchanged, the Order remained unable to settle on any one candidate. Each person of the Order pushed their nominee. With a compromise impossible, the Order deadlocked until the First Lord took the rare step of offering his "unofficial" support for Lilly. She had not been in earnest consideration up to then, but none of the Order's members could afford to deny the First Lord his choice.

Razoal counseled First Lord Jerithan on the selection of Lilly, aiming to cement the support of Marvo and many Prudents in his faction. With the appearance of unity and respect for his once-rival, the Order's choice of Lilly Marvo proved effective in securing Prudent Marvo's loyalty. The First Lord was reasonably sure he understood the man well and expected nothing less than total obedience from Marvo in the exchange. Jerithan had created the need for compromise, seeing the members of this year's Order of Teth comprised itself of individuals whose character flaws included stubbornness, one and all. Jerithan then sat back and allowed events to play out, creating the conditions for Lilly Marvo's dark horse selection and Prudent Marvo's allegiance.

Watching Lilly Marvo as he followed in behind her, Jerithan briefly glanced across the room to see Prudent Marvo smiling proudly at his granddaughter. The First Lord was also proud of himself for what he had accomplished with a simple gesture.

"You've done well," the Voice broke through Jerithan's thoughts.

Jerithan silently replied, *Yes. Thank you,* soaking up the praise that, from what he believed, came from Father Sun, the one true God.

The Voice added, *"This is better than I thought you might do. Prudent Marvo at your side will have a measurable impact on our plans to create the Empire of Tartica, and at such a small expense. I am proud of you."*

Jerithan craved the adulation of his inner companion and blushed at the compliment.

Lilly Marvo, as the maiden-incarnate-Teth, stood before the holy congregation of Prudents. Jerithan was a step behind on her right, and the Temple of Life's Second Lord was to her left, followed by ten young boys and ten girls all adorned in ceremonial white robes and flowers. The Prudents remained standing as maiden-incarnate-Teth gently removed the left strap from her shoulder, letting it drop from her arm. Slowly and gently, she lowered the strap of her gown from her right shoulder, letting it fall. The ceremonial gown dropped to the floor.

As a reenactment of Teth's actions—done at the founding of the city—Lilly stood naked before all who had gathered for Firstmeal. Stepping out over the fallen gown, her feet gingerly walked down three steps into an opening in the middle of the table. All eyes fixed on her as she represented the Temple's goddess. She epitomized Teth's innocence and beauty. Reaching the center of the confine, she raised her outstretched arms with palms upward, and turning to face the flowered children and the Council of Prudents, she spoke the ceremonial lines: "Children of the world. The few left to seed our future, join me in a new beginning. Thrown off are all our ties to the past. I stand here naked, as in a new birth, to accept from Mother Earth only what she willingly offers us, to clothe us, feed us, nurture us, our spirits, and to lead us in a new direction as we, the chosen survivors, repopulate humanity. Children, join me."

"*She is beautiful.*" The Voice broke in on Jerithan as he watched the ritual unfold. "*Do you think Marvo knows how lustfully his brothers look upon his granddaughter? Look at him. He is so proud of her. It blinds him. He does not see it. These holy men and women, with the Book of Teth as their guide, should better understand the Gift of Flesh is about love and purity. It is proof, faith is no match for the Torment of Lust. Not even in the holiest of men."*

You know what I see, First Lord Jerithan replied in thought. *I see a means to an end. I see the face of Prudent Marvo, and I know that we have moved our cause one step forward by eliminating a powerful obstacle. I am that much closer to achieving the impossible, Emperor of Tartica.* At that moment, Jerithan's unquenchable lust for power trumped his lecherous desire for the heavenly form before him.

"*That is why you are the right man for what we have to do. You do not see the lovely Gift of Flesh or the Maiden Teth reborn. You do not see a goddess. You see an answer to our Prudent Marvo problem, standing in the center of the room. I have always known why you are my chosen. Now don't you have a ceremony to continue,*" the Voice concluded.

With the thought of the lovely Lilly Marvo standing before the Council of Prudents, Jerithan stepped to the top of the three short steps, coming to face them all.

"As it was at the dawn of time," he began. All but a few eyes looked up to meet his gaze. "Eurithian, Father Sun, roamed the heavens, racing across the universe as he pleased. Until He came upon Simurmure, Mother Earth, who was wandering alone in darkness. Eurithian, with all His might, ensnared Simurmure to Him. She struggled to break free, but to no avail, and they became entwined, but He could not pull her to Him. Eurithian relentlessly drew her closer year after year. And so, it has been since the dawn of time.

"Each day, Eurithian rose to continue the chase until exhausted and sleep fell upon him. Each day, Simurmure raced across the sky, pursued by her would-be lover. But she longed to regain the freedom she once knew. Eurithian bathed her in His warmth, and over time, she came to appreciate His gift."

While Jerithan paused and looked about the faces of the Council of Prudents, the Voice in his head reflected, *"I know you have Marvo the Elder on your mind, but look at that lovely body. She is a lovely gift to the eyes. Is there anything more exquisite, is there nothing greater, in all of Eurithian's creation and amongst the Six Gifts, than the sight of such a woman?"*

Maybe the Voice's words were a test, but the First Lord ignored him, and kept on, "Simurmure came to love the warmth but would not relent. Freedom, more than anything, drove her each day. Over epochs, He pursued her through the heavens, and still, she would not give in. Eurithian was mad with a passion for Simurmure, so He set His seed upon the solar winds with the hope His seed would reach His unrequited lover. Settling upon baron lands, Eurithian's seed yet bore fruit. And so Satrin, god of water, was born of the fruit of Eurithian and Simurmure, and she was pleased. The Sun God's seed brought her a child whom she loved so. Seeing her pleasure with Satrin, Eurithian again released His seed tenfold to bring his love, Mother Earth, even more children. And it was so. With a great eruption, Efros broke from the loins of his mother. He broke free of the physical touch, as he desired to roam the heavens. Yet she would not release him to his father because she loved him deeply, and he loved his mother deeply. She hides Efros from his father by day and loves his mother each night.

"And so, it was that Simurmure came to love Satrin and Efros. She was grateful to Eurithian for these gifts. She stopped racing through the heavens to escape His advances and settled into a peaceful and quiet place in the heavens. But still, Eurithian rose each morning to set His warmth upon her and longed for more. Father Sun saw this in her.

"And it was at the dawn of the First Age of Man, a massive release of the seed in the form of sunlight from Father Sun reached the womb, the open barren lands, of Mother Earth. And the children of the Earth sprung forth from the barren lands.

"Simurmure saw them grow and multiply. She loved them as her own, but Eurithian grew jealous. As the children of Earth spread across the world, Eurithian could take it no longer. They worshiped her, not Him, and commanded His son Satrin to bring rain down upon all the children of Earth and sweep them away."

Jerithan again paused, looking out over his audience. With all the Prudents watching him and Lilly Marvo still standing among the flowered children, Jerithan motioned all eyes toward the encircling fresco.

"For although Satrin was compelled to obey his father, he loved his mother so that he whispered in the ear of only a few, warning them to prepare for what was to come. The First Age of Man ended with the Great Flood set upon the Earth by Satrin. And with those few who Satrin hid from his father, the children of Earth and the creatures of Earth again grew and multiplied for many millennia to come."

With the flowered children becoming restless, as children often do, Lilly took it upon herself to gather them to her side. Her naked form before them was of no concern, having been brought up in the faith and having been accustomed to all people in their natural state.

"But the children of Earth grew demanding on Simurmure, taking from her all she could give. And yet, they demanded more and more of her until devastation fell upon the children of Earth over what little resources remained of what Mother Earth could provide. Father Sun saw this, and He was not pleased. Efros wept for his mother and the children of the Earth. He saw his mother was distraught. He loved his mother so deeply that he committed a great sacrilege. He whispered to just a few, so Father Sun would not find him out, to gather the seeds of life throughout the world and to hide them away from Eurithian. For Efros knew his father's wrath would soon be coming. And so it did. Father Sun brought down His anger upon all the children of Earth, and so it was with the second Great Destruction, He sent fire on the solar winds to destroy the great cities and to wipe the children of Earth from all existence."

Turning to the maiden Teth standing before them, Jerithan continued the story of the Ages of Humanity. "So it came to be, the beginning of the Third Age of Humanity. Yet, Eurithian had come very close to succeeding." As all eyes turn to face the maiden Teth, standing in the center of the open circular table.

She looked up to the fresco to point to the rise of Teth while Jerithan continued. "Eurithian's wrath had destroyed so much, but even that was not enough. He rained down upon the remaining children of Earth, poison in the form of rain, and then he set darkness upon all of creation. For generations, He set cold upon the world so much it chilled even the bones of Mother Earth. Eurithian was certain He had finally succeeded, and so He rested."

Jerithan looked at Lilly in the form of Teth and smiled. "Out of the ashes of what remained from the Great Destruction, a child of Mother Earth was born—Teth, the savior of our world. Eurithian had all but succeeded. Yet Teth traveled the world to find those who had survived the Great Destruction. There were so very few. She gathered them unto herself with the aid of Satrin. It took many years, many years fraught with destitution. Finally, when she found all she could, she brought them all here to our home, our city, the birthplace for the Third Age of Humanity."

Lilly, taking her cue, stepped forward. "And it was the word of Teth, to the few who survived and gathered about in this place after the Great Destruction and its aftermath, all should love one another without fault, without shame, without jealousy to give joy to Mother Earth once again. We all commit to her and respect the gifts she offers without hesitation, without greed, without the desire to demand more than Mother Earth can give to nurture us, to spread the seed of humanity freely and with love in our hearts until such time we are called upon to return the borrowed Gift of Flesh to our Mother Earth, to her soil, in the Circle of Life, so she may offer our flesh to nourish others throughout her kingdom. That Nature may be replenished, and others may be born to love her as we have.

"I stand here bare before you, before the city, before the Temple of Life. I stand here proud of the Gift of Flesh she has given upon me. Upon all of us. To share it as I want, to love as I will, and to serve all of humanity with joy to our Mother Earth by bringing forth from my loins the future children of our world.

"I stand here before all, as I was on the day of my birth, as a symbol of the rebirth of all humankind. And it is through the Gift of Knowledge that we conceive of what we want, what we expect, what we can achieve, and then consciously or otherwise unknown to us, such thoughts create our reality, either in an instant or over the long stretches of time. But know this: it is in the moment of thought we create the future. It is here we conceived of a new beginning for humankind, and it is here we recreate it this day."

One tear rolled down Prudent Marvo's face. Clearly his heart surged beneath his green vestments at the sight of his granddaughter as the maiden Teth reborn. Lilly was beautiful. She looked so much like her mother in her youth. Jerithan took pleasure in seeing his fellow Prudent Marvo; knowing his heart hurt watching his granddaughter, and most certainly Lilly would conjure up thoughts in Marvo of Lilly's mother, his own dead daughter, whom he repeatedly reminded to all who would listen, he missed so much. Lilly was perfect in both her recital and in the part she played in securing Prudent Marvo's loyalty to Jerithan. Jerithan was proud of himself for his well-orchestrated manipulation of Prudent Marvo.

Serco, standing alongside the proud grandfather, put his arm around his fellow Prudent. "You should be proud, Marvo. That's a very special granddaughter you have there."

From his perch, Jerithan caught the exchange, and it irked him. This performance would be done again for the entire city at the end of the parade. He would have to make sure Razoal did not station Serco near Marvo next time. It was the only flaw in an otherwise perfect morning.

Jerithan stepped down into the center, draped a robe over Lilly, and kissed her on the cheek. "Your mother would have been so proud of you today. You were perfect," Jerithan said, holding her hands in his as he turned to look for Prudent Marvo, who was making his way toward his granddaughter. "Go to your grandfather. He is so proud of you. As we all are, my dear."

Lilly thanked the First Lord, offered him a quick curtsy, and rushed to her grandfather's arms. "Did you see me, Granddaddy? I did good, huh?"

With more tears in his eyes, Prudent Marvo said, "Teth herself could not measure up to you today." Sacrilege, maybe, but he was a proud grandfather. Surely, Teth would forgive him.

She wiped the tears rolling down his cheeks with her thumbs. She leaned in, speaking softly in his ear, "I love you, Grandpa."

Razoal looked at Jerithan, and they both grinned. Razoal, standing at the top of the steps, clapped his hands together and announced, "Let us eat. Firstmeal awaits."

Jerithan spontaneously threw in, "Children, Lilly, please join us as my honored guests." No one was prepared for the invitation Jerithan offered—the event administrator, the cooks, the waitstaff, the Prudents, the children, Lilly or Second Lord Razoal. Firstmeal was a time for informal Temple business. It had always been that way.

The invitation caught the waitstaff off guard more than all the others. There wasn't enough room. Not enough plates. More utensils were needed. More glassware. And food—would what they had already prepared be enough?

Jerithan cared little for the event manager's concerns. He didn't want to give Serco a platform or any opportunity to address the Council of Prudents in a formal setting.

Nothing positive would come of that, he thought. *Better to take the win and stop the game while I'm ahead.*

"*That could not have gone better, my friend*," the Voice made its observations known to Jerithan. "*It will pay dividends. Brilliant call inviting the little urchins to the table. Let us see Serco sow his seeds of dissent with the beautiful little flowers seated between them all.*"

The woman overseeing the details of Firstmeal was exceptionally good at her job. To Jerithan's surprise, the waitstaff recovered quickly, and servers entered the hall with chairs, plates, glasses, and tableware. Soon after, they brought elaborate trays full of food and drink for the gathered to enjoy. It was so well organized that it might have looked like the impromptu invitation was planned.

It wasn't planned, but that didn't prevent First Lord Jerithan from patting himself on the back. He was well skilled at recognizing when he did well.

One of the flowered children tugged on Razoal's vestments. She stood only as tall as his waist. Looking up, she asked, "Please tell us the story about how Jhonay spread the seeds across the empty land! Please. Please," she pleaded.

Stroking her head, covered in white petunias, Razoal deferred. "We'll get to it later, little dove. We'll get to it later. Come on, you sit next to me. I'll tell you Jhonay's story over Firstmeal." She beamed at being so honored to sit with the Second Lord.

"Please find seats for all our flowered guests," Jerithan ordered the waitstaff. He inconspicuously directed the event manager to seat several young children between Prudent Marvo and Prudent Serco.

Jerithan did not know it then, but a new tradition was born that morning. They would remember it as an insightful, kind, and benevolent gesture to the city's children, mirroring Teth's own behavior. No one would ever recall it was born of one man's insecurities.

The Voice broke in. "*Once again, you have done well. There was nothing more to gain. A wise decision to bring those young ones into the lion's den. Who amongst these vultures would pursue their private agenda with these sheep at their sides? I am impressed. Now, what about the Chancellor? Is he dead?*"

Old Habits, New Dangers

Owls Neck: 27th day of the Salmon Moon

Mithany | Arek

Mithany, Arek, and Neladith had barely traveled fifty yards when they heard the mysterious sound again. The blood-curdling growl. Louder this time, if possible. The three travelers froze.

"Shit, that's close," Arek observed.

Mithany was scared. They were all scared.

Neladith asked, "What do you think it is?" Fear dripped from her every word.

Mithany stood silently.

"Damned if I know," Arek whispered.

The three stood looking about, searching the forest for a sign confirming movement of any kind.

Nothing moved.

"Listen."

"I don't hear anything."

"Exactly."

"Whatever made that noise has every living thing in the forest scared shitless," Mithany noted.

Arek pointed to a clearing off in the distance and about twenty yards up the road. "It came from over there."

"Okay, so we all agree, we don't go there," Neladith demanded.

Arek took two steps in the direction he was pointing when Mithany grabbed his arm. "No."

"I'm going to check it out."

"No way."

In a whisper, Arek told the two women, "I'm gonna go over by that tree. Might be able to make out something."

Neladith joined in, adding support to Mithany, "No."

Mithany's facial expression posed a question for her brother, "What, to impress a girl? To get laid? Are you crazy?"

He replied to them both, Mithany's unverbalized query and Neladith's spoken demand, "It's what I do, ladies."

Mithany was right, of course, or so she guessed. This level of stupidity could only be to impress Neladith. Then again, he was always the first one out of hiding whenever their mother got close to finding them. He always stepped up and took the beatings to protect Mithany from their mother's wrath.

"If anything happens to me, you two run," Arek added, this time less confident.

About to take his first careful steps towards the danger, Mithany squeezed his arm. She looked him in the eye. What she read on his face almost brought her to tears. *It wasn't to impress Neladith. It's for me.* She thought, *Shit! He's doing it again. To protect me.* Experience told her there was no stopping him.

He leaned in close, putting his lips close to her ear so only she could hear. "Old habits die hard. Run like hell if you have to, and don't look back. Love ya, kiddo."

Arek kissed his sister on the cheek and took his first steps toward the awful sound.

Arek reached an opening in the brush close to where Mithany and Neladith were standing. He spied something moving further along in the forest, near the top of several enormous boulders. A head, completely covered in thick, matted, brown hair, perched atop enormous shoulders, bobbed up and down. Its head stopped moving. The hairy, brown face turned toward him.

Its eyes locked on him. Mustard-yellow irises encircled dark, almost black, large pupils. Arek's own eyes bulged, and his mind reeled, gripped at the beast's discovery of his presence. Adrenaline shot through his body by the force of rapid hammer blows thumping inside his chest. Unable to control a single muscle, his brain scrambled.

He almost shit his pants.

He might have.

Just a little.

Blood pounded in every artery, in every part of his body, but none more than in his head, threatening to burst apart his skull with explosive force at each contraction of his heart. He wished he'd never gotten this close. But more than anything, he wished he could move.

He'd seen nothing like it in all the world, nor had he ever experienced such incapacitating terror.

Poked out above the tops of boulders that themselves stood a good eight or nine feet from the forest floor, the head of the beast stopped moving. *Whatever comprised the rest of the hairy, brown body hiding behind the huge boulders gotta be enormous.*

Arek was afraid to move—even if he could.

Panting heavily, half scared to death, he gazed at the object of his terror. The object of his all-consuming fears glared back at him with angry, yellow eyes.

Looking like a giant hairy man, its piercing eyeballs stared him down, nailing him to the spot where he stood. His heart pounded so loudly the monster almost certainly heard it beating.

Seconds passed. A minute passed. Neither of them blinked. For a moment, Arek's mind escaped the dread bewitching him. A simple realization slipped through the blind terror obscuring all other thoughts.

The beast wasn't howling.

It wasn't moving.

And it wasn't attacking him.

The giant, hairy, man-looking creature kept glaring at him. Terror faded to a degree just above scared shitless, giving him the slightest chance of getting out alive.

Arek never understood how he gathered whatever bravery he had buried deep inside. But for Mithany, he called up, from somewhere in his soul he'd never accessed before, all the courage he could muster. He inched towards the monstrous creature, one careful step after another. He kept a suitable distance between himself and the beast. With each slow step, the giant thing studied him as Arek circled around. The enormous, hairy, man-like being didn't move, but it kept its eyes locked on him.

The brave young man changed his path from a wide circle and took a few steps forward. The closer Arek crept forward, the more he realized this was something he'd never figured he would see. It had to be a Great Yetgnal, like the one carved into the frieze on the wall of the Forest Maiden. Arek, standing several feet from the real thing, marveled at the massive size of the Great Yetgnal and was appalled at the smell it gave off.

Time passed impossibly slow for the two women waiting for Arek's return. Neither had moved in the minutes following Arek's disappearance into the clearing. They'd made out bits and pieces through the openings between the leaves, enough to tell them he was still alive, but not enough to know what was going on. Mithany reached out for Neladith's hand.

It was then the blood-curdling sound rang out again. A ferocious, deep, penetrating growl rolled over and through anything alive or dead. Bones, trees, and the ground rattled as the penetrating vibration of waves passed through everything in their wake. Pure terror washed over Mithany, and she expected the same response in Neladith. The piercing howl reached into her and seized her heart. As if a large hand compressed it inside a fist, struggling for its freedom, it stopped beating. Breath fled her lungs, and try as she might, she couldn't get it back.

She couldn't lose him too, not knowing what had become of Reyne and now Arek. It was too much. She almost collapsed in Neladith's arms. Seconds passed, and with a hard-fought gulp, air filled her lungs, bringing life to her heart.

Neladith appeared to be shouting something her mind couldn't put together. Mithany's attention followed the direction of the woman's arm, pointing at a large blob of brown fur moving quickly away from the clearing, showing itself for a few seconds before escaping out of sight.

Without realizing, Mithany ran to the clearing where she expected to find her brother.

In the span of just a few minutes, her heart stopped again. Sheer horror washed over her, too much for her to comprehend. Half propped up against one of the large boulders, a limp, lifeless Arek lay before her eyes.

Lies on Parade

Teth: 27th Day of the Salmon Moon

Tomelai

The Adelleian entourage prepared to assume their place in the Grand Parade. Derr rode up alongside Chancellor Tomelai. "Your entire retinue is in position and is set to go. If you're ready, Rotti, I'll have your Chief of Staff get this show started."

Chancellor Tomelai, with First Lady Kaythlin by his side, sat atop two of the largest tribian horses the crowd had ever seen. "Do it. Down the Grand Protisium another year, Drew."

After a nod to Derr, the First Lady turned her attention to her husband. "You and I haven't spent this much time together in quite a while. Reminds me of when we were first married. Before your father died. I miss this," she said, reminiscing about the life they shared before Madrotti assumed his position as Chancellor.

Twenty security agents of the KCG rode the edges on either side, creating a barrier between parade onlookers and Chancellor Tomelai. Tribian horses of the Chancellor's Guard were draped in a resplendent summer green. Adelle's crest, proudly embroidered on each side, depicted a snow-capped Mount Tandure. The Chancellor's sigil spoke to the formidable and ever-present strength of the nation-state of Adelle. The tribians stood eight feet tall from hoof to head, carrying the girth of twice a normal steed.

"It has been nice. Hasn't it? If only the demands of running the country would allow us more time together. I miss it too. I have missed you. Glad we are here together," Tomelai said, always the statesman, even in his marriage.

Tomelai tried to put the incident at The Stand out of his mind. He couldn't afford to look concerned for the crowd. First Lady Kaythlin by his side helped him put a warm smile on his face. Kaythlin Tomelai, the former Kaythlin F'Siyn, held men's eyes at a single glance, and the women's as well. Born into a high station, with all the privileges commensurate with wealth, she took full advantage.

The Chancellor rode side by side with Kaythlin, arms stretched across the gap between horses, holding her hand in a sign of unity and love. Neither felt the intense love they had once shared as when first wed, but a measure of affection existed between them now, more because of her efforts than of his. The affection he offered just wasn't love anymore. In a moment of introspection, weighing power against love, he wondered whether he'd made the right choice. The fleeting thought died quickly.

Years of ruling had ground away at the deep feelings he once held for Kaythlin. Power in Tandure, the capital of Adelle, was his and his alone. What he willingly shared of his authority was minor at best. His love for the First Lady waned as the years passed them by, yet his lust for her never wavered.

Hiding it well from others, the unrelenting sacrifices perforce of holding on to power exposed him as a selfish man. Maybe in fairy tales love always came first. The pursuit of power proved stronger than love.

Despite his own failings, he knew First Lady Kaythlin still loved him. She wanted him to love her again. The way back was littered with years of sacrifices. He'd succeeded at one and failed at the other. Both were committed to rule in Tandure as Chancellor and First Lady. He told himself it was for the good of Tandure he kept the reins of power. Love slipped silently through his embrace, drip by drip, as the years rolled on.

Could he love her once again, he wondered?

In the absence of love, he still needed her to rule the kingdom, to hold on to power. There were also their two children to consider: their daughter, the Heir Apparent, Tane, and their son, Loseff.

“Do you think the children will be ready to join us next year? We’ll ride down the main thoroughfare of Teth together as a family?” Kaythlin’s motherly love for her children remained firm through all their challenges.

“Tane’s more than ready. But we needed her to hold down the fort while we are here. It was because of your encouragement I left her in charge. Should be an eye-opener for her. Her first time at the helm. Who knows, perhaps she can do this next year and we can stay home. Of course, depending on whether we still have a country when we get back,” Tomelai joked.

“She will do fine, my love.”

The First Lady was not without her own power base. Toadies and flatterers made up much of Tandure’s elite society. Many of them proved useful, knowingly, or unwittingly. Lady Kaythlin was intelligent and charming. What power she had, she took.

Tomelai followed her dealings closely, keeping tabs on her through the KCG. She was his wife, the mother of his children, and she was as formidable as she was beautiful.

“Don’t forget smiling is part of the show,” she said as they proceeded through the streets of Teth, holding hands for all to see. Only those closest to the imperial couple had knowledge of the layers beneath the public lie.

“You look beautiful as always, but ever more so today,” Tomelai tenderly offered his wife, lifting her hand to his lips. He did not stretch the truth.

A young Kaythlin F’Siyn learned how to walk, to speak, to act, and to control how she appeared to others. She learned how to form the image she wanted to project. Above it all, she learned how her own actions controlled what opinions others would form of her.

The young Kaythlin F’Siyn learned history, religion, and anything she could study or read. She learned how to dress, use makeup, hair and, above all, she came to understand how to enhance an already beautiful facade. With the best teachers money could buy, Kaythlin became more intelligent, more beautiful, and more graceful than any person had ever been in all of Adelle.

Of all her qualities, the common folks of the kingdom who deeply loved the First Lady spoke of her graceful manner. Though loved throughout the country, just not by her husband anymore.

"Dear, what do you think of removing the blue dagger depicted beneath the snowcaps of the KCG's crest? The dagger says everyone in the KCG is in the shadows of the night, the enforcer behind the Chancellor. Behind you. They are feared, and I am concerned it reflects on you."

Swords hung from the side of each man and woman of the KCG as they rode along the parade route. Dressed in dark blue formal suits with black leather boots, they showed their faces for all to see. To the crowd, each presented a vision that spoke to the fear in people. The KCG offered the inhabitants of Teth an ominous and powerful reason to respect Tomelai and his KCG.

"Our protector, Drew, might object. But for you, I will think about it when we return." They both were certain he wouldn't.

Following behind the powerful image of Chancellor Tomelai and First Lady Kaythlin was half the senior administration of the Kingdom of Adelle.

"I'm pleased you did not take me up on my offer to remain behind to help Tane," said the First Lady.

"You are my wife. The nation's First Lady. All Teth has come out to see you. They want to see the beautiful First Lady of Adelle more than they desired the sight of a sovereign from a foreign place."

He kissed the back of her hand and continued, "My dear, you are the stuff of dreams for so many little girls and women, whether in Tandure or Teth. You are the desire of men. You have kept your youth. You are beautiful and you are a leader. You have the talent to run the country better than I. As much as I would choose no other to rule in my place, you are too valuable as a symbol of our greatness together. And most of all, I would miss you."

He imagined Lady Kaythlin believed he almost meant every word.

"No, my love, they are here to see a great man. You are the object of their eyes."

There was truth in her words. She was beautiful, and she commanded as many eyes as him, probably more. Everyone they passed along the Protisium would see and envy First Lady Kaythlin. She just wouldn't flaunt it in front of her husband, the Chancellor. He knew Kaythlin allowed him to think he was the center of the crowd's attention. They both knew otherwise.

As they rode together, they smiled and waved to the clueless onlookers.

At a predetermined location along the parade route, the entire Tandure procession dismounted and began walking. It was tradition. The tradition fit Tomelai's needs to be seen as a man of the people. Teth's citizens welcomed Chancellor Tomelai and First Lady Kaythlin with adulation as they passed.

Derr watched for threats from atop his steed. His plain-clothed staff mingled in the crowd. If a second attempt on Chancellor Tomelai was in play, it would happen while he walked amongst the throng of spectators.

Tomelai had just crossed the threshold into uncertain danger.

He Shit His Pants

Owls Neck: 27th day of the Salmon Moon

Neladith | Mithany

"Arek! Arek! Answer me!" Mithany pleaded for her brother to show any sign of life.

He didn't move.

No reaction.

Eyes closed.

Arms limp.

Neladith stood back and watched as Mithany petitioned and begged. The red-haired woman was more interested in Mithany's behavior than for Arek's status amongst the living.

During the hours spent on the road between Owls Neck and Hensdale, Mithany hadn't spoken to her much. *Okay, maybe the girl is thinking about her boyfriend, Reyne,* Neladith considered. Although, she got the distinct impression Mithany's silence held more meaning.

The bitch doesn't like me, Neladith concluded. *Now look at her. Not so high and mighty, are you? Well, the feeling's mutual. I don't like you either.*

"Are you just gonna stand there?" Mithany screamed at Neladith, pulling the her from her thoughts.

Amused at her opponent for Arek's attention, Neladith responded in soft tones to Mithany. "What can I do that you're not already doing?"

After the words escaped her mouth, they hit her ears, and she realized how dreadful it came across. Before Mithany's stunned face put together a retort, Neladith quickly followed up. "I mean, you're right there. What can I do?" Which didn't seem to be much better given she intended to offer support. Her second attempt came off even more insensitive.

Mithany, jaw wide open, turned away from Neladith.

Neladith gave up. She stepped forward. Her foot came down on noisy leaves.

Mithany swung her head around much quicker than it seemed humanly possible.

Her face hissed with anger.

Her eyes threatened danger.

Neladith grasped the peril and stopped where she stood. She struggled to decide which posed the greater risk: the brown beast whose howls terrorized an entire forest or the petite woman currently leaning over Arek's motionless body. Thinking it might be the diminutive woman, Neladith realized she needed to change the direction of the conversation.

Neladith switched up her approach. She consciously slipped into her little girl's voice and said, "I'm sorry, you get it. I'm scared too. Is he going to be alright?"

Mithany snapped at Neladith. "I don't know."

"Is he at least breathing?" Neladith blurted out.

"Yes. Shallow," Mithany shot back with a curt reply.

"That's good, right? I mean, he's breathing," Neladith responded, trying to sound like a concerned schoolgirl.

"Yes. He's breathing. At least that much is good," Mithany said, trailing off.

Standing a few steps from the siblings, Neladith's eyes narrowed, watching Mithany holding Arek's face in her hands as though she was intruding on something intimate.

Mithany pleaded with the motionless body, "You can't leave me."

Neladith resolved to add her own support. "He won't."

"Stay out of this." Mithany's tone struck Neladith as a command. Neladith calculated the advice offered, and complied.

With Neladith quieted and off to the side, Mithany never took her eyes off her brother. One of his eyelids twitched, and for the third time, Mithany's heart almost stopped. She witnessed the corner of his lip curl up, obviously trying to hold back a smile. One eye popped open. They both opened.

Without saying a word, and before Arek said anything, Mithany planted her lips firmly on his and kissed him. She pulled back, looked into his, and said, "Say something!"

"You two've got to knock that shit off," he said, followed by a big, toothy grin.

"You bastard! You had me scared to death. You've been awake this entire time." Her fist came down with one not-so-gentle blow to his chest.

"Ouch! Well, I heard you coming, and well, you know." Arek rubbed his chest where she punched him. "Thought it might bring you two together. You know, worrying about little ole me. Guess that didn't work out as planned."

Neladith stepped forward, directing her words at Arek. "We heard the thing and then saw that big, brown, hairy thingy running from here. When we got here, well, you looked hurt or something. What happened? And what's that smell?"

"Well, it turned out to be a Great Yetgnal. Can you believe it? No shit. In the flesh. Or in the fur, I guess. Thing hadda be eight or nine feet tall. Smelled awful."

Still standing almost on top of her brother, Mithany demanded, "Get to the point. How are you still alive? And by the way, you don't smell so good yourself."

With her attention on Arek, Reyne's situation escaped her thoughts. She was happy to see her brother unharmed. Flooded with joy for the second time that day, she felt good, if only for a moment.

"Well, his foot was stuck. Him, her, how do you tell? Do those things have tits? If they do, I didn't see any. So, I figured it's a guy."

With a nod toward Neladith, Mithany said, "That's my brother. Facing death, all he can think about is breasts. Don't say I didn't warn you."

Just then an idea popped into her head, and she turned back to Arek. "What, you didn't look to see if anything was dangling between his legs? Wouldn't that have been easier?"

"No. No. I didn't see anything there either. I guess I didn't look that hard. I was just trying to figure out if it was a guy or a gal Great Yetgnal. Or Great Yetgnal woman, if that's what they're called. You know, a lady Yetgnal. It was all fur and hairy down there. Who could tell?"

"Sure. Sure," Mithany said, half laughing to herself.

Neladith shrugged. "Hey, stay focused. Get back to the story. What happened?"

"Alright, so, we'll call it a him. You know, no tits. He watched me, but he wasn't comin' for me. I was careful tryin' to, you know, circle around him. His head followed, but not his body. I got to a point I could see why. Like I said, his foot was stuck."

"So, what happened? Get to the point already," Neladith said.

"Well, if you'd just hush down over there, I'll tell you. I found a decent size branch and used it as a lever to get this big-ass rock off his foot."

"How did he let you get close?" Mithany asked. "Those things are supposed to be mean."

A huge smile bloomed across Arek's face. "See, Sis, you also called it a he."

"Shut up," Mithany said, conceding the minor victory to Arek over the gender issue.

"I don't know. I moved real slow. Mimed what I was goin' do with the branch. Pointed to the boulder I was goin' use to wedge it under, you know, to lever it up. Guess he just let me. Maybe those things are smarter than we think."

"You must have been scared," Neladith said, still coming off in her little girl persona.

"Part of me was terrified, but some part of me felt bad for the thing. So, I gave it a shot. It worked. But"—Arek paused—"after he got his foot free, or after I got his foot free, he came right at me. Ugh, he smelled like shit. His breath was even worse. He put his head right up to mine," Arek said, holding his hand just an inch from his face in a demonstration.

"His nose—I mean his nostrils—were so big and dried snot was hanging from them on those little hairs in his nose. Anyway, he sniffed me. Took in a deep whiff, and then growled at me with his big yellow fangs and disgusting teeth. His mouth opened wider than my entire head. Thought I was gonna die right there. I tried to scream, but nothin' came out. Then he let out a growl. Guess you heard it. And that's when I closed my eyes. Terrified, waiting for him to bite my head off. And that's when I shit my pants! That's right; I shit my pants. Laugh if you want to. You would've done the same."

Both women exploded in laughter.

Arek ignored them and continued. "After a few seconds, when I realized I didn't die, I opened one eye and saw he wasn't there. I looked around. He was gone. Then I heard you coming, and well, you know the rest."

Still laughing, Mithany leaned forward, giving him a sisterly hug. Neladith stepped forward to join in with her arms wrapping around them both, apparently not wanting to be left out.

Mithany broke the three-way embrace, stepped back, scrunched her nose, and demanded, "You gotta change those pants. You smell."

With no outward signs of embarrassment and having just admitted to defecating in his own clothing, Arek said, "Way ahead of you, Sis. There oughta be a pair of leather pants in the samples you brought with you that might fit. And we'll just leave this pair I'm wearing right here. By the way, go ahead, laugh, but remember, I faced down a Great Yetgnal. I'll be the hero of Hensdale." His chest puffed out in the proud proclamation of his deed, the smell coming from his pants notwithstanding.

"They might fit you. Will be a little tight. They're women's pants," Mithany said with a devilish giggle that lasted but a few seconds. Her amusement ended abruptly. Thoughts of Reyne came flooding back. Her body posture shrank, and her head dropped. "And please make it quick. We still have some way to go before I find out what happened to Reyne."

Reunion of Sorts

Hensdale: 27th day of the Salmon Moon

Daedyn

Daedyn found the Doc just where the drunken Trell suggested. Confident that Reyne was more than likely to return home at some point, Daedyn was pleased with the decision he made. And with Doc Brenal now in tow, the pair approached the family homestead. The place looked empty, and Daedyn felt hope drain from his body.

After climbing the four short porch steps, Daedyn anxiously opened the heavy treestone door. It swung on its hinges without a sound. Daedyn pulled the cover off the lume crystal jar set on the wall just inside the door. A gentle light illuminated the small entrance. He turned and pulled the cover off the lume jar on the other side of the door as well. The room filled with the soft, warm, green glow given off by the radiant mineral. The treestone walls glimmered as absorbing the gift offered by the lume crystal.

Both Brenal and Daedyn were taken aback to find a man sitting in the shadows against the wall across from the door. The mysterious man stood.

"Who the hell are you, and what the fuck are you doing in my house?" Daedyn demanded, crossing his arms over his broad chest. Almost twenty-two, Daedyn was muscular in his youth, even more so now as a young man. Years farming the orchard contributed to his well-chiseled physique. His six-foot frame stood firm and motionless, staring down at the intruder.

Something looked familiar about the stranger. The man rose to a familiar stance, one that reminded Daedyn of the beggar. Yet, he wore a traveler's leather attire. Boots laced up to his calves and a short waistcoat looking worn but appropriate for the outfit. A leather scabbard for a knife, tied to his belt, hung down the side of his mahogany-brown leather pants. Was it the old beggar? It almost looked like him. The man's face offered a younger appearance than the old vagrant's visage Daedyn had grown accustomed to seeing over the years. Daedyn guessed the man looked to be in his mid-forties instead of the seventy-ish-year-old beggar-man he thought he knew.

The stranger put out his hands with open palms.

Daedyn remained firm, with his arms crossed over his muscled chest.

The stranger said, "I'm Meratoruc. Please call me Mera."

"And where's Rey?" Daedyn asked.

The man introduced as Mera paused a few beats before continuing, "Reyne's okay. He's sleeping in his bed. There won't be any need for your skills tonight, my friend," Mera said, looking towards Doc Hollid Brenal. Then, turning to Daedyn, he offered, "Reyne will be fine. I've taken care of him."

"So now I know your name, but it still doesn't answer my question. Who are you, and what are you doing in my house?" Daedyn demanded, ignoring Doc Brenal's friend reference.

"Excuse me," Mera spoke softly. "I'm here to help. That's all." He smiled facing Doc Brenal. "How're you, my old friend?"

"Nice to see you again, Mera," Brenal replied.

Before Brenal could say anything else, Daedyn did an about-face, and fled down the hall to Reyne's room. With the front door still open, sunlight spread down hallway before giving way to the shadows.

Daedyn opened Reyne's bedroom door slowly, knowing the hinges were likely to squeak. He spied Reyne sleeping. Relief flowed through him. He stood holding the door handle. While watching Reyne resting peacefully, he listened to the two men talking in the other room.

"He's over the worst of it," the man calling himself Mera said. "I worked my healing skills on him. The mark on his neck appears to be the point where spiderworm venom entered his system. And not by chance. I suspect someone tried to kill him. The poison will stay with him for the rest of his life, albeit ever so small. Lasting side effects are always possible but, oddly, only a small amount appeared to have been delivered. Uncommon and a bit strange. Good news for him, though. I hope there won't be any noticeable change like the way some people manifest behavioral issues when hit with a large dose of the stuff. Anyway, I think he'll be okay. He should be over the worst of it for now."

"I should've guessed, my friend. By the way, you look—you look great. Every time I see you, I'm amazed. I keep getting older, and you, you never seem to age." A second later, Mera's words caught up to Brenal's thoughts, "Wait. What did you say? Someone tried to kill him?"

"Friend" surprised Daedyn, but not as much as the idea that someone tried to kill his brother. It hit him hard. A punch to the gut. But he was there when it happened. He didn't remember seeing anyone try to kill Reyne.

Daedyn raced back down the hall to confront the stranger. "What did you say?"

"I dressed like a bum all these years whenever I visited Hensdale. Didn't want to be noticed and didn't want anyone following me here. I've been coming and going all these years, keeping up on your brother."

"What? No, not that. Someone tried to kill my brother? I was there. That didn't happen," Daedyn spit out, struggling to understand.

"That's for another time. Right now, let's focus on making sure Reyne is doing okay," Mera said.

"No. It's not for another time. It's for right now." Daedyn's fists clenched.

"I'll share it with all of you, but not before the good doctor gets a look at Reyne, and not before I can explain everything to Reyne first. I'm sorry, but that's final. And just so you know, I'm here to prevent any harm coming to Reyne. I must ask that you allow me to share my suspicions with your brother at the right time. Not right now and not without him here."

"Fuck that. Here. Now."

"No."

Daedyn pushed. He wanted answers, but they weren't forthcoming. He resigned himself to the fact he'd have to wait.

Daedyn glared at the two men standing in his home. There appeared to be some warmth between Mera and the Doc. The old vagrant had been stopping in the village a few times a year for as long as Daedyn could remember. Daedyn never thought much of him and didn't recall ever seeing him and Doc Brenal together or even talking between themselves. He was confused, but at least Reyne seemed to be alright, resting in peace. Daedyn decided he'd let it ride for the moment, but he would get all his questions answered.

Preparations

Hensdale: 27th day of the Salmon Moon

Quith

On the day the people of Tartica celebrated the Feast of Teth, Quith and his unit spent part of it reducing the continent's population. The day meant nothing to them but for their objective to eliminate Reyne Brenton. Their first attempt earlier that morning had failed. Later that same day, the team of Evidarian assassins gathered, minus the operations manager Dylla, to regroup before their next attempt to murder Reyne.

The safe house sat along a quiet stretch on the outskirts of Hensdale, a few miles from the market square. The small family farm consisted of several meager barns for equipment storage needed to support the insubstantial apple orchard. The older couple had worked the fruit grove and eked out a simple yet satisfying living. That is until Selundra Quith and his fellow agents needed a sanctuary to hide out and a central point from which to prepare their covert operations.

No one would miss the older couple for the two days Quith's unit expected to occupy the deceased's homestead. It wouldn't be until after Quith and his team departed Hensdale that the lifelong farmers' whereabouts would begin to worry the community. Quith was certain their bodies would never be found.

"Gentlemen," Quith offered his security detail, "we've been in this world too long. I'm exhausted with all this daylight, as I'm sure you are."

Tylus, the cinnamon-blond, rugged-looking, dedicated operative in his prime spoke up. "Gotta agree with you, boss. Makes it a lot harder for us to do our job."

Agent Grafph, more bulbous around the mid-section than the others of the team, saw life away from Evidar a little different. "But you have to admit, you're not looking over your shoulder every minute for someone coming at you all the time. Not sure it's how I would run things over here, but I've enjoyed the reprieve from fighting for my life every day."

Quith reveled in Evidar's brutality where Grafph simply survived in it.

Evidar was a dark world from a different reality, a place where only minimal light reached the surface. Quith found freedom in the lack of organized civilization—a place where the strong wrestled control over their environs. A place where everyone else cowered under a strong-arm's sphere of influence.

A place without laws.

A place without order.

A place of unchallenged freedom.

A place where one could kill or be killed at any moment without consequence.

A place where the powerful excelled and the lesser were subjugated.

It came as no surprise that Quith and Grafph perceived their lots in Evidar from different perspectives.

Quith warned Grafph, "Keep up that attitude, and you'll be fighting for your life here too."

Grafph slinked back, and his body seemed to shrink in stature in response to Quith's threat. The mild-mannered yet deadly Grafph was a contradiction to his occupation. Highly skilled at killing when directed to do so, submissive otherwise.

"So why did you ask to see us, boss?" Tylus asked.

"I spoke with Dylla earlier today in Owls Neck, where she's stationed herself. I filled her in on our efforts this morning. She could be happier. She confirmed Plan B, the follow-up to the Brenton op, is a go. That is, if he doesn't die before nightfall."

"What's the chance of that happening?" Grafph asked.

Tylus said, "I've been watching the guy all day. A lot of commotion at his house these past few hours. He's still alive, but from what I gather, he's had a rough go of it. My guess, it's fifty-fifty that he's dead by the end of the day."

As the unit leader, Quith issued the orders they'd follow. "Dylla wants us ready to go. That means we activate the backup plan and set it in motion as though we have the intention of seeing it through to completion. If Reyne Brenton dies before we take final action, all's the better."

Grafph steepled both hands in front of his mouth. "The same plan we've all been briefed on?"

Quith nodded. "There's a firepit between the house and the orchard. It's used to clear out debris, branches, and rotten nuts to keep the rows of trees empty. They burn there every day. And every evening, Reyne Brenton walks out to that fire pit just after sunset and puts it out. He's always alone. That's our strike point. Plan hasn't changed."

Grafph asked, "But he's sick. You think he'll follow that same routine?"

"If he shows up to kill the fire, we kill him," Quith stated matter-of-factly.

Tylus asked, "What about the new girl Dylla briefed us on when we did that thing back in Jarouhar? Haven't seen anyone new yet, and shouldn't she be here for the briefing?"

"She arrived. Dylla caught her up. She's in Hensdale already," Quith said. "I'll meet up with her at the kill site just as it gets dark. You two will be on lookout duty."

Grafph asked, "Have you met with her yet, and what do you think of her?"

"Dylla has confidence in her, and that's all you need to know. She's been assigned to our unit, and she's supposed to be excellent. Everything we do tonight will be in support of her completing this mission."

Tylus noted, “Let’s hope she’s that good. I don’t know about the rest of you, but I’m ready to go home. Let’s get this last one finished so we can get the fuck out of here. All the rules in this place—enough already.”

Quith followed, “I couldn’t agree with you more. Let’s nail this down and head home. Let’s go through the plan one more time.”

Quith, Tylus, and Grafph walked through every detail of the op. Each man outlined their respective assignments and what was expected of them. They recited each other’s roles in case anyone needed to fill in for the other or to account for any unforeseen variables.

Only after Quith was satisfied did he allow Tylus and Grafph to finally settle down for a meal.

Quith passed up a chance to fill his belly. Superstition kept him from eating before a kill. He reflected, *Reyne Brenton will be dead, one way or another, before this day ends.*

The Faithful

Teth: 27th Day of the Salmon Moon

Jerithan | Razoal

Not long after Firstmeal wrapped up, Jerithan, pleased with himself at the results of the ceremony, met with his co-conspirator, Second Lord Razoal. The pair sequestered inside a private room within the Temple Palace to analyze, regroup, and plot their next steps in the aftermath of Chancellor Tomelai's failed assassination.

The First Lord took hold of Razoal's shoulder, looked him in the eye, and said, "We failed this morning. But we cannot be stopped. The world needs us to unite everyone in Tartica under one banner. Father Sun and Mother Earth are as good a cause as any. If I do nothing else with this life, I *will* bring the faithful together under our leadership without secular interference. This Gift of Life given to me drives me to complete my God-given task. With the power and tools of this Lordship, I must bring them all together under one roof for the good of humanity."

For all the questionable things the two had done in the Temple's name, at least in this, Jerithan believed himself to have noble intent.

Killing the Chancellor was supposed to be the opening stage of the campaign to create the Empire of Tartica. Parts two and three of the campaign would address the other world leaders, Dimenk and Larsed. The First Lord expected the plan to usurp Dimenk's authority would be wrought with difficulties, but anticipated Larsed's downfall would unfold easily.

"Now that Tomelai's piece is still on the board, we're going to need to rouse the passions of our followers even more to pull this off. We are going to need their support," Prudent Razoal offered Jerithan the obvious observation.

"Why do you think they listen to us, follow us? The faithful masses, I mean," Jerithan asked his Second.

The quizzical look on Razoal's face didn't slow Jerithan, who continued without waiting for a reply. "Is it because we are their friends? No. Is it because we give them shelter, freely disperse grain rations to feed them? No. We barely affect the miserable existence most of them live other than to placate them."

Razoal opened his mouth to speak, but he was too slow.

"No. They follow us because we offer the easiest path to Hope. They need Hope to get through life every day. Otherwise, there would be chaos in the streets. Do you think people would continue to live like they do, absent a promise of something better? The Circle of Life, after they die, is the 'better' they desire. The good join the Community of Souls."

"Part of a better life in the next round," Razoal added.

"Not just that," Jerithan continued. "We make Hope easy for them to follow. We are like water. Hope flows through us, through the path of least resistance, to the masses. If we make our faith too hard for them to follow, we are no better than the secular rulers who tax and judge them every day."

"We are Hope made easy."

"Exactly. If anyone threatens to take their only Hope from them, that will get them riled up. *That* is our path to rouse our troops. And we will begin scaring them into submission right after the annual Council meeting. Marvo is going to plant a few seeds of dissention in the next several days."

Jerithan took a quick breath, but before he could finish, Razoal began, "I've laid out Marvo's speeches. And I'm exceptionally pleased about how Firstmeal turned out with the Council of Prudents. I agree. It couldn't have gone better."

Both men smiled, recalling the success they achieved at Firstmeal only hours earlier, before First Lord Jerithan Cree put in, "Oh, that fat bastard Serco. We just might have to delete him from the equation before this thing is through."

Razoal cautiously replied, "That is one option, yet I fear martyrdom might make him even stronger in death."

"Maybe."

"Killing Serco, while both the easiest and most desirous way to solve the problem of his open opposition, has many drawbacks. The biggest disadvantage is that the rest of the Council of Prudents would see your hand in it. To protect you, I fear we need an alternate approach to eliminate your chief rival now that we've neutralized Marvo. I'm sorry I failed you with Chancellor Tomelai inside The Stand this morning. I still don't understand what went wrong, but I will find out," Razoal offered.

"*Killing a pain-in-the-ass Chancellor, sure, why not? But killing a Prudent? An obvious adversary, no less. There is much to consider before striking.*" The Voice paused—"*First Lord.*"

Jerithan stopped, frozen in place. The implication was clear. As First Lord, he existed as the living symbol of the Temple of Life, the voice of the faithful on Earth. Killing Serco was a risky move, but only if blame could be hung around his neck. Besides, he was clever enough to deal with Serco in other ways. Though he had to admit, the idea of killing him carried in it more than a degree of satisfaction.

Jerithan said to the Voice, *Serco must be removed, that is obvious, after the show he put on this morning. As we move forward to wrest secular authority away from Dimenk, Larsed, and Tomelai, Serco is going to oppose our efforts every step of the way.*

"No. They listen to us because they are lazy," Jerithan said to Razoal, keeping the two conversations he was having simultaneously separate, trying to think of other options other than murdering Serco. "Serco does not understand human nature. He thinks the flock must all be staunch believers. If we had to rely on true believers, Communion of the Circle would be convened in a small tavern."

Razoal's head tilted in thought, then replied, "Since we received notice Tomelai lives, which leaves Serco in play. The two are allies. We would have eliminated two threats with one death—Tomelai's. But we failed. So now, we still have Tomelai *and* Serco to deal with."

As though he didn't hear his Second's words, Jerithan said, "We tell them what is moral. How to behave. How to pray. When to celebrate. Do it, and you will have a better life. We provide a simple path to salvation."

Razoal nodded his agreement. "I get all that. But why don't you think there are that many true believers, given everything you said?"

"Most get it. It is a simple allegory. Father Sun, Mother Earth—some being living like a star, chasing after another being, a living planet, Earth. There is a god, maybe not the one we tell of in our stories, but a god to answer to just the same. We worship the Cycle of Life and rebirth through the natural process. The sun gives life, and the Earth nourishes us. We consume what the Earth offers. We die, replenish the resources of the Earth, and it starts over again. All the aspects of life fit the story we tell them wrapped in the religion of the Temple of Life."

Jerithan paused a thoughtful, long moment before adding, "Did you ever wonder why we mourn when a loved one dies? The reaction to death seems antithetical to the core of our faith. In death, joining in The Circle, one with the Community of Life, one with all things followed by rebirth in whole or in part. In the belief that we are judge-worthy, of course. It always amazed me we do not celebrate each passing, that we are not happy for whoever's died, since they would pass into a much better state of being. Should not each passing be a celebration? Instead, it is mournful. It is tearful and burdened with sadness. That, my friend, is my proof why there are so few true believers."

Razoal looked at his friend with understanding eyes. "That's always puzzled me too."

"But it is easier to follow the path we give them... just in case."

"*What does that tell you about humanity and, even better, how do you use it to defeat Prudent Serco?*" And then the Voice yelled in his head, *"You think of me as an allegory!"*

Jerithan thought in reply, *Serco just might be a hardline true believer, and using that could play into our hands. So maybe we do not kill him but show his followers he is a fraud. And surely, you are no allegory. You stand as something beyond, as proof there is a consciousness that transcends the physical host. The Circle of Life does not merely dump our bodies as resources back into the pool. Your existence is my Hope that we are more than the sum of our minerals haplessly wandering through time without purpose.*

Turning his thoughts from the Voice, First Lord Jerithan addressed his Second. "Razoal, we have an idea. Taking out Tomelai was a misfire. But concerning Serco, there may be another way to neutralize him without killing him."

"We? What we?" Razoal looked around the room. "And how do *we* propose to remove Serco from blocking our path?"

Quick to react, the First Lord, not letting on to Razoal that there was another presence speaking to him, "Yes, we. You and me. There *is* another way. Do you see it?"

Razoal lied convincingly, "Yes. Alright. I see where you're headed with this." He didn't know where Jerithan was going. As close as the two men were, Jerithan had never seen through his Second's lies. As Second Lord of the Temple of Life, Razoal found lying to be part of the job. Lying wasn't of any real consequence since it was done to support the Temple's holy leader.

Butting heads with the First Lord every time he spoke untruths or offered factual inaccuracies would accomplish nothing but to cause himself to be replaced by another and then another and still another until someone was found who would serve the First Lord faithfully. Why bother? Razoal lied as well as anyone. At least this way, Jerithan had a friend by his side, and, as Second Lord, he'd pick the important battles to fight. He had to speak in untruthful ways now and again in the service of the holy Temple of Life. He had done much worse than lying over the years.

A practical man, Razoal believed Jerithan wanted loyalty more than he wanted the truth. So Razoal gave his friend loyalty above all else without breaking the word of Father Sun, "Give truth to all who seek it."

In Razoal's calculation of the man, Jerithan, as First Lord, perceived himself as the truth—in whatever words he spoke. So, Razoal played along, hoping to glean the details from Jerithan as time unfolded. They both agreed on the need to bring down Serco. To achieve it, the First Lord was suggesting something new. Whatever the plan, Razoal could adjust; limiting the blowback was the best he could hope for.

As for Tomelai, Razoal wasn't ready to give up on killing the Chancellor of Adelle. Death would come to Chancellor Tomelai. Of that, Razoal was certain.

Check-up

Hensdale: 27th day of the Salmon Moon

Brenal | Daedyn

Brenal's eyes opened to the darkened room. After some much-needed shut-eye, nestled in Daedyn's bed, he woke slowly, as old men often do. Old age afforded Brenal few benefits, and stealing a cat nap while waiting for Reyne was one of them.

Doc Brenal hadn't taken part in any holiday celebrations since the passing of his wife years ago. This Feast of Teth was no different. His concerns were for Reyne. Brenal hoped the young man would be awake by now, so he could finally attend to assessing Reyne's condition.

The numbness in his hands—he always experienced it upon waking—usually passed after a few minutes. He reached out, wiggled his fingers, probing for anything solid, yet found only a chill in the air. He recalled seeing the lume crystal jar on the end table. Waving his hand about in the darkness, he found nothing but empty space. *Where is that thing?* he wondered.

He swiped at the air once more. This time his hand made contact. Brenal pulled the cover off the jar housing the light-giving crystal, releasing a gentle green glow upon the room. But not without cost. A sharp pain shot down his side from his shoulder to his hip. An old injury from a fall he'd taken the time he raced to his wife's side in her last moments.

The energy of youth had fled him long ago. Each time he woke brought new and recurring demands on his body. Lying in bed, struggling through his many aches, Brenal raised his right arm as though he were reaching for the ceiling. A routine he came to accept as necessary if he wanted his hands or fingers to function at all.

He fanned out the fingers of his raised hand, stretched them apart and, with only the slightest discomfort, bent his elbow back and forth several times. After a few rounds, both arms were prepared to face the rest of the day.

He turned his attention to those stubborn legs. His body creaked and cracked, but he managed to roll into a sitting position in bed. To his delight, the seated positioning tugged at the muscles easing the tightness in his spine. Swinging both legs over the edge, the weight of his feet pulled them to the floor much like an anchor sinks to the bottom of a lake.

The floor wasn't just cold; it was freezing. Warming his feet wouldn't be easy—it never was. His body and especially his feet generated little warmth anymore. His toes and fingers were at the end of the line of whatever little internal radiance he generated. The cold floor reduced both feet to clumps of icy flesh.

Brenal was determined to leave his feet on the floor for as little a time as possible. He eased into his pants and pulled the waistband up over his ample belly. Short, heavy, and mostly bald, his look matched his age. For a man of such little means, his overweight outline was an enigma to everyone who knew him. He had few possessions beyond the tools of his trade and did little to plan for his next meal. Food supplies were nowhere to be found in his run-down dwelling, yet here he was, heavier than ever.

Brenal did so much to help others his entire life. He assisted everyone in the small community whenever called to do so and even when not called to do so. Yet, there wasn't a damned thing he could do for himself to relive the feeling of ice blocks attached to the bottom of his legs. As quickly as he could manage, he pulled up one foot, willing heat into it as he rubbed. His actions did little to relieve the discomfort, but at least his hands were getting a little more limber from the effort. He wasn't sure how long he rubbed, but he knew if he was ever going to get out of bed, he needed to get moving.

Brenal slipped on his socks and then his boots. He pulled a shabby top over his head while still seated and let the hoody drop behind his neck. The wool pull-over had faded to a light brown from either the lack of a good scrubbing or because the dyes leached out long ago. The edge around the collar was frayed, much like the cuffs, but not too much to cause the old healer to take up its repair.

His head popped through the neck of the garment. He flinched, noticing Daedyn standing in the doorway. "How long you been there?"

"Not long."

Brenal stood up and stretched out his hand towards Daedyn. "Good afternoon, my young friend," he said. He didn't think it through. Brenal realized too late that he hadn't secured his pants around his waist. His britches fell too fast to be stopped by the slow reactions of an overweight old man. With his pants now around his ankles, he pulled them up once again, only this time slightly embarrassed.

Daedyn laughed at the display. "Good afternoon, Doc. Have a nice nap?"

It wasn't the first time Brenal unintentionally offered comic relief, but when it came to healing, no one in the region was better. Finally fixing the drawstring around his waist, pants secured, Brenal flopped his butt back onto the bed.

"I guess this thin little waistband has some hefty work to do." Laughing at himself as he often did, Brenal wasn't taken to flattery, just the opposite. He had a way of putting everyone at ease with his self-deprecating manner. Hidden behind his good humor existed a brilliant medical mind. He willingly gave up a promising career as a big-city surgeon to marry the love of his life and live out his days a simple country doctor. A decision he never regretted.

What few hairs he had were pointing in every direction. Brenal moved across the room and dipped his hands into the nearby washbasin, then fanned the fingers through his hair, matting down the few remaining gray strands.

He asked Daedyn, "You seen your brother? I want to check on him."

"No. I was about to search for him when I heard you stirring. Come on," Daedyn said, walking over to the washbasin to assist Brenal in moving the process along faster. "Let's go find out how he's doing." Pausing for just a moment, he added, "And I want to know more about this Meraturoc fellow."

Brenal let the comment about Mera fall away without addressing it. "It's still light out, at least. Well, that's good news." His stomach grumbled, letting him know a satisfying meal would be the next thing he did after checking in on Reyne.

Daedyn and Brenal continued down the short hallway of the treestone home. Daedyn ran one hand along the cool, transformed-wood stonework. Almost like granite, the treestone was as hard as it was smooth.

His hand glided over the rock-hard, creamy, silk-like surface. It was a mindless habit, soothing to his soul, transporting his thoughts to a time when he was seven years old. He fondly recalled when the house was built, at being mesmerized looking on as workers extracted harvested ironwood trees from their brine bath, converting the otherwise ordinary wood into treestone. He remembered being amazed the sawyers used entire trees—minus the branches, trimming each only for height as they were placed side-by-side, and stripping the bark from the home's interior surfaces.

Up over the lintel of his bedroom door, Daedyn's fingers touched every curve of the transformed trees of the inside walls. He caressed every dip, every nick, every bump for the thousandth time. The message from his fingertips, this is home; this is safe.

The homestead belonged to him and Reyne now, ever since their parents had passed away. Making a physical connection with the wall surface comforted Daedyn as he girded himself on his way to find out his brother's fate. Daedyn's head told him Reyne would be fine given Brenal's healing skills, but thoughts of Reyne's death and a life without his brother scared the hell out of him. He was taken aback that he could even let himself think about such things. He worried it could actually come to pass. And the words Mera spoke earlier in the day, that someone tried to kill his brother, were hard to believe—but what if it were true?

His fingers continued to glide across the cool surface, setting an anchor for his drifting nostalgia and his growing fears.

As they walked, Brenal silently watched Daedyn's hand glide over the treestone surface. The hand seemed to explore, fondle, and caress the wood, suggesting something sensual to Brenal, like a lover's touch. A feeling he could only vaguely recall. He was fascinated at Daedyn's concentration, at the obvious pleasure. Brenal longed to feel that way again. He missed his wife, Sura.

Stepping through the front door, Brenal stopped to bask in the warm sunlight caressing his face and hands. But his hands fought the warming rays to deny the full measure of the kindness nature offered them. Cupping his hands to his mouth, the old man breathed heavily into them. It proved a futile attempt to deliver even a small amount of heat to his fingers. His feet weren't any better off.

Brenal thumped closed fists against his chest. "Old age isn't the gift they led me to believe in my youth. Ah, Sura, if you could only see me now." His steamy breath leaked through his fingers as he gave another go at it. Hiding his words inside the small enclosure before his mouth, he lamented, "I do miss you so, my dear."

"Hey there," Daedyn said, stepping out onto the porch, "if I gave you the choice between warm hands or a warm woman, which way would you go?"

"I'd take whatever you could provide, but know this, my young friend, either would only deliver a smile to my face if the results could warm up these stiff, icy fingers," Brenal replied, releasing another hot breath into his frigid hands. Facing Daedyn, lowering his hands from his mouth, he said, "Well, that didn't work. Where's this warm woman you've been talking about?"

Daedyn slapped him on the back. "You'll live. Look across the tops of the trees. The sun's still got a way to go. When it does go down, those fingers of yours ain't gonna do any better."

Looking up from his wizened hands, Brenal scanned the horizon and there, beneath the first line of alphen trees, sat Reyne and Mera. The men faced each other with their backs resting against opposing alphen trunks. Mera had one leg bent up while the other lay straight out. Reyne positioned himself with knees apart and ankles crossed, facing the man he once knew only as "the old beggar."

The tree line of the alphen orchard was only fifty strides from the front porch. The grove was laid out in an orderly pattern. Trees appeared dense when seen from afar, but up close there was plenty of space for working between the rows of the nut producing plants.

"Nothing's really changed on this nut farm since I can remember, and I gotta lot of rememberin' in here," Brenal said as he tapped a bent finger against his temple. He'd known the boys since they were born, having delivered every newborn in Hensdale for decades. "Let's go see how Reyne's doing."

"Wait," Daedyn said. "First, tell me, who the fuck is Meratoruc? We didn't get that settled yet."

"Oh, nothing to worry about. You'll see. He's not such a bad guy."

Daedyn squinted. "Do I need to worry?"

Brenal continued down the steps of the porch, holding onto the handrail as though he was holding onto life itself. He stepped out into the open space between the house and the alphen grove, finally answering Daedyn, "No."

Daedyn picked up the pace, yelling out to Reyne, "You alright?"

Brenal grabbed onto Daedyn's shoulder. "Slow down. Have mercy on an old man. I can't keep up with you young ones."

As Brenal approach with Daedyn as his guide, Reyne put his hand to the ground, the other against a tree. Standing, he rubbed the back of his neck. "I'm fine, Daedyn."

Facing his sibling, Reyne swept his arm and bowed in jest, "Let me introduce you. Daedyn, meet the old beggar. Calls himself Mera now. Seems we have a new friend."

"We met. We ain't friends." Daedyn's reply was curt.

Daedyn gave his brother a hug, ignoring Mera. After letting go of the sibling-embrace, Daedyn stepped back, and punched Reyne in the arm before complaining, "You're a pain in the ass. You had us all scared shitless, you fuck. Where the hell did you go... I left you on the bench in town, and you disappeared. Real nice. You couldn't tell me where you were going?" Daedyn rambled, and it was obvious to Brenal he was happy to see his brother safe—before Daedyn punched Reyne again.

Reyne exclaimed, half playful, half serious, "Ouch! Do that one more time and I'll knock you on your ass, you little prick. That hurt!"

Daedyn smirked. "Good. I wanted it to hurt."

It appeared things were getting back to normal, but Brenal stepped between the brothers, nonetheless. He looked sideways to see Mera studying Reyne. The vagabond had watched the boys grow up during his inconspicuous, frequent visits over the years, and it was over those many visits Brenal had come to know Mera well.

"Now, let's have a look at the bruise on your neck," Brenal said in his fatherly way. "What a beautiful day to be alive." Brenal opened his arms wide and took in a deep breath. "Wish these hands could only warm a little." He slapped them together and rubbed, hoping to generate anything resembling warmth. He shook his head. "Didn't work."

He placed a hand on Reyne's neck. "Lower your head. Let me see."

Reyne bowed down, but Brenal, still unable to see the details of the wound, said, "Come on, you've got to make this easier for an old man. Let's move over to the porch."

They walked the well-worn dirt path to the house nestled in a clearing within the alphen grove. The sun continued its march through the sky, now touching the tops of the trees. It was a sight the brothers knew well.

The deck that wrapped around the front of the house to face somewhere between sunrise and sunset. Daedyn and Reyne—with Mithany by his side—often started their workday with a cup of coffee, sitting on the porch, talking about the plans for the day while watching the sun coming through the trunks of the alphen trees. Two rocking chairs looked like sentries guarding the front door, while two smaller wooden chairs acted as an offering to anyone else fortunate to share the experience with the brothers.

Daedyn, along with Reyne, Mithany, and occasionally Brenal as their guest, spent many evenings with friends on that same porch. It was one small part of life in bucolic Hensdale Brenal loved.

He'd witnessed the brothers grow into men and knew the siblings shared almost everything. Brenal reflected, *Except for Reyne's coat. It was once their father's.* It amused Brenal that Reyne refused to share it with Daedyn. Brenal suspected the coat held a special meaning to Reyne as an unspoken connection to the boy's deceased parent.

As the four men stepped onto the porch, Brenal said, "Now let's see how the patient is doing this glorious day." His arms spread wide in a gesture to show his appreciation for the day. "A gift," he said to the others, all now watching him.

"Well, let's get to it then," Reyne replied. "I want a clean bill of health if you can ever get around to it. I'm gettin' married next week. Think you'll be done by then?"

Taking a few steps towards Reyne, holding on to the porch railing, the old healer approached a rustic wood chair next to Reyne. Doc Brenal plopped himself into the smaller seat with little finesse.

Reyne continued rocking. "Why are you sitting down? I thought we came up here so you could get a better look at the bite mark on my neck."

"Oh, yes. Yes." Placing his hands on the chair arms for support, Brenal pushed himself up with all the effort his hefty frame could muster. "These old bones," he lamented as he raised himself into a standing position. "Now stop that rocking if I'm gonna get a good look at that."

Reyne looked up, shook his head, and lowered it as if to bow to the village elder. Brenal ran his fingers along the back of Reyne's neck, searching out the target of concern.

"Shit, your hands are cold," Reyne said and pulled back.

"Be still," Brenal huffed, and went on examining Reyne. He found a tiny, pimple-like bump. Doc Brenal used the tip of his index finger, moving it in a circular motion around the injury. With old, bent fingers, Brenal felt the skin around the mark and pressed along the bite several times. He pursed his lips. *Strange. It should be worse,* he thought, but didn't say so aloud. *I'm not sure why.* He tilted his head at Mera as if to ask, "Did you do something here you didn't tell me?"

Mera stepped forward. "I can understand there's some confusion about what you're seeing. I haven't filled in all the details of the time I spent with Reyne before you two arrived. I had eyes on you both," Mera said pointing to the brothers. "Even before you arrived at the market and before the incident with the horses when you went down, Reyne. When you were sitting on the bench, and then you passed out, there wasn't time to do anything but get you home and treat you. I figured Daedyn would get back here soon enough. Thankfully, your body responded to the antivenom. As best I could tell, most of the venom pooled close to the surface and not much had spread. You were lucky."

Mera returned a respectful nod to Brenal, and the nod was all the country doctor needed. The two men understood each other.

Daedyn put out his arms, turning his palms up as if to ask, "What does that mean?"

Brenal ignored Daedyn. "Put your head back down," he instructed Reyne in his mild, yet familiar, bedside manner. "I need to get a better peek at this."

Pushing his patient's neck around to face the best lighting, Brenal moved his face closer to the tiny mark. He reached into the front pocket of his well-worn shirt and pulled out a small, round lens from a soft pouch. Moving the eyepiece close to the bite, Brenal closed one eye and moved the other up against the lens. Studying the mark through the clear glass, Brenal said, "You're a fortunate young man. I don't see any significant discoloration, and the skin isn't raised too high. Both good signs."

He studied it for a minute longer as Mera and Daedyn hovered over his shoulder. Brenal ran his crooked fingers over the area slowly. "Okay. Pick up your head. Let me see your face." Brenal raised one hand and extended his bent index finger straight up—or what passed as straight, given its gnarled shape. "Follow my finger," he directed his amused patient. He moved it across Reyne's field of vision from left to right and back again. Brenal inspected the eye movements of his patient as they tracked his wandering finger.

While following every movement of Brenal's knurled, wrinkled, bent finger, Reyne said, "I feel a lot better. I'll be alright to get married next week. Right, Doc?"

"Well, that knock on your head did little to improve you in any way," Daedyn said and showed his teeth in a broad smile, apparently proud of himself for making an amusing observation. No one smiled except Daedyn, who lowered his head, shaking it. "And as for getting married, well, not sure Mithany was in her right mind either when she said, 'Yes.'"

Brenal continued, "Alright, I don't see any manifestations lingering here, but my experience with spiderworm bites..." he trailed off, staring out into space. Mera, Daedyn, and Reyne waited.

"And?" Daedyn prodded.

"Oh, he's going to live. But I have a balm I think should be applied over the next couple of days just to be safe. It will draw out whatever poison's still in there."

Daedyn let out an overly loud sigh. "Well, that's great news, but does the little eyepiece of yours tell you anything about whether he's gonna be able to get his lazy ass off the porch and do some work around here?" he said pointing over to the alphen grove full of nuts. "It's almost time for the harvest."

Without hesitation, Reyne gave a short yet powerful smack to Daedyn's arm.

"Ouch. You dick. That hurt." Daedyn rubbed his arm. "I owe you. You know the rules. Anytime, anywhere—dickhead." Daedyn curled his lips in an evil yet playful grin aimed at Reyne. "And you ain't gonna know when it's comin'." The grin grew wider. "Well, there's good news, anyway. You're gonna live, so I won't have to bring in this harvest all by myself. At least no more than usual."

"Screw you. I do all the work around here," Reyne responded.

It was good for Brenal to hear Reyne acting himself. Life was going to return to normal, and Reyne was going to be alright. It was a scare. The poison could have done considerable damage. After delivering his "all's clear" prognosis, Brenal had put them all at ease.

The old healer smiled. He lowered his head as though embarrassed and drew back a few paces while palming the eyepiece. Brenal slipped the lens back into its pouch and then into his shirt pocket.

Reyne looked up at Brenal. With a smile, a nod, in heartfelt words, he said, "Thank you."

"I've had enough of this romantic foreplay between you two. Anyone hungry?" Daedyn asked, rubbing both hands together.

"I can go for a bite," Mera said.

Before they got to the business of eating, thundering hooves grabbed their attention. Four heads snapped to face the dirt road. Brenal saw the tithe master racing towards them—atop the very wagon that struck down Reyne earlier.

Surviving Pomp and Circumstance

Teth: 27th Day of the Salmon Moon

Derr

Teth's name-day festival—in the city that bore her name—was tracking toward a tremendous success, a great day for the Temple of Life, the faithful and the nonbelievers alike. Performers, musicians, exotic animals, food vendors, and Lilly Marvo as the Maiden Teth excited the masses beyond all expectations. Ignorant were they all of the attempt on Chancellor Tomelai's life only hours earlier. Even if the crowd had been aware, it would have had little impact on the excitement the Grand Parade generated as it passed through the center of the city. The parade featured Chancellor Tomelai, President Dimenk, Prime Minister Larsed, and Teth's own Provost Kwuinan. Each had their expectations of the pageant, none more than the Captain of the KCG. Derr had one goal for the Grand Parade: get through the event with his Chancellor still alive.

From moment to moment, threats were detected, evaluated, or dismissed. Several suspected threats required closer inspection, initiated with a look from Derr to one of the plain-clothed KCG operatives sprinkled amongst the onlookers. Others of the KCG fanned out in their official garb. Intel gathered from the Agents of Derr made him aware the other nations-states' security teams had their people similarly placed.

Every inch, every person, every balcony, every movement warned of danger making the parade a miserable fucking experience for Derr. Derr had no option but to endure it along the entire three-mile length of the Grand Protisium, ending only at the gates of the Temple Palace.

The Temple Palace was at the heart of the city in both its location and in its importance to the inhabitants. It was there that the First Lord and Council of Prudents would ceremoniously welcome the secular Heads of State at the conclusion of the parade. Only then did Derr expect a temporary reprieve from his perpetual state of heightened alert.

Nation's rulers, whether chancellor, president, provost, or prime minister, all made their way towards the Palace at midday, and Derr knew any one of them could have been behind the events inside The Stand.

His thoughts jumped from threat to threat, evaluating each as fast as his mind could process. Derr observed President Dimenk of Greenlin reaching out to Prime Minister Larsed. In less than a heartbeat, Captain Derr reflected on an internal Adelleian dossier and concluded President Dimenk's style of personal diplomacy—which earned her the reputation as a thoughtful leader—was of significant concern. She would overwhelm the inexperienced Larsed to the detriment of Adelle.

Simple threads in time, such as they were, held the opportunity for nations to rise or fall, depending on the skills of their leaders. Others may have considered Greenlin fortunate to have at the head of government, one as personable and skilled as President Dimenk, but Derr's evaluation placed her on a different scale, one defined by threat levels.

Derr watched them all, including First Lady Kaythlin, who remained radiant throughout the day. He placed her near the bottom on the same scale but considered moving her up after this morning.

Residents of Teth and visitors from every village, hamlet, or city across the continent lined the Grand Protisium over its entire length. Tens of thousands packed the causeway as the Heads of State rode as equals towards Tartica's spiritual leader, First Lord Jerithan.

Mixed in amongst the adoring hordes, packed twenty and thirty deep along the city's main thoroughfare, retailers offered their wares, food, drink, flesh, housing, games of chance, all raking in coin brought in from the four corners of the continent. Refreshment vendors outnumbered every other mobile street merchant. Of the food carts, none were more popular than the sweet-eel sticks for which Teth was renowned. Peddlers of a different type offered illicit drugs if one knew how to identify a Thuggery dealer. Derr identified them all.

Conditions on the ground created an impossible security challenge for Derr. There were too many people, too much movement, too many variables and too much chaos to lock down security; it overwhelmed Derr and his team. If the unknown grandmaster made another assassination attempt, it'd happen along the chaos of the Grand Protisium.

By tradition and by law, the Covenant should have been enough to ensure the safety of everyone. Derr knew better. He understood the law, understood the traditions; he almost respected them, but he didn't trust them to be the safety net they pretended to be. The attempted assassination earlier in the morning, despite the second Absolute Universal Obligation of the Covenant not to take a human life, proved his point. As his eyes darted from person to person, from every jerk of an arm, from every turn of a head, he wondered who orchestrated the attempt.

I will find you. Maybe not today, but soon.

He'd have to wait until later in the evening or even the next day to lay eyes on the KCG's assessment report of what had occurred inside The Stand. Derr would have to wait even longer before taking action in response.

Amongst the sundry shops along the great causeway, Celebratoria, cathedral-like buildings, represented each of Teth's Six Gifts to humanity: the Gift of Love, the Gift of Knowledge, the Gift of Flesh, the Gift of Life, the Gift of Renewal, and the Gift of Nature. All welcomed believers and the curious alike.

The Feast of Teth offered the collective Celebratoria a day to attract new followers as much as it was for the merchants to extract coin. Each Gift Celebratoria, like the merchants, street performers, and Thuggery opportunists, sought something from the throng of prospects.

Derr looked on as a small woman, dressed to look like a teenager, deftly reach into the handbag of an impeccably dressed older woman. The mark appeared otherwise engaged intently on the antics of a lively mime. The thief pocketed her gain and moved on quickly to her next victim.

Derr knew the mime would get his cut later when the coconspirators divvied up the day's haul. He watched, but as it posed no danger to his Chancellor, he moved on as quickly as the pickpocket.

Derr reflected on pre-visit assessments prepared by the KCG as well as on his own experience. Teth counted among its inhabitants the holy, the faithful, the indifferent, and a small group of people devoted to taking whatever they could from whomever they could take it from. The city wasn't just the center of faith. Teth was known for both its purity and its depravity. A city balanced between forces capable of driving it into chaos and those capable of soothing the soul of any who pass through its gates. Teth, like any other big city, reflected the human condition for better or worse. Each experienced Teth through the lens of their own economic or social status impacting their perception of life in the city—glorious or brutal.

Derr had no choice but to endure the miserable parade. Traditions and pomp dictated the activities of the day. Choreographed as though a delicate ballet, each step by the leaders, at each stop along the Grand Protisium, each speech and each offering to Teth was planned for the benefit of the crowds. The leaders of Adelle, Greenlin, and Kantos played their parts but had their own agendas.

The Grand Parade stopped at each of the Celebratoria along the Grand Protisium with solemn offerings. The honors fell to Dimenk, Tomelai, Larsed, and Provost Kwuinan.

At the first Celebratoria honoring the Gift of Love, the parade stopped and President Dimenk of Greenlin spoke. She was adorned in a lime-green gown laced with gold fabric. Her bustle rounded at the hips. At thirty-five years of age, she was plump from years of well-prepared meals at too many state banquets. Her hard gaze almost obscured semi-attractive underlying features. Credit for her stately appearance went to the herculean efforts of the well-trained image-makers and talented make-up artists. None of that mattered in Derr's estimation of Dimenk as he concluded she didn't trade on her looks. President Dimenk was a born leader who demanded respect: respect she earned with a commanding presence. Above all, she was smart, strategic, calculating, and opportunistic. In Derr's assessment, it was her political acumen that made her formidable, respected, and dangerous.

Dimenk had the potential to threaten Derr's friend, Tomelai. But Derr held something important over her head, and he made certain she was aware—to Adelle's advantage. Her husband of ten years, Tague Dimenk, didn't match her ambitions, her intelligence, or any of her many appetites, including her ravenous hunger for the Gift of Flesh. She took many lovers, both openly and secretively. The men, openly, whereas the women, all secretively. Not that sex with someone of the same gender was forbidden in Greenlin or anywhere in Tartica—under the right conditions.

The Covenant demanded procreation as an Absolute Universal Obligation first. As her nation's childless President, she failed to deliver the requisite progeny, as demanded by the Covenant. Until she did, she wasn't free to share her bed with other women. The occasional dalliance with other men was overlooked and even encouraged in the hopes of a successful pregnancy. Sharing the Gift of Flesh with other women before delivering a child into this world would have ruined her political career. Even worse, repeat offenders faced service in one of the "birthing farms."

The Covenant wasn't fair in its unforgiving framework to rebuild humanity. She had the duty to procreate just like everyone else. She was thirty-five and without children. Until she produced offspring, Derr continued to dangle the affairs with other women over her head.

The parade paused, as did Derr, but he kept up, ever vigilant, ever watching. Dimenk dismounted and approached the Celebratorium. She spoke with a powerful voice. A voice demanding attention, like so much else about her. "We give thanks," she said as she kneeled at the steps of the Celebratorium of the Gift of Love, folding her arms together, palms open, her head bowed low.

Opening her arms wide, she spoke to the crowd. "To Mother Earth, for the life she gives us. And for every day, we give thanks to Teth, a child of Mother Earth and Eurithian, Father Sun, the one true God in all the heavens. Teth, conceived out of the undying love of Father Sun, His gift to Mother Earth, the Gift of Love. And the love of a mother for her child, to nurture and to provide for. From Her love, all love flows through Teth to us. Through Teth, we can know love. Love of family, of a mother, of a father, brother, sister, and the love between us all."

After a long pause for effect, Dimenk continued. "And the special love between whomever we hold close to our hearts as a choice we openly make." With those words, the President stood and reached out to take the hand of her husband Tague, who had just stepped forward, as planned, and dutifully stood by his wife. "As I have chosen my love, my husband, my Tague." They lifted their enjoined hands above their heads to the roaring approval of the crowd.

The President had planned to say more, but as she and Tague stood there, hand in hand, she had the crowd. The multitudes roared. Both turned in unison, entwined hands held high, waving to everyone and no one in particular. They loved her at that moment. Derr could see it, and he was certain she could as well. It came as no surprise to Derr she ended it there with nothing more to be gained. She had done well, Derr admitted to himself.

Derr's protective efforts continued as the nations' leaders, each in turn, stopped to make dedications at the various Celebratoria of the Six Gifts. The day proceeded as expected. The leaders enthralled the gathered crowds, who welcomed the chance to brush up against such important people. All the while the pageantry reinforced the Temple of Life's political influence.

Derr observed money flow throughout the day in small transactions. Many, many small exchanges that added up to vast amounts. Merchant's coffers overflowed by the end of it all, turning untold profits. Children delighted at street performers and loved the pageantry of the parade. The underground economy flourished as well. Though it mattered little to Derr, Teth's place of honor was secured for another year. The only outcome that interested Derr was the survival of his friend.

Through it all, Derr watched. He watched President Dimenk. He watched Prime Minister Larsed. He watched Provost Kwuinan. He watched his own First Lady. He watched the crowds, the street performers, the acolytes, the merchants, and he watched his unit as they performed their duties.

Through the efforts of his vigilance, his calculating mind, the KCG's exhaustive planning, and his relentless watching, as the parade concluded, Chancellor Tomelai was still alive.

Home Is Where the Heart Is

Hensdale: 27th Day of the Salmon Moon

Mithany | Mera

Tithe masters weren't accustomed to doing much for the faithful save picking their pockets in the name of the Temple of Life. It came as quite a surprise to Mithany when Tithe Master Fegmin abruptly stopped along the road on the trio's return trip from Owls Neck to Hensdale. He unexpectedly offered her, Arek, and Neladith a ride. The trio had completed over half the mentally tortuous journey and welcomed the offer. Midday on the Feast of Teth had improved considerably for Mithany after the pair of heart-stopping events she'd endured earlier.

Uneventful as the ride back to Hensdale proved to be, the lack of further excitement gave Mithany the chance to share Arek's attention along the way. After arriving in Hensdale, dropping Neladith off at the Forest Maiden Inn—telling Arek she had something to do and would catch up with him later that night—Tithe Master Enlist ferried Mithany and Arek to Reyne's home.

Tithe Master Fegmin waved as he approached the four men seated on the porch. "I have something for you," he yelled out to Reyne and the others.

Mithany leaped off the back of the wagon in a flash, running with open arms. Reyne sprung from the porch and sprinted to his soon-to-be wife. Stumbling, she almost went down, but there was Reyne, arms extended, to catch her.

In the clasp of Reyne's tight embrace, joy coursed through her every pore.

He's okay. The thought rang in her mind like a tower bell clanging again and again. *He's okay.*

The world was right for all she cared. Tilting her head back, looking up at Reyne, she held his face in upstretched hands. Tears filled her eyes. Shaking uncontrollably, her teeth almost rattled. Being in his arms untethered the passion she'd kept in check hiding behind the fear of uncertainty.

Reyne lifted her off her feet. She smacked her lips forcefully against his, and the kiss seemed to go on without end. She poured everything she had in her small frame into that kiss.

"Agghh, you two have to do that in front of everybody?" Daedyn frowned. "Nobody wants to watch that."

Indifferent to Daedyn and the rest of the world, Mithany playfully bit Reyne's lower lip as she gradually released him from their embrace. Her feet remained off the ground, either because Reyne still held her tight or she was floating on air at the sight of him.

"I was so worried about you. You're okay. I'm so relieved," she repeated in the excited squeal of a schoolgirl.

"What happened? Were you knocked out? Where was Daedyn?"

She rattled off question after question, happy to see the man she so deeply loved but curious about what took place while she was in Owls Neck.

The tithe master interrupted the enthralled lovers from his position on the cart to address Reyne, "I didn't know I'd bumped into you earlier, near the square. I'm so sorry. I didn't see you. People told me about it after. I honestly didn't even know what happened. I would have stopped. You got to understand, I would've stopped," he said apologetically.

Fegmin's words filter into Reyne's consciousness, which was otherwise intently focused on Mithany in his arms.

"You know it goes against all Temple regs to give anyone a ride. Picking up Mithany was my way of apologizing."

Reyne scowled at Fegmin, but Mithany gave him her soft, round puppy eyes, and his expression quickly changed. He said to the tithe master, "The heck with it. Don't worry about it. We're even now that you gave Mithany a ride."

Arek objected, "Hey, what about me? He gave me a ride, too."

Reyne beamed at Mithany without turning to face Tithe Master Fegmin. "Apology accepted."

"I was on my way back from a quick tithe collection trip in Owls Neck when I came across the three of them. You've got to hear Arek's story about a Great Yetgnal."

Tithe master was mostly a descriptive title the Temple of Life used to lessen the blow of paying taxes to the Temple. A tithe master was the Temple's tax collector, and everyone knew it plain and simple. When tithing became part of the Temple of Life, no one in Hensdale could say. It was a practice Reyne grew familiar with throughout his life. Based on the stories his late father told, it was part of his father's life and his father's father's life before that.

Reyne and Daedyn believed in the cause of feeding the poor, donating as much as they could every year to the Temple of Life as their tithe contribution. The brothers ignored the demands of the Temple bean counters for even more, without fear of consequences. There weren't any, if only for alphen producers. So, it was quite a surprise to Mithany, who did most of the financial accounting work for the brother's business, when Tithe Master Fegmin offered her a ride.

Fegmin said, "I wanted to see if you were alright. Seems you are. Again, I'm sorry for what happened. I'm gonna head back now. We'll settle up after the harvest."

Mithany laughed to herself. It seemed Fegmin didn't have the courage to ask the brothers for the expected exorbitant payment of one hundred barrels of alphen nuts after almost running Reyne over.

Waving one hand high in the air, Fegmin shouted with his back to the small gathering, "I'll be back in a few weeks after the harvest."

Daedyn and Reyne took turns recounting Reyne's accident, bringing Mithany and Arek up to speed. They spoke of Mera as well and how he helped Reyne.

At a different time, she might have been more interested in Mera, but with the excitement of finding Reyne up and about after the frightening news she had heard earlier, Reyne was all she could think about.

With great interest, Mithany listened. She anchored herself next to Reyne, holding his arm in hers with her head nestled in his shoulder. The Goddess Teth couldn't move her from his side.

Arek was milling about, not seeming to care for the details that Mithany ate up with every word.

"Would you stop pacing!" Daedyn insisted upon Arek.

"Daedyn, you gotta listen to this. I got a great story. You won't believe what I saw," Arek said, continuing to dance around, much to Mithany's amusement.

"You have to forgive him. He didn't return alone. Our boy here met up with a pretty young thing while we were over in Owls Neck. He spent the night with her. I'm not sure why, but she came back with us. She elected to get dropped off at the Forest Maiden Inn. You'll get a chance to meet her at some point, I suspect, given how fond Arek is of her. I'm surprised they've been apart this long." Poking a playful jab at her brother, she added, "And I suspect he is eager to get back to her."

"Oh, come now, Sis. Of course you know why. For some more of this." Arek ran his hands over his body. "And besides, who's the one who had to run back here even before we did what we went to Owls Neck for?" A smirk aimed at Daedyn and Reyne crossed his face. "You know what it's like with a woman for the first time."

Shoulders shrugged, hands apart and pointing in Mithany's direction, Reyne shot back, "Hey, dickhead! That's your sister. No, I don't know."

Whether it was true, it was the right thing to say. At least it's what Mithany expected of him. The Gift of Love held the expression of physical love as one pillar of faith, but Temple doctrine didn't give the engaged couple free rein as far as Mithany was concerned. In her heart, she knew Reyne felt the same. Having grown up with both Reyne and Daedyn, she had heard more than a fair number of first-time experiences the brothers boasted about while in her presence—before she and Reyne became an item.

Thinking it was mostly truthful, Mithany appreciated Reyne's reply for his fellow studs to hear. She understood men well, better than most, and certainly better than other women her age. She fathomed Reyne's acquiescence cost him standing in their boys' club, and that was just fine with her.

"It's okay, choirboy," she told Reyne, stroking his back and almost laughing as she spoke. "I'm here for you now. I'm all the first-time you're ever goin' to need." She paused for effect, then added, "Or you're ever goin' to get," before kissing him devilishly on the cheek.

Reyne blushed. "Right you are, my dear. Right you are."

She heard more than words in his reply. His sincere tone touched her down to her bones. His gaze said he wanted nothing more than to spend the rest of his life with an exceptional, intelligent, attractive, and funny woman—her.

Reaching for Reyne's hand, sliding her palm into his, she looked up at him. *It's always in the eyes, and his seem to be smiling at me*. She could see all the love she ever wanted in the way he looked at her. Warmth tingled in her body, and as it coursed through her, it settled in her loins. She mused, S*ometimes it's not in the eyes.*

Walking past the two young lovers, Daedyn slapped his brother on the back. "You two need some time alone. We can all get outta here for a while." Looking over at Arek, Daedyn gave a knowing head nod and a wink. "Let's leave these two alone."

"What's the matter, no one special in your life?" Mithany said to Daedyn in response to jabs he aimed at her man. Turning to her brother, she added, "And as for you, I'm guessing the moment you leave this little gathering, you're heading back to the Forest Maiden Inn to find your new friend."

Arek observed, "She's smarter than she looks."

"I've got to give him credit for this one," Mithany said. "She's got quite the body, long auburn hair, and those haunting eyes. I've never seen eyes like that before. Almond-shaped, and they come in captivating red. She's got him under her spell." Looking over at her brother, offering him an evil little smirk of her own, she teased, "I can guess what she used to cast her spell on you, and it wasn't just those red eyes."

Daedyn jumped in, "Red eyes. Never seen that before."

Reyne followed with, "Me neither."

While unnoticed by the others sitting on the porch, Mera's head snapped around mid-sentence at Mithany's description of Neladith. He was otherwise engaged in conversation with Brenal but stopped listening to the old man when his brain caught up with his ears.

Brenal continued talking, but Mera was no longer listening. He strained to hear the others, waiting to confirm what Mithany said. The coloring of the woman's eyes meant nothing to anyone else other than the curiosity of a rare affectation.

Mera knew better.

Daedyn and Reyne roared in laughter at Mithany's observations of Arek and Neladith. Arek gave a look back at the five of them that told them he didn't care if they laughed.

"Spell or no spell, and regardless of what wonders she used to cast it, Sis, I'm a lucky boy. And yes, those eyes aren't all that makes her so special."

Mithany wanted to say, "Oh, little brother, you're a pig. The Gift of Flesh has its purpose—to produce children." But she didn't.

There wasn't condemnation in her thoughts. She came to expect little from most men his age. Her brother was no exception. Reyne was, though. And then there was the Gift of Flesh to consider. It no longer fulfilled its original intention, regardless of what the Temple of Life leadership taught.

Nestled close to Reyne, Mithany told her brother, “Reyne is different. And in a few days, we’ll be married.”

“Oh, I still gotta tell you a story about a Great Yetgnal and me,” Arek excitedly announced, looking about for the correct hour. “Shit. Don’t have time. Can’t tell you right now. Gotta get back to town. You understand. And, Sis, don’t go tellin’ ‘em anything about the Great Yetgnal. I want to tell ‘em myself. Promise.”

He didn’t wait for her reply. The eager young man leaped down from the porch, running off, heading for the Forest Maiden Inn where he expected to enjoy his favorite of the Six Gifts the Temple of Life encouraged all to observe.

Mithany pursed her lips and shook her head, watching her brother run off. “There he goes. Off to find his new plaything.”

Ignoring Mithany, Mera’s thoughts raced. He locked on the words Mithany used to describe Arek’s new friend. *Red eyes.*

That changes everything!

Anything Is Possible

Teth: 27th day of the Salmon Moon

Derr | Tomelai

Derr let himself relax the tiniest bit, with Chancellor Tomelai safely back in the Temple Palace complex. Safer, anyway, than the streets of Teth. The suite of rooms provided to the Adelleian delegation were as spacious as they were remote. Derr's team made the arrangements with Razoal, requesting lodging for Tomelai, himself, and the Chancellor's top courtiers in the Palace's remotest settings.

Why Razoal accommodated Derr's request without tit-for-tat puzzled him, yet he accepted the gesture. The relative isolation afforded Derr the opportunity to implement even tighter security precautions. The safety of Tomelai was his only concern, regardless of Razoal's out-of-character acquiescence.

Like many of the guest suites inside the Temple Palace, scenes from the Book of Teth adorned the Chancellor's room. Derr paid it no mind. Tomelai unbuckled his sword belt, dropping the ceremonial rapier and scabbard to the ground. Derr watched it fall from his perch near the door. "I like you better with ornamental steel, Rotti. You shouldn't have jumped into the fray this morning. You almost got us both killed. Keeping you alive is my job. You fucked it all up."

"We are alive, Drew. That is all that matters."

"Hard to argue with. By the way, where's Kaythlin?"

"I sent her out to mingle with my entourage. She's reviewing the day's events and reveling in my performance at the Celebratorium of Knowledge. She's setting the tone for Adelle's elites, subtly demonstrating how they are expected to speak of this day and of her husband's grand performance when they all return to the capital city of Tandure." Tomelai bowed and followed with abroad sweep of his arm. "Her script will say I was magnificent."

"At least you will be in all the stories, Rotti. Like sheep, they'll follow her lead. The desire to remain in her good graces is a strong motivator. Good idea sending Kaythlin."

"She will see to it they dare not stray from the glowing terms she is only now so gently laying down as the official view of the day's events. It is funny, Drew. An off-handed conversation with Kaythlin, so seemingly fortuitous, so gracefully presented and so well spoken, will have such force behind it they dare not contradict her account."

"Not unless they care to see their standing jeopardized. She may not hold office but she has your ear. A woman of power, intelligence, grace, she not only captivates the ruling class, but she plays them all so well."

"Kaythlin and I are a well-matched team. Who works the court for every foible, flaw, desire, or ambition better than her? How many times have you two chatted over the weaknesses she uncovers and how best to exploit them? She is a gem."

"That she is, Rotti." Derr reflected, First Lady Kaythlin was a woman well-matched to suit the needs of her Chancellor. All his needs. Her acumen to satisfy her Chancellor did not stop at the bedroom door. "Whatever's good for the Tomelais is good for the Kingdom of Adelle."

Derr's words brought a smile to Tomelai's face. "The Tomelais are Adelle and Adelle is the Tomelais. It had been that way for generations and will be for many more to come."

Captain Derr was pleased Kaythlin had not returned before he arrived. He needed time to speak to his Chancellor openly and without the necessity of holding anything back in the presence of others. When the two men spoke in private and alone, they held nothing in reserve, or so they told each other. As much as the Chancellor encouraged his partner in life to offer her opinions and insights, Derr was certain Tomelai was also thankful for the duo's private time without her.

"Rotti, I have to ask, back in the passage this morning, I thought I saw something that suggested you knew more than you were saying. You killed their only survivor before we could get anything out of him." Derr questioned his sovereign as though he was just another man by the good graces afforded him in the special relationship they shared. They had known each other since childhood before Madrotti Tomelai, the privileged heir apparent, and Druin Derr, a commoner, grew into men. Chancellor Tomelai rarely imposed his stature on their relationship. They were the closest of friends and could say anything between them as close friends dared to offer.

Tomelai, caught off guard, snorted. "Who else could accuse the Chancellor of Adelle of plotting his own staged assassination attempt for publicity but Druin Derr, Captain of the KCG? Come on, Drew, that guy was not going to give us anything. It was obvious he couldn't speak."

Tomelai crossed his arms, and with bent knee, rested the sole of his shoe against the wall to mimic Derr's stance. Derr immediately broke formation. He never enjoyed being mocked. For all his stoicism, for all his inner strength, for all his cold blue eyes offered as a defense against the world, Tomelai could always playfully get a rise out of him.

Pushing away from the wall with his foot, Derr turned to face Tomelai. "You're good. Nice try, but you still didn't answer my question. Did you set it up this morning? You could've killed us both."

Druin thought he had gained the upper hand as the two men parried. With his back resting on the wall, Derr crossed his arms and returned his posture to bent knee, foot against the wall. Derr offered his friend the Chancellor a visual yet unverbalized, "Fuck you!"

It only made Tomelai laugh even more.

"Drew, how long have you known me? Maybe I am crazy enough to stage that for my benefit, but I would never put your life at risk." The Chancellor's foot pushed off from the wall.

Derr thought for a second. His eyes drew in tight, then he stated flatly, "You're equivocating. You still haven't said yes or no. I've questioned too many people over too many years to tell when someone isn't answering me, and besides, I know you too well."

"Who says I have to answer you? I am the fucking Chancellor." Tomelai's smirk stretched from ear to ear.

Dropping the playful back-and-forth, Derr asked softly, "You having fun with this? This is serious. Come on, Rotti, enough of this bullshit. Did you or did you not put someone up to make it look like an assassination attempt?"

The two stared at each other. Derr broke first. He'd won his fair share of these little stare-down contests. Just not this one.

Walking over to his friend, Tomelai put his arm around Derr's shoulders. "Of course not, Drew, but some bastard did try to kill us today." The Chancellor dropped his arm from Druin's shoulder and stepped forward to face his Captain.

Derr replied, "Well, not really. They were trying to kill you. I just happen to be there."

"Touché! And lucky for me, you were. You saved my life once again. You sure you want nothing your Chancellor can give you?"

"No. I'm good."

"We do this all the time. I beg you to take more coin. Hell, take any woman in the kingdom you want. Let me say thank you for this and all the times you have come through."

"You know my answer. I need nothing. I have enough. When and if I ever do want more, I'll let you know. Until then, our deal stands. I'll take whatever I want from your treasury whenever I want it. That's my compensation."

With pursed lips, cocked head, and raised eyebrows aimed at Derr, the Chancellor said, "That is good. Just take more next time. You live like shit."

"We've been through this a thousand times. You appreciate me. I appreciate the offer for more. Enough. Let's move on. And besides, everyone lives like shit compared to you."

Although his friend Druin Derr was being sincere, Tomelai looked upon the man with sadness. He wanted to heap riches upon him. Tomelai wanted to settle the debt he owed. He didn't enjoy having it hanging out there. Derr was a weapon Tomelai used to keep himself in power. The man sought so little in return compared to the service he provided. Tomelai felt guilty. He owed his friend more than his friend realized and more than his friend was willing to accept.

In his heart, Tomelai considered Druin Derr the better man. He would have been the better Chancellor. Not that Tomelai would give up power. No, that would never happen. Druin Derr was the man Tomelai wished he could be. He had inner strength like no one Tomelai had ever known. Himself included.

Tomelai had been hurt by Derr's accusation. It could have been because Derr was the better man, or it could have been that if Tomelai was being honest with himself, he was capable of such a stunt. Well-practiced at burying his emotions when he didn't like what he felt, Tomelai was a stoic to the core. He swallowed hard and drove his hurt deep, beyond conscious thought, avoiding any need to face it ever again.

Tomelai heard Derr continue, "Let's get back to who could have done this."

The Chancellor began, "Alright. There's the possibility it came from within, and if so, we have to ask two questions. First, who would have the most to gain, and second, who could have pulled it off? We have the long list of wannabes. You and your network always keep close tabs on them. Is it possible any of them slipped past your notice in pulling off something like this?"

Derr considered it for a second, and said, "I always start from the position that anything's possible. It leaves nothing out. In this case, the likelihood it's one of them is remote. There are other, more likely candidates than the wannabes. We can circle back to them if we come up empty. Either it's someone we didn't have on our watch list, or the mastermind is from outside Tandure."

Steepling his fingers in front of his face, Derr's cold blue eyes stared out at nothing and everything. He added, "And I don't like the idea it was someone we didn't account for previously. We go over this shit often enough. We didn't miss anyone who should be on our watch list unless you've been keeping information from me.

"How are things on the home front? Tane wouldn't be the first Tomelai to step into the shoes of Adelle's Chancellor before Mother Earth intended to reclaim the sitting occupant. Your family has a history of chancellors dying unexpectedly young. Tane's not on my list of likely suspects, but what do you think?" There was no fear in Derr of questioning the Chancellor. No pretense of sovereign and subject.

"I do not think so. She is not like that. If it were Tane, her mother would have to be involved, and between the two of them, I do not see it happening. Kaythlin has not given up on me. Regicide... to what purpose?"

"Kaythlin is definitely someone you need to keep happy. Your wife is about the only person who might even outplay me."

"You and me both, Drew. She's one hell of a gal."

"What about Loseff? He's shown little interest in anything, but I'm not around your family from minute to minute to watch him."

"Drew, I do not have to tell you that you did not fail me today. You know better than to think because an attempt happened, you failed. You saved my life."

"I'm aware. But I failed you today because I didn't stop it before it happened." Derr dropped his head.

He failed. All his watching, information gathering, all his planning and not a single source within his vast network of agents, spies, and informants offered anything pointing him in the right direction. Derr had to admit that either his network was inadequate or there was a double agent in his ranks.

Tomelai gave emphasis to his words: "Do whatever it takes to find out who is behind this. My opinion, I think it is related to our proposal on electrics. As for failing me, it is true we did not stop it before it happened, and that is concerning. My concern is not about you. I am concerned my death is in play. Today was just the start. We stop them, or they will stop me from living. Whoever they are, these people are not just going to walk away after one try."

"True. And these may be new players on the board. Over the next few days, mull it over, Rotti. I'll go over the names on my watch list again to see if anything was overlooked."

"I know you like to keep them around, Drew, even though they want my job. It might be time to dispose of the more dangerous amongst them. We have a blind spot. We got poked in the eye today, and we do not know whose finger it was."

Madrotti Tomelai occasionally added and removed names from Derr's watch-list in myriad ways. Derr quietly removed threats from the world of the living from time to time; often, but not always, delegating the chore to one of his trusted lieutenants. Keeping the Chancellor in the seat of power was not a simple task and not for the faint of heart, despite the Covenant's demand to preserve life above all else.

Druin Derr puffed his cheeks, mulling over Tomelai's comments. "Not just yet. Let's watch them even closer. They failed today. There might be some fallout. Someone knows something, and whoever is pulling the strings, they may need to dispose of some unwanted loose ends. Someone might lead us to the puppet master. I'll shake the trees. Something might fall out." Lips pursed, giving the Chancellor time to consider his suggestion, Derr stood silent and waited.

Tomelai pause at Derr's suggestion before finally saying, "Alright, make it happen. Now, what about my fellow leaders from Kantos and Greenlin, or that prick Jerithan Cree? I do not see the Prime Minister of Kantos doing anything of the sort. He is too new to the game, and I doubt Dimenk would take the chance. I am leaning toward First Lord Jerithan Cree."

Derr continued the exploration, "I'm not inclined to rule out the First Lord either. Although, early reports from my people suggest there may have been a few arrows from the Anatese in several of the dead would-be assassins. If the Temple leader, as much of an asshole as he might be, was involved, why would the Anatese help us? They answer to him alone. They wouldn't have come to our aid. Unseen, I might add. Unless, of course, he was so confident he could pull it off and didn't give the Anatese, those monkey men living in The Stand canopy, any heads-up. We'll never know. They won't talk to us. Never do."

"Maybe."

Derr continued his line of inquiry. "There's also Jerithan Cree's lackey, Razoal. My people watch him closely. He's given nothing away. Either he's that good, and I doubt it, or the Temple wasn't involved. On the other hand, we might have missed it, and that means we have holes in our intel." Derr stopped to give Tomelai time to consider his words. He watched Tomelai evaluating his insights. He was always watching even his Chancellor.

Shifting the discussion from the Temple, Tomelai said, "What do you think about Dimenk? Excuse me, Madam President Dimenk. We have strained relations between Greenlin and Tandure of late. What with the ongoing squabble over the rights to the mineral deposit at the base of The Razors? It's in unclaimed territory, and our people were there first. She's tried to make the case its nearer to her border. Would she risk everything over mineral rights? There is a lot of money at stake, and she hates, utterly hates being made to look weak. What does your intel tell you? What information don't I already have?"

With an exceptional memory, Derr pulled up in his mind the report about Dimenk. "I'll get a copy for your review. It's common knowledge she hates to lose to men more than anything. It could push her to take a shot at you over the Razor's find. But she knows we know of her preference to dabble in women. And she isn't licensed to partake in that particular Gift of Flesh since she's produced no offspring. She wouldn't risk the exposure. It'll cost her everything. A national leader violating a core directive of the Covenant. She'd be ruined. My instincts tell me to focus elsewhere."

"But if it is her, you'll need to find your way to extract quiet revenge. Your people could do it," Tomelai stated directly, then added, "but we're getting ahead of ourselves."

Before the two men could explore any further, the door to Tomelai's room opened, and First Lady Kaythlin stepped in. Dressed as she was for the parade, she looked like a polished jewel. Her smile met both men and her charm quickly unarmed them both.

"Boys," she said playfully. "I know you both too well. Put your game pieces away for now. Druin, please allow me a few private moments with my husband."

"Kaythlin." Derr dutifully proffered a respectful bow. He wanted to continue the conversation with the Chancellor, but he knew better.

Kaythlin walked over to the Captain of the KCG. She hooked her arm inside his. His needs and wants were no match for her charm. He'd lost too many times to fight it once more. Druin Derr did what he'd rarely ever done for anyone else: he surrendered to her. With her arm gently under his, she walked him politely towards the door.

A stunning woman of unmatched elegance, she was hard to deny when she wanted something. The power of her beauty, matched with intelligence and grace, did a funny thing to man or woman. Derr was no ordinary man, yet he couldn't deny Kaythlin. It was obvious to Derr he wouldn't be continuing his conversation with Rotti. He could protest, but he wouldn't get a reprieve.

Tomelai aimed an impish grin at Derr, as if to say to him, "The Lady has spoken. Time for you to go."

"Druin, I thank you for keeping my love safe today, but we have a banquet to prepare for." Walking him through the archway leading into the hallway, she slipped her arm free. She leaned in close and kissed him on the cheek. Kaythlin whispered in his ear, "I owe you more than you can imagine. Thank you, my dear Druin," and turned away. The door closed, and Kaythlin was alone with her husband, the Chancellor.

Standing in the Temple Palace hallway, staring at the door just closed on him, Derr turned and walked away, leaving two KCG posted at the entrance to the Chancellor's chamber. Derr didn't give his KCG guards a second thought.

He was thinking about Adelle's First Lady. *I know Rotti doesn't think so, yet maybe I should look at her more closely.*

Not What It Seems

Hensdale: 27th day of the Salmon Moon

Mithany | Mera

Reyne and Daedyn spent the remains of the afternoon regaling Mithany, Brenal, and Mera with stories. Tales mostly about Mera as the butt of the boys' childhood pranks. Mera proved to be a good sport about it. While Mithany heard them all before, she enjoyed the retelling and laughed along with everyone else. She especially enjoyed the pleasure it gave Reyne reflecting on the good times he and Daedyn shared.

Reyne still exhibited side effects from the spiderworm venom in his system, highlighted by the almost imperceptible differences in his movements and his speech. Mera, she suspected, saw it too.

Doc Brenal had assured them that Reyne would be back to his old self soon enough, but he wasn't there yet.

Mithany used the gathering as cover for the opportunity to study Mera. While she laughed through the afternoon, as did they all, Mithany kept an eye on the newcomer. He was a mystery she needed to solve.

With dusk's approach, story time ended and everyone headed inside except for Reyne, who told the group he needed to check on one or two things in the orchard.

Inside, Daedyn slapped his hands together. "I'm gonna start fixin' some dinner. Mithany, you think your brother and his new girlfriend will be joining us?"

"I don't think so. He's been gone a long time. I'm gonna say that's a good sign he's found her. Knowing the things that interest my older brother, his plans for tonight won't include food, or for that matter, any of us."

"Well, the way you described her, I don't blame him. Brenal, can you give me a hand? You don't want Reyne cookin' if any of us wants to eat tonight. My brother has a few outstanding qualities, but cookin' ain't one of 'em."

"Sure. Why not? I've eaten more than most in my day." Brenal patted his well-nourished belly. "Cooked less for myself than I care to admit, but I know my way around pots and pans."

Brenal and Daedyn headed off to the kitchen, leaving Mithany alone with Mera. She was a little unnerved by the way Mera looked at her, as though sizing her up. She could see it in his eyes. *It's always in the eyes.* "Can I help you with something, Mera?" she asked.

The previously disguised beggar leaned in close and whispered in her ear, "You've been studying me all afternoon. You don't have to worry about me. The time for fear is coming, but not of my doing."

Mithany's smile opened wide in a welcoming gesture. "I'm just getting to know you. Not the ragged old bum from the stories we just heard." She paused, wagged her finger at him, and continued, "I'm keeping my eyes on the new you."

Mera put his hand on her shoulder. "Good, challenge accepted. Reyne's a lucky man to have someone like you."

"You bet your ass he's a lucky man. And, yes, he damn well knows it too." Trust remained unsettled between Mithany and Mera, but together they took their first steps in the right direction.

"I like you, Mithany. Always have. There's a lot I want to share with you both. When's that fiancé of yours coming back inside?"

Before Mithany could answer, Arek burst through the door. "I'm back!" he proclaimed, throwing his arms open wide as though making the entrance of some honored guest.

"I didn't expect to see you this soon, brother. Didn't find her, huh?"

"Oh no, I found her. We had a fantastical afternoon." With excitement in his words, delight lit up his face. "But it all ended too soon. Not that *I* finished, you know, too soon... hah... hah. She said she had something to do. So here I am. Happy to see me, Sis?"

"Do you always have to be so obvious? No need to announce it; we all figured you were getting laid."

Mera ignored the sibling banter. "Arek, did you run into Reyne on your way in?"

"He's out by the tree line," Arek said, pointing towards the grove. "You guys eat yet? I worked up a powerful appetite."

Mithany's head slumped forward and she closed her eyes, shaking her noggin from side to side, mildly amused. "Sometimes you're just a little boy inside an overgrown body." Popping her head up, she opened her eyes and spread her arms apart. "Now get over here and give your sister a hug."

Arek swept her up in the big, tight embrace she wanted, lifting her off her feet. Short, dangling legs whirled in the air as Arek enthusiastically spun her around. With his face close to her ear as they twirled through the room, he said, "Little? That's not what she said."

She tried to react, but with Arek's arms wrapped tightly around her, her hands were immobilized against his chest. "Agghh, you." She struggled to get free. Her wiggles and squirms only made him laugh all the more—and he didn't let go.

With apparent amusement at her reaction, he kissed her cheek. "You know I love only you, Sis."

And just as quickly, he put her down. As her feet touched the floor, he loosened his hold, and she pushed herself away. "Yeah. I know, you big goof." Her hand shot forward, grabbing one of his nipples through his shirt and, securing it between her thumb and forefinger—she twisted hard.

"Ouch. That's no way to treat your big brother. Suppose I did that to you?"

"Like you never have."

Mera approached Reyne, who was pulling nuts off a low-hanging branch. Reyne didn't look up, mesmerized by the alphens he'd gathered in his palm.

"See here, these husks are starting to split." Reyne poked a finger at the samples and rolled them in his hand like a pair of dice. "Haven't opened all the way yet. They're a little green. They're gonna be ready in two weeks. They'll be ripe for the pickin' by then." His voice trailed off, and lifting his eyes from the nuts, he stated flatly, "I just love this place." The harsh glare he gave Mera screamed in no uncertain terms he had no intention of doing anything but harvesting the orchard when the time came.

Reyne tossed the nuts into the burn pit and stared into the flames. Without looking away Reyne said, "You're here for a reason. I'm not sure what it is, but I'm gonna bet this ain't a social call. Revealin' you're not that beggar person we'd known over the years tells me you want somethin', and I've got a feelin' it's about me. So, what do you want?"

Mera thought for a moment. He'd played out the conversation in his mind a hundred times over the past few days: how he'd carefully outline the truth for Reyne, men from an alternate Earth in another dimension with evil intent, enjoining the young man to his cause. Now that he stood before Reyne, seeing him, feeling the young man's desire for a simple life, to make a home with Mithany, Mera understood convincing Reyne to leave Hensdale for a larger objective, a dire purpose, wasn't going to be easy. But that didn't change anything. It had to be done.

"You've lived in Hensdale your whole life." Mera dangled the words in an inflection that left them ambiguously somewhere between a statement and a question.

"That's right."

"Well, not exactly."

Silence hung in the air.

Reyne slowly took his eyes from the flames to face Mera. He tilted his head as if to say he wasn't sure what he heard.

Mera searched Reyne's face for clues, like he was studying a treasure map but couldn't find the X.

Mera waited.

Reyne said nothing.

Mumbling under his breath, as though struggling to set a hook with a fish on the line who wasn't biting, Mera said, "If you only understood how much depended on you."

A hint of annoyance struck Mera's ears in Reyne's reply. "What's that supposed to mean?"

Ignoring the question, Mera asked one of his own. "Do you know what's going on in the rest of the world?"

"Who gives a shit? Let's get back to what you said."

"*I* give a shit, and so should you. And it's got everything to do with why I'm here and what I said about that 'not exactly' comment. It's all tied together." Mera mixed in small intrigues for Reyne, hoping to tweak his interest, his desire for answers. He wasn't ready yet for the big reveal; Reyne wasn't primed. More foundation-of-understanding needed to be laid down first. "Tartica could use your help."

In a calm voice, Reyne explained, "I'm a simple businessman. Don't give much consideration to the rest of Tartica. I got enough in my life to keep my mind focused right here in Hensdale. I got a business to run. Lots of people depend on me and Daedyn. And Mithany and I are gettin' married in a few days. I don't need you or anythin' you're about to shovel my way to upset those plans. I don't care what the rest of the world is up to or where it's goin'. Life around here's been the same for a hundred years. Nothin' out there is goin' to change that anytime soon. So, keep your 'not exactlys' to yourself. I ain't interested in hearing whatever you came here to say."

Reyne turned and walked away.

Hum, where did that go wrong... Comments about the rest of Tartica I suppose. The realization gave Mera pause before taking another run at Reyne.

"Please wait," Mera said in a calculated, heartfelt appeal. Mera understood people. If he offered anger in response to resistance, Reyne would dig in his heels. But, it was difficult for Reyne or anyone to shut out a weak, pathetic reply as though kicking someone when they're down. Some could. Mera counted on Reyne not being one of them.

Mera waited.

Reyne stopped after a few paces. He paused without turning back. "Why should I?"

"Because your dream of a quiet life with Mithany on this outpost of reality is in genuine danger of being destroyed." He let the threat germinate before continuing, "Soon."

Reyne turned, took several strides towards Mera, and looked the former vagabond in the eye. Close in, face to face, Reyne exploded, "What, you think I'm an idiot?" Spittle flew out with each word, and his arms flailed about wildly. "They need us. Alphens feed the poor all across Tartica. Hell, just five nuts a day is enough to fight off fatigue and hunger. There ain't nothin' any of those morons would do to upset alphen production. We're not the only ones producing 'em, but we contribute our share. They leave us alone because they need us. I'm just a small orchard, but the powers-that-be need me. It suits them the way things are now. Nothin's gonna change that." Reyne drove his finger into Mera's chest.

Mera didn't blink when sputum slapped his face, and his chest accepted the offense. He took every bit of Reyne's anger and didn't back down. He softened the look in his eyes to show Reyne he wasn't hiding anything. "At least hear me out. Will you do that much?"

"Know this. I haven't heard one word of what you're sellin' that interests me. But I'll listen because you may have saved my life. After that, we're done." His voice trailed off. "I'm goin' back inside. We'll finish this later."

Well, that went a little better. He's open to listening. One step at a time.

Reyne started to walk away again. Mera reflected, *No, it can't wait till later. Gotta do it now while I have his attention.* Mera looked around, making certain no one else was about. "Reyne!" he called out.

Reyne stopped and turned around. Mera rolled up his sleeve and plunged his bare arm into the burn pit. Reyne gasped and ran towards the open fire. In the few seconds it took for Reyne to bridge the gap, Mera's arm was deep in the flames. Reyne tried to grab him to pull it out, but Mera held out his other hand as if to say, "Stop."

Like a statue without feelings, Mera stood unmoving, without fear, without pain, as the fiery heat flickered against his arm. It commanded Reyne's full attention. His jaw hung open and the look on his face made it clear: Reyne couldn't fathom how the arm appeared unmolested by the intense heat or why Mera wasn't withering in pain.

"That's some trick," Reyne said, moving his hands towards the flames as though to prove to himself it wasn't real, but quickly yanked them away from the hot sting biting into his skin.

"There is so much more to reality than you know. No trick, my young friend. There is life everywhere, in everything. Believe it or not, in these flames, too.

"I show you this to open your eyes in the hope I can make you listen, make you understand, make you trust and believe. To change your mind about walking away from me." Mera's arm remained plunged in the pit of fire and tongues of flames licked at his limb as he spoke. "Things are moving faster than I had hoped, and you need to come up to speed. You and I don't have the luxury of time I'd hoped for. The woman with the red eyes, Arek's new girlfriend, is not what she seems—she's here to kill you."

The Firaché

Hensdale: 27th Day of the Salmon Moon

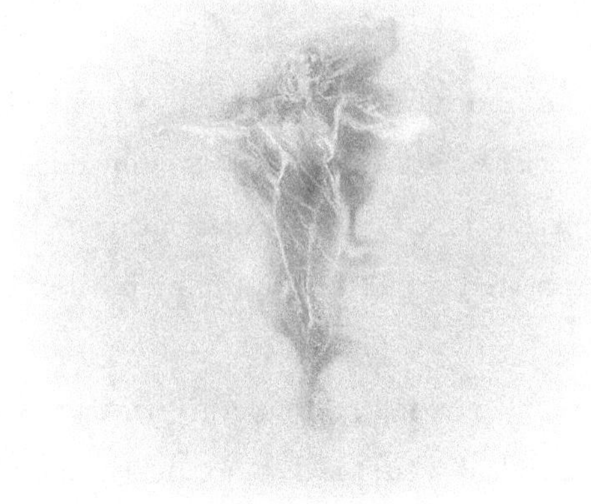

Reyne

The words of someone wanting to kill him seemed to burn away in the flames that rose and fell all around Mera's arm. Reyne's thoughts were locked on the yellow and orange flares slapping and rolling over Mera's limb as it hung like a ham hock roasting on a spit. To Reyne's astonishment, Mera's arm resisted every effort of the intense heat to seer its flesh. Slowly, Mera pulled his arm from the burning pyre.

Reyne immediately grabbed it in both hands. Confusion gripped him, realizing even Mera's tiny arm hairs escaped unmolested. Reyne ran his finger over its length, searching for any signs of burn marks, but there were none to be found. The door guarding Reyne's understanding of reality had been pried open—if only just a bit.

"How's that possible?" Reyne searched Mera for any sign of falsehood, coming away empty in the effort. Again, he stuck his hand toward the flames, yet quickly pulled it back from the intense heat.

"I showed you this because I need you to understand. There're events taking shape that threaten everything you know. I'm hoping to stop those behind it, and I need your help to succeed." Mera's plea sounded desperate.

"What, I'm gonna give everything up just because you can stick your arm in a fire? Not gonna happen, Mera. You're gonna need more than some magic trick."

"Magic? Magic is what you can't explain. Things you don't understand. Magic is a word that describes something everyone thinks impossible when they see it happen. What you witnessed is real. So accept it and understand this: what you know about reality is incomplete—and it needs to change. To that end, please, indulge me one more time. There's more I need to show you. Gather up some small branches and a few twigs, then place them here next to us."

Reyne considered the request a moment before giving in and went about gathering wood. Mera pulled two stumps closer to the pit and sat down. Reyne dropped the pile and Mera patted the stump next to him, inviting Reyne to take a seat.

"I'm going to introduce you to a life form you never knew existed. You're going to have to accept some things that, in your current state of mind, you'll think impossible. I'm going to show you one of those impossibilities right now to open the door for what I'm going to tell you later."

Mera reached out to touch Reyne's forehead. Reyne slapped Mera's hand away. "No, please," Mera shot back as he tried again, only to get the same result. "Please trust me. I need to access your Eye of Heaven so that you might see."

"Eye of what? Another trick?"

"Please allow me," Mera asked as he deliberately placed two fingers on Reyne's forehead, "it's called the Eye of Heaven. Some call it the Third Eye. It's a part of the brain people never consciously use. Right here in the front of our brains, a part of ourselves we give away freely to the forces around us but never access what it sees. With it open, we can see the hidden reality all around us, or at least part of it. I just need to open yours a little," he said, with fingers resting on Reyne's forehead.

"What nonsense are you sellin' me? Did you do somethin' to me?"

"Do you feel any different? Do you see differently? Think, hear, smell anything that's not the same?"

Sheepishly, Reyne replied, "No."

"Good. I would like to introduce you to the Firaché. They're fierce and short-lived communal beings that have much to offer. But people never see them. Their minds are closed to such things. Almost everyone I've ever known, their Eye of Heaven is closed." Mera moved his arm once again into the flames.

"I still don't see nothin'."

"You will," Mera commanded as he closed his hand around a single column of flame. Then opened it again as though releasing something unseen.

In disbelief, Reyne saw flames taking on human-like shapes dancing all about the pit. Red, blue, orange, and yellow insubstantial forms coalesced from within the pyre. Mera's arm swept through and mingled in with the creatures made of fire. They reacted by moving aways from Mera's open palm—as it probed for something within the blaze. Reyne scrutinized Mera searching through the flames with outstretched fingers.

Without warning, Mera snapped his hand closed as though he snatched a fish in water, struggling to wiggle itself free of its captor.

A hot arc shot out through the fingers of Mera's tightly held grip. It flickered and squirmed about like a man being held around the throat. Reyne flinched in disbelief as flames struggled to free themselves from Mera's clenched fist. He couldn't believe his eyes, watching the effulgence fight for its release.

He heard a woman's voice coming softly somewhere from within the enflamed wood. Reyne jerked back and fell off his stump.

"Who calls to me and my people?" They were words in their own way, somehow formed from the sounds of the burning, hissing logs rising out through the flames.

Volumes of fiery phantoms mixed in with—and became one with—the blazing specter held tight in Mera's grip. "It's only me, your old friend Meratoruc." And he loosened his hold.

Dusting himself off and settling his buttocks back onto the stump, Reyne sat—his jaw hung open. He saw apparitions take shape as they flickered and danced: human-like forms in the fire, small, tiny, and large. Bodies swaying as flames incarnate. He saw what looked like arms held over heads, waving wildly about, swaying from side to side, growing, shrinking, constantly moving.

He saw faces, large and small, appear from the base of the blaze and sink slowly back into the mass of fire. Reyne saw small creatures, all naked forms, men and women, in an orgy of ecstasy. Hips of all different shapes and sizes, thrusting, then swallowed up by larger flames.

Fire-shaped bodies, all naked, racing about in physical form that looked like ghostly demons existing somewhere between flames and humans. Other fire-beings pounded at the logs with their flame fists, ripping at the wood with flame-like claws, sending embers into the sky.

He stared deep into the fire where the flame creatures, a hundred, maybe more, entwined in seductive dance. Flame men with erect phalluses chased down nubile flame maidens. Fire-hands groping fire-breasts of all shapes and sizes. Others making passionate love, causing the fire to grow larger, hotter.

Humanoid shapes starting out as small embers, growing larger as they rose up, growing even larger, almost half the size of a child, reaching up at the sky, wildly waving their flame arms before dissolving back into nothing. A face the size of his own rose out of the inferno to stare at him briefly, only to turn away and to bury itself between the thighs of another Firaché. Flame hips thrust up and down against the flame face. As a flickering tongue lapped between the other's thighs, hair of fire-threads danced along the back of its head before being swallowed up by even larger flames.

Fiery lovemaking was everywhere, dancing everywhere, fire-figures of men and women of all sizes, everywhere. A large phallus pushed higher from the small log, fiercely flapping about until a mouth from out of nowhere took it all, and flames instantly exploded all around it. How long Reyne stared deep into the phlogiston, he couldn't be sure, but it was a voice he heard that pulled him back from his trance. Arms waving, rising, reaching out with fingers of fire, searching for something to grab. Reyne couldn't look away.

"I-We am-are the Firaché, and I-We speak for all," the voice said, as the form of a woman's head the size of his own took shape and rose from the base of the conflagration. A word that sounded like "I am we" hissed at him. Flesh so well defined yet fluid red, orange, and yellow swirling on the surface to form fire-skin. As her head reached further above the pit, her hair of white fire flickered wildly upwards, ever upwards.

Her neck rose out of the melee. Fire-skin roiled over fire-breasts and hips as they too rose from the bed of coals like a body rising from a pool of water taking shape before Reyne's eyes. Finally, thighs of fire pushed up out of the wildly dancing forms, fire-arms resting on her fire-hips.

"Tribute, Meratoruc. You must pay tribute," she demanded while burning wood spit against the force of the flames.

Tossing a small branch on the heap of the inferno, the fire-maiden's eyes, deep red and black, blinked open. Her head rolled back with laughter that burned at Reyne's core. "No. You tease me, little man, with morsels. I-We demand tribute," she screamed, flames shooting from her mouth. Tilting her fire-head back, she roared, releasing a blaze high into the air.

"My friend, I will pay your price, but first tell me of what you know of the brothers on this farm," Mera replied.

"No!" she howled again. But this time, Mera pulled his arm back from the flames, her full figure now standing within the conflagration. Beautiful and terrifying, yet mesmerizing to Reyne as both the spectacle of a fire-being that spoke and of the most sensuous female form he had ever seen. Eddies of red, deep yellow, orange, whirling, riding, shifting intense colors played along her skin, forming:

Her face.

Her hair.

Her neck.

Her breasts.

Her torso.

Her thighs.

Her legs. Her long, sensual legs.

It all held Reyne's attention. He couldn't look away. Again, Reyne noticed her voice. It spoke and hissed words. At times it sounded deep, sultry, crackling, and at other times rose to a high-pitched whine, but it was always alluring to his ears.

"These brothers, one of them here with you, tends us well. Now, tribute." Other flame beings, one after another, rose by her side up to the height of her hips. Tongues of flame licked at her thighs and in between them. She moaned in delight before the smaller beings fell back into the orgy pit.

"The young man here does not believe his own eyes. Tell him something only important to him he might not know, and I'll pay your price. Tell him something secret, special. Prove to him your type reveals all that is locked away in the wood, the living matter that sees all that goes on around them. Prove to him you *are* real."

This time, she took a more seductive approach as she held out her hands and reached for Mera's face. He didn't flinch. Orange, red, and yellow flame-skin reached out as smaller flares flickered off her fire-fingertips. She stroked his face, yet the heat did not burn him. He smiled as she reached to pull his lips to hers.

"Tribute," she hissed in a whisper.

Mera held out his other hand. It appeared to touch nothing of solid substance, melting in between her ample breasts. Yet he pushed the fire-woman back with little effort.

"Meratoruc," her words softly slithered and crackled, "please, I-We am-are dying as we speak. I-We need tribute."

"I will feed you well tonight, but first tell him as I asked."

An arm shot out from the base of the bonfire as though reaching for the pile of logs, but the fire-arm couldn't remain formed as it moved further from the pit. "Ahhhh," flames shot out of her mouth as she screamed in a high-pitched screech, having failed to gain the pile of branches.

"So be it." The fire queen closed her eyes, tilted her head back before snapping it forward. Both eyes shot opened—burning a look into Reyne's soul. "Of the girl. They both love. The other brother, not here. He hides his feelings." She stopped. Waited. Then demanded, "I-We speak true of what I-We know of what the wood reveals. Now, tribute!" she shrieked as a conflagration of a thousand Firaché shot upward at her command, taking shape, cavorting, screaming before dying down to a flicker.

Reyne's eyes bulged in reaction at the manifestation. Stunned at the revelation, his mind reeled. Nausea reached up from his gut and threatened to explode at what she claimed. *Daedyn? Mithany? No...*

Mera spoke to the fire-maiden: "You've done well. I will speak with your kind again and will offer praise of you when I do." Mera let go of her fire-form, releasing the Firaché queen.

She slipped through his grasp. The fire queen's form settled down into the communal pit. A multitude of fire-bodies descended on it. En masse, they licked, lapped, fondled, and thrust against it in a feast of carnal pleasure until her form disappeared from Reyne's eyes. Her words spit out from the center of the fire in orgasmic release, "Tribute."

In a single motion, Mera threw the entire pile of branches onto the bonfire. With a roar of embers and flame, Reyne thought he heard laughter. Fire flickered high into the sky, turning back the approaching dusk.

"They haven't gone, you know. We're just not seeing them as we did a moment ago. I released them, but the lives you saw are still dancing and playing as we speak. They are celebrating the brief lives they have. What you saw, you might think of as debauchery. It's not. They're just making the best of what little time they have trying to reproduce and grow their community. They revealed themselves in forms you and I can understand. They don't exist in the human-like shapes you and I saw. They live in the natural state you see now."

"Is it possible that I just saw that? That was real? And Daedyn has feelings for Mithany? I'm not sure which one is more unreal."

"They're as real as you and I. And what she told you is true as well. I showed you the Firaché so you might look at the world and know there is so much more to it, and well beyond. I am challenging what you believe, so you might accept what I have to say. It'll be hard to believe any of it. If things were different, if we had more time, if I got to you sooner, perhaps there's a different way. But the girl Arek called Neladith is a problem. She's a dangerous assassin who is here now, and she wants you dead. I can guarantee she's not alone. I have to take you away from here so they can't find you."

"My head is spinning, and I can hardly believe any of it. And that shit about Daedyn. You said it's real. How can you know that?"

"I don't, but I know the Firaché speak the truth, and they've never lied to me before. I believe her every word."

"Now you say someone wants to kill me. Why? What did I ever do? Doesn't add up. And that fire-babe, holy shit, I can't believe what I saw. Nothin' makes sense. I need time."

With his head hanging low, Mera stated firmly, "*We* don't have time. *You* don't have time."

"Leave me alone!" Reyne's face couldn't hide his inner devastation at the revelation about Daedyn's feelings for Mithany.

"Promise me, before the night is out, we'll finish this conversation. There's so much more I need to share with you."

"Maybe."

"Before we go, let me—"

"How can that fire-babe be real? How could she know Daedyn's still in love with Mithany after all these years? He wouldn't do that to me."

"The Firaché showed you something real. They knew more than you about Daedyn's feelings. Or was it something you already guessed? You said it yourself. He's indifferent to this marriage. Why isn't he happy about it? If the Firaché are right, your brother's been hiding it from you. If they spoke true, you must accept that what you saw was real. And if the Firaché are real, consider the danger you are in... is very real."

"I gotta admit, I thought he just resented her, you know, rejecting him. All these years later, I never guessed he still carried a torch. He took his shot, lost, and gave up. So I took my shot with her. She picked me."

"Understand this: she spoke of you beyond what I know." Mera rubbed this hand along the arm just pulled from the fire. "And it wasn't without a considerable cost to me to show you the Firaché. They don't burn my flesh, but let me tell you, their bite hurts like hell. It takes a considerable effort to do what I did, and I'll pay the price over the next few days."

"Okay. I'll admit I saw something. What, I don't know."

Mera nodded as the two men stared into the fire. "Talk to Mithany and Daedyn later tonight. Yet, in this moment, I shared the Firaché to open your eyes. More than you know is going on. I think—no, I know—you're in danger."

Reyne's head was spinning. The Firaché captured his attention. Their reality couldn't be denied. Mera played that card just right. There was more to the world than Reyne understood. He wondered if Mera's Firaché gambit earned just enough trust between them to listen to the rest of what Mera had to say.

However, Reyne didn't want to hear anything else. The implications for what he believed could all come undone. He was going to get married, have children, grow alphen nuts, and live a happy, quiet life with Mithany by his side. He wouldn't let anything change that more matter what Mera said.

While thoughts of the Firaché wouldn't let go, with his love for Mithany his anchor, he resolved to take whatever Mera threw at him. He could listen and stay the course.

Leaving the fire pit and the Firaché behind, Reyne and Mera walked toward the house. Mera did most of the talking. Reyne didn't believe everything Mera told him, but he listened. The Firaché earned Mera the right to say his piece.

Reyne struggled with one revelation more than anything Mera said. It reset Reyne's life story. His stomach clenched at the revelation. He didn't believe Mera. He couldn't. From that point on, Reyne's mind fought Mera at every word. He gathered his resolve and did the only thing he could. With steel in his voice, Reyne said, "Mera. It don't matter. I ain't goin' anywhere with you."

"Then you're as good as dead."

Belle of the Ball

Teth: 27th Day of the Salmon Moon

Kaythlin

Kaythlin and her husband Madrotti Tomelai were among the honored guests of First Lord Jerithan Cree at the Feast of Teth Banquet, the premiere event of the day. High-ranking religious and secular leaders from the four corners of Tartica, accompanied by their respective staffs according to custom, were all in attendance. Whomever orchestrated Chancellor Tomelai's assassination would be in the gathering of dignitaries; Kaythlin was certain of it and, even more so, determined to ferret out their identity.

First Lord Jerithan held the fete in the Palace's Grand Glen Hall. Kaythlin, with her arm locked under her husband's, marveled at the walls, the ceiling, and even the floor as each contributed to an extraordinary mural scene, reminding her and every attendee of the power of nature and of humanity's place in it.

A basic tenant of the Temple of Life placed humankind as only one of the many creatures of the world, all created as equals, beholden to Mother Earth for sustenance, shelter, and life. The room dwarfed Kaythlin—as it did all in attendance—under a dome masterfully crafted, sitting one hundred feet above the floor. Her eyes followed the giant sequoias of The Stand depicted across the main wall with an opening resembling The Gate at the main entrance to the room.

She reflected on the army of long forgotten artisans who painstakingly reproduced every needle of every tree in such exactness that it proved difficult to discern the reproduction as an artifact.

The unbroken mural rose from the floor, flowed up the walls to reach the top of the dome—every inch in vivid color. Treetops seemed to change hue based on the light penetrating through the strategically placed windows high off the ground, as a ring of glass encircling the dome. On the far wall, opposite the depiction of The Stand, stood the Razors: an impenetrable mountain range bordering Teth to the north. The Razors dwarfed both the city itself and even the majesty of The Stand. Its peaks, many over twenty thousand feet, stood as a reminder of the power of Mother Earth. The Bay of Synn, as recreated on the western floor of the Grand Glen Hall, served as a transition from The Stand and the Razors. The Bay of Synn, a natural wonder, afforded access to the city-state for the vast commerce moving in out of Teth each day.

Kaythlin swept her red high-heel clad foot over the view of Teth as though seen from above like the goddess herself looking down on the city. Tile inlay expertly recreated the Grand Protisium as it traversed the length between The Stand and the Temple Palace, including the spoked roads leading to and from the Palace, the hub of the city. The fields and farmlands standing between the city proper and the Razors, which made up the natural basin sitting between the Razors and the Bay of Synn, were a breathtaking representation of the outlying communities.

Kaythlin caught sight of Jerithan Cree huddled with his supporters, including several of the Prudents who made up his power base. A stroke to Tomelai's hand, signaling to him she'd noticed something he should take note of. Amused at how they fawned over the First Lord, she collected and stored away the insights she gathered from her observations.

Kaythlin kept her ears piqued as the festival banquet afforded every attendee the opportunity to impress any other attendee. Played right, the evening offered the chance to propel a lesser Prudent to a higher status or, for the more carnally focused, a chance to acquire mating privileges for the night. Played wrong, doomed one to the back-benches of Temple leadership for years to come or at worst, one more evening in an empty bed.

Kaythlin mused, reflecting on those who usually played the game of flesh and others whose lust ran deeper than skin and played for nothing less than power. As the Feast of Teth Banquet rolled along, and the candidates vied for position, Kaythlin took it all in. She and Tomelai, arm-in-arm, weaved in and out of the players as they roamed the room, soaking in the sights, the words, and the whispers.

She observed Prudent Serco intentionally turn away from Prudent Hansel's approach. Moments later, she watched Serco catch sight of Prudent Beezup, and head off in his direction.

Tomelai leaned in, whispering into her ear, "Watch for clues. We still do not know who amongst these vultures sent those men in after me this morning. Secrets and powerful forces are at play. The game master is somewhere in this room."

He didn't need to remind her of their shared objective of the evening, to flesh out candidates. With her arm under his, she pulled him in close and teased, "Oh, my love, you know I only have eyes for you." She ran her long, thin fingers through the graying hair of his temple. "It makes you appear distinguished."

"You sure I am not just getting old?"

"You wear it well, dear. It gives off a stately, experienced leader vibe. So does the black suit, the long tails, the white shirt, and I love the sash."

"Now I know you *are* fucking with me."

"No. Maybe. Well, you are so handsome. You have me, you are correct, I've always hated the sash. But you pull off the entire ensemble nicely. You men have it so easy. You put on a dark suit, white shirt, and you appear so polished. What I had to go through, not even close."

"And the results are a testament to your natural beauty and not of the effort."

"You are too sweet, my love."

"The two of us standing here, the Chancellor of Adelle with the First Lady on his arm. Who do you think they are looking at? It certainly is not the guy with the distinguished graying temples."

"Of course they are." Lady Kaythlin raised up on her toes, scrunching them into the front points of her high-heels, to kiss Tomelai on the cheek.

The dressmaker slit Kaythlin's long silk gown up the right side, intending to expose one long, slender, silky-smooth leg—just as the First Lady commissioned it. The effect commanded attention with each step she took. Thin, sheer material clung to her upper frame, only releasing its grip from her body just below the hipline. Fabric, shaped and colored to resemble the yellow and orange leaves of autumn, adorned her dress.

The vivid colors seemed painted on as fabric rolled over her backside. Her dress clung there, rounded and perfect, before gracefully falling loosely to her ankles. Curved hips, set in motion when she walked, created the impression of flowing liquid amber. Form-fitting silk clung to her bosom, accompanied by a low neckline that afforded an ample amount of cleavage to compete for attention. Thin straps of her sleeveless gown crossed along her back, far below the First Lady's shoulders.

Kaythlin understood the effects the female form could have on both men and women alike—and she counted on it. Although the male physique could achieve a similar level of notice—just not this night. While overt sexuality pervaded Tartican culture as a consequence of repopulation insisted upon civilization, its ever-present display didn't inure human nature to its prurient appeal or release any who Kaythlin ensnared in her trap. Once in her grasp, as the ambushed spewed mindless chatter, attempting to impress her towards their own ends, she readily disarmed her captives, extracting unguarded tidbits of information.

To Kaythlin's way of thinking, sexuality, like intelligence or ambition, were mere tools to be employed by those who possessed them and were both willing and skillful enough to do so. She possessed all three, and put all into play as she wandered the room, supported by her co-conspirator husband at her side—a choice she made—as a means to an end.

She was like no other. A brilliant tactician, a consummate observer, and a skilled conversational inquisitor. What she gleaned from watching, listening, and extracting from others was unmatched, unless one considered Druin Derr. But Derr lacked the physical assets of Lady Kaythlin.

Kaythlin overheard the ambassador of the Temple of Life from Kantos tell another, "The couturier who designed that dress is exceptionally skilled." With an imperceptible nudge, she brought the exchange to Tomelai's attention.

However, it was the man standing next to the ambassador whose observation gave rise to Chancellor Tomelai's knowing smile aimed at Kaythlin, when the man said, "Yeah. Maybe. But you gotta believe in the One God, because who else had the power to create such a woman? It is perhaps the pinnacle of all His creations across all of time. If He saw her first, He might not have chased Mother Earth across the heavens. He would have given up on Mother Earth for her. I know I would."

Finishing his admiration of Eurithian as the One God, and of his handiwork, the man drew the sign of the Temple of Life, the Signum Circulus, tracing a circle around his heart with his thumb before resting his palm over his heart.

Tomelai beamed at Kaythlin. She hardly imagined anyone in the room looking in the pair's direction even noticing he existed, let alone he was smiling. She squeezed his hand in a knowing gesture. Kaythlin appreciated that her husband thought her beautiful, admired her for her grace, her charm, but above all, she saw he appreciated her even more for her mind.

Breaking away from the constant attention of onlookers, she said, "Listen to that, Madrotti." She closed her eyes, rested her head on his shoulder, and melted into his arms. "Musicians playing an elegant classic of forest life. Orchestral instruments producing the sounds of chirps, calls, rustling leaves, croaks, and all in a captivating melody. And how they string it all together in harmony as one musical score of mathematical and natural elegance. It's beautiful, Madrotti."

He kissed her on her forehead. "Yes, my dear, it certainly is."

Kaythlin appreciated the talents of musicians who could work in unison to make forest sounds into a full orchestral piece sounding so natural.

She listened as they played her favorite. "If for no other reason than to hear those exceptional musicians play 'The Dance of The Morning Dew,' I am happy to be here tonight. Even our own musicians can't match the talents of this orchestra."

Tomelai whispered in her ear, "I will acquire the Temple Palace Orchestra for you. Not sure how I will get the First Lord to release them. But, for you, I will make it happen."

Pulling herself from the reverie of the orchestra, and Tomelai's promise, Kaythlin glanced across the room to First Lord Jerithan, who continued to hold court. "Madrotti, look over there." She nodded with her chin. "See how the First Lord soaks it up? He loves the fawning attention. The small little clutch of Prudents is attending to every word. Watch his face."

"What is it saying to you?"

"It's saying the leaders of the world and the Temple are all in one place. His place. At his invitation. He thinks himself the belle of the ball. He believes they've all come for him. Of course, the Temple is part of the reason we all attend. Temple followers across the continent expect their leaders to pay homage to the Goddess Teth on her appointed day. But the First Lord firmly believes it is his stature, more than anything else, that is the main attraction this night."

"You get all that from the look on his face?"

"Not just the look. The way he smirks more than smiles when they respond to him. There are no lines around the eyes when he smiles. Real laughs and genuine smiles make lines. He is pleased with himself more so than he is with those he is holding court with."

First Lady Kaythlin and Chancellor Tomelai followed the movements of the First Lord as he pranced around in his adorned, dark-green vestments. Green, the color of nature, the color of life, and the symbol of Jerithan's power.

"You think you are getting a glimpse inside his mind? He thinks all this is about him? The magnificent First Lord. The power behind the rulers of Tartica. It is all about him. The center of society, the center of influence... Jerithan. That is what you read? That is what you are telling me he thinks of himself?"

"That is exactly what I am telling you, my love."

"That is one delusional bastard."

"I must leave you now, my love. It is time." With a soft kiss to her husband's cheek, Kaythlin set off in First Lord Jerithan's direction.

Dance of the Maiden

Teth: 27th Day of the Salmon Moon

Kaythlin | Jerithan

Kaythlin left her husband's side, cut through a trove of banquet attendees, and aimed herself at the gathering around Jerithan. Holding her arm out as she approached her target, she said, "First Lord, will you do me the honor of escorting me through the maze of guests?"

She had one objective: determine if Jerithan had knowledge of who commissioned her husband's death—or, worse, if the First Lord was involved in any way.

As Kaythlin intended, she expected Jerithan interpreted her approach as a self-deprecating act by another of his flock. Not that she believed either she or her husband were subservient to Jerithan's position as First Lord, but if he believed it, so much the better. She had learned early in life how susceptible some men could be to manipulation by beauty spiced with flattery. Jerithan Cree was one such man.

Accepting her arm, Jerithan quipped, "If I may be so bold, together you and I embody the symbols of beauty and power."

"You flatter me, First Lord," she said coyly as the two continued walking through the crowd. "Funny, I don't feel that powerful."

Jerithan's free hand rode down the side of his velvet robe like a peacock preening its feathers. "Then I am left to conclude it must be my beauty that holds their eyes in such captivity. Do you suppose it is my lovely vestments?"

Kathlyn looked back, with Jerithan on her arm, to spy Tomelai nodding his approval.

As the pair navigated the crowd, she extracted updates from Jerithan on each of the Prudents they encountered and who was fighting with whom, although none of the information covered new ground. Jerithan was being careful, but Kaythlin had a knack for extracting savory tidbits from even the most guarded. She considered her next move and thought back to the information Captain Druin Derr of the KCG outlined for her and Madrotti in preparation of their visit to Teth.

Derr had advised her that, although Jerithan had not married, he had sired three children before becoming First Lord. Unlike President Dimenk, his association with voluminous and anonymous lovers fit within Covenant norms. And while visits by a First Lord to a Celebratorium honoring the Gift of Flesh was part of his or her duties, *this* First Lord frequently took pleasure in sampling their offerings. He was also known for repeated inspections of the high-class, secular brothels owned by the Temple of Life. The regularity of both went beyond simple administrative visits.

It was all part of information Derr had provided in a dossier on Jerithan for the Tomelais. Kaythlin considered another approach to loosen Jerithan's tongue—flattery alone hadn't delivered. She reflected on Derr's concluding assessment in the report:

First Lord Jerithan Cree can't be seen as having a favorite amongst the Six Gifts. Not as First Lord. It has too many implications for the flock. His actions are examples for others to follow, and his actions speak for the entire Temple of Life leadership. The religious Order can't afford to be known only for indulgence and fornication. His passion for flesh is one of this First Lord's triggers. We classify it as "a weakness." We can use this to our advantage. Prudents in the highest levels of the Temple hierarchy are aware of Jerithan's proclivities and will at some point use it against him if they have enough support to make a move. The major faction lining up against him, led by Prudent Serco, does not appear strong enough at this time. We developed more on Prudent Serco's faction in part 2 of this report. We can use Jerithan's weakness against him in specific scenarios to our advantage. Our conclusion: the First Lady would be best positioned to line up against the First Lord in a one-on-one negotiation.

In preparation for attending the banquet, Derr, Tomelai, and Kaythlin agreed she stood the best chance of finding out if Jerithan knew anything of the failed assassination—pairing her strength to his weakness. Set to her purpose, gifted with grace, beauty, and elegance, she moved through the room as though a prima ballerina performing a well-choreographed dance with her partner Jerithan, the premier danseur, at her side.

Kaythlin and Jerithan came to a sudden halt, pulling her from her thoughts. Standing before the duo, a Temple of Life novice bowed in a show of respect. "First Lord Jerithan, Prudent Serco said that it would be appropriate for me to let you know how grateful and honored I am to be invited here tonight." The youthful novice, there as part of the service staff, continued, "By the grace of Teth, it is such an honor to meet you."

"What is your name, young man?" the First Lord asked with a hint of annoyance in his tone.

Fumbling with his hands inside the crossed sleeves of his light green robes, obviously nervous, she felt sorry for him. He was beyond his station to interrupt a First Lady and First Lord engaged in conversation. Anyone else of high stature would have put him in his place. They made First Lady Kaythlin Tomelai of different stuff. Kaythlin saw it as an opportunity to take measure of the First Lord. *How will he handle it?* she wondered. She remained silent, looking down at the adoring eyes of the fawning novice, waiting for Jerithan's reaction.

"*Careful, my friend. She is studying you,*" the Voice spoke to Jerithan as he prepared to reprimand the novice.

Jerithan replied in his own mind, *Who is this peon? Who does he think he is, interrupting me, the First Lord? What balls.*

With lips parting as a prelude to the First Lord's expected rebuke, the Voice broke through Jerithan's thoughts, *"Now, now there, play nice. You do not want to distract the lovely lady on your arm. You have a more important game to play tonight."*

The suggestion stopped Jerithan in mid-thought. *"Besides,"* the Voice said, giving him another option, *"we can always crush the boy tomorrow... away from the judgement of others. And let us not overlook that Serco sent him in to get a rise out of you."*

Jerithan liked the idea. *Your point is well taken. I will admonish him tomorrow and blame it on Serco.*

Heeding the Voice's suggestion, Jerithan backed off. "Well, my young devotee, I thank you for your kind words and am pleased that our Temple has one such as you." With his free hand, the First Lord thumbed the Circle of Life on the novice's forehead, saying the words, "From the Gift of Life from Mother Earth, we give thanks by returning to Her that which is Hers and to be joined with Her in the community of everlasting life."

Bowing with both hands still joined under the cuffs of his robe but now much more settled, the novice reverentially said to his leader, "Life from Life, we return our Gift." Having concluded the sacred reply, he couldn't help adding, "Thank you, First Lord. I will remember this meeting for the rest of my life."

"However long that might be," the Voice jumped in for Jerithan to consider.

"Your honor is more than I deserve," Jerithan directed at the novice. "Go with the grace of Teth."

"You lie with conviction and dignity. You make me proud."

Jerithan quietly stepped away from those who stopped to watch.

The First Lord and the First Lady moved on. Placing her hand on Jerithan's, Kaythlin nodded. "Very well handled. I can see why the Temple of Life chose such a magnanimous leader. Others might have been tempted to rebuke the social faux pas the young man made. But you were gracious instead."

She looked into his eyes as though searching for something. It unnerved him as he wondered if her inspection found him lacking. Not letting on what she found in his visage, she said, "What a wise and caring man I have escorting me tonight."

The surge of pleasure at his own handling of the novice's offense was cut short by the Voice. It was one of those rare moments the First Lord wanted silence from the Voice. He hoped to enjoy the time he had with the First Lady of Adelle.

"She is playing with you."

Let me have this, Jerithan rasped. *Let me enjoy this evening. This is MY night.*

He searched his thoughts for the Voice, who was his friend and silent confessor. The Voice that guided him through troubles was gone for now. Turning his thoughts to the striking woman on his arm, Jerithan said, "Now, what were you saying, something about me being wise, or words to that effect? Let's hear that again."

The two of them laughed. Jerithan fancied envious eyes upon him at that instant. He played it for all the attention he could squeeze from it and laughed even louder. Few had his stature, none could compete with his position as First Lord, and in the arena of intelligence, he imagined he had few equals. Bringing it all together in one complete package, as human beings go, he was amongst the rarest of specimens—at least, that's what he believed.

While Kaythlin loved the dance of seduction, she loved the payoff even more.

She breathed deeply. A distraction tactic, intending to appeal to his "weakness" and disrupt whatever thoughts occupied his mind.

Jerithan leaned in and spoke softly into her ear. "You know, I might share some things I've found out about that incident this morning."

She imagined he stole a glance at her cleavage, hiding his purpose for the unnecessary whisper. Yet, in his offering, it appeared to Kaythlin Jerithan wanted to impress her, to let her know he was a man with considerable reach; he was a big man, a powerful man, and well informed.

She had expected their verbal foreplay to last much longer before either approached the main event—the attack in The Stand. Disappointment in him reflected her expectations for someone in a position of power having the air of experience in such matters, more than Jerithan as a man.

Readily willing to accept his early misfire—before she herself put in much effort—she wondered if an additional move on her part could deliver the payoff she wanted. Deciding it worth a try, she stroked his ego. "First Lord, you are a man of many surprises. I would be forever in your debt if you could help me, not as a First Lady but as a worried wife who wants to understand better the dangers her beloved faced today, and maybe beyond."

She imagined Jerithan translated that in his mind to mean: You are such a big man. I didn't think anyone knew about the attack at The Stand. You have sources that reach deep. You are very impressive.

"Please come see me tomorrow," Jerithan offered. "We can talk more about this when we can be alone. Here, there are too many ears about."

With his words, Kaythlin understood their dance was over for the night. Yet, she had partly achieved her objective with the First Lord.

He knew something about it.

She wanted more.

He hadn't satisfied her yet. She wondered if he could deliver more with additional stimulation from her. Slowly stroking his arm, taking another deep breath, exhaling bit by bit, she watched him steal a glance at the fabric stretching tightly across her breasts. "You are so gracious in your offer, Jerithan. May I call you Jerithan, First Lord?"

He beamed an impish grin as though a little boy who got away with swiping a cookie from an off-limits jar. "Of course, Kaythlin. Will you join me for breakfast tomorrow?"

Accepting his invitation, Kaythlin inwardly smirked. Derr had him pegged. An approach to her breakfast meeting with the First Lord began to take shape. She had him, but would have to wait for the information he would certainly share.

Jerithan was rambling now, yet Kaythlin listened to every word. Most of it was of little importance. She kissed him on the cheek, thanked him for his attention. "I cannot keep you to myself all night, Jerithan. Thank you for your precious time. Until tomorrow then."

Their dance had ended.

Kaythlin released the First Lord and walked away. She expected he didn't take his eyes off her. There was no need to turn around to confirm it. She had the measure of the man.

Meeting up with her husband, he filled her in on his night. Tomelai was not idle while Kaythlin probed the First Lord's defenses. Tomelai informed her that he didn't get much from Razoal, but Serco and a few of the other Prudents were freer with their criticisms without Jerithan listening. "You did well to keep him occupied, Kay."

She thanked him. "My love, your toolbox has more power behind it and your results proved more immediate… though less important," she teased.

"Kay, even so, I could not have done none of it without you."

"It all comes down to my breakfast with Jerithan tomorrow. The game is set. He knows something."

He Dies Tonight

Hensdale: 27th Day of the Salmon Moon

Quith

Quith arrived early at the kill site. Across Tartica, the Feast of Teth was waning, but for Selundra Quith hidden in the weeds at the Brenton Family Orchard, the most important part of the day had just begun. The hot-shot young shooter and the team's newest member, Agent Arrow, hadn't arrived. She wasn't late—not yet anyway.

Moments after settling in, Quith glimpsed Reyne walking back from the burn pit accompanied by Meratoruc, confirmation for the Evidarian that Reyne was still alive. If all went according to plan, not for much longer.

The advance setup enabled Quith to ensure he wasn't followed. Careful that way, his attention to detail saved more than one mission from being aborted or worse. In his experience, ops broke down when people failed to carry out their assigned tasks precisely as planned. Early arrival at the agreed-upon location afforded him the chance to watch his team approach and to confirm they too arrived without unwanted escorts.

The two members of the ops security contingent positioned themselves at their strategically designated marks. With security in place, no one could approach Quith unnoticed. The detail of Tylus and Grafph had been with Quith for more than a year and accompanied him on dozens of engagements. Both men were experienced, trusted, and capable. Either could jump in to fill any position if needed. Not as experts, but with sufficient skills to complete the op.

With the advance team in place, they waited. Inactivity, even with purpose, was not Quith's strong suit; he was eager to complete the mission. With Reyne dead, the last of the Tartican Tweeners posing a threat to his version of Earth would be eliminated. It meant he'd be free to return to his world. Quith fared well in Evidar's brutal environs as a man to be feared, a persona he cherished. Most of all he longed for release from the constant sunlight. He needed Reyne Brenton dead to punch his ticket home.

Dusk was fading, and the sweet release of night would soon bathe him in darkness. Quith watched the sun slide below the horizon, round and orange as it dipped. Lighting the trees from behind, it appeared to set the leaves of the alphens on fire in the color of green blood. He welcomed the coming night, preferring the sun do its business and be done with it.

He'd been in the reality of Tartica long enough for his eyes to adjust to the constant daylight and for their redness to leach away, but, like a predator in the dark, he trusted only the black veil of night.

All the while he kept a lookout for Agent Arrow. He'd never worked with her before and preferred not to bring her on this late in the operation, but Dylla forced her on him. The Devil's Blacksmith wanted it that way. Agent Arrow was an unknown variable that made him uneasy. On a precise operation to kill a man, Quith didn't like feeling uneasy. He had his doubts about the high praise for the untested assassin.

How could anyone be that good at such a young age, he wondered.

If late or unable to fulfill her assignment, Tylus would take her place, Quith decided. While he waited, Quith settled in a tall patch of weeds marking the edge of the open field just beyond a line of trees, one hundred forty-two yards from the brothers' home. The switchgrass had grown tall with autumn's approach, and its coloring afforded the perfect camouflage for the wooden tripod support. The setup blended in perfectly.

Quith anchored each of the three-legged supports with long spikes biting deep into the hard dirt. Standing three feet off the ground, the tips of the switchback reeds barely reached the top of the tripod head. Quith stayed low to the ground as he slipped out of his tan and brown camo. Well-suited for daytime, but with evening rapidly stealing away the light, he preferred the operational blacks he wore underneath.

The sun's complete departure, escaping below the horizon, announced evening had arrived. Now, he thought, Agent Arrow was late. With an eerie likeness to a cicada mating call, he reached out to his security team to ask if they detected any movement in the area. Both replied in kind. Quith understood their cicada-like answers; the new agent wasn't anywhere in sight.

As he lay in the tall grass, contemplating Tylus's skills at filling Agent Arrow's assigned role, he felt something crawling up his right thigh. His hands, being quicker than his head, slapped at whatever it was. He smacked the object with the faint sound of skin to skin—only one was his.

A human hand.

Security failed.

Training took over.

Reflexes kicked in.

In a snap, he rolled away from the hand. With amazing speed he spun back. He threw one leg over his assailant, straddling his prey. His knees and full weight came down hard across the intruder's wrists. One hand grasped his opponent's throat, the other readied to strike the attacker. He felt little resistance to any of his maneuvers.

He looked down to see Agent Arrow, the young woman he'd been waiting for. Quith moved one hand over her mouth, but that didn't stop her laughter from leaking through his fingers.

She said in a whisper, "Okay, okay, let me up, Mister Whitetop. Isn't that what she called you back in Owls Neck?"

Quith lowered his head to her left ear. "What the fuck's wrong with you, agent? You were supposed to be here already, and now you pull this shit. You could've given us away with that stunt."

"Oh, be quiet. Besides, what about that crack security team of yours? They never saw me sneak past them."

Quith took her meaning. With that one deception, she had established herself better than the lookout detail he'd put together.

"Get off my wrist, or do you want to take the shot yourself?" Evidar's Agent Arrow—Neladith Karlis—demanded.

Clearly pissed off, Quith never played games when on an op, nor did he accept nonsense from anyone. Not about to start now, her actions were unacceptable. Although disappointed with Tylus and Grafph, he had to admit he didn't detect her approach either.

He rolled off her, letting go her wrists, permitting her to move out from underneath him. "Don't pull any shit like that again. And, if you fail tonight, I'll see you never get a second chance."

Quith put out a different cicada call, notifying the security duo Neladith had arrived.

"Keep your britches on there, Mister Whitetop." Her expression showed no sign his threat had any impact on her.

Calling him Mister Whitetop for a second time set him off. He grabbed her by the collar. Lifted her head off the ground. Yanked her in close. Face to face. Like a rag doll in his hands, she offered no resistance. "I'm your team leader, and I expect you to behave professionally." He shoved her away. "And enough of the Whitetop shit. It surprised me to see you in Owls Neck at the inn this morning with that guy. Is it all just fun and games for you? We have business to get to. I heard you're very good. A prodigy. Maybe so, but I'm the one who has final say in the here and now. This is my op. Don't fuck it up."

"I was ordered to get my ass to Owls Neck. My handler instructed me to wait there for Dylla on news of the success or failure of the first attempt on the target. Oh, I'm sorry, *your* first attempt. *I* wasn't part of that. If needed, Owls Neck was close enough to call me in for Plan B. While you spoke to that girl Mithany at the table when me and Arek showed up, Dylla gave me the nod. I walked here today, out in the open, right under their noses. So here I am, pulling your cajones out of the fire. And, no, it's not just fun and games, and yes, I *am* that good. But why does it have to be all serious and uptight? Killing can be exciting. Plus, we're away from that place. Why not enjoy the peace while we're here?"

"This is your first trip to this world. It's all new the first time in. But it wears on you. You might be enjoying it now. Trust me, it gets old fast. By the time those red eyes of yours fade back to their natural color, you'll be sick of Tartica."

"I'll have to take your word on that."

Her words set off red flags. She liked the time spent away from Evidar. Something he'd have to keep on the lookout for. They'd lost agents in the past to the lure of Tartica's easier way of life. And Quith tracked them all down, one by one. He'd kill her too, if circumstances required.

Dismissing her attitude with the wave of a hand, Quith demanded, "Why are you late?"

"I'm not late. It ain't completely dark yet. You've set up, and the target isn't anywhere to be seen. Second of all, I was quite enjoying the boinking Arek—the guy you met me with in Owls Neck—was giving me. Or I was giving it to him? Doesn't matter." Tipping her head back, rocking it from side to side she added, "Arek's good at it too. I'm goin' back there after we put this Reyne guy down. Killing always gets me all worked up."

Rolling his eyes and lifting himself up on one knee, Quith looked down at the young operative and wondered if she was that good, both in bed and as an assassin. He wasn't sure which excited him more. Killing, and fucking right after, was something he too enjoyed. He saw a lot of himself—as a younger man—in Neladith.

"Get up," he ordered, offering her a helping hand, "and don't call me Whitetop again. Focus. Let's get this done."

Not knowing when to give up—irritating Quith all the more—Neladith poked at a sore spot. "You know, I wouldn't have to be here tonight if you'd gotten the job done with that spiderworm poison." Up on one knee, she attached the two-bow to the tripod.

With a sneer, he swallowed his anger, intent on getting the op back on track. "I was told you prefer the two-bow," Quith stated, evaluating her technique as she secured the two-bow to the tripod.

"Yes. It's unmatched in the force it produces and has excellent accuracy." Handling the bow, she was all business. "See how it's constructed? With two upper limbs and two lower limbs, spaced a hand's width apart, both arms of the bow come together as a single piece at the riser. The two-bow delivers more thrust, providing the opportunity to take the shot from a greater distance. Two-bow strings gather at the center, as though a single bowstring at a precise point. The two-bow design does, however, require precision stringing by an expert not to create a pull left or right. The two-bow requires more arm strength than the standard bow, and it requires endless practice to master."

"By the way you caress that thing, looks like you care for your two-bow better than you do for people."

"The two-bow treats me better than most people. It's dependable, reliable. It's never let me down, unlike everyone else I've ever known. Given the op assigned to us, the two-bow is the weapon of choice. The level of difficulty for the planned shot demands an exceptional weapon. Other than me, that is." She paused, then threw in, "This one ain't mine from home. Dylla let me try it out earlier in the day after she briefed me. It'll do."

"I'm glad it meets with your highness's approval." He paused before continuing, "Reyne didn't die in his bed like we hoped, so Plan B's a go. I caught a glimpse of Reyne with Meratoruc at dusk, out in the orchard. He'll be well enough to attend to the burn pit tonight, just like he does every day. That can happen at any moment, so stay ready. He dies tonight."

Revelations

Hensdale: 27th day of the Salmon Moon

Reyne

Mithany, Reyne, Daedyn, Brenal, Arek, and Mera busied themselves inside the brothers' home. Daedyn, standing alone in the hallway outside Reyne's bedroom door, said something that Reyne and Mithany—lying together on the bed—both ignored. With attention on his fiancée, sharing a pillow, face to face, Reyne delighted in their time alone.

Her fingers fondled the back of his neck. "I'm so happy you're alright."

"Of course I'm alright." He pulled her in, and their lips met.

She ran her palm along his cheek. "So, what's all this nonsense with that Mera character?"

"Now don't go getting' yourself upset. I'm just tellin' you what he said. He thinks someone is tryin' to kill me, as ridiculous as it sounds. He says I gotta go away with him to keep it from happenin'."

He moved in to kiss her.

Her jaw hung open, and she pushed him away. "What?!"

"I don't know what to believe. He's got my head spinnin'."

"Do you trust him?"

"I trust you and Daedyn."

He thought he trusted Daedyn, but the revelation from the fire-queen made him question even that. He considered just how much to share with the woman he loved, not wanting to further upset her. He dared not reveal what the Firaché fire-babe said about Daedyn's hidden feelings. "It's probably all bullshit."

Puzzled and fearful, Mithany's look melted his heart.

He kissed her again. Her soft lips drew him dangerously close to spilling everything. He couldn't withhold anything from her—never could.

Reyne was about to crack with the Daedyn revelation on his tongue when Mithany asked, "Was it about this morning?"

Seizing the opening as a reprieve, "Yeah. Mera says it wasn't an accident. But the way I saw it, it had to be a mistake. I did a dumb thing when I stepped into the wagon passing by."

She held his face in her palms and said, "Because of that, he wants to get you far away from here. That's crazy."

Daedyn pounded on the bedroom door. "Enough already with you two. Rey, let's get this conversation over with. You, me, and Mera. We got things to clear up."

Reyne shouted through the door back to his brother, "I'll be right out! Calm down."

But Daedyn didn't let it go. "Any day now, little brother. If you two are done doin' whatever it is you're doin' in there. Finish up. Get dressed and get your fat ass out here."

Reyne hated being called little brother.

Releasing a kiss, Mithany bit at his lower lip. "He's talking about you. I have a lovely ass."

Reyne ran his hand over Mithany's behind and grabbed a handful of her butt cheek. "Not an ounce of fat here."

She squealed. "There'll be time for that later." She kissed him again. "You're going out there with Mera. Promise me, whatever he says, you're staying put and we're getting married next week. Besides Arek, you're the only one who understands me, and I'm not givin' you up."

"Of course. There ain't nothin' he could say that would stop us from gettin' married. I'm yours, my dear, for better or worse. For the rest of our life, it's you and me. Okay, maybe Daedyn too, 'cause I don't think he's ever moving out."

Reyne rolled on top of Mithany and after the long, passionate embrace, he rolled off.

"I got *my* Reyne back. Stay here with me for the rest of our lives. Besides, who's gonna pull you out of those dreamlike night terrors when you're asleep? You can't leave me."

Her hand slid underneath the waistline of his pants. Teasing, she gave his privates a squeeze. "I'll be waiting here for you. We'll finish this when you get back." Withdrawing her hand she said, "Now get outta here and go tell him you're not goin' anywhere."

"Come with me. We'll face him together. We're always stronger together."

"You flatter me, honey. But this is somethin' you gotta do by yourself. I'll be waiting here for you when you're done. You're gonna make it up to me tonight. Scaring the shit out of me like you did; we're gonna get rid of all this built-up tension. Don't be too long, or I'm gonna have to begin without you."

"You always know just what to say. I like your idea better. How about we get this show started and leave them to themselves and deal with it tomorrow?" He reached under her blouse.

"As much as I love that idea," she said, removing his hand from her breast, "the sooner you talk it out with Mera, the sooner we get him out of our lives. And, I promise not to start until you get back." Mithany ran her fingers through his hair and planted a firm kiss on his waiting lips. "Now get your ass out there, mister."

Reyne walked away, leaving Mithany behind. Joining Mera and Daedyn in the kitchen, he asked, "Where's Brenal, and I thought I heard Arek's voice?"

"They're on the front porch, Bro."

Reyne faced Mera with a hard stare. Stern and determined, he left his feelings of love in the bedroom.

With arms crossed over his chest, Reyne rested the back of his foot against the wall. "Alright. I said I'd listen. So here I am. Let's make this short. You stay, Daedyn. You gotta hear all this, too."

Mera began, "I'm here because of your father."

"What about my father?" Reyne's tone announced he was in no mood for games.

Reyne rubbed at the source of pain coming from the back of his neck. The effort brought no relief, and while it hurt less than earlier in the day, it still hurt.

"Gwerther and Pachelle were as much a father and mother to you as anyone. They raised you and, from my reckoning, loved you as much, if not more." Mera stopped.

"Pachelle and Gwerther are my parents. Because they're dead doesn't change a thing."

Grabbing Reyne by the shoulder, Mera said, "This isn't how I planned to tell you. But it's all the time we have. The presence of Evidar hunters changes everything. You and all you love are at risk. And yes, that includes Mithany and Daedyn. Not just you. So listen." Mera paused and lowered his voice. With open arms he pleaded, "Please, just listen."

The thought of putting Mithany or Daedyn at risk terrified Reyne. It steeled him against Mera's words. He hadn't come to terms with the revelation of the Firaché woman suggesting Daedyn harbored unrequited feelings for Mithany—or if he believed a word of it—or if Firaché were even real. He had no idea how to reconcile any of it. He brushed Mera's hand away from his shoulder. "I'll listen."

His head pounded.

His heart hammered.

A strange fury roiling within threatened to be unleashed on Mera. Something was different about him around this man. Reyne, the nice guy, was being pushed into the recesses of his soul. A different, angrier Reyne emerged in Mera's presence. He didn't like himself this way, but losing his entire reason for being, getting married and having a family, stoked his deepest fear. Those fears fed his growing anxiety, cocked and ready to explode.

Mera spoke slowly. "Just weeks ago, I was racing to a small coastal town, Jarouhar, well south of here, to reach someone just like you. Her name was Lorique. She was a few years older than you. She married a nice fella. They were enjoying a pleasant life together. Like the one you and Mithany want. That's until Evidar hunters showed up. By the time I got to her, she was dead and gone. Her plans, her wants, her desires meant nothing to Evidar's hunters. Like you, Lorique had no clue she had any special talents. Assassins knew what she didn't even know about herself. I thought no one besides myself was aware of either of you. Two others before Lorique had also disappeared in the weeks prior. I got here as fast as possible. To save your life. You aren't safe."

Squeezing his fists tight, Reyne said nothing as Mera's words sank in.

Mera continued, "Please, I mean no disrespect to Pachelle or Gwerther. They were my friends well before I brought you to them. Pachelle was pregnant, about to give birth to Daedyn. The timing was by chance. I arrived here with you a day before Pachelle gave birth to Daedyn. Gwerther waited until Daedyn was born and announced twins to the village. Brenal was there at the beginning. He delivered your brother, Daedyn. I asked him to look over you. Your parents raised you as their own. You were theirs in every way but one."

Reyne didn't want to believe. He couldn't allow himself to. The pounding in his chest grew louder, thundering in his ears with each pulse.

Confusion overwhelmed him.

Fear gripped him.

He readied to strike.

Daedyn blurted, "Reyne, what the fuck is he talking about?"

Daedyn's voice and sudden interruption snatched Reyne back from the precipice. "Believe it or not, this guy says we ain't brothers. Well, not by blood. I got different biological parents. Conveniently, they're dead, and this guy here says he dropped me into Mom and Dad's lap a day before you were born. It's a bunch of shit." Reyne's face burned red hot. Reyne could see the anger in his brother as well.

Daedyn said everything Reyne was thinking. "That's bullshit, old man. Look at us. We're not all that much different. Mom wouldn't have lied to us all those years. Get the fuck outta here."

"You have the same frame, body type, only by chance. Gwerther was a good man—" Mera began before being cut off abruptly.

Reyne spit out, "Stop playing games. Get to the point. What do you want from me?"

It was hard to back off from the discussion about his lineage, but Reyne held back, determined to ferret out Mera's true intentions.

Mera started again, "We worked together, me and the man whose seed gave you life. He wasn't the father who raised you, but nonetheless, he sired you. I don't say these things with any pleasure. It's just what is."

Reyne's heart stirred when he thought of his mother, Pachelle. "You're tellin' me Pachelle's not my mother." Reyne wanted to say more, but the words got stuck in his throat. He loved her and struggled with her death, more so than Daedyn. He didn't press Mera; Pachelle's death hurt too much, even after all these years. Reyne took the conversation down another path. "You're tellin' me, some guy I never knew was my father."

"Yes. I had a close relationship with the man. To put it bluntly, he had the reputation for being a prick. A harsh, demanding man, but loyal to his friends. He took care of the people he loved. He loved your birth mother, and you had a sister. She was barely three. That didn't matter to the Evidar assassin who wiped out your family. Your birth father was also a talented leader, and a man dedicated to—"

Reyne cut Mera off. "Horseshit! Why should I even listen to you?"

"Because it's true."

"Fuck off!"

Outraged, his muscles tensed, his fists clenched. A wild beast lurking in his soul threatened to break free. Yet, somewhere buried below the rage, Reyne harbored an undeniable desire to understand the truth, even if he didn't like it. Reyne's anger protected him from opening a door he didn't want to walk through. If rage stood in his way, he didn't have to look past it to see the truth of a hidden reality buried in the past he didn't want any part of. Someone else would have to knock down the door for him.

Mera said, "I take no offense. When you're ready, I'll continue."

Mired in ire, hurt, and a reluctant longing to know more, Reyne hung his head. His words escaped as a whisper, as though not wanting them to be heard—or answered. "What proof do you have?"

"None."

"Then what does it matter? Pachelle will always be my mother. Gwerther will always be my father. Daedyn... my brother. Why do I have to be someone else's son? Can't you just get to your point regardless of who you say my father is?" As the words came out, a pang in his chest stopped him. He wasn't sure of anything.

Mera slowed his pace and lowered his voice. "It matters a lot. So very, very much."

"What? You gonna tell me I'm some long-lost prince from some fallen king? I'm the long-lost heir to some stupid throne?"

"I wish it was like that, but no. This isn't some fairy tale about a man who would be king. You don't have a secret signet ring, a unique birthmark, or a princess for a sister. You're none of those things, and you aren't the fruit of a kingly dalliance. None of that."

"Then what am I to you?"

"You're the son of a special type of man: a man who did so much for this world even though no one will ever realize how important he was. He was demanding, unforgiving, but he had a unique ability. It's because of that rare ability I hid you away and tried to protect you. Delivering you here to two lovely friends of mine, your adoptive parents, Gwerther and Pachelle."

"I don't believe any of it. And even if I did, so what?"

"You inherited his genes. And because of your lineage, you likely inherited his unique abilities as well. One talent he had, that, in part, helped keep our world a little safer from a foreign place called Evidar. He protected Tartica, all of us, for a lot of years."

"So what am I, the prince in waiting? I take over for him? Is that your plan?"

"The only thing you'll ever be a prince of are these alphen trees, I'm sorry to say. Although, I'd bet you'd make a better ruler than any of the men and women who claim those titles now."

"And now you rub elbows with kings too! Ha! I'm the Prince of the Alphens." Reyne spun about with open arms. "Wait. Evidar? Where is that? I've never heard of it."

"None but a few alive in Tartica today have. Yet the threat from Evidar is no less real, my young friend."

Reyne's face soured. "I'm not your friend."

Ignoring the remark, Mera went on, "Had events gone differently, I'd hoped never to reach out to you. I hoped to watch you live your life a happy nut farmer. To watch you raise a family and grow old. To my dismay and to Tartica's misfortune, it didn't turn out that way."

"Tell me the rest of your tale, beggar." The derogative title was intended to strike out at Mera. "Tell me your fairy tale. Amuse me. I'm a little too old for kiddy stories. Spice it up as you go. Make it interesting. I'll get you started. Once upon a time, there was a beautiful maiden... You take it from there."

There it was again—an anger Reyne couldn't control. The fury lurking in his soul popped its head out. He didn't like himself this way. He didn't recognize who he was becoming. All Reyne wanted was to get back into his bedroom, safe in Mithany's arms.

Mera didn't reply.

Although the silence afforded Reyne the chance to settle down, instead he continued his sarcastic retorts. "Did you promise the King you'd lock me away while he lay dying in your arms? Trot me out only when his kingdom needed saving from some crazed evil dark lord despot?"

Mera's lips drew tight, and he looked down. "It's not like that."

Daedyn remained silent.

Reyne shrugged. "Continue your tale."

"Your biological father died thinking his entire family was dead. Murdered. He never even knew you were born. He deserved better. You were a newborn when I stole you away. Your father and sister lay dead just a few feet away from your mother, who was also dying. They thought they'd finished her off too. I got there too late to stop it, but we were lucky. She still lived, but barely. I had to cut you out of her to save your life. In the end, she held you to her chest just before she passed. Her last breath was your name."

Reyne hung his head. Neither he nor Daedyn spoke a word.

"I would like to say I did it because of the respect I held for your father and the loyalty I had for your mother. I owed them that much and more. Those weren't the thoughts racing through my mind as I secreted you away. Then, I brought you here. A place where my friends, Gwerther and Pachelle, would raise you to be the morally strong man you are today. A place where Brenal could keep you well. They did such an excellent job raising you, and for that, I will always hold them in my heart."

Tears welled up in Mera's eyes.

After a long pause, Mera continued. "Bluntly, Reyne, I need you, Tartica needs you, in Evidar. You're not remotely prepared for it. It's a different world. Dark, dangerous, and deadly. Uncivilized. It holds the threat of destruction over our heads. Of undoing all we know. They've been better at killing than we have. Taking our important pieces off the board. I've tried to protect others like you but, somehow, they had knowledge of all of them. How they acquired it, I've yet to piece together.

"You're the last of those I've tried to hide. Maybe there's more like you, but I haven't found them. You're at risk of being killed by Evidar assassins. They crossed over into our world, and they are hunting Tweeners. And I'm sorry to say they're very good at it."

Daedyn interrupted with only a word: "Tweeners?"

"Tweeners have a rare talent: they're able to move between our reality and Evidar's. It's related to physics, the Many Worlds Interpretation. Two Earths. It's not supposed to happen, the ability to share information between distinct planes of existance. But somehow it has. That's not important right now. Anyway, it's no simple task to move between dimensions. With preparation and guidance, Reyne, like your father, you—"

"And even if I made it to this mythical place, Evidar, once there, what then?" Reyne asked. His words dripped with contempt.

"Maybe you can't," Mera said flatly. "Then again, if you can, you can have a tremendous impact. It's a struggle that's been ongoing for a long time. It's possible that the end of the Second Age, the Great Destruction, caused this duality. Tartica is in danger of being merged with an alternate, disturbingly darker version of Earth, to be consumed by a reality you don't want to know. As shitty as that sounds, there isn't anyone else left from our side who can transition between here and Evidar. Your father did it. You have his genetic makeup and I'm hoping you can do it too. There are people in Evidar who need to die to stop what's coming."

Looking down at his feet, Reyne stated flatly, "I'm not your man." He lifted his head to meet Mera's gaze. "And if I believed half the nonsense you're sellin', I still couldn't leave this place. Can't leave Mithany. Like I said, we're gettin' married next week. Can't leave Daedyn. Can't do it. You want me to go someplace dangerous and kill people I don't know just because you say so? I don't really give a shit whatever your plans are. I'm not leavin' here, and I'm not gonna be part of your cockamamie scheme."

Reyne saw his brother's relief at the rejection of Mera's request.

Mera made one last attempt to sway the young man. "Before you make your final decision, there are three things you need to understand. First, the red-eyed friend Arek met the other day is not of our world. She's not from our reality. She's from Evidar, and the red eyes give them all away. It takes time in the light of day for their eyes to adjust to the constant sunlight here. The red in their eyes fades over time. They don't leave Evidar with red eyes—it's the sunlight they aren't used to. Goes back to their natural coloring, eventually. Evidar is a dark place. Extraordinarily little natural light. They fear the light of day, like human instinct is to fear the dark of night. It's a realm opposite ours in many ways.

"But they're people just like us, living a different paradigm. It's their reality they want to impose on our world. To make this place theirs. Your father-by-birth helped keep Tarica safe from that ever happening. He spent time in the realm of Evidar eliminating those who threaten us. Since he's been dead, things have gotten worse."

"You got no way of proving any of that," Reyne demanded.

"Except for her," Mera shrugged. "The one with the red eyes. For her to be here and to expose herself before allowing the redness to fade… something's going to happen soon. Their only hope was to hide her from me; red eyes mean nothing to anyone else. But they failed at that. I'm here to save you. She's an assassin. Put two and two together. You think that poison in your neck is by chance? You're their target. They want you dead, today, not tomorrow. That's what I fear."

"I ain't sayin' I'm buy any of this, but you said you hid me here in Hensdale. How'd they find me?"

"I don't understand how they could. But, somehow, Evidar knows you're Edruk's son. Yes, that was your father's name. You're in some serious shit, and so are the people around you. If you love them, you'll listen to me on this. You'll take my words seriously. I need to get you away from here. Today is already too late. Tomorrow is even worse. I can protect all of you: Daedyn, Mithany, and Arek, but not all here together. Something bad's been set in motion. Evidar hunters have killed the other Tweeners, like you. Most never knew what they were. I've been too late to save the others. I'm here for you. And there's something else I have to tell you."

Not giving Mera's words time to register, Reyne calmly cut in, "What's this other thing I need to know?"

Deadly Calculations

Hensdale: 27th Day of the Salmon Moon

Quith

Night held its grip tight on the Feast of Teth and had not yet let go. With Reyne and Daedyn inside their childhood home, Neladith and Quith waited outside to steal that very life from Reyne.

As effortlessly as water rolls off a leaf, Neladith had pissed off Selundra Quith. Her offhanded reply and dismissive, "Well, I'm here now," did the trick.

Quith said nothing. The assignment was more important than his pride. He'd deal with her later. He pushed down his anger for the good of the op. When it came to killing, he was a professional, a proven commodity. The op came first.

Neladith made adjustments to the two-bow. It stood secured in the tripod and ready for action. "How far? Exactly?" she asked.

Such a young-looking woman, Quith thought. "You seemed to change in an instant from a disrespectful, insolent whelp into a consummate pro. You're all business now."

She ignored the comment. "Distance?"

"One hundred forty-two yards to the porch stairs. Tylus paced it out a few days ago, and Grafph confirmed his measurement. Just like you practiced for, one hundred forty-two yards."

"Air speed?"

"There isn't any wind, and there's been none all evening."

"Elevation?"

"The change in elevation is a five-foot drop from here to the target area." Quith pointed and said, "You can see the porch from here."

"My natural dark-sight is still one hundred percent. At least this place didn't fuck that up. I think I have a touch of light-sickness but I'm adjusting." Neladith looked up at Quith and added, "I see the red in your eyes is all gone. Aside from all the sunlight, this place ain't so bad. A helluva lot more civilized." Neladith looked out to the porch. "Give me the updated recon report since my last meeting with Dylla."

Quith filled her in on the details leading up to the present moment.

Surprising Quith, Neladith want more details. "Which one, where?"

"I stationed Tylus forty-five feet behind us at twenty-five degrees to the right. Grafph is ahead by fifty feet at three o'clock from our position. As I'm sure you already know," Quith replied. He was impressed by the way she paid attention to every detail. "Tylus to the right and Grafph to the left. They've spotted no one since we set up."

"You sure that's accurate? I slipped through."

She had a point. He had thought the two were as good as any. Now he had to reconsider; unless, of course, she was that good. "Focus on the shot," he ordered, changing the subject.

"The rest of your report, please," she asked, half as a request and half as a command.

As team leader, Quith was in charge. However, in the field, everything and everyone's actions went to support the operator.

On this op, it was the shooter.

On this op, the shooter was Neladith.

Her direct, abrupt tone did not offend Quith. Just the opposite. He respected Neladith more because of it. What he couldn't get over was her age, her looks, or that body of hers.

Selundra Quith had been doing this too long to believe this child-like, red-haired operative was as good as Dylla had promised. He'd seen too many hyped-up newcomers who never measured up under the real-world pressure of an on-site operation. The slightest tension or unsettled nerve threw them off. Success or failure inevitably turned on the little things.

The position from which the shot would be taken was difficult at best. The setting limited the choices of locations, given how far the tree line was set back from the house. There wasn't any other plausible option. Quith wasn't sure it could be done. They'd been assigned the op to kill Reyne Brenton. Dylla gave Quith and his team the order. It had to be done.

This would be their second attempt. The first attempt would have created a better outcome, leaving everyone to believe the young man died from the venom of a spiderworm. Since the poison dart attempt failed, the powers-that-be tapped Neladith. Brought in as a guarantee. It was risky, but Dylla surmised they wouldn't get a chance at a third. Plan B had to work. Failure wasn't an option.

Quith continued his report, "There is a group of people gathered inside the house. Reyne, his brother, the girl from the inn who is Reyne's girlfriend, as well as Meratoruc and the old man, Hollid Brenal. And your boyfriend. You've been briefed on Meratoruc. He showed up earlier today looking old and grungy, but has since changed into the familiar man I've encountered before."

"Any insights about the gathering? Will any of it affect how we're to carry out our op?"

"No. Intel says the target goes out alone to attend to the burn pit. That's still the kill box."

Neladith pushed for more. "Do we know what's going on inside?"

"They've been in there for some time now, eating an evening meal, I suppose. Meratoruc and the target were out earlier by the pit, but I couldn't make out what they were doing my view was partially blocked. I couldn't move, didn't want to be discovered."

He described what time they arrived at the house, their comings and goings, and the clothing they wore. He described each of their heights and approximate weights. Overall, he provided a thorough report.

Neladith came prepped with details on Reyne and Daedyn, along with Mithany—and Arek she knew from firsthand experience. The new variable was the unexpected presence of Meratoruc and Brenal. "I can see two people on the porch. One looks to be Arek, and the other doesn't match any descriptions from previous briefings. He must be the old man Brenal you mentioned."

Quith gave her a quick assessment of the impact of the two new variables. "He's Hollid Brenal who, along with Meratoruc, wasn't expected to be on site. Brenal won't impact us, but Mera's presence could affect our exit strategy and our efforts for up close confirmation of the kill. I'll adjust our after-action on the fly depending on the outcome. I'll make those decisions when needed. If Arek and Brenal are still on the porch when Reyne comes out, you're still taking the shot."

"Roger that. You say it's one hundred forty-two yards with a five-foot drop," Neladith stated, reconfirming the data for the shot. With the two-bow attached to the specialized tripod, she changed the angle of the two-bow three clicks up.

Quith watched her make the adjustment after pulling out a small notebook. Paging through the charts and figures, she recalculated the settings and concluded, "Yep. Three clicks up." She bent down to look through the site. Her hand seemed to follow the arrow's flight, or as she imagined the exact path it would take. She stepped back, studied the scene, and turned back the adjustment by one half-click.

Again, Quith was impressed that she did the calculations in her head, whereas even after all his years of real-world experience, he still needed pencil, paper, and charts to do the complicated mathematical calculations to reach the same conclusion. "Wait, what arrow are you using?"

"The leaded-glass arrows Dylla and I agreed on."

Selundra Quith could plainly see the leaded-glass arrow. "Good."

Glass arrows were delicate and not used often. Failure rates were high given the forces an arrow endures as it bows and flexes after release. Difficult to make because of the annealing process, which was done over and over to strengthen the long thin glass while retaining enough flexibility so as not to shatter. It challenged the skills of an expert glassier to create such an arrow.

Glass arrows were difficult to produce but more accurate than their wood cousins. A thin string of fine lead was embedded in the core along the length of the arrow to combat the natural proclivity of glass to break against the flex forces upon release. Neladith gave him the impression she was not even the least bit concerned she would release it incorrectly. Quith was.

Neladith reflected, "I like the glass arrow because it shatters on impact. Broken glass shards hurling forward with all that momentum, ripping through everything those sharp little pieces encounter. Devastating and deadly for anything living."

Quith watched the delight in her eyes as she spoke of death.

"Double check. Wind?" Neladith asked.

"Still none," Quith replied, having just scratched out the math in his own journal.

"With three up and a half-click back, you're telling me you're calculating a seventy-pound pull weight. That's extraordinary for someone your size. Not a fingertip more or a fingertip less. You expect a drop of eight feet on the pull of gravity over one hundred forty-two yards down, plus five feet down for the elevation difference. With the weight of the arrow and no wind, are you sure you sighted it properly so as not to drift off center?"

"Four-hundred-grain arrow over four hundred twenty-six feet at three hundred fifteen feet per second should be in the air exactly 1.35 seconds, and gravity's pull has been factored into my calculations," she added confidently.

"Check."

In her professional assassin persona, Neladith thanked him for confirming her mental calculations. "I've sighted dead center where we expect the target given his height. With no wind, there shouldn't be any left-to-right drift."

"Now we wait," Quith said. "Settle in. He'll be dead soon enough."

Secrets Laid Bare

Hensdale: 27th Day of the Salmon Moon

Mera | Daedyn

With the hour growing late, Brenal and Arek popped through the front door of the brothers' home to join a heated discussion in progress. Ignoring Arek and Brenal, Mera slapped his hand down on the table.

Daedyn jumped back.

Motionless, Reyne stared down Mera.

Mera lowered his eyes in a gesture directing Reyne to look down. He slipped his hand away from the table, exposing something from underneath his palm. The mysterious item looked to be a dead spiderworm.

"What I'm going to say affects all of you," Mera explained. "Unless Reyne objects, I'll to spell it out for everyone. Do you want Mithany to join us before I start?"

"No. Go ahead. Say what you have to say," Reyne replied.

"*This* dart caused *that* pain in *your* neck. Not some spiderworm. Someone tried to kill you with poison. They wanted it to appear to be a fatal spiderworm bite. They were clever. Tipped this dart with lots of venom. Lucky for you most of it was still on the dart when I found it near the side of the road where you went down this morning. I grabbed it before Daedyn chased me away."

Reyne reached behind his head to rub his neck.

Mera continued. "For the millisecond the dart bit into your neck, it didn't have time to drill deep enough into flesh. The wagon must've knocked it off just as the dart reached you."

Arek piped up in a tone somewhere between his usual effervescence and disbelief, "That's some story."

Mera shifted his eyes to Arek and back to Reyne. "Not a story. The dart says it's real. If you didn't bump into the wagon, we wouldn't be having this conversation. So believe me when I tell you"—he paused and looked at each of them, one by one—"all of you are in danger because there are people out there that want Reyne dead."

Brenal looked to be studying the dart Mera left sitting on the table. "It's true. The spiderworm leaves two tiny fang marks. I saw only the one when I examined you, Reyne. I figured it was an odd spiderworm with a missing fang. Although, I'd never seen a one-fanged spiderworm. The poison dart is right there on the table, and it seems to me Mera's explanation fits together."

Reyne leaned a shoulder against the treestone wall, crossing his arms. "Is that all you got? How do I know you don't carry that thing around with you? Blow darts with poison tips aren't something we come across too often in Hensdale. Makes for a delightful story."

Mera had played out all he had in his arsenal. He hoped the dart would open Reyne's mind a little. It didn't. He had no choice when he said, "I'm sorry to bring this up, but today Reyne and I learned that there is something you brothers share. Yes, you're brothers, maybe not by blood, but brothers just the same, despite all we've talked about here tonight."

Reyne shot Mera a hard look. "Don't."

Mera ignored Reyne's protestation. "You asked if I had more to offer. The Firaché aren't a mind trick. If I can get you to accept that, I hope you can accept the rest." Not giving Reyne an opportunity to counter, Mera turned to speak directly at Daedyn. "Daedyn, it was said today—"

"NO!" Reyne demanded.

Paying no heed, Mera continued. "Let's say I heard this from someone I trust to speak the truth; you hold feelings for Mithany. It wasn't said to cause problems, but offered as an observation."

Daedyn stood silent against the accusation in Mera's voice.

The revelation sent Daedyn's world crashing in.

He'd never admit it.

He never had.

He never would.

Hammer blows struck inside his skull. Explosive forces built up against the adrenaline coursing through delicate arteries struggling to hold it in.

He'd spoken no such words to anyone.

Confessed his love for her to nobody.

Shared his deep secret with not another human being alive.

Ever.

How could they know? How could anyone know? They couldn't. It's a trick. A gambit.

Daedyn's eyes drew tight. "Who said that shit?"

"The Firaché," Reyne replied, giving no further explanation.

Brenal and Daedyn looked at each other and in unison asked, "What's a Firaché?"

Reyne rolled his eyes. "I'll fill you in later. Let's just say Mera wants me to accept that fire can talk! You believe that shit?"

A stillness gripped everyone in the room.

Thanks be to the Goddess Teth Mithany isn't here, Daedyn thought.

As much as Daedyn wanted to hear Mera out concerning the brother's lineage, for both his own and Reyne's sake, he didn't want this part of Mera's so-called truth to be revealed. It would drive a wedge between himself and Mithany and maybe even between himself and Reyne.

His gut retched.

Panic washed over him.

His face burned red hot.

His entire being, body and soul, numb.

Daedyn opened his mouth to speak. His scrambled brain fought to get words out. His reaction would be as important as his words, so he didn't dare hesitate. With every bit of internal fortitude he could muster, he pushed aside the deluge of fear threatening to expose him, for his brother's sake, for his own sake, for Mithany's sake, and for god's sake, he'd never tell his younger brother the truth, no matter the consequences. Reyne and Mithany mattered more. They were to be married. He wouldn't let Mera put a wedge between them with the revelation of his true feelings for Mithany.

Daedyn pushed out the words, "No. What bullshit is that?" Adding a snicker his brother would expect from him.

"Don't you lie to me, Daedyn!" Reyne demanded.

Daedyn held Reyne's eyes in a hard stare. A true bluff. Neither let go for the longest time. Brenal, Arek, and Mera sat back and watched the duel between brothers play out.

Reyne blinked first.

Daedyn heard Reyne let out an uncomfortable laugh.

"You fucker! I almost believed this old beggar," Reyne exclaimed, and with a hard slap to Daedyn's shoulder, turning his face from his brother.

He bought it. It's over, Daedyn sighed to himself. Relief flooded through Daedyn.

Pants on Fire

Hensdale: 27th Day of the Salmon Moon

Reyne | Mithany

Daedyn was a decent liar, but never good enough to fool Reyne. How the Firaché witch had come to know Daedyn's hidden feelings for Mithany didn't matter. Reyne saw the truth of it revealed in Daedyn's false denial. The Firaché had to be real and that meant Mera's tale of assassins might just be as well. More devastating than Mera's belief someone tried to kill him, Daedyn still loved the woman Reyne planned to marry. Under the best of circumstances, either problem on its own threatened to over-match Reyne's ability to rise above it. But with both life-altering revelations crashing in on him at the same time, he was trapped. Walls were closing in all around him—with no way out.

Reyne cared about Daedyn, yet did that let him off the hook? *Do I allow him to think his secret's safe? How long did Daedyn hide this from me? All the way back to when we were kids?*

Reyne lived it. He stood by as Daedyn chased after Mithany. Reyne himself had desires for her too back then, but pushed them down because Daedyn claimed dibs as the older brother. Not that Mithany would have agreed to the brothers' claiming rights, but they had their sibling rules; dibs were dibs. A system worked out between them as young boys as the alternative to settling conflicts through fisticuffs. While the unknowing prize in the childish brotherly arrangement, nevertheless, Mithany held all the cards.

It didn't take long for her to reject Daedyn's advances. After being denied, Daedyn had no choice but to step aside and let Reyne take his shot. Rules were rules. In little time Reyne had won her affections and a loving relationship blossomed. He and Mithany connected as soul mates. In the years that followed, Daedyn never said a word, never showed jealousy, and never made any attempt to break them apart.

He let her go for me. He never let it show. Wow!

The impact of the Firaché revelation didn't have the effect Mera desired—just the opposite. In the realization of Daedyn's sacrifice, Reyne loved his brother even more.

Daedyn gave up so much of himself for me... so I could be happy. Who could do that? Only a man who cares for a brother more than anything else in the world.

Reyne concluded he had to stay in Hensdale for Daedyn's sake, for Mithany's sake, and for his own sake. This was his reality—this was the world that needed saving.

Reyne glanced across the room to see Daedyn, still flushed, breathing a sigh of relief. Daedyn proffered a smile to them all, certain he'd pulled off the lie, but Reyne knew better. Daedyn's unrequited love for Mithany would stay hidden. Reyne didn't see the need to out him. Clear to Reyne, his brother didn't detect he'd seen the truth of it. Reyne suspected Daedyn was too consumed hiding himself from everyone to be aware Reyne had seen beneath the lie.

Pushing off from the table, Mera tipped his chair back and put his hands behind his head. "Reyne, so much depends on you."

Reyne simply said, "No."

"What do you mean, 'no'?"

"Just what I said."

Reyne desperately wanted to go to Mithany. He wanted her comfort. A big, strong, muscled young man, yet he wanted to hide in her arms and feel safe. He longed to hold her and protect her from all the evils in the world Mera spoke of. More than anything, Reyne desired the life he dreamed of with Mithany—and Daedyn at his side.

The sound of a hand slapped hard against a tabletop. It came from the other room. Or at least that's how Mithany heard it when it jolted her from her nap. She'd been drifting in and out of sleep, but was now wide awake. Yet she didn't move. She remained in Reyne's room, curled up in his bed, confident her future with the man she loved was secured.

Muffled voice filtered through the walls and door. She didn't get all the conversation. Sound struggled to find a passage through the dense treestone.

She overheard Mera speak of some revelation. Her breathing stopped when Mera said to Daedyn, "... you hold feelings for Mithany." Straining to listen to every word that followed, she rolled the discussion over in her head. Reyne demanded to know if Daedyn hid feelings for her. She wondered what Reyne thought of it and if he believed Daedyn's denials. She didn't. She'd always known. She never told Reyne. How could she?

She made out parts of the conversation about Reyne leaving Hensdale behind, and how Mera wanted Reyne's help to take on some threat to the world. Mithany didn't understand what lay behind the menace. She listened and gathered in the gist of it: whether or not Reyne offered his help, people were going to do their best to kill him. She didn't get all the words, but she put together enough. Finally, she heard Reyne say "no," and his one-word reply filled her with joy.

Mithany wanted to sleep, to wake up and find the past day had been a dream. She wanted to go back to a time earlier in the day. She wanted to return to the point earlier in the day when she arrived in Hensdale to find Reyne sitting on the porch, when all the world was right.

Reyne abruptly rose from his chair and started to make his way out of the kitchen.

"Where are you going?" Mera asked.

Daedyn shouted towards Reyne, who was disappearing down the hallway to where Mithany awaited him. "I'm glad you're stayin', Bro, but I thought you were gonna make sure the fire in the burn pit is out. There's a lot of trees out there. You just can't leave it unattended all night. Put out the fire. That's one of your jobs. Not mine."

Reyne turned the knob and reached out to push open his bedroom door just a little. He intended only to peek in on Mithany, not wanting to disturb her if she was sleeping. Reyne poked his head from around the door. Her delighted, warm, smiling face grabbed at him from across the room, stealing his attention with just a look.

Reyne reciprocated. Mithany pulled back the sheets, inviting him to join her. Reyne closed the door behind him, and without saying a word, he moved towards the bed.

Mithany's position about leaving her behind, while he and Mera ran away somewhere presumedly to hide, was clear enough to Reyne. Mithany wanted to get married, and so did he. Not at some date in the future, but next week: just like they planned. She was kind in her words but firm in her heart when he left her alone in his room earlier. She wanted him to stay.

With the others locked out on the other side of his bedroom door, Reyne heard Daedyn say to someone, "She can make that boy do anything."

"I can still hear you," Reyne shouted back without turning his gaze from Mithany. Once more, he yelled over his shoulder towards the closed door, certain Daedyn would hear him, "The fire pit can wait. I'll get it later." For Reyne, it wasn't a hard choice.

"Fuck it. I'll put out the fire," Daedyn said, mostly to himself, but loud enough for everyone in earshot. "We're not done with this," he said to Mera.

Take Aim

Hensdale: 27th Day of the Salmon Moon

Quith

The day honoring the Feast of Teth slipped further into night. A short distance from the brothers' front porch, Neladith and Quith remained positioned in the tall grass—waiting. The pair of assassins, having already set up, were prepared to strike from just beyond a nearby tree line in the dark, the way they liked it. They needed only for Reyne to emerge in order to accomplish their deadly assignment.

"Nothing's happening," Quith said, stating the obvious. He pulled his field glasses from their case. Darkness prevented scintillation from the sun's reflection bouncing off the glass lenses. "You want a look?"

"No. I trust your assessment."

"You sure it's balanced perfect?" Quith asked.

"Balance perfectly. The hardest part of this shot is going to be the timing. If he moves down the stairs, it's going to affect my judgement. It's only four steps. Not a lot of time to calculate the target's speed to lead him properly."

"You making excuses? You haven't even missed yet. Where are the extra arrows?" A concerned look grew on his face.

"No excuses, just want you to know how difficult this shot is so that when I make it, you'll be in awe. Oh, no other arrows. Only the one. It's all I'll need. It's all I've ever needed," she said confidently.

Cocky bitch, isn't she, Quith thought. *Hope she's that good, and my missed attempt on Reyne Brenton will soon be forgotten.*

The evening grew dark, and the moon hung low just above the tree line. The ops leader monitored the unfamiliar orb hanging in the sky as it creeped on through the night. The moon, the stars, and even the sun hid from them in their world. He shot out a cricket call to his security team. The expected reply came back, music to his ears.

"You know, I didn't expect to see you at the inn in Owls Neck, and I certainly didn't expect to see you with that boy," Quith said.

"Well, compared to an old guy like you, he's a boy. But he isn't, not really. He may appear young, but he has all the skills of a much-practiced older man. Skills I definitely appreciated and expect to again," she replied with a grin. "You're right, though. In other ways, he acts like a boy, grabbing my boobs in public because he loves playing with them and thinks no one's looking. Not the behavior a young lady expects. If I'm being honest, I kinda like the thrill of getting groped in public."

"Either way, it all worked out. You're here now."

"I made it here without a hitch. What better way than out in the open with the fiancée of the man you're gonna kill, along with her brother? Great cover. And he was quite attentive to me on our walk back to Hensdale. Oh, here's an interesting thing we encountered on the trip. Came across something they call a Great Yetgnal. Big beast, nine feet tall. Hairy fucker and smells awful. But, the guy you call a boy, he couldn't have been better. Don't worry, I'm not attached to him. If he gets in the way, you'll have no objections from me. Remind me after to tell you more of that story about how he stood up to a Great Yetgnal. Delightful story. Ends with someone shitting their pants."

"Good," was all Quith said in reply. He couldn't help thinking how he wished he was that young man, then added, "Young lady? Lady? Who would that be?" he laughed.

"Fuck you. I am so a fuckin' lady."

Quith shot one finger to his lips. "Shhh," then pointed. "Look. The door is opening. Get ready."

Consequences of Deceit

Hensdale: 27th Day of the Salmon Moon

Brenal | Daedyn

After Reyne slipped away to join Mithany in his bedroom, Mera and Arek sat at the table with Brenal. Daedyn paused at the door he'd just nudged open. It looked as though he was about to leave to tend to the fire pit, but the engrossing conversation between Mera and Brenal anchored him where he stood.

Brenal said, "Mera, it seems there's much you haven't shared with me over the years. I've seen a lot of unique wonders in this world, but what you just spoke of to Reyne is beyond what I can come to terms with."

Mera, his friend of many years, didn't trust Brenal enough to share the truth with him. It hurt Brenal.

"When you brought the newborn Reyne to Pachelle and Gwerther, you asked me to watch over the boy, to keep him healthy and to keep you posted on his developments. Now I feel used more than anything."

"You *are* a dear friend, Hollid, and have been for a long time." Honesty tinged with sadness mingled in Mera's words. "I didn't share this important information with you for a reason."

Brenal couldn't hide the hurt he felt, and pain was written across his face. Thoughts came and went of what he might ask Mera to find a small measure of comfort in what felt like betrayal. None seemed sufficient to the task.

"You must think me a terrible friend," Mera declared. "I asked you to watch over Reyne all these many years, only sharing with you he was an abandoned newborn. I didn't lie. The murder of his parents left him an orphan"—Mera paused—"I wanted to share the truth of it, but didn't dare risk it. Your counsel and keen mind would've been a great resource and an even greater comfort. But I couldn't do it without putting your life and that of Sura's at great risk."

Still feeling the sting of betrayal, Brenal cut him off. "And now you feel no such compunction. What? I'm expendable now that the job's finished. Having done your bidding over these past twenty-odd years, I'm no longer needed? So you can tell me now?"

It was apparent to Brenal his words hurt Mera, as he intended. Brenal did what most people do when someone hurts them. He hurt Mere right back.

A *tsk* escaped Mera's mouth. "Of course not."

Those words hung in the air as the moments seemed like hours. Brenal was defiant. He would not be the one to break the silence, the one to fill the void as demanded by human nature.

In the end, Mera breached the quiet. "I've always known what I do puts my life at risk, and I accept that for myself. I couldn't do that to you. Not to a friend. How could I ask you to jeopardize what you had with Sura? Even now, what price would you pay to have her back?"

Brenal had always been a kind and gentle man, but not at that moment. "You can't use her like that. She cared about you, too. You can't!" he demanded in anger.

"And what if I did?" Resentment leaked out in Mera's reply. "What if I did share with you all this? And what if Evidar agents discovered you were my confidant... like they discovered Reyne's whereabout? What if Sura paid the price of our secrets? What then?"

Mera went on, but his tone faded back to one of empathy, "Would you have understood? Would you have been willing to forgive me? With a pain in my heart, I kept this and more from you. If it costs me your friendship now, then that's a price I don't want to pay, but I'll accept it with great sadness, knowing it was best for you all these years."

Understanding came slowly to Brenal. Seconds passed into a minute or longer. Time seemed to move so very slowly when there was nothing but an empty void staring down at troubled friends. Brenal ultimately came to understand Mera's point. He missed Sura too much.

With a sense of finality to the understanding they'd reached, Brenal felt Mera's hand on his shoulder, in an unspoken acknowledgement of their reconciliation: a reconciliation born of need.

Mera smiled. "Now these kids are in a helluva lot of trouble. And I need your help to save them."

Standing in silence with his hand still on the doorknob, Daedyn hadn't moved during Mera's and Brenal's tense exchange. From his position, he could see the door to Reyne's bedroom was closed. Feigning anger at his brother, Daedyn yelled loud enough for Reyne to hear. "As usual, little brother, I'm doin' your work. I'll tend to the firepit. And I'm taking your special coat. Dad's old coat. I'm keepin' it. It's mine now."

No reply came back, but Daedyn didn't think he'd get one. He knew his brother too well. It bothered him every time he gave it any thought: Mithany chose Reyne over him. He was also jealous of the influence she had over Reyne. Influence he once had.

Or maybe it was the one thing his heart never accepted?

She wanted Reyne.

She didn't want him.

Thinking about it, Daedyn was getting more annoyed with each passing moment. He wasn't mad at Reyne, not really. And he wasn't mad at Mithany. But it wasn't the way he wanted it. His anger wasn't pretend anymore. It was real. Daedyn turned his attention away from Reyne's bedroom. The pain of what lay behind it stung more than usual.

Pushing open the front door, he muttered, "Pussy-whipped little prick." Yet, he admitted to himself, *Guess I'd be doin' the same thing if I was alone in a bedroom with her.*

Just before stepping through the doorway, he reflected. *It's good Reyne ain't leavin' Hensdale. You'd think I'd be used to them two by now.*

He stepped out, closing the front door behind him.

He paused for a moment on the porch, looking out over the alphen grove in darkness, thinking about the changes to come after Reyne and Mithany got married. Mostly, he felt sorry for himself. He feared the bond between him and Reyne was starting to slip away. Years ago, he'd accepted losing Mithany to Reyne—forever. Now Reyne and Mithany were getting married. They'd still be brothers, but Mithany would be living with them permanently. Things were going to be different.

Looking out, Daedyn noticed the flames had faded, yet the embers lingered. *Ironic*, he thought, *much like the dying flames of hidden love.*

Daedyn let himself pause there on the porch, consumed in self-pity. Not that Reyne was going anywhere with Mera, but losing him to Mithany was an even greater forfeit. Grief filled his heart as he stood there—alone in the dark.

A Shot in the Dark

Hensdale: 27th Day of the Salmon Moon

Neladith

"You sure that's him? Your call, leader," Neladith questioned Quith.

Quith's team gathered the intel.

They scoped out the target.

They chose the location.

As team leader and on-site spotter, it was Quith's job to confirm the target and to tell her whether to proceed with the kill order.

Three short chirps escaped Selundra Quith's cupped hands. A moment later, the same three short chirps came back. Confirmation from the security detail the package had arrived.

"You heard the reply. You can almost make out his face. And look, the height. The shoulders. That hair. The jacket. He had it on when I saw him earlier at the pit with Mera. The target wears it to go out at night and sometimes in the morning. That's him. Take the shot," Selundra Quith ordered.

Making only a slight adjustment for the target's position on the porch, with the arrow nocked on the bowstring, Neladith drew back the leaded-glass missilette. There would be no pull to the right or left. The four bow strings, two from above, two from below, came together at a single spot—dead center. Sighted in line with the target's body, but above the target's head, Neladith accounted for gravity's pull on the arrow as it sped through the air.

She calculated it over again in her mind: drop rate, weight of the arrow, pull weight, speed, and distance of travel. The target's position changed from the strike zone they'd anticipated at the bottom of the steps to the top of the step where he now stood. The target remained motionless. All the better to shoot at a still object.

She released.

The snap and twang of the bowstring sounded perfect to her trained ear.

Neladith admired the way Tarticans measured time—a concept absent from her home world—it added an extra layer of precision to her skill set. She and Quith could only hope the target wouldn't move in the next 1.35 seconds.

Childish Games We Still Play

Teth: 27th Day of the Salmon Moon

Kaythlin

The Grand Ball hosted by First Lord Jerithan was breaking up. The Chancellor of Adelle, along with his First Lady and captain of the KCG, walked together towards their sequestered rooms inside the Temple Palace. The halls deep inside the palace were empty save for the three Adelleians. Noise drifted on the evening air, delivering muffled voices fading ever further with the growing distance between the Palace's Grand Glen Hall and its departing guests.

Enough real estate to offer private conversation separated the Tomelais and Derr from the other retiring Ball attendees. The appearance of isolation moved Derr to say, "Good. We can finally talk. Rotti, someone tried to kill you this morning. To remove your playing piece from the board. It can't go unanswered."

Kaythlin slipped her arm through her husband's. She nestled her head into his broad shoulder as the pair walked arm in arm.

"They will try again," Derr stated flatly.

Tomelai stared down the long hallway.

Spoken in dulcet tones, Kaythlin said, "My dear Druin, you are not going to let anything happen to my love."

Madrotti Tomelai moved his free hand over his wife's arm.

"Gentlemen, I have been thinking," Kaythin began. "Perhaps there *is* a way to put an end to it before any further attempts are made."

"I defer to that strategic brain of yours," Derr said, making a bowing gesture as he walked. "Let's hear what you have in mind."

Kaythlin looked around, making certain they were free of prying ears. "Follow my line of thinking. Take yourselves back to the time you were boys. Well, you are both still boys in so many ways. You are just playing more dangerous games."

A chuckle rolled off Tomelai.

Derr's face showed no reaction. It rarely did.

She continued, "So, what did you two do when you were off playing some silly board game as children? Madrotti, as usual, you were losing. Forgive me, my dear husband. I am certain Druin exaggerates." She squeezed his hand and laughed. "In any event, how many times, Madrotti, did you grab the board and throw it up in the air? You ended the game and denied Druin victory. It is exactly what you need to do in the Council of Nations tomorrow."

Tomelai and Derr turned to face each other. Two pairs of eyes narrowed in unison. Tomelai tilted his head to the side. The men engaged in what looked like a silent discussion, and both reached the same conclusion. Derr announced their mutual decision, "The Covenant. Of course. That'll work."

Tomelai's forehead wrinkled, apparently rolling the idea over in his mind before a broad, evil grin took over. "Kaythlin, that is the answer. You are brilliant." He wrapped his arms around her, lifting her off the ground, and affectionately twirled her as though dancing in the empty hallway. "And Drew's version of those childhood stories—well, he is full of shit."

Derr ignored the retort. "We still need to determine who was behind the attack this morning. When we do, we *will* exact our payment, of that, there is no doubt. That game hasn't even been set up to play yet. And I have to agree with Rotti. Kaythlin, you are an exceptional gamemaster. You may have just saved your husband's life."

Kaythlin's feet once again touched the ground. She looked up into Madrotti's eyes. "It has never been attempted. It will create complications, unforeseen consequences. But I do not see any other path to put a stop to further attempts to assassinate you. You, my love, are strong. You will weather the storm that follows."

Till Death Do Us Part

Hensdale: 27th day of the Salmon Moon

Neladith | Quith

On the porch, standing alone in the dark, the man hadn't moved. If Neladith had done the math correctly and if she executed her shot precisely, he had mere moment left to live. The slightest error would mean failure—her failure.

The arrow took all of 1.35 seconds to reach its target. Exactly as Neladith calculated. She did everything right.

Good for her.

Bad for him.

Without a sound, the leaded-glass arrow entered the back of his neck, just below the base of his skull. The arrow shattered on impact. A multitude of broken razor-sharp shards ripped through his flesh. The target didn't cry out; he couldn't—it was already too late.

With excitement rushing through her, Neladith pumped her fist as the target's body slumped forward. His torso hung over the railing. With limp arms draped over the banister, blood dripped, gushed, and spurted from deadly, ravaged wounds. Slowly, the body slid down the balustrade, stopped only by the newel post at the bottom of the stairs. Debilitated, dying, or maybe already dead, it came to rest.

"Nice shot!" Quith exclaimed in hushed tones.

Neladith smiled. Her shit-eating grin spoke well enough to her meaning. She allowed herself a few heartbeats of quiet adulation from Quith, to revel in the glory of her success, before responding, "Of course it was." Joy leapt from each word, proud at the death of another by her hand. "Yep, I'm that good," she added, blowing across fingertips bent back against her palm.

"How in the hell are you able to achieve such accuracy? That porch is four hundred twenty-five feet away, and you dropped the projectile into an area no bigger than my thumbnail. Amazing." Quith gave away his true underlying appreciation for her skill. She reveled in it.

As though taking a celebratory lap, she explained, "It's a rare thing I do. It requires precision, specialized equipment, planning, mathematics, understanding dozens of variables, and endless, relentless, unforgiving practice. And you helped as a spotter. But more than anything else"—she paused for effect before delivering the grand finale—"it's my skill as a marksman that made it possible." She bowed, sweeping open arms across the scene.

No other operative under Quith's command could have made the shot, and she knew it. She saw Quith did as well. This extraordinary result, she thought, proved her value to the team and made her indispensable. Her first *official* kill couldn't have gone better.

Neladith hit the target with flawless accuracy, but this was Quith's operation as the team's leader. He intended to reap the accolades from Dylla and the Devil's Blacksmith for its success. His own failed attempt to poison Reyne would soon be forgotten.

The new agent, Neladith, while overconfident and even a little arrogant, did back up her bravado with results. He allowed himself to be proud of her. However, as well as she performed, Neladith had one more lesson to learn. Quith expected it to go down hard; Reyne Brenton was dead, and he would make certain all the glory accrued to him. "Let's get outta here," he told her. "We stay here too long, someone will spot us. They'll discover the body soon enough."

The duo broke down the lethal setup in a flash. Slipping behind a row of dense trees, Quith and Neladith met up with the other team members.

Quith congratulated them all before issuing after-action orders. “I’ll meet up with Dylla in Owls Neck in the morning and debrief her on the op. Again, nice work, Neladith, and you guys too. Good to work with you all. Neladith, these two are heading back, but I want you to stick around a day or two with this Arek guy. We can’t do a body inspection with Mera there. He’s too dangerous. But we still need post-op intel and kill confirmation. You have any problem with that?”

She nodded in acceptance of the assignment and asked, “Do you want to leave one of the security guys behind to confirm whatever I report?”

Quith continued, “I’d like to, but Mera has too many tricks up his sleeve. As soon as he realizes what just happened, whoever stays behind will be in danger. Not you, though. You’ve got excellent cover with the Arek boy. In any other op, but not this one with Mera out there. You stay, confirm the kill. Let’s see what the fallout is. Find out what Mera does in response. See if he has anyone else that we don’t know about. Neladith, I’ll find you after I’ve talked with Dylla. Good job everyone. You all have your orders. Now get the fuck out of here.”

“You sure, boss?” Tylus offered. It sounded more like a demand than a question. “I’ve been doing this a long time. I respect the threat the man’s skills bring to the dance, but I’ll be alright. We need to confirm we got our target, especially after what happened on the first try.”

Anger flared in Quith at being reminded of his own failed effort. He tamped it down. “Nothing to confirm. Two heartbeats in the air, and it landed dead center.”

Neladith added. “I’ll be fine on my own.”

“He’s dead for sure. I’m leaving only Neladith behind. She’s well-placed. I don’t want to hear anything else about it.”

Neladith, Quith, Tylus, and Grafph went in different directions. Staying low, working their way through the trees, it was doubtful anyone, even the most well-trained operative, could make out their movements.

Reyne was dead. Selundra Quith was certain of it.

A Grisly Discovery

Hensdale: 27th Day of the Salmon Moon

Mera

With Reyne and Mithany huddled together in Reyne's bed and Daedyn out on the porch, Brenal and Mera, with Arek looking on, had come to terms about Mera's withholding of information of Reyne's true origins from Brenal all these years.

Changing the subject—after Mera and Brenal faced the difficult emotional breakthrough that threatened to undo their decades-long friendship—Mera blurted out, "Hey. What about Arek over there? He's been quiet. Arek, tell us about your new friend."

"Don't worry about me. I'm doin' fine. As for my friend, her name is Neladith, and—"

A muffled thumped coming through the front door from outside stopped the discussion cold. Curiosity overpowered the trio, and Arek left talk of Neladith behind. "What do you guys suppose that was?"

Mera shrugged. "Daedyn's still outside. I'll go take a look."

Brenal stood. "I'm coming with you."

"Sure, leave me here alone," Arek complained. "But if it's anything exciting, give me a yell."

Brenal was the first out the door, and it took less than a heartbeat for the men to realize what lay before their eyes. Daedyn's body hung over the banister. Blood was everywhere. One droplet, then another, dripped from his neck into the gruesome red puddle below. The horror of it locked out the rest of the world. Brenal appeared fixated on the drips, oblivious to Mera's gyrations.

In a panic to get around Brenal, Mera leapt down the stairs to Daedyn's limp body slumped over the railing at the bottom. He grabbed Daedyn, lifted him off the newel post, and spun him around. Mera came face to face with Daedyn's bloodied and torn flesh with lifeless, open, empty eyes staring back at him.

Daedyn was dead.

Mera wanted to yell out for Reyne, but didn't. Nor did he carry Daedyn's body up to the porch. Settling it back down, his anger flared, *Fuck! Fuck! Fuck!* His head bobbing up and down with each internal utterance.

In all his years Mera had seen life's tenuous hold fade from the living too many times. With clear intent and due respect, Mera carefully turned Daedyn's body over, leaving it in the exact position where he'd found him.

His blood curdled at the seemingly cold maneuver.

His gut twisted knowing what he had to do.

With fists clenched, he knew he'd failed.

I told these kids I'd keep them safe... protect Reyne... his family. If I could only have convinced him to leave with me. Fuck!

Without warning, Mera was burning hot. He'd lost control over the effects of the Firaché on his body. Normally, he dissipated the heat built up with each Firaché encounter over several days. Facing Daedyn's death, he let down his guard and the resulting stress-induced anxiety opened the door for the residual Firaché-infused heat inside him to pool near his heart.

Mera struggled to endure it.

He had claimed victory over the side effects of conjuring the Firaché every other time. Bearing down with considerable mental strength, he quietly dissipated enough heat to gain control of the residual energy he absorbed from the Firaché still coursing through him.

Several minutes of pushing through the exerting heat-releasing process brought him back from the edge. He'd continue to disperse more in the days to come, but he'd done enough to return to the only purpose driving him: to save Reyne from his brother's fate.

What he had to do next would tear him up. But it had to be done.

Mera composed himself and turned to face a visibly shaken Hollid Brenal, who hadn't moved. "Hollid! Hollid!" Mera's words were sharp and harsh, trying to break his friend from the trance that gripped the gentle old man.

"He's gone, Hollid."

Hollid Brenal stood motionless, dazed, staring at the bloodied, lifeless body of his friend. "My god. Why? And when did it get so hot out here?"

"Never mind the heat… Hollid, look at me. I need your physician skills right now. Reyne needs you. We're going to walk into that house in just moments, and we're going to tell the young man inside his brother is gone. I don't expect it will be easy or that Reyne will handle it all that well. So please, pull yourself together and tell me what you make of this. I know what I see and need to know if you see the same thing. We've got to be on the same page, so I can offer Reyne an explanation he won't question."

As Hensdale's only medical authority, Brenal examined every dead body in the small village over the past several decades. Mera knew that since the passing of Brenal's wife, facing death was hard for the old man. Every death reminded Brenal of what he lost. Mera suspected Brenal's medical training and years of experience was all that enabled him to push through his inner torment.

Brenal said, "What explanation can you offer him? His brother's dead. There's nothing you can say to that boy inside that will mean anything. But I'll share with you what I can. These marks *almost* look like claws ripped through Daedyn's neck."

After a long pause, pointing to the ground, Brenal continued. "But it wasn't an animal. You see these broken shards scattered about? They tell the tale. See this puncture hole right here?" Brenal said, pointing at a spot on Daedyn's bloodied neck just a few inches below his ear.

The country doctor walked around to view the body from below Daedyn's lifeless head. "Look here. The same round puncture came all the way through. It's not a natural wound. Couldn't have been made by—"

Before Brenal finished his thought, Mera interrupted. "Yeah. I saw that too. And those glass fragments confirm your assessment. I've seen this before, but not in a long time. These are fragments from a rare weapon, a glass arrow. Can't be any doubt. Death was the intent but not meant for Daedyn," Mera told his companion. He looked up from the body to scan the area. "I'm sure they're gone by now," Mera concluded as he gazed out over the landscape.

"What're we going to do?" Brenal's head hung low, as though searching the ground for answers.

The only reply the dirt offered either man was the guilty broken shards strewn about.

Mera gently rested his arm around the hunched shoulders of the visibly shaken, sweet old man.

"Reyne needs to comprehend the danger he and his remaining loved ones are facing. Cruel as it might be, Reyne must see this scene just as we found it."

Mera's heart sank at the idea of using Daedyn's death. "We don't have any option, Hollid. Daedyn's wasn't the first death I've witnessed. And trust me, there will be many more. Too much is at stake. Reyne has to experience all the horror you see before you, without either of us lessening its impact on him."

"That's an awful idea. When did you become so heartless?"

"This isn't heartless. It's necessary if I'm going to save his life. You think I like this idea? It rips my heart out to do this to Reyne. It tears me up inside. But there isn't any other way. Or do you want to be the reason that young man in there suffers the same fate? It hurts me to do it. It hurts me to even say it. But it's got to be this way."

Brenal offered nothing in response, and in looking away from Mera he appeared to be studying his boots.

Mera shook his head. "I think it best you tell him that his brother is dead. He'll focus his anger on me if I'm the one who tells him. He might get violent."

"I know," Brenal answered without looking up.

A Lesson in Power

Teth: 27th Day of the Salmon Moon

Kaythlin

Inside the Temple Palace bedchamber assigned to Kaythlin and her husband, the pair prepared to turn in after a long day.

Madrotti Tomelai dropped his sash, got undressed, and wrapped a towel around his waist. "The evening went well, Kay. Did you enjoy the ball?"

"Yes, I did, my love. Mostly for the time we spent together. Yet, we have the unfinished business of identifying who ordered you out of the way. In the morning, I will do my best to find out what Jerithan knows. He's invited me to some one-on-one time with him over breakfast."

Tomorrow she'd focus on Jerithan. Tonight, she'd have Madrotti.

Madrotti plopped into a sitting position on the bed, wrapped only in a towel. He'd held on to his muscled physique despite his advance into middle-age. He angled his arms behind his back with knuckled fists pressed into the mattress, as though striking a pose. Kaythlin's eyes took in his carved torso, broad chest, defined pecs, and wide biceps. She enjoyed the view.

She slipped out of her dress and stood motionless for just a second, sans clothing, knowingly stoking his desire. Madrotti appeared to be consuming her with his eyes as he scanned her from head to toe. She reached for a robe and slid one arm into its sleeve.

"No, don't," he pleaded.

With a telling smile and a tilt of her head, she ran her other arm through the other sleeve. She shifted her hips, whirled the robe's white cotton belt in circles a few times before securing it in front. Taunting him, she pulled tight both ends into a knot as though accentuating an answer to his unspoken desire.

"Down boy," she teased. Kaythlin had control. In the moment, all the power in their relationship belonged to her, and she wasn't going to give it away that easily.

"You are perfect, my dear, in every way."

She didn't have to be told, although she did enjoy hearing it from the man whom she craved would love her once again someday. In a playful, less-educated affectation she said, "Ya ain't so bad yourself, big fella." In her role as First Lady, always a pillar of charm and grace, now alone with the man she loved, she was free to express the playful inner woman she hid from public scrutiny.

He slapped his hands together in prayer and rocked them back and forth.

"Let's return to the discussion of breakfast tomorrow." Refocused on business, she strung him along. "I am happy to contribute to the cause. I do not mind putting my assets to use at breakfast with Jerithan Cree," she said, wiggling her fingers, spread wide apart, while riding her hands over her breasts and down along her hips. "We are in this together." Her words spoke of business, while intentional movements reeled him in.

An intimate advisor to her husband, Kaythlin regularly took part in the formulation of plans and strategies more than anyone other than Derr. The First Lady was insightful, having the talent to glimpse what people hid behind their masks. Dedicated to her husband, she wanted their love to be like it was before he became Chancellor. Her hope for love's return meant she would never betray him. Although the path back was blocked by his single-minded desire to hold on to power, she never stopped trying.

While he may have let love slip away, it was always clear, he still needed her, wanted her, and desired her. She understood he wanted to love her, yet his kingdom demanded too much from him to hold on to both power and love. In the crucible of life—as the married Chancellor of Adelle—after all else burned away, his true love, power, remained. Kaythlin, the intelligent, compassionate optimist, understood her husband simply lacked the ability to manifest love and to hold on to his kingdom at the same time. She also accepted her husband's limitations—being born of human frailties—knowing few people could. It was a choice only the most powerful ever had to make.

She made a choice, too. But unlike Madrotti, she chose love.

Kaythlin, accepting his failings, lived on hope, and waited for moments like these. She had his undivided attention and intended to use every bit of the fleeting power she held over him to pry open the doors to his heart in order to secure evermore territory on the beachhead of love. And capturing new ground had other prurient rewards that delighted and enthralled her.

Knowing she couldn't lay siege this soon, she continued driving Tomelai into the open. "It's Jerithan's meeting, so he's expecting something in return."

"He will want information from you, Kay. He wants to learn if I have anything up my sleeve when it is my turn at the Council of Nations. He is going to want you to tell him how hard we are willing to push for electrics. Tell him we will go all the way. He is not going to like what he hears, but you will deliver it in a pretty package. As you have said before, distract them with something to focus on in the one hand while hiding what is really going on in the other."

Kaythlin joked, "Are you suggesting breakfast with me is not enough for Jerithan? The man obsessed with the Gift of Flesh? An enjoyable morning meal with a pleasant-looking woman whose full attention is on him? When does he often get such a chance?"

"It would be enough for me. I wouldn't be able to think about anything else."

Love may have escaped over the years, but the lust between them remained strong. She was not only smart and attractive; she was exceptionally talented in ways only a husband might experience. In turn, she appreciated that his bedroom skills could match hers—talent for talent. It kept their lust alive while she waited for love's return.

Pursing her lips while puffing her cheeks, she replied, "I know you too well." With one hand flat against his chest, she felt his heart pounding like a schoolboy's.

He slid his hands down along her hips, trying to reach under her robe.

"You'd never be able to finish your breakfast." She smirked, removing his hands and returning them back to his lap. She looked down at his pleading expression before walking across the room.

"Suppose I owe you a bit of thanks for wearing that robe. Otherwise, we would never get through this discussion."

"So that is what you think this is? A robe. It is no such thing. It is gift wrapping for your present."

Turning slowly around to face him, she let the loose-fitting garment drop to the ground, revealing her naked form underneath. She gracefully stepped over it. She moved towards Madrotti in careful, dainty steps.

From his place, sitting on the bed, Madrotti looked up at her approaching. A devilish grin took shape and stretched from ear to ear.

She was slow to reach the bed, teasing him with each soft, intentional placement of a foot. Kaythlin rolled her hips, accentuating her feminine qualities with every step, teasing him with the object of his desire at the center of it all. Each step gingerly placed with purpose: she wanted him to take her all in. With exceptional confidence and style, she glided across the room. She followed his eyes. He didn't blink. He couldn't.

Stopping in front of Madrotti, seated on the edge of the bed, she wanted him to explore her with his eyes, for her own pleasure as much as for his. She watched him do so, ever so slowly. The intense desire in his eyes fed her own.

But not yet.

To her purpose, she required him ravenous.

He reached up to place his hands on her hips. She stepped back. Out of reach. She turned from him. Walked away. She headed for the drawing-room.

As Kaythlin sauntered further and further from Madrotti, she smiled, confident he burned red hot with desire at the sight of her from behind.

"Hey!" Madrotti pleaded, sounding like a spoiled child whose toy had just been taken away, his hands still hanging loosely in the air. "Where are you going? Oh no, do not leave me like this," he said, looking down at the rise in his towel.

Power comes in many forms, my love, Kaythlin reflected, strolling away from him with every step.

She held all the power at that moment and didn't intend to give any of it away. Kaythlin remained sequestered for a few brief minutes. She had no real reason to leave the room except to heighten his anticipation and to make certain he understood she was in charge, not him.

Kaythlin reentered the room, adorned only in a smile. Slow in her approach, with all the intention of agonizing him, ever aware he was in awe of her. Her eyes followed Madrotti's as he studied her. She must've made the same approach a thousand times, and yet his face spoke as though it was their first.

She was smart enough to recognize she had other strengths. But this one pushed past his lust for power. She held this one authority over him. With his guard down, what she did with it once he let her in, well, that was her chance to claim additional territory in his heart.

Kaythlin remembered Madrotti's own mother—in the woman's prime. She refused to use sex appeal as a tool because she believed it degraded women. She couldn't stomach being treated as an object of desire. The logic of it made Kaythlin laugh. When in love, fires cannot be left unattended to die. Kaythlin understood the impact of desire on the heart. When it yearns to be quenched, denial does not extinguish its hold. Like water, it will seek the path of least resistance. Madrotti's father frequented the beds of many other women throughout his marriage.

Silly woman, Kaythlin mused. She would not see Madrotti turned away like his father had been. Love may have slipped away, but Kaythlin had a firm grip on Madrotti's want for flesh.

Enticing a man's desire is but a single arrow in a woman's quiver. It's ours to be pulled out when we want to use it. If Father Sun would chase Mother Earth across the heavens for eternity, hoping to have his way with her, it speaks volumes about who really holds the ultimate power.

Kaythlin saw the truth of it regardless of its unsavory social construct. It was an unfair advantage that some women held over some men. Like the raw force of nature she was, it would be silly not to use it. She had one purpose, well maybe two, in drawing the naked arrow she aimed at Madrotti's heart. *Power is power, in whatever form it takes.*

She stood before her husband, who hadn't moved from his seat at the edge of the bed, and put one of her hands on each of his knees. She spread his legs apart. Kaythlin lifted one of her own legs, rested a foot on his chest, and with her toes, she pushed him down flat on his back. She tossed his towel aside and lowered herself to her knees between his.

As their lovemaking progressed, she didn't surrender herself to him. They took turns leading. The expression of their mutual desire went on long into the night, demanding much to fully satiate the lust they had for each other.

Kaythlin hoped she'd capture new beachhead. Madrotti was worth saving. In the morning, breakfast with Jerithan Cree came next—he wasn't.

What Can't Be Unseen

Hensdale: 27th Day of the Salmon Moon

Reyne | Mera | Mithany

At the instant Daedyn's death registered in Reyne's mind, his life changed. His reaction was born in a place beyond his control. In less than a heartbeat, unfathomable grief exploded in his core, radiating through his frame, out through his arms, down his legs, up through his gut, and impaled into his brain. It ripped love, joy, happiness, and every pleasure he'd ever experienced in his near-twenty-two years from his consciousness as though any of it ever existed. The agony coursing through him burned white-hot. It denied him control of his limbs; his thoughts; his breath.

His legs buckled. He gasped for air.

Reyne's soul was on fire, in searing pain, demanding release.

With the end of the first heartbeat, Reyne's pain found purchase in an outlet he could not restrain. He screamed in anguish with every burden his body suffered to give voice to—in releasing his all-consuming grief. The awful sound paled compared to the conflagration of anger, as though a demonic beast incarnate tried to devour his soul.

An endless wail poured out of Reyne.

Terror spread through the orchard as the creatures of the night scattered at the horrific sound.

Reyne's left hand started to tremor. Then the other. His eyes rolled back into his head. His legs no longer kept him upright, and he plunged forward. His face crashed into the ground. Mera reacted fast, but a full-body convulsion had overtaken Reyne by the time Mera reached him.

"Fuck!" Mera spat, turning Reyne over on his back. Blood flowed freely along a gash on Reyne's forehead. The deep cut held little interest for Mera.

Reyne's back arched high off the ground. His legs flailed wildly. Boots kicked at the hard dirt with his heels. His pupils aimed somewhere hidden from sight; his eyes exposed only the whites.

Mera's head whipped around to face Doc Hollid. "Hollid, it's the poison!"

Hollid, heartbroken over Daedyn's death, stood motionless, as though frozen in time.

"Dammit! Hollid! He needs you. It's the poison."

Brenal snapped to, "It could be... but it might be shock. It might be both. His body, reacting to the trauma of seeing Daedyn, would've forced his blood pressure to spike. The high blood pressure could've pushed whatever poison's still in his system through his body. Or, it could be an extreme panic attack. It could be any of them or could be all of them."

"Fuck! Fuck!" Mera's head jerked up and down with each utterance.

Hollid warned, "Mera, his tongue."

"Mithany, grab me a twig. I need to keep his mouth open,"

She didn't move.

Mera shouted, "Now, woman! He doesn't have much time. Move your ass!"

The demanding tone in his voice broke her trance, and she jumped to find a twig nearby. Breaking it into a smaller size, she handed it to Mera. He struggled to pry open Reyne's mouth fighting against the young man's spasmodic thrashing. Mera forced it open only to lose the battle a moment later. Reyne's jaw snapped shut, slicing open Mera's fingertip. Blood flowed from the wound, but Mera ignored the bleeding. He jammed the broken stick between Reyne's teeth, preventing him from biting off his tongue.

Mithany looked on in horror, powerless to do anything for the man she loved... helpless... again.

Still flailing, Reyne faced the danger of broken bones.

His head rocked back and forth, slamming into the ground with tremendous force. Once, twice, three times, the back of his head crashed into the hard ground. The impact threatened to fracture his skull.

Mera threw his full body weight against Reyne's forehead. Changing position, he carefully held Reyne's head down with his palms and sat atop Reyne's chest, pinning the flailing arms to the ground with his knees.

"Dammit, Arek. Help me. Hold down his legs."

It took only seconds for Mera and Arek to gain control. Reyne took deep, hard breaths. The grunting continued from a place buried within his gut, as if a wild beast, struggling for its life, trying to escape the deadly maw of some unknown predator. Howls spewed out as unintelligible sounds. Reyne's unconscious body battled to free itself from Mera's hold, as though something inside Reyne had taken control. It fought back with the strength of three grown men.

Against all odds, Mera and Arek held him down. With Reyne's arms pinned to the ground, Mera turned Reyne's head to expose the poison dart wound. With his right thumb, Mera pressed hard on Reyne's neck, where the deadly venom entered. A droplet of blood forced aside, with his thumb against the puncture site, Mera began circling movements. Slowly at first in imperceptibly small orbits, then faster and faster he spiraled it around. Reyne's eyes shot open and then his eyelids slammed shut. The beast within seemed to surrender as Reyne stopped moving.

Arek released his control over Reyne's legs and stood alongside his sister. She slipped her hand into Arek's.

Reyne's eyelids flickered open, then closed, then open, over and over, while Mera's thumb whirled too fast to be seen by the naked eye.

Mithany, Arek, and Brenal watched it all as Daedyn's dead body lay only feet away.

Mera was Mithany's only hope of keeping Reyne from joining his brother in death.

Mera, straddling Reyne's chest, commanded Mithany's attention.

Her body shook uncontrollably. Tears flooded her eyes. Her heart pounded. Her chest heaved, as though ready to explode.

She'd lost Daedyn only moments ago, and now Reyne was seconds away from death. It was more than she could withstand. She loved them both. But she chose Reyne. She wrapped her arms around Arek's and held him tight.

Mera stood as her champion, fighting against an unseen force was locked in battle over the outcome—Reyne's life. Mithany didn't really know this mysterious man, and yet Mera was her only hope.

Faint and light-headed, awareness of everything around her began drifting away. Shadowy figures replaced the solid images of Mera and Reyne. She pushed back against the monumental grief threatening to steal consciousness from her.

Her legs betrayed her.

They went lax.

The world around her grew darker.

Her mind reeled.

Everything was spinning around at lightning speed. Dizzy, a haze descended across her vision. She was losing the battle.

Mithany fought to hold herself together, and like Reyne, she was in danger of failing. There was no one to save her. They had all their attention on Reyne. Consciousness began to fade. She mustered every ounce of inner strength her meager frame allowed and clung onto Arek more tightly than she ever held on to anything in her life. Pressed tight against his body, his heartbeat anchored hers in a momentary reprieve. She had to be strong for Reyne.

He is going to make it. I have to be here for him.

With determination, she focused on Mera's vibrating, circling thumb. Reyne's eyelids suddenly stopped flickering and slammed shut.

His body went limp.

Mithany screamed.

Mera lifted his thumb off Reyne's neck a fraction of an inch. A thin thread of a sticky, pale-yellow liquid stretched between the site of the puncture wound and Mera's thumb. Less than a single droplet made up the tiny strand of powerful poison.

Mera moved his thumb further away from Reyne's neck. The wafer-thin yellow substance stretched even finer before snapping, jerking the liquid from Reyne in the process. It came to rest entirely on Mera's thumb.

Mera inspected the toxin, then moved it nearer to his nose, sniffing at it as though searching for clues. With finger and thumb, he rubbed and squeezed what little remained of the venom, releasing the foul stink it offered. Mera continued the delicate kneading procedure until the material spread so thin it evaporated before Mithany's eyes.

Mera sat on the hard ground. He pulled his knees to his chest, closed his arms around his bent legs, and rocked back and forth, never moving his gaze from Reyne's limp body.

Mithany took a seat next to Mera. Tears flowed freely down her cheeks. Agony invaded every cell of her body.

She wept, fearful death held the man she loved in its grip.

Her mouth hung open in a silent scream.

Mera looked over to her. He rested his hand atop hers.

"I've done all I can. All we can do is wait."

Plans Within Plans

Hensdale: 28th Day of the Salmon Moon

Mithany

Midnight came and went for those gathered at Reyne's home. It was no longer Daedyn's home. Tension pervaded the group in the ever-present morass that hung in the air as Reyne threatened to join Daedyn in death.

Earlier, Mera and Arek moved Reyne's unconscious body to his bedroom, where Mithany now laid beside him in tears. Puffy eyes followed his chest as it barely rose and fell hundreds of times before she caught the slightest twitch of an eyelid. Breath fled her in an instant. Her hand shot to cover her mouth. She dared to hope.

Then nothing.

She waited.

Minutes passed.

Hope faded.

The knot in her stomach squeezed even tighter. Mithany called out, "Doc, can you come here?" Most of all, she yearned for Reyne to hear her plea and spring to life.

In short, Doc Brenal joined Mithany in Reyne's room. Following close behind trailed Mera.

"Doc, his eyelid twitched. It moved. That's a good sign, right?"

The village doctor looked to Mera before offering consolation to Reyne's betrothed. "Yes."

Even if Mithany hadn't read the facial cues exchanged between the two men, the tone in Brenal's one-word reply told her it reflected nothing more than a kindness.

Brenal walked to the washbasin, dipped a hand towel into the water, wrung it out, and handed it to Mithany. "Here, keep this on his forehead."

"I'm not an idiot."

"No, you're not, my dear. Quite the opposite. But it will help," Brenal told her.

Mithany snatched the damp, cool cloth from Brenal. Mera moved to sit along the edge of the bed with Reyne's unconscious body between them. "Hollid, can you give us a minute? If he moves, I'll get you."

Brenal looked down at the floor and, without saying a word, walked out of the room and closed the door behind him.

"I think he feels useless," Mithany said.

"We all do."

"You got Reyne this far. Thank you."

"I think his love for you got him this far. Not me. I think that's all that is keeping him holding on."

A single tear escaped down the side of her face.

"You're a strong woman. Intelligent. There's a good reason you're his anchor."

"But—"

"You see, that's what I mean. Intelligent."

"Say what you have to say."

"You know he may not make it through the night. But neither of us is willing to accept that. So, let's talk about what happens tomorrow. Well, I guess it's already tomorrow. Let's talk about the rest of today."

"You want to take him away from me. I'm sorry. No."

"Alright then, let's do this now. I could tell you all the reasons he has to leave, but I'm guessing I'd be wasting my breath. So, if you'll indulge me, I'd like to tell you of how I think it should go if Reyne comes out of this."

Mithany's brow furrowed, and her eyes drew in tight.

Much to Mithany's surprise, Mera brushed her transformation aside. "I'm sorry it has to be this way. You deserve better. You both do. But you don't understand what we're up against. I do and, believe me, our chances of keeping Reyne alive aren't good even if he does survive the night. If you care about nothing else, think about Reyne. If they've got to hurt you or even kill you to get to him, it would be like a man flicking a fly off the back of his hand. It'll mean nothing to these people. Look what they did to Daedyn. They won't stop until Reyne's dead. They must continue to believe Reyne's gone, that they killed him here tonight, if you have any hope of protecting him."

"I thought you said you weren't going to give all your reasons Reyne has to leave?"

"The killer or killers cleared out temporarily to prevent detection, but they'll circle back. Within hours or, at the very least, by dawn. They'll return to confirm the facts on the ground. They *must* believe it's Reyne who they'd killed, because if they don't, they'll do everything possible to track him down and finish the job. Anyone you've ever cared about will be at risk until they finally put him down. I'm sorry this sounds harsh, but you have to hear it."

Mera rested his hand on hers. She pulled away.

"Alright then. Here's what has to happen. We'll hold a brief ceremony at the family's Cycle of Life, tonight, while it's still dark. I'd expect they'll be mourners over the two-day traditional Celebration of Return. You, Arek, and Brenal will remain here to welcome those paying their respects. Tell anyone who asks, Reyne was mauled. Daedyn's so overcome with grief he's gone into seclusion. Everyone must believe Reyne's passed, and Daedyn remains with the living. Folks will accept it given how close they were. I think it'll buy time for Reyne and me to get far away from you and Arek."

With arms crossed over her chest, Mithany sighed. "I'm not agreeing to any of this, but go on."

"The local Judjurex might be a problem, but with Doc Brenal and his official documentation of Reyne's death, it should be enough to dissuade any investigation. The Judjurex will never suspect Daedyn is really the one in the family plot."

"Tetrip's not a stupid man. He's been Judjurex a long time."

"Just tell the Judjurex the story. He's judge, jury, and the sole authority to execute his decision. Convince him a wild animal ripped Reyne's face and throat open when he checked on the fire pit near dusk, like he does every evening. Hell hounds have been in the area. You got Brenal out of bed in the night, but it was too late. If he ever gets to the point of exhuming the body, with the damage to Daedyn's neck and parts of his face so damaged, I can't figure how he'd make any other identification. The examination will hold."

Mithany flinched at Mera's words. Recovering, she said, "Tetrip will be suspicious of the midnight burial."

"If he asks about the sudden burial in the dark of night, tell him Daedyn demanded it so he could go in seclusion but still give his brother a proper send-off before going away."

It offended Mithany to hear Mera talk so callously. She forced herself to listen. "Not that he is going anywhere, but where did you intend to take him?"

"I can't tell you in case things don't go as planned. They'd have ways to get information from any of you."

Mithany reinforced her position. "Again, not that he's leaving with you. Just curious. How come I'm not going with you and Reyne on this little trip of yours?"

"You can't follow where he needs to go. In the end, neither can I. Also, you're needed here to cement the deception that it's Reyne that's buried in the family plot."

With lips pressed tightly together, struggling to hold back tears, Mithany shook her head. "He's not going with you."

"Mithany, remember when Reyne's father passed, and both boys were still too young to run the orchard? Their mother took over. Then when she passed, Santander managed the place after that. Sorta like a steward. The brothers still rely on him to manage most of the day-to-day operations."

Mithany opened her mouth to speak, but Mera jumped in.

"Yes, yes, a harvest is coming. Mithany, talk with Santander, tell him Daedyn gave you instructions before taking off for him to take over the day-to-day obligations until Daedyn returns from mourning. Give him a chunk of the profits until Daedyn gets back, and I can assure you the farm won't miss a beat."

Mithany studied Mera. "And if I don't go along with any of this and Reyne stays put once he wakes up? What then?"

Sadness painted his face at her words. "Then it doesn't matter if he ever wakes up. He'll be dead either way."

The threat had little time to germinate.

The whisper of a sigh escaped Reyne.

Mithany froze.

Reyne opened his eyes.

A Whirlwind

Hensdale: 28th day of the Salmon Moon

Mithany | Reyne

The second Reyne's eyes opened, Mithany exploded across the bed, threw one leg over Reyne's chest to straddle him, and grabbed his face in her hands. With childlike joy, she planted kiss after kiss on every inch of his face. His nonexistent reaction paused her mid-celebration. His arms lay flat on the mattress making no effort to return Mithany's embrace. Lifeless eyes looked back at her. Slowly pulling back, while holding his head between her palms, Mithany scanned his face for clues. As though in an emotional coma, his expressionless reaction to her matched the emptiness lurking behind his eyes.

What she found stunned her, hurt her. She expected love but didn't find it. Reyne was alive, awake, aware, yet his heart hadn't returned from the depths of despair—it remained somewhere dark.

On the verge of tears, awareness came to her slowly; he'd been sequestered in an unconscious state since seeing Daedyn's body. In the timeframe of his mind, not the agonizing hour she awaited his return from unconsciousness, only seconds had passed since the unfathomable, incomprehensible, and horrific discovery.

"It's been almost an hour since you—" Mithany paused, uncertain how to describe his convulsion in reaction to Daedyn's murder. Fearful the wrong words threatened to cut even deeper into his wounded soul, she said, "You've been out for some time. Your body reacted poorly to the venom and—" Mithany failed to finish her thought and buried her face in Reyne's chest as she let loose a torrent of emotions. "I'm so sorry—" She wrapped her arms around him as he laid there, staring at the ceiling, unmoving, unflinching, and unresponsive.

Mera rose from the bed, and stepped back from where he sat, affording the couple a little space.

Mithany shifted her head from Reyne's chest to look up at Mera. Fear, hurt, pain, confusion, and a plea from deep in her core escaped to her face, begging Mera for help. Reyne's disregard of her affections proved more devastating than anything she'd ever experienced, including Daedyn's death.

Mera settled his hand on her hunched shoulder. He spoke to her as though Reyne hadn't reawakened. "Reyne's in there. He's alert. He needs time. It isn't you. If you'd like me to see what I can do, leave us alone for a little while. I'll call you back when I'm finished."

Speaking in short bursts between gasping for air and sobs, trying to form sounds, devastated, Mithany hung her head. "I'll be in the kitchen."

She rose off Reyne, who didn't look at her. With a nod at Mera, her large, round, watery eyes implored him to bring Reyne back to her.

With a clunking sound, the door closed behind Mithany, leaving Reyne alone with Mera.

Mera, it appeared to Reyne, disregarded Mithany's pleas and dug in with his own agenda. "I know you're listening. I'm so very sorry about Daedyn. I'm not a cold-hearted bastard, but you need to know assassins did this to your brother, intent on killing you. I need to get you out of here. Tonight."

Behind Reyne's implacable facade, indignation sent sparks along the pathways of his brain. With his brother, dead, Mera shot off about things that didn't matter. Not even a simple, "How are you feeling?" or "You were a little rough with Mithany"... No, not Mera. He went right after the issues important to himself. Reyne's fists clenched.

Mera grabbed him by both shoulders and shook him. "You're not ready for this but, there's no other option. Come with me."

Reyne pulled away. Mera grabbed him again, this time much harder, and dragged Reyne out of bed. Forced along through the hallway, like a prisoner on his way to the gallows, Mera manhandled Reyne past Mithany and Arek, pushing him out the front door.

Spectators to the tension-filled display, Mithany and Arek followed Mera and Reyne outside. Insistent, Mera told everyone to get back in the house for their own safety, he had something to show Reyne... and Reyne alone.

Mera hauled Reyne step-by-resistant-step the entire way to a spot about one hundred fifty yards from the house. They paused at a location just at the edge of the tree line.

"What the fuck, Mera?" Anger spat out in Reyne's words.

"I cared about your brother, and I care about you. Whether or not you believe it, there's nothing I can do about that."

"Like I give a shit what you think."

"I'm sorry if I seem callous. Time is running out. Evidar hunters will be back before dawn."

"What am I doin' here? Another talk with the fire?"

"No. Something we must do now. I'm sorry it can't wait." Mera shoved Reyne forward.

Mera stopped just behind the line of trees where the weed grasses appeared matted down. "I believe this is where the people who murdered Daedyn set up. You're not ready for this, but you have to see it. Kneel here with me. I need to open your Eye of Heaven again. Your Third Eye. Wide this time."

Reyne didn't move.

Mera yanked Reyne's arm downward, forcing him into a kneeling position.

Reyne felt Mera's hand on his forehead. "Get the fuck away from me with that Eyeballs in Heaven shit." Reyne slapped it away, "Another trick, like the Firaché! I gotta get back to Daedyn and Mithany. Now leave me alone." Reyne moved to stand.

Mera seized his arm. "Daedyn's gone. That's why I brought you here."

Reyne tried to rip free, but like a block of granite holding him down, Mera's grasp proved unbreakable. The lack of success didn't curtail Reyne's efforts.

"Stop," Mera demanded harshly. "I know you're hurting. We all are. Yes, go to Mithany. She needs you, and you need her. But give me two minutes. It's all I ask."

Reyne reluctantly settled down.

"You don't understand. None of you do. You need to see this... life forces all around us... right here," Mera waved his arm over the spot. "Life is everywhere, in all things. You, me, birds, trees, rocks, dirt... it's in everything."

Reyne squinted but remained.

"You see life in the forms you're familiar with. But everything, everywhere, consists of the same quantum particles. That's where life resides. Everything is alive because it is the quantum particle that harbors life. *They are life.* Anyway, not now. I don't have time to explain it."

"Quantum whaticles?"

Mera didn't reply. He placed his palm flat on the ground between them. He ran his open palm in small circles, still pressed to the ground, slow movements at first. While on one knee, Mera, ever so gently, rested three fingers on Reyne's forehead.

"What the fuck," Reyne complained. "My head already hurts like hell."

"Give it a second."

With his other palm pressed firmly on the ground, Mera's hand started to vibrate. Mera's fingers began rising from his down-turned palm as though bent backwards from another hidden hand. Exactly what shape his hand retained, Reyne couldn't make out. Mera's hand vibrated too fast for Reyne's eyes to follow. But his middle finger rose out of the blur to take on a solid shape. Faster and faster, Mera's hand moved with the lone finger, impossibly motionless. An inconceivable sight, if what he saw qualified as real. Then another finger joined the lone sentinel, then a third.

Hand movements pressed against the ground gave Reyne the impression Mera was trying to push away the undergrowth. Still, Mera's arm and three fingers did not move, as though made of granite, fixed in place, while Reyne stayed focused on Mera's hand, appearing as nothing more than a blur the color of flesh.

The world began to change before Reyne's eyes. Like a stone dropped into a pool of water, wave after wave radiated from the union of Mera's palm and the earth beneath it. Inch by inch, then, foot by foot, it radiated outward from Mera's palm, transforming reality in its wake.

Fluidity ruled within the circle. The new here and now, at first confined to a small space around him, grew wider and stretched further in every direction. Sounds within the space of altered reality became less distinct, blending into one indefinable voice of the forest. Reyne shifted his attention away from the changing world unfolding before him to look down at Mera's hand. It vibrated and moved at speeds beyond human comprehension.

All of creation in the tight circle rippled in waves, generated from the spot Mera touched the ground. Everything shifted, swelled, heaved, and fluttered around them. No longer solid, the landscape rose and fell like an angry ocean. Wave after wave of ever-changing corporeality crashed against Reyne's mind.

Mera had transformed the physical world inside the circle.

Reyne's eyes bulged as he struggled to understand. Shapes appeared wind-blown as though a watercolored painting with edges bleeding against drops of the silvery liquid. Brush strokes pulled the scenes away from their painted core. Colors shifted. Bits and fragments of scenes—entire forests, people, all on immense scales—appeared on the tiniest slivers of light. The physical world whirled about in a tornado of infinitesimally small packets of reality whipping around in every direction. Reyne saw worlds inside every speck of dust. Hundreds upon hundreds, thousand upon thousand and millions upon millions of dust-sized scenes of the past, both solid and windswept, struck at his mind. Impossible and yet so real.

As Reyne looked on, Mera searched through the impossibly small fragments, brushing them aside one by one, thousands by thousands, with just a momentary glance that took milliseconds yet allowed time for Mera to study each scene carefully.

Nothing remained static: images whipped in the wind as though blown away like sand flowing off the crest of a dune. The Brenton orchard rippled across the ground and through the trees, undulating with each passing wave. Scenes large and small whirled about in tiny grains, each a reality unto themselves.

Every grain, every windswept brush stroke held an event.

Millions upon millions of realities tried to break free of the chaos and return to their natural state. None succeeded.

The broken reality inside the vortex grew more complex. Reyne fought to stay focused on anything as he grappled to anchor his mind. Undulating waves radiated from anything he fixated on, and there were always images, memories—not his—just out of reach. Like bedsheets pinned on a clothesline, writhing and whirling about in a strong breeze, Reyne lacked the ability to grasp onto any single one of them.

Ghostly forms took shape.

At what point Mera withdrew his touch from Reyne's forehead, Reyne didn't recall. Thousands of years of forest-memories-incarnate flooded into his mind and images formed before his eyes. Unable to determine if they existed only in his thoughts or in his sight, Reyne understood, whatever it was, it was real.

And still reality continued to evolve. Forms and light shifted, changed, grew, disappeared, and reappeared at a phenomenal rate. Misshapen human forms flickered like wild dancing flames. People took on the specter of ghosts solidified. Shadowy avatars of Daedyn, his mother Pachelle, and many others who he didn't recognize took shape. Each rose from the ground. Three, ten, one hundred different Daedyns mulling about and people, themselves at all different ages, rose and fell. He saw many images of himself at every age come and go. People formed, then dissipated at an incredible rate. Trees grew from sapling to maturity, only to fall to the ground in a fraction of a second. Leaves grew on branches, changed colors, fell to the ground over and over hundreds or thousands of times in a matter of a single heartbeat.

Reyne found himself able to follow it all, even though it was happening so impossibly fast. Without warning, the ground from beneath Mera's palm radiated a shockwave that blew away the visual chaos.

The silent shockwave carried no force in the physical world. Yet, the tremor from the wave struck Reyne's mind like a hammer, knocking him off balance. Reyne fell to the ground, caused by the single powerful massive shockwave as it rippled out across everything, clearing the way for him to see why Mera brought him here.

The surge washed away the chaos, all the uncertainty. Between the oscillations, the scene snapped into normal time. Reyne understood, Mera had found a single memory in the quantum whaticles he'd hoped to reveal.

Reyne witnessed an older man whose white hair whirled about his head. His face first appeared solid, then stretched. His form proved difficult to make out, vacillating between crisp and windswept. The white-haired man took on a solid form, only to be blown away like dandelion seeds in the wind.

Reyne looked upon a young woman whose red hair stole his attention. Long strands trailed away from her face, whipping hard in all directions. Stunned by the red of her eyes, she seemed to look right through him, striking fear in his gut. His heart hammered, sweat dripped from his brow, and the woman began to dissipate like smoke drifting upward.

Suddenly, the red-haired, red-eyed apparition snapped into solid form with an arrow in her hand. The horror of it gripped him as she nocked it in a strange-looking bow. Reyne knew what came next. Hatred flooded through him. Something inside his soul screamed to break free to attack the red-eyed murderess.

He struggled to hold on to the woman's image as, piece by piece, she broke apart and flittered away in the wind.

Other phantoms appeared, and Reyne strained to keep their shapes in his consciousness. The images continued shifting from solid form to gossamer wisps back and forth, over and over. Reyne labored to hold it together in his mind. The ever-constant wind was pulling apart everything. Then, a blurred-then-solid-then-ghostly, windswept image of the red-eyed woman reappeared. She drew the bow and let the strange, clear, almost invisible arrow fly. Rage howled inside Reyne and burned away at his control. The arrow raced through the altered reality to dissipate as it pierced the edge of Mera's creation.

Before Reyne was ready, a tornado took hold of the entire scene. Shapes, forms, and whatever color there was, all swirled into a single funnel, and as Mera pulled his hand away from the spot on the ground, it all disappeared.

The world before Reyne snapped back into the reality he knew.

It ended too soon. Reyne was certain of what the arrow would do in the altered reality Mera conjured for him, but the vision whipped away before he could see his brother struck down. Reyne craved to see more yet shuttered at the thought of following the arrow's path to see it strike down Daedyn.

Before Reyne had the chance to ask how, Mera jumped in.

"That was the woman who killed your brother, and you just saw her and her accomplice." Mera stopped. The images Mera called from the past bit deep into Reyne's heart. A small part of his own humanity died with Daedyn.

"Remember the white-haired man. Remember the woman, her eyes, her hair, her face. Sear those images into your mind. Not today, not next week and not even next month, but soon, when you're ready, we're going to find them and kill them."

Reyne's mouth hung open. What he witnessed stunned him. Words eluded him. Nothing came out. He wanted to ask how Mera did that. How'd he pull the past out of thin air?

Reyne almost asked if it was real, but somewhere in his soul, he knew the truth of what he saw. His gut twisted, threatening to retch. He'd never get Daedyn back. Reyne remained silent, unable to capture the words buried in the thoughts racing around in his head to express the depth of his loss.

Reyne locked onto Mera's words, wanting to believe him. He needed to believe one day he'd kill the woman who took his brother from him.

Mera lifted himself from the ground, brushed his hands against his pants and stood. "And the woman with the red eyes is a hunter from Evidar sent here, into our reality, for one purpose. To kill you."

"To kill me." He thought his about brother. "Instead, Daedyn's dead."

His mind kept going back to his decision not to heed Mera's advice when first presented with the demand to leave Hensdale. How could he have known it was poison? Mera showed him the dart, and even then, Reyne didn't believe him.

Mera's voice broke through Reyne's introspection. "If Mithany and Arek were to know Neladith killed your brother, how do you suppose they'll react to her? Will they be able to pretend to accept her condolences when they stand vigil? Or will they want to strike back at her?"

Reyne sat back and wrapped his arms around bent knees. He didn't answer Mera. He didn't need to.

"No. We can't let them know for now. Mithany and Arek's reaction must be real for Neladith to accept the deception. These Evidar hunters must believe they succeeded at killing you."

Reyne understood Mera's point, but flinched at keeping it from Mithany. "I have to tell her."

"You can't. Do *not* share any of what you saw here with Mithany, Arek, or even Brenal about the red-eyed archer who brought down Daedyn. If you do, you'll put their lives at risk."

Reyne's bulwark against leaving began to crumble. His head hammered inside his skull, and the pain in his neck wouldn't release him. And all that didn't compare to the darkness invading his soul.

Mera continued, "We're going back inside. Speak nothing of this. Tell them I took you out to the spot where they fired the shot. That's all. Nothing more. We have to prepare Daedyn for internment before the sun comes up."

Mera stuck out an arm, offering to pull Reyne off the ground.

Everything he ever wanted from life, his wedding to Mithany… only days away.

Before dawn arrived, a life-altering decision hung over his head like a noose.

Reyne grabbed Mera's hand. If a way out of leaving Mithany existed, he had only hours to find it.

UNSEEN IN THE NIGHT

HENSDALE: 28TH DAY OF THE SALMON MOON

Mithany

Half of Daedyn's face was an unrecognizable mess. Blood soaked his clothes. His neck and jaw, along with a part of his cheek, appeared more like raw meat. Skin, muscle, and even a small piece of his brain stem hung exposed by the damage caused from the fragmented shards of glass tearing through body tissue indiscriminately.

Mera and Mithany stood alone on opposite sides of Daedyn. "Mithany, if you're up to it, I could use your help prepping Daedyn's body for interment."

"I'll do my best," Mithany said, visibly shaken. Concern for Reyne tugged at her. He survived the convulsion, but was weak and looked haggard. And, if Mera had his way, Reyne would be leaving within hours, even though he was in no shape to do so.

The body lay on a table Arek set up near the spot where Daedyn died. Mithany and Mera disrobed his corpse. Tears dripped slowly down her cheeks as she tried her best to help. Every few minutes, she wiped runny mucus from her nose. Without warning, she released the contents of her stomach all over Mera's boots.

The man who'd loved her as far back as she cared to remember laid dead on a makeshift mortuary table. She'd never returned his romantic affections, but loved him like family just the same. As kids growing up, Daedyn frequently taunted her, as little boys often do to little girls.

Mithany opened up to Mera while staring into Daedyn's face. "I overheard part of the conversation when you were all in the kitchen. It's true, Daedyn made the first move on me. Reyne may have felt the same back then, but Daedyn's the one who took the initiative. Besides, there was nothing Reyne could do about it. Daedyn called dibs, or so I've been told. It was the brothers' way."

She pulled a comb through his hair clumped together by the sticky, coagulating blood, and continued combing as she spoke. "At first, I'd been open to the idea. But never felt that spark. We were young. Guess Daedyn might have been no more than thirteen when I broke his heart. I was about the same age. Too young to realize what I did to him or that it would last to this day." With delicate care, she arranged his hair as he always wore it. "You know, I would catch Daedyn watching me still. He'd steal a glimpse here or there. I wasn't supposed to see it. But, us girls, we notice when we're being watched. I don't know... maybe guys don't catch on to that sort of thing. Reyne never did."

With the backside of her fingertips, she gently stroked the undamaged side of his face. Looking down at Daedyn as though speaking to him, not to Mera, tears cut along her cheeks. "Even if I hadn't noticed every time you stole a glance, it was always in your eyes. It was written on your face." She paused, looking deep into Daedyn's eyes, just beginning to cloud over. Soft and tender words escaped her heart. "You couldn't hide your feelings from me, they were always so clear. I saw your desire, your torment, and the sadness in you knowing your brother had the woman you loved. I'm so sorry I didn't feel the same for you." She leaned close and whispered, "Daedyn, I always kept your secret. I never told Reyne."

Mera reached out to put his hand over hers, but said nothing.

Mithany broke her gaze from Daedyn to face Mera. "It's only one of the two secrets I ever kept from Reyne. He seemed oblivious of Daedyn's feelings for me. Maybe because he couldn't face it, or maybe because Daedyn did everything to make Reyne believe he was indifferent. He put up a good front for Reyne. I never let on to Daedyn that I knew his heart. Maybe he knew I knew, maybe he didn't." She wiped away the water in her eyes. "Sometimes it's a curse being able to read people. I've tried to teach Reyne how to read faces. It never took. He's not all that intuitive."

Mera let her speak uninterrupted. She needed to get it off her chest to anyone other than Reyne. It was cathartic for her to let it all out after years caged inside, never spoken of to another human being.

"I understood why Daedyn was aloof around me. He had Reyne convinced. But I knew better. We gals always know better. And now he's gone." She bent over the body, kissing Daedyn's cold forehead. It was more than she could handle. She spun in a jerk and retched again.

"I'm so sorry, Mera."

"You have nothing to be sorry for." He handed her an empty container. "When you're up to it, can you go for another bucket of water so I can rinse off Daedyn?"

She suspected it was so he could wash the vomit off his boots and give her something to do other than looking at Daedyn's ravaged corpse.

Upon her return, Mera grabbed the handle of the bucket from her. "Thank you, Mithany. Leave the pail here and, if you wouldn't mind, please check up on how your brother and Brenal are doing."

Arek and Brenal had been working diligently on Daedyn's final resting place beneath the Big Alphen, as it was called by generations of Brentons. Brenal did what he could, although Arek did most of the work. The digging went slow. Mithany arrived and took up a spade to join them, hoping to distract herself from Daedyn's lifeless body and Reyne's withdrawal.

The men dug their hole near the large three-hundred-year-old alphen, not more than fifty yards from their homestead, where Daedyn and Reyne played as children and grew together into men. Several generations were laid to rest in the shade of the sacred family tree.

"Not needed, Sis. The two of us got this. A third spade will just get in the way."

Heeding Arek's advice, she stopped.

Daedyn's family ancestors embedded a memorial stone monument in the trunk long ago. While the Big Alphen stood almost thirty feet tall, the stone monument appeared small in comparison. Mithany stared at the plaque and read the simple words carved into the memorial's stone face:

At the end of my journey, I hope not to say,
I wish I had but one more day,
To do the things I've not yet done,
To sing the songs I've not yet sung.
Such an ugly vision would Death portray.

Upon completion of all my goals,
With nothing left in future's hold,
With nil ahead but barren straights,
Looking back on fading lights,
Then welcome Death, my tired soul.

It's not by choice, this Gift of Life.
The terms of Death are neither mine.
The terms are in living, where choice is made.
The best to hope for, a life well played.
It was in my life, my Death's defined.

Mithany reflected on the stone's etched words. Death held an ugly vision for Daedyn. So much ahead of him cut short in such a horrific manner. She wondered what life would have been like had she chosen Daedyn when he was at the beginning of his journey, starting on the path to make the choices that would define his life. Robbed of the opportunity to glance back as an old man on his life and whatever brought him joy. He'd never be that old man. Daedyn would take his place with his parents and generations of Brentons beneath the shade of the Big Alphen, to be consumed by its roots and the other forces of nature reclaiming everything that was once Daedyn. Such an ugly vision had death delivered to him.

Upon her return to Mera, she discovered the body had been cleaned, as were his boots, and prepared for its ultimate resting place. With a call that echoed through the orchard, Arek, Brenal, and Reyne joined Mera and Mithany as they walked out to the awaiting grave site.

Mera appealed to them, "Please understand this will not be the traditional Cycle of Life ceremony. Exigencies demand all our efforts focus on preserving the living. I'll do the best I can."

Mera's rushed treatment appeared to offend Reyne to his core.

Reyne yelled at Mera more than once, starting when Mera demanded Daedyn be buried immediately after the body was cleaned and the grave completed. In response, Reyne coldcocked him, knocking him off his feet.

As things settled down, Mithany asked Mera to speak with her in private.

Reyne gave her a hard expression, but she offered soft eyes in return that said to him, "Trust me, my love." She expected little in return from Reyne, given his foul mood, and that's exactly what she got. Reyne remained emotionally distant, and while she understood, it still stung.

Mithany privately explained to Mera, "You need to express yourself with greater care given Reyne's raw emotions. As much as you need our little band to take action with dawn approaching, please promise me you'll do better. For Reyne's sake."

Mera said, "I'm sorry, and I promise to do better."

The two returned to the gathering only a few feet away.

Mithany sidled up to Reyne, and taking a risk, she slipped her hand into his. Their fingers intertwining, she gently stroked his arm. The minor grin she got from him she claimed as a major victory.

Daedyn's interment took place at the Brenton family's Cycle of Life burial plot, where his parents and ancestors were laid to rest so many years ago. Mera began, "This is the place where Gwerther and Pachelle offered their life force back to Mother Earth, completing the Cycle of Life. As dictated by tradition, all living things must return to the Earth in order to re-enter the Community of Life. Mother Earth is the source of all living things and the creator of all of life's manifestations. As offered in the Book of Teth, a common energy interconnects all living things in the Community of Life, shared over and over throughout millennia, reincarnated in many different forms through the Gift of Renewal. Daedyn, like his parents before him, gives back to Mother Earth the life energy borrowed from the Community of Life. The life energy Daedyn had only temporary ownership of."

The Mera-led ceremony came off more like a lesson than as a solemn goodbye. "Daedyn's life energy isn't all he returns to Mother Earth. Daedyn returns his flesh to the Earth in its natural and free state to be shared with future generations of Nature in the Cycle of Life. Daedyn gives back to the Earth as he entered this world, naked, and is returned naked with no encumbrances upon it." Mera paused and turned to Reyne. "Unfortunately, the traditional burial shroud wasn't available, and I'm sorry, Reyne, for the use of a white bedsheet."

The disrespect at Daedyn's expense had been building up since Reyne's last eruption. It was the final blow, and he lunged at Mera.

Mithany jumped between the two men, with Daedyn's naked body as a silent witness. Obvious to Mithany, but not to Reyne himself, he had only one real option: where to point his anger. He wasn't truly angry at Mera. He was angry Daedyn was dead, and angry Mera demanded he leave Mithany behind to run away like a coward. While Reyne didn't realize the internal forces driving his behavior, Mithany understood the man she loved.

She told Reyne, "Honey, please, not here. Don't make this something you won't want to remember when you think back on this moment." Reyne glanced down at Daedyn's body. The emptiness pouring off Reyne touched her soul and bit into her heart.

The small group stood at the Big Alphen with their palms resting on its trunk. The shortened ritual completed, with the white bedsheet in place of the burial shroud, Mera, Mithany, Brenal, Arek, and Reyne offered the Signum Circulus with a thumb drawn in a small circle over their hearts, palms resting over it at the end.

After lowering Daedyn's body into the newly dug hole, to be consumed by nature and returned to the Community of Life, Reyne and Mithany stood silently, hand in hand, staring at the plot of land that would take their loved one back to Mother Earth. They couldn't let Daedyn go.

Mera put an arm around Reyne's shoulder, letting it rest there for a moment before softly offering Reyne heartfelt words. "He will always be your brother and will always be a part of you. You are who you are, in part, because of Daedyn. Be proud of that. Be proud of him for who he was. Keep him always."

Mithany half expected Reyne to strike out or push him away, or at the very least, brush him aside, but Reyne didn't react.

Mera and Arek began the awful task of filling over Daedyn's body with dirt. Brenal joined in to help. Reyne's eyes filled with tears. Mithany clung to him as though it was Reyne himself she'd said goodbye to.

With the dreadful task completed, five people stood muted in the dark, all eyes fixed on a mound of dirt. No one uttered a sound. Nothing except for the noises of the forest followed for a few minutes before Mera spoke up.

"Evidar hunters are about. Daedyn's death proved that point."

Mithany squeezed Reyne's arm as she felt him tense at Mera's insensitivity.

Mera directed Mithany, who hadn't agreed to Reyne's departure but spoke to her as if she had, "The tricky part will be selling people on why Daedyn is absent from Reyne's vigil. Follow the plan. Tell everyone Reyne's death resulted from an animal attack. Took him in the night. Daedyn's in seclusion. Grief-stricken and inconsolable. Hopefully, the agents of Evidar will never catch on, and Reyne and I will have days or weeks of a head start."

It just seemed wrong to her, not allowing others to mourn Daedyn's passing.

Mera continued, "People see what they expect to see. People hear what they expect to hear. It's always easier to accept what's expected than to look deeper to see the truth of it."

Mera's explanation suggested he had people figured about right—in Mithany's mind anyway. People usually followed the path of least resistance, not all... but most.

Deception based on "the expected" was the essence of Mera's plan. Mithany and Arek would make the people of Hensdale conclude it was Reyne who'd been killed. The mourners will accept it because they'd expect Mithany to mourn. People will believe because they will expect Arek to be at her side. People will believe because it will fit into what they expect to see if Reyne had died.

The scene Mera tasked Mithany and Arek with creating wouldn't be too hard to paint. Mithany experienced the grief of death. She experienced the pain of death. The good folks of Hensdale would believe it because her pain was real.

Mera reminded her, "As Reyne's fiancée and with Daedyn in seclusion, they would expect it of you to hold a vigil at the family burial plot."

With eyes drawn in tight, Mithany said to Mera, "You speak as though Reyne's leaving with you."

Goodbye My Love... Goodbye

Hensdale: 28th Day of the Salmon Moon

Mithany

Daedyn's body rested six feet below where the struggle over Reyne came to a head. Mithany challenged Mera's plan that at its core—for whatever good intentions it espoused—ripped Reyne from her life. Mera made his position clear in a tone as harsh as he'd ever spoken to her. "Reyne must survive. He must leave. No discussion."

Crinkles broke out across the bridge of her nose, and she bit down hard as her jaw clenched. The two were locked in a battle over Reyne's future. Neither Arek nor Brenal could do anything but watch. A nonreaction from Reyne didn't help Mithany's cause.

Mithany hadn't agreed to it, and there hadn't been a group discussion. However, Mera appeared to proceed as though leaving with Reyne was a foregone conclusion. Placing Daedyn in the ground profoundly impacted each of them, and the danger Reyne faced, Mithany well understood. Mera's actions pushed them all, begrudgingly, towards the inevitable—Reyne's departure.

Except for Mithany.

With urgency in Mera's voice, giving up on diplomacy, he demanded, "Mithany, there isn't time. I'm sorry."

"Reyne," she pleaded, "you're goin' along with this?"

With a statue-like gaze, fixed and off somewhere else, Reyne remained silent and stone-faced. He said nothing, nor signaled his support nor opposition to either Mera's or Mithany's demands on him.

With a muffled huff, Mithany dropped her eyes and shook her head in disbelief.

Mera continued as though he'd been declared the victor. "Mithany and Arek, you two'll stay behind and stand vigil at the family plot, mourning Reyne. It's going to be hard on all of you. I'll do everything I can to keep Reyne safe. I'm sorry, Mithany, you can't come with us. You're the linchpin in the deception for Evidar hunters. You've got to be the one they see mourning."

Bending her knee behind her, the sole of her boot scraped across hard ground. Her arms folded over her chest and her upper body leaned back. She pulled in a deep breath through her nose and her chest rose as her lungs filled with the night air. Mera appeared to be waiting for her acceptance, but she had none to offer.

Mithany and Mera glared at each other. She didn't give an inch. Mera shot a hand forward and grabbed her wrist. He led Mithany by the arm far from Reyne and the others—out of earshot, where he made his final push. "Unless you want him dead, I have to take him away. He knows in his head he has to go, but his heart won't release him. Neither of you can let go of the other. You have to be the one. It has to be you. He can't... You have to. There is no later... He'll be dead if he's still here when later arrives."

"I didn't agree to any of this."

"That doesn't matter."

"You want me to be the one to push Reyne out of the nest? We're days away from a new life together as husband and wife."

"Scary people want to kill Reyne. He's walking around with poison in his body from the first attempt. He won't be so lucky next time. Reyne must leave, otherwise they'll kill him."

"... unless I let him go."

"Yes."

"It ain't fair! It ain't fair to either of us. And by that bitch Teth, it wasn't fair to Daedyn!"

A *tsk* escape Mera. His tone softened. "You're right, it's not fair. That doesn't change what you have to do."

"Why?! Why is this happening?"

"Why's got nothing to do with this anymore."

Without giving Mera the answer he demanded, other than the sour expression on her face, Mithany turned away and made for Reyne's side.

She stopped, took Reyne by the hand, breathed slowly to calm herself, and looked down at Daedyn's final resting place, contemplating the finality of death. Clarity of thought inched forward, taking over from where anger previously held ground. As difficult as it was to admit to herself, Mera was right. Accepting what she had to do did little to placate her fears—the harshest amongst them, losing Reyne forever.

"Give us a moment alone," she said without turning to face Mera.

Mera nodded, and with Brenal and Arek in tow, they all walked far enough away to give the two a modicum of privacy.

Neither Reyne nor Mithany spoke for what seemed like a lifetime. Their eyes, filled with tears, fixed on the spot enveloping Daedyn's shrouded body. The indifference she experienced previously radiating off Reyne was gone.

"He's there with Mom and Dad," Reyne said, breaking the silence. "It's all my fault. I should've listened to that miserable fuck. I should've listened." He lifted his gaze to meet Mithany's. Holding her face in his hands, he delicately kissed her. "I can't lose you too."

It's in his eyes, Mithany reminded herself. *It's always in the eyes.* His beheld love, yet in there she also detected grief, sadness, confusion, and so much more.

Mithany glimpsed all of it behind Reyne's tear-filled green orbs. More than she wanted to believe, she spied unfathomable pain lurking there.

She had to let him go.

Yet, Mithany needed him now more than ever: to lie with him, to hold him tight, to wrap him in an embrace that would last forever.

Where would she muster the inner strength to do what Mera asked of her?

His eyes wouldn't release hers. Love poured through their gaze. Her heart pounded. *Oh god, I have to let him go.*

Mithany turned away. It hurt too much. She couldn't bear her pain. Even worse, she couldn't bear his. The anguish he tried to hide from her proved too much for her gentle heart to bear. A future of profound loneliness looked back at her and almost broke her then and there.

All her love for him... all his love for her... burning into their souls—laid bare for her to see. *Have strength*, she told herself. *Be strong for him.* But she wasn't—she couldn't.

The diminutive young woman waged an all-consuming internal struggle to summon the courage for what came next. If she demanded it, he would stay.

She witnessed his inner ordeal about leaving her behind. Comprehension of the tremendous heartache Reyne silently endured throughout her protestations leached into her heart. The realization Reyne's torment was all about her crushed her like a boulder dropped on her chest. And she understood, losing Daedyn fed into Reyne's fears. The premature passing of his parents, the progenitor of the primordial fear driving him in life—to hold on to what he loved before death stole it from him.

The only option to protect her from the same fate as Daedyn was for Reyne to get far away. The internal conflict rendered him apart. To hold on to all he loved, he had to let it go. Protecting her drove him, and leaving her was the only way to achieve it. But she hadn't let him go, and her demands on him fed the torment in his soul. He wouldn't leave unless she released him. Mithany came to understand all of it. She came to recognize the inner struggle thrashing at his very being. Unless she released him, this pain would kill him, if the hunters didn't do it first.

While Reyne struggled inwardly with his unsolvable dilemma, she and Mera openly battled for his soul. They both argued to possess his future. She demanded he stay. Mera demanded he leave. Written all over his face, torment, driven by the opposing forces of love and terror, lay bare before her. She finally accepted what she had to do.

She had to save him.

She yearned to hold the love they shared through touch. Her heart burned to physically connect. As Mithany kissed him, his lips gently warmed hers. Love poured through them as their souls reached out to join as one. His kiss told her he never wanted to leave her, but he couldn't live with himself if anything happened to her.

He had to go to keep her safe.

He had to stay because he loved her so much.

His eyes didn't raise up to meet hers. She knew he didn't have the strength.

She decided for them both.

She had to do it for him.

Mithany cradled his face in her hands and looked into his eyes. It was in that look he spoke to her in a way his words failed to. He told her he had to leave, but he didn't have it in himself to do it.

Mithany had to gather all the inner fortitude her petite frame afforded to let go of her hold on him. Not for her sake, but for his. The intense consequence of her decision seared agony into her chest, as though someone had cut her open, exposed her beating heart, and ripped it from her trembling body.

She loved him even more because he couldn't leave her. He was willing to face his own death to stay by her side, but he wouldn't—he couldn't—face her death. Mithany hurt so much, yet she had permitted herself to be the reason for his anguish. She loved him too much to let it continue.

It took all the courage she had to let the words escape her mouth, "I love you... but you have to leave me."

Reyne's head hung limp before her.

Mithany waited.

When he lifted it and their eyes met, she saw puddles had gathered in his. Words clumped in her throat as she held back the force of emotion choking off her voice. She would never have the strength to speak the words again if she didn't speak them now. Mithany compelled them onward through strength of will, up through her heart, out through the tears, and into her throat. A faint hint of sound escaped. "It's alright, my love, I release you."

Water in her eyes clouded her vision. It was time for Reyne and Mera to leave. They had about an hour before the sun would be up, and Mithany understood Reyne had to be out of Hensdale long before.

The two lovers faced each other. Bringing his hand to her face, with his thumbs, he wiped away the water trailing down her cheeks. A single tear formed in the corner of Reyne's eye. He told her, "I love you with all my heart, and no matter how long it takes or wherever I have to go, I will return to you."

Gently at first, she pressed her lips to his. As her passion grew, she pressed against him harder and harder while her fingers rifled through his hair. One kiss to hold her desire for him until they were together again.

They pulled apart, and she reached down to clasp his hand in hers. Their eyes locked, and nothing on Earth or in all the heavens had the power to distract either of them in that moment.

In what sounded like a whisper, he said, "I'm ready, Mera."

The sound of it tore her heart from her chest.

So much more than just his hand slipped through her fingers as he walked away. Looking back, he didn't need to say the words. She saw it in his eyes. Love was always there when he looked at her.

Remember that look, she told herself, *those beautiful green eyes*, unknowing how, or when, or if, she would ever see him again.

When Reyne turned away, her life changed—never to be the same.

Alone at the base of the Big Alphen, crying a flood of tears, with her face a concoction of salty water, snot, and mucous, she gulped at the air, grasping for breath.

She watched the two men walk away.

As the dark of night stole him from her vision and he faded from her life, her legs grew weak, and they failed her. Mithany fell to her knees. She turned to the heavens, clenched her fists, and poured out a soul-piercing scream of anguish.

At that moment...

... she broke.

Breakfast Games

Teth: 28th Day of the Salmon Moon

Kaythlin | Jerithan

Bells chimed throughout the Temple Palace announcing the eight o'clock hour and an end to morning devotions. Jerithan and Kaythlin sat alone in the First Lord's private dining room. Each came with their own agenda, determined to dominate the other.

First Lady Kaythlin reflected on how she so enjoyed the challenge of a head-to-head diplo-speak battle for information. She didn't expect the impending mental engagement between herself and First Lord Jerithan Cree to move her to the same level of ecstasy Madrotti took her body to—over and over—only hours earlier. Although, she hoped the rewards of the mealtime encounter held the promise of an altogether different type of fulfillment from what she anticipated as an intellectually satisfying indulgence.

With battle lines drawn, the metaphorical combat broke out over breakfast between the Temple of Life and the Kingdom of Adelle.

First Lady Kaythlin approached the contest, as would any soldier facing an enemy, donned in proper battle attire and armed with appropriate weaponry. Kaythlin selected her civvies but was born with her weapons. She approached the imagined theater of conflict in a red-colored top, standing out in stark contrast to the greenery of the room's decor. Most camo functioned to blend into the surroundings, but Kaythlin selected hers to stand out. Dictates of the psychological attack she planned required his full attention on her. She was armored in a fine, loose-fitting silk blouse that left her ample breasts to sway freely, untethered by the absence of restrictive undergarments.

Nipples, experience taught her, could be quite distracting, and she planned to bring hers to bear. Deployment took little effort, a body shift here, a sway there to brush them against the silk fabric with the slightest of movements. She expected they would manifest as tiny weapons, once armed, aimed directly at his ability to concentrate on the business at hand. A tactical strategy born out of her enemy's weakness, lechery, aimed to disrupt his powers of unbroken, clear thought—if only moment by moment.

A veteran of an untold number of diplomatic and other high-societal engagements, Kaythlin knew well that a momentarily exposed flank could doom an opponent.

A black leather skirt, comprising little material, completed her would-be uniform. With Kaythlin seated at the breakfast table, the very short dress remained sequestered as though in a foxhole during most of the battle-meal and didn't expect to see much action. Kaythlin considered its potential deployment in retreat.

Her hair pulled back in a tight bun exposed the delicate yet gracefully aging features of her face. Deep-red lipstick intended to playfully tug at his keenness. She wanted him distracted, disarmed, and vulnerable once engaged in the arena, and getting and keeping him off-balance was the goal of the clothing she selected.

Astute enough to maneuver the political waters to anchor his ship in the harbor of the First Lord's velvet chair, she knew he had weapons of his own as an intelligent, shrewd, cunning, and strategic thinker.

Look for the trivial things. He won't make the big mistake. It will be the small missteps that will give him away. She needed every advantage she could get.

Based on years spent in the political trenches, she learned to never underestimate an opponent, none more so than Jerithan Cree. Yet, self-assured in her assumed superior intellect and matched with her god-given assets, all pointed at a probable victory in Kaythlin's mind—if all went as planned.

Plans were only plans, and few survived intact upon first contact with an enemy. Kaythlin and Jerithan had to let it play out on the imaginary field of battle:

the breakfast table. This was his game, and on the fictional chessboard, he played the green of his vestments in place of white, and instead of black, she played the color of her lips—red.

She appreciated he'd expect something from her in exchange for the information he provided at the Feast of Teth Ball last evening. Just how much information concerning Adelle's push for electrics at the upcoming Council meeting would she reveal, she had yet to decide. A decision she'd make in the ebb and flow of battle.

Skilled at diplomacy and with a reputation amongst the congregation of being thoughtful and pious, the public held the First Lord in high esteem. Kaythlin went deeper in her understanding of the man. Reputations are often the product of well-planned marketing campaigns for people in the public eye. Well-placed Adelleian informants and years of experience dealing with Jerithan exposed the First Lord's true nature to Kaythlin. A man consumed with his own self-importance, and a bit of a letch, formed the foundation of her assessment of Jerithan Cree. The Gift of Flesh stood out as his weak flank. Her approach focused on that very weakness as an opportunity to be exploited.

Time to deploy.

Kaythlin arched her back, taking in a slow, deep breath. She could feel her body strain against the silk fabric. Covertly, she spied his eyes dart across her chest ever so discreetly and caught the corner of his lips rise ever so slightly.

Got you.

She laughed to herself and held back the urge to roll her eyes. She might have been disgusted with him but for the importance of the outcome.

"My dear First Lady, you must call me Jerithan."

"Thank you, First Lord—excuse me, Jerithan." She allowed silence to linger a moment before proceeding. "And you must address me as Kaythlin."

"Now that we've gotten that out of the way, perhaps you and I might enjoy a friendly meal." The First Lord grinned.

Kaythlin smiled back. "Jerithan, thank you for inviting me to share this delightful meal with you this morning."

"Kaythlin, I'm pleased to have you all to myself."

"I am happy to be here, just you and me. Besides, Madrotti's off to some meeting, preparing for his opening address to the Council. There isn't anywhere I would rather be." She let that sink in. "I would not have missed breakfast with you for anything. I am grateful to have the opportunity for this one-on-one time. Just you and I."

As the imagined chess game began, Kaythlin theorized he desired to control the mood by selecting a light, non-aggressive, nonthreatening setting, hoping to put her at ease. She considered it, his first mistake. Few across the continent of Tartica could match Lady Kaythlin in grace and charm. Jerithan dreamed he played in the same league, and his overestimation of his own skills was to her advantage.

Delicate diplomacy abandoned him. Flustered at the sight of strained fabric holding back heaving breasts, Jerithan blurted out, "Electrics. Why now?"

He'd advanced his symbolic opening move, deploying a piece to the center of the board.

Kaythlin tilted her head to the side and brought out her own piece to challenge his. "We can most assuredly discuss that issue. However, with your approval, may I offer a topic dearer to my heart? I am interested in hearing what you have to say about events of the other morning involving my husband and some unexpected guests inside The Stand."

Jerithan's eyes lingered perhaps because of the small protuberances making themselves known through the loosely fitting silk top. Constant brushing against the thin red fabric brought them to his attention.

The Voice broke through Jerithan's preoccupation, "*Good thing the Chancellor's not here today, huh?*"

Startled by the Voice in his head and all too aware he'd lingered much too long with his look, First Lord Jerithan returned his focus to her words. Looking up discreetly to gauge whether she was aware of his indiscretion, he concluded she was not. He felt proud, like when he was a little boy stealing hotcakes from the baker, getting away with something that he should not have. It delighted him. It emboldened him. It pleased him more than anything.

"Of course, you appreciate this is of great concern to me, as a friend of both you and Chancellor Tomelai. From my position as First Lord of the Temple of Life, having such a terrible event occur to someone I invited to join me to celebrate the Feast of Teth is an affront to me as well."

Two servers entered the room. Jerithan turned back to First Lady Kaythlin and offered, "Ah, this would be coffee and tea. I prefer tea myself, however I am given to understand you enjoy coffee."

"How thoughtful of you, Jerithan. Yes, thank you. I would love a cup."

"I have done my research, Kaythlin. My staff tells me you quite enjoy kumquats and ptarmigan eggs for breakfast."

With the kumquats, Jerithan made another move on the metaphorical chess board.

Electrics. Just blurted out. No foreplay. Right to it. Kaythlin interpreted it as a man a little overanxious. Unable to hold back. She allowed herself to muse over the Gift of Flesh he so keenly desired and the implication his quick-draw behavior implied. She laughed to herself then turned her thoughts to a more serious concern. *The kumquats, a mistake?*

She moved another imaginary piece forward, threatening his control of the center, when she said, "Kumquats in Teth this time of year, and you did so just for me. You are quite the exceptional host, Jerithan. I appreciate the forethought you put into our breakfast together."

She took another deep breath, intending to distract him, hoping for something unintentional to spill from his unguarded thoughts.

Words, most likely intended to reenforce his lead position, did not. "Well, yes. I must confess, I hoped you would appreciate them. I made special arrangements. Just for you. These are the only ones in the entire city, I imagine."

And there it was. The admission left him exposed.

First Lady Kaythlin wasn't sure he was obtuse or plain ignorant of the implications of revealing he'd prepared for this unscheduled breakfast meeting weeks before the attempted assassination of her husband inside The Stand.

Implications raced through Kaythlin's thoughts. *He had to plan for kumquats well in advance. They are only available halfway across Tartica. And they do not store well. Jerithan had to know he was going to invite me to breakfast. And this meeting was not part of either of our pre-planned itineraries that were orchestrated down to the minute.*

Why? Under what circumstances did he envision for us to be alone? Unplanned yet planned private one-on-one time together? But surely he knew Madrotti... No!

Is it possible? Did Jerithan have foreknowledge of the attack? Even worse, did he plan it? Is he that stupid or just that bold?

A red herring? Or the seeds of proof in a little green fruit?

Aware eyes can betray one's thoughts, First Lady Kaythlin looked down and prodded at the kumquat slices. Before reaching any conclusions, Kaythlin needed to confer with her husband. She took a bite. "These are delicious. It is so very thoughtful of you, Jerithan. You cannot imagine what this act of kindness *really* means to me."

Hidden behind a smile, peering up, she searched Jerithan's face while poking her fork at the food on her plate. She caught the corner of his eyes squint ever so minutely.

"You impress me, Jerithan. This is a wonderful breakfast. I would never have expected such a far-reaching gesture as these little green and black speckled slivers. This means more to me than you realize. You have surprised me." The First Lady offered a soft expression, feigning the gratitude she meant to convey.

"*She has your number, you know. She is quite clever,*" The Voice broke in with his own insights of the First Lady.

Jerithan replied to the Voice before verbalizing a response to First Lady Kaythlin. *Perhaps she does, and perhaps she doesn't. We will see.*

"Kaythlin, I was going to find any excuse to have you here at the palace for breakfast, one way or another. Official itineraries be damned."

*Let her chew on that for a while, t*he First Lord offered to the Voice in his head.

"*I like it. Quick recovery. I thought she had you. It is both subtle and confusing. Nicely played,*" the Voice observed.

Jerithan beamed at the compliment and symbolically captured one of her pawns.

She reflected on his last move. *Never underestimate your opponent. Time to regroup.*

"Jerithan, you surprise me. I am here at your gracious invitation, and I welcome the opportunity to learn more about what you might offer concerning the failed attack on my husband. It hurts me to think there is someone who tried to assassinate him." She paused, mostly for effect, but also to buy a little time. "And to disregard our sacred Covenant."

"Kaythlin," Jerithan said, reaching his hand across the table. He laid it on top of hers. "I cannot imagine how difficult this has been for you. If I can help root out those behind the attempt on your husband, and to unearth the blasphemers of our most holy dictate, I am at your service."

She observed him closely but couldn't detect anything that gave him away. Although he left out the word "failed." *Perhaps he's very good at pretense.* She'd evaluate his words and actions with more scrutiny later. She held his look, making her tone as sweet as possible. "Thank you."

One hand rose above his head, followed by the snap of his fingers. "More coffee for my guest." It came out harsher than she thought he intended.

She studied him as he switched roles from consoling friend to lord of the manor in nothing flat. It told her his hand-on-hers gesture was all an act.

"Thank you so much for your offer, and I have enjoyed our time this morning." She proffered him a draw.

"Oh, but you do not have to leave so soon. We must talk more about electrics. You and the Chancellor believe it is time to unleash them on Tartica, I gather."

In his words, she concluded the First Lord declined her offer of a draw. *He wants to play on. I'll oblige him.*

"You men and your politics. Yes, my husband requested electrics as an agenda item for the Council to consider."

"To consider?" First Lord gave nothing away with his questioning reply.

She offered Jerithan only information he would already have. "It is an important proposal for all nations to consider. Madrotti foresees its development as having a positive effect on humanity. Civilization has reached a population size that can sustain itself from this day and beyond. My husband believes this is the right time to advance our culture. For the betterment of all. Is it possible someone wanted his voice silenced?"

"I agreed to the agenda item. Silenced? No. We owe it to everyone to hold an open debate. Wouldn't you think it possible I could support the idea?"

Kaythlin pondered his move. A defensive action evident in his selection of non-responsive words.

"My husband would welcome your support—the Temple of Life's support. It is such a monumental decision."

She moved to attack, asking him to reveal a decision. If a physical chessboard had been set before them, she advanced her knight to threaten his hold on the center.

"My support may be possible in time. We have explored the Temple Archives and, as you are aware, there are many books created by the survivors of the Great Destruction sometime after their arrival here on Tartica. Of course, not in their original form, but what we've copied and recopied over time. Books of the things they recalled of life before the Great Destruction. Amongst the many wonders of the Second Age they put in writing, there are several books related to electricity. My people are still studying them and want to hear what the other leaders think on the subject."

He blocked her attack with another noncommittal response in his declination to reveal his position. Kaythlin concluded Jerithan's move a deception, as Derr's intel had surmised Jerithan did not support electrics. She prepared for Jerithan's attack. He wanted specifics on Madrotti Tomelai's vision for electrics across Tartica.

Jerithan's wants didn't concern her; a position she easily defended. It was the Temple Archives that interested the First Lady of the Kingdom of Adelle. Kaythlin had knowledge of the books the First Lord referenced. Many of the Temple Archive books were available for public consumption, but there existed several subjects Temple lords considered taboo, such as electricity and volumes of alternate religious practices. As guardians of the volumes created by the Great Destruction's survivors, Temple of Life leaders held back all such books from public access in the rebuilt civilization of the Third Age.

Over decades in years past, the Kingdom of Adelle secretly paid off Temple scribes to copy every book in the secret archives. Kaythlin was certain Jerithan was aware of the Tomelai duplicate library, but didn't let on.

"You must be much more educated than I am on the subject. I welcome your insights, and I am sure my husband would as well. I am hopeful you can share them with us."

To distract his thoughts and loosen his tongue, she took another long deep breath, stretching the limits of the fabric's ability to hold back her heaving chest. She looked away to a server bringing coffee to give Jerithan a long look. She considered, *The Gift of Flesh is his favorite*, and hid her eye roll from his view.

"*That's 'check', my friend,*" Jerithan heard the words from the Voice in his mind. "*She is good. I like this one, Jerithan.*"

Not so fast. This is far from over, Jerithan said to the Voice.

"That may come to pass, Kaythlin. In the meantime, I look forward to the debate. We will all learn more about your husband's vision of how electrics will advance society without doing damage to our commitment to live a life dedicated to nature."

I think that moves us out of check, Jerithan offered the Voice.

"Well played. What other surprises do you hold for the First Lady?"

Jerithan replied in his thoughts, *That will all depend on her. Let's see where this takes us.*

"I am quite enjoying myself this morning." The Voice may have even laughed if Jerithan heard it correctly.

"Thank you so much for breakfast, Jerithan, and for your thoughts on the upcoming Council debate on electrics. You are a very thoughtful leader. However, I must be going. You know how all our schedules are so tightly packed on these state visits. This impromptu meeting makes my schedule all the tighter."

Jerithan understood her offer to finish the game later. To leave the pieces where they lay.

"*This one is quite the devil,*" The Voice in his head noted, but Jerithan paid no notice, being otherwise fixated. He didn't listen as she thanked him for inviting her to breakfast.

Up from her seat, she walked over to the First Lord, who remained in his. Jerithan turned his face towards her as she approached. She bent down to kiss him gently on the cheek. As she did, the scoop of her neckline, pulled down by gravity, gave the First Lord an unobstructed view of all her fullness.

He'd known many women, but none with the beauty, grace, warmth, and physical appearance of First Lady Kaythlin Tomelai. She was special. *If I could only have her,* Jerithan offered his observation to the partner in his head.

The Voice replied, *"You are surely not alone in your desire, my friend."*

First Lord Jerithan accepted Kaythlin's offer to finish the game later. He wanted to play on, but the view gained from her low hung top engaged his thoughts with other imagined activities. *Live to fight another day*, he concluded.

She witnessed the smile on his face, born not from the social grace she offered his cheek. The exposure she permitted him burned into his mind and assured her untethered access to him in the future. She laughed inwardly at how easily she could manipulate a man of such high stature yet of such low, lecherous proclivities.

The outcome of the breakfast battle didn't end in the all-out victory she had hoped for. Yet, she captured an important game-piece; First Lord Jerithan may have played a part in the failed assassination attempt. In the exchange, she gave little away of Adelle's plans at the cost of a few stolen glances. An acceptable outcome measured against what she gained in this first round of engagement, she decided.

She had one more piece to play and one last tease to proffer. Prepared to do serious battle armed with a strategy to attack his vulnerability for the Gift of Flesh, her short, tight-fitting skirt emerged from the fictional foxhole. One last parting shot across the battlefield as she rose to leave—a direct hit.

Kaythlin put extra femininity in her step, certain he'd explore her in every detail as she walked away. With more than her fair share of confidence, she lifted one arm without turning back and waved goodbye.

Success Has Many Fathers

Owls Neck: 28th Day of the Salmon Moon

Quith

"You're telling me it's done," Dylla said, confirming Quith's statement.

Selundra Quith smiled, prideful of his accomplishment in dealing death to Reyne Brenton, while trying to ignore another idyllic morning in Owls Neck. Like a spider exposed in the open, he hated the fucking sun. The only negative to an otherwise great start to the day.

Quith traveled through the dark of night to arrive at his appointed meeting with Dylla. He thought it best for his comings and goings to be done away from the prying eyes of small-town busybodies, or maybe it was just an excuse to travel under the cloak of darkness a life on Evidar instilled in him.

He and Dylla sat at the same table they had the day before. On this occasion, they shared the open café deck with other patrons. The conspirators, careful how they spoke in the open environment, selected vague code words for only a trained ear to understand.

Quith appreciated Dylla's sense of style, even her overabundance of confidence. She spoke slow and direct with an air of command—a born leader who didn't need to threaten or raise her voice to earn respect. Her past successes were well known to Quith, as were the stories about those who disappointed her. She wore her authority understated, but as hard as steel in its application. For the people on her good side, she rewarded them richly. Those not rewarded didn't last long enough to share their stories.

Quith, a frequent beneficiary of Dylla's positive reinforcement approach, looked forward to his return home, where her appreciation for the Reyne Brenton op would be properly recognized. Quith considered her management style another ironic twist of fate—the role positive reinforcement played in making him a better killer.

Pleased with himself, Quith reveled in this, another successful op under his leadership. "To answer your question, yes, it's done," he said, looking about for the server. "I'm starving. When's our food getting here?"

A few heartbeats later, Quith said with a grin, "Ah, there's the girl now." A local, looking not much older than Neladith, stepped forward, carrying two breakfast plates.

The waitress placed the meals before the conspirators. Dylla nodded to the young woman, accompanied by a warm smile. "Thank you, dear. That will be all for now."

Not waiting, Quith attacked the assortment of food on his plate, but then suddenly paused. "Why do you treat these people nice? They aren't ours, and when it's over, they're all fucked."

Dylla rested her chin on her interlocked fingers atop steepled arms. "I've treated you well in all our years together. You haven't failed me yet. Neither has the girl serving us. When one of you *does* disappoint me, I'll stop being nice."

With a mouth full of toast, he said, "Whatever. Agent Arrow is cocky"—referring to Neladith—"but she's good. She hit the target... one shot."

"Four eggs. Eight sausages and three slices of toast. Are you sure that's going to be enough?"

"Haven't had anything to eat since yesterday afternoon. No, it might not be. We'll see," Quith said, cutting into a fat sausage link and releasing a squirt of grease. "Besides, I got it done. Let me savor this." He stabbed it with a fork and jammed it into his mouth.

"*You* got it done?"

"My team."

"You're absolutely positive it's finished?"

"One of our security guys quickly moved to confirm delivery at a distance. He reported seeing an unmoving item hanging over the porch railing. Our man tried to move in when Meratoruc and another old guy came out of the house. Our man heard them confirm the package had reached the end of the line, terminated. Our guy backed off. He didn't take any chances. Meratoruc's got too many tricks up his sleeve to risk lingering."

"Good, you confirmed something terminated upon delivery. Did you identify the package accurately?"

Quith gulped down a few bites. "Yes, moments before everything came to an end." With a quick look around to confirm no one appeared to be listening, Quith's eyes darted back to Dylla's. After picking up a piece of toast and devouring it in an instant, he wiped his mouth on his sleeve and leaned in close. In a whisper, Quith detailed his report. "We confirmed the target before the kill. It was Reyne's outline. Reyne's physique. Reyne's height. Reyne's hair. He was wearing the same outfit as earlier. He went outside to put out the fire in the burn pit. Like he does every night. It was the only time all evening he was isolated in the kill zone. Tylus reported hearing Meratoruc say, 'Hollid, he's dead.' Hollid's the local doctor."

"Yes, I know who Hollid is. More importantly, is Neladith still assigned to the fiancée's brother? I've received a message from our principal. He is anxious that we don't let him down. He wants absolute confirmation, as do I."

Dylla, not willing to concede to Quith's confirmation of Reyne's identity *moments before*, inasmuch as *after* is the only accepted method of confirming a successful kill, held back her acceptance the operation was over.

With a deep breath, Quith stopped eating and put down his fork. "This principal you want to satisfy is a Tartican. What do we give a shit about satisfying Tarticans? We know who we answer to. It's the Devil's Blacksmith that matters." Looking down, dismissing her concerns, he returned his attention to the food on his plate.

Dylla didn't respond immediately. Her eyes followed him as he stuffed half a piece of toast into his mouth. "It's the way the Devil's Blacksmith wants it handled, Quith. We pretend to play their game to achieve our goals. Harder for Meratoruc to figure out who's moving the pieces. Again, is Neladith in place?"

Allowing a moment to swallow, he spoke up, "Yes. She's to attend the mourning ritual tomorrow at Reyne's gravesite. She'll pretend to comfort the girl's brother. If there's anything out of place, we'll get word about it quick. Funny, isn't it? Neladith delivered the fatal strike, and now she's going to be the one to comfort them through it." He paused, shoved the last piece of sausage into his mouth, and before swallowing, he muddled, "You've got to love the irony."

"Alright. Get your people together after their silly ritual is over. Get Neladith out after day two. She won't need her boyfriend as cover after that. We know a package has been delivered. But... I want absolute proof you delivered the right one. No further delays, Selundra, you know what's at stake. Our world's future depends on this op. I have confidence in you."

He looked up from the last morsels remaining on his plate. "I've never given you any reason to think otherwise. I won't this time either."

"I'm happy to hear. I'll be even happier after your next report confirms your success."

In Quith's experience working for Dylla, she believed people responded better being told what they could achieve rather than threatening a subordinate with the consequences of failure. A credit to her approach, people often rose to meet her expectations.

"Nothing to worry about, Dylla. Confirmation is but a formality. We'll all be going home soon."

Besides, Dylla's reputation for dealing with failure didn't require constant reinforcement; the penalty was well understood. There was too much at stake to suffer incompetence. Those who failed didn't live long. Quith never gave it much thought, given his track-record of success. To his way of thinking, what became of operatives who fucked up, well, that was their own fault—*Not gonna happen to me.*

Nightmares in the Real World

Hensdale: 28th Day of the Salmon Moon

Mithany

Exhausted, even before venturing out to meet the new day, Mithany woke from a difficult sleep in Reyne's bed. She opened red, puffy eyes from crying most of the night. She propped herself up, letting her feet drop to the floor. Although much of the morning drifted away before she rose, the new day delivered Mithany into a new paradigm. One without Reyne.

Her heart sank.

The events of yesterday were all too real.

A nightmare had escaped into her reality.

This particular yesterday, as yesterdays go, had been a long one for Mithany. It ended for her just before dawn, only a few short hours ago. The traumatic events of the prior day seemed unreal, not possible, a dream, a nightmare. Mithany's head started spinning from the moment she overheard Mister Whitetop back at Owls Neck speak of an accident in Hensdale.

As though trying to experience their last kiss, Mithany flittered her fingertips across her lips. She'd released Reyne from his torment only moments before her legs gave out and her heart broke. How long Reyne would be gone, Mera didn't say. She wondered if he'd ever return to her.

Knowing Reyne left to protect her, in a way he didn't protect Daedyn, did nothing to fill the emptiness in her soul. If she was lucky, someday, Reyne might return. It was her only solace aside from the support of her brother Arek.

Mithany took some comfort in being in Reyne's bed, though it seemed empty without him despite Arek's presence next to her. The siblings had a special bond. Arek had always been her rock, especially through the brutality of a lost childhood. Physically the stronger of the siblings, Arek looked after Mithany throughout their difficult early years. He took their mother's blows, from iron-like hands, in Mithany's place whenever he could.

She loved her brother, her protector. Sure, he could be a rogue. A little too easily infatuated with women and the Gift of Flesh, but she forgave him for all his faults. Without him, she wouldn't have survived her mother's inexplicable anger at the world. Amazingly, and more importantly, she came through it intact because of Arek. Well, almost intact. She would be forever in debt to her older brother.

She was happy to have him by her side, in the bed she shared with Reyne, on the day she began her new life. Having Arek to lean on would help her through the difficult days ahead—especially standing vigil for Daedyn even though the villagers would be told it was Reyne buried at the family plot.

Mourning "a death" was the only part of Mera's plan she judged appropriate. She missed Daedyn and loved him as a brother. Her pain would be on display for all to see. Mera had confidence she'd be able to pull it off, but Arek was the wildcard. Mera considered taking the impetuous young man with them just to keep him out of the way, but Mithany convinced Mera she needed Arek by her side.

What the people wouldn't realize was that she'd be grieving the loss of both Daedyn and Reyne. She wanted to embrace Reyne in her arms and to hold Daedyn close to her. But Reyne was gone and Daedyn was dead. All that remained was Arek at her side, abandoned in Hensdale as a sacrificial pawn in whatever game Mera played.

Mithany didn't believe Mera when he first offered his outlandish tale. Not sure if she accepted it even now, but that mattered little anymore. Mera was her only hope to keep Reyne safe and to bring him back to her—one day—if he lived through it.

Maybe she didn't trust Mera to keep his word, but Mithany trusted Reyne with all her heart. Awake in Reyne's bed, she told herself: *I've gotta be strong.*

Arek stirred next to her. As short as it was, he'd slept through the remains of the night. His voice drifted into her ears from what seemed like a thousand miles away. "Sis... Sis."

Sitting up on the edge of the bed, she turned her head back towards Arek. His familiar cadence, his warming tone, anchored her. Mithany reached over to brush his wild bed-head-looking hair from his face. "Where would I be without you?" she pleaded.

All the usual playfulness abandoned him. Reaching for her shoulder, he said, "Sis, we've always been there for each other. You don't have to say anything. This is gonna be difficult, but we're gonna get through it together, just like we always have."

He didn't need to say more. She understood it all too well.

"I know. It's just so hard," she said and started to weep again.

Arek's hand guided her head to his chest. She crumbled into him, shaking. Arek held her as an overwhelming sense of loss invaded her soul.

In Arek's arms, a spark of joy touched her heart basking in the familiarity of his comfort. She dreamed of Reyne holding her, igniting emotional memories of the intimacy they shared. They so enjoyed their mornings together—enjoined as one. It was their special time. In a heartbeat, the imagery of lovemaking fled her, evoking even a deeper sadness to wash over her. Some unnamed hormone pulsed in her veins, sapping the physical strength from every muscle fiber in her body.

She looked away from the man holding her, not because it was her brother, which was nothing new, but because of the shattered promises of her own desires in the empty life she faced without Reyne.

Darkness bled across her soul like black ink infused into a pool of white.

No longer would she be there for Reyne, to care for his needs, to satisfy his desires.

No longer would he be there to care for her—or to satisfy her own desires for him.

Up quickly from the bed, Mithany exited the room in haste, before grief stole even more from her. She raced through the hall and out the front door onto the porch, hoping the light of day would deliver a small measure of relief.

Sunrays streamed through the trees delivering warmth and color to the morning. Sweet notes of alphen wafted across the orchard. Mithany experienced none of the uplifting joy it offered. Daylight failed her. Not because her eyes, puffy from the constant strain of tears, clouded her vision, but because the malignancy growing in her consciousness obscured the beauty in everything—heartbreak overwhelmed her.

Mithany spent the rest of the day in quiet bereavement putting in place all the necessary arrangements to stand vigil on the morrow. She prepared herself mentally and emotionally for the mourners to come, in anticipation of one of the hardest day she'd ever face. Maybe even harder than today—the first day of a new life without Reyne.

Failure Is an Orphan

Teth: 28th Day of the Salmon Moon

Jerithan | The Voice

"*Failure is not acceptable.*" With anger the Voice chided Jerithan, reflecting on the botched assassination attempt of the prior day. Alone in his bedroom, sequestered in the Temple Palace, First Lord Jerithan pondered the meaning of the Voice's words.

The Voice demanded, "*You might think you can remain silent, but I am in your head. I can explore everything in here. You can hide from yourself, but not from me.*"

Jerithan threw up his arms and spoke aloud into the empty room. "What do you want from me?"

"*You failed.*"

"I did. I fail at a few things every now and again. I am only human. What are you?"

"*The Chancellor still lives.*"

"For now. But we can still do this. I have given this some thought since yesterday and concluded he did not need to die. We can still consolidate all authority on Tartica. Harder, sure, but still doable."

"*There is nothing in here in this head of yours about a follow-up plan. You cannot deceive me.*"

"No deception. We haven't regrouped to figure out how just yet."

"*He CANNOT be allowed to succeed in the Council tomorrow. He must be stopped. Tomelai is going to propose moving away from civilization's commitment to remaining all natural. This arrogant Chancellor is going to propose electrics. That cannot be allowed to happen. We must not permit the seeds to another Great Destruction to take hold. Tomelai must be stopped. You do not have time to regroup."*

"He will fail. The votes are not there. Yes, Tomelai lives. But I have looked at how we might still get past this problem. I don't care one way or the other if electrics get approved, except there would be too much upheaval in our shared way of life. Consolidating power at the same time electrics take hold, impossible. We agree, Tomelai must be prevented from getting his way. But even alive, I have him stopped. I have secured Kantos's and Greenlin's votes. They will not support the proposal. It will die on the table. I had to give a lot away, but I got them on board."

"You sound sure of yourself. Are you certain there can be no other outcome? President Dimenk of Greenlin might go for electrics. Electrics would be the beginning of the end. If they get approved, amassing authority under the Temple banner will take decades, centuries, or even a millennium, but however long it will take, everything we have done to lay the groundwork towards creating the Empire of Tartica will be lost. Electrics must be aborted before it takes on a life of its own."

"Yes, I am positive the proposal will not pass the Council vote. Chancellor Tomelai's efforts will fail."

"Dimenk was leaning towards a yes vote and Larsed was on the fence."

"Where were you when Razoal and I were speaking with these leaders last night at the Grand Ball when I got them on board?"

There was a pause in the exchange. After searching Jerithan's memories, the Voice said, *"I see. You did some clever work here. Yes, they will align with us, and you gave away a bit much, but that's the price for failing not doing it right the first time."*

"Where were you when I was meeting with them?"

"Never mind that. Not important," the Voice replied, not giving anything of himself away.

"And besides, we were successful with the nut farmer. Your Agent Arrow joined up with Dylla's crew. My spy rode through the night. I received word this

Reyne Brenton fellow is dead. Let us celebrate a victory there too."

"*This is good news.*"

"I still do not understand how a businessman from Hensdale plays into this. But I trust you." Jerithan made the statement hoping to get a better explanation from the Voice. Jerithan ordered someone's life to end based only on a voice in his head. To ease his conscience, he fished for information from the Voice that might have justified the young man's death.

The Voice, in return, said nothing.

"What about the others you asked me to eliminate? The girl from Jarouhar, the old man from Dead Crow and—"

The Voice cut him off. "*Yes, yes. They were all necessary. There are things about the future you cannot understand, but trust me when I tell you, all of them were a threat to our plan to consolidate civilization under your rule as Emperor of Tartica. They would have all been threats in the future if you did not take care of them now.*"

"It is obvious there are things you are not sharing with me."

The Voice, hiding his own thoughts from Jerithan, reflected, *And I never will. It is all a lie, my friend. Reyne Brenton, Tomelai, Lorique posed no danger to you, but they posed an enormous threat to me, people capable of wreaking havoc on my world's timeline. I could not have that. You have never seen through my veil, and you never will. You have been blinded by ambition to sit on the throne of your fantasy Empire of Tartica. It will never happen. My friend... I am coming for your world.*

Surrender to the Beast

The Woodlands: 29th Day of the Salmon Moon

Reyne | Mera

A cold, damp, gray mist hung over the camp, much like the gloom that filled Reyne's heart. The effects of the rising sun brought a glow to the fog enveloping them. Silhouetted trees, like the ghostly shadows of his mind, painted the landscape. Reyne lay wrapped in a blanket on the chilly, wet ground. Motionless yet awake, he had no desire to face another day.

Spiderworm poison entered his body two mornings past, followed by a life-threatening convulsive reaction only thirty-six hours ago. Deposited here to face another dawn, his second without Daedyn or Mithany. Drained, and fatigued in body and soul, his head throbbed with every pulse, and his mind raged at the birth of each new thought.

While not a single reason existed for Reyne to open his eyes, he did so reluctantly. Surrender came easy to the day that started out offering so little, keeping itself from him, hiding behind a veil. He didn't care to pull back the shroud, and he cared less of what the day had to offer. Reyne saw little beyond the campsite in both his field of vision and of his future. An impenetrable miasma clouded both.

The sun would rise to burn away the physical cloud hugging the ground. Expecting anything to incinerate the misery enshrouding his soul offered only false hope.

Wet hair hung matted about his face as the dank strands clumped together like soggy rope. His clothes held chilly dampness against his clammy skin. He existed as a sodden mess of cloth and hair, but didn't give it much attention. Into another place, in another time, his mind escaped to a life with Mithany and Daedyn at his side. Mind and body had become disconnected, separated by distinct realities. Reyne struggled to face the new, miserable existence that now imprisoned him.

Memory failed him about the time spent walking along the forest trail with Mera for however long it had been. Numbness sapped every fragment of ardor from him. The two journeyed towards something, or escaped from something. He didn't care much either way.

During the entire time since they left Hensdale, Reyne hadn't spoken a single word, scarcely looking up for endless hours as they walked. He'd become nothing more than a pale lump of flesh aimlessly limping forward, one excruciating step after another. The only thing that kept Reyne going, a single cause playing over repeatedly in his head, was that he'd left Hensdale behind to keep Mithany from suffering the same fate as his brother. They killed Daedyn, and he wouldn't put Mithany in harm's way, even if it meant he had to leave her. Both Daedyn and Mithany had been ripped from his life. He hoped to find his way back to her one day soon, but Daedyn was never coming back.

Why assassins from an alternate version of Earth wanted to kill him didn't matter. What did matter: they killed his only brother, or if he accepted Mera's story, a foster brother. He didn't accept that either, not now, not ever.

Rage, anger, fury, all-consuming sorrow, and morass competed for territory, pushing aside whatever else tried to occupy his thoughts. Reyne experienced loss deep in his bones, his muscles, his gut, and with every breath he took. He spent his entire life, moment by moment, day by day, year by year, with Daedyn at his side. Everything either of them did, they did together. Daedyn was part of him; he'd been part of Daedyn as though the two brothers shared a single life. When Daedyn died, a part of Reyne died with him.

He didn't understand how to go on as half a man through the pain or the overwhelming sense of loss. Utter confusion battered about under his skin with every passing second. It repulsed his senses. He didn't want to feel anything. He didn't want to see where he was going because he didn't care. His only purpose in life, the life left to him, was to put distance between himself and Mithany. Where he was or how he got there didn't rate as all too important.

Mera gave the distraught young man his space.

Reyne has to find a way out for himself.

Pointing that out to Reyne, Mera thought, sounded like an empty platitude. Like the stupid, insensitive words people often say to grieving friends. So many times, words intended to console served only to offend. It would be a mistake Mera couldn't afford to make. He committed himself to silence. A quiet he would maintain until Reyne took the first steps to break free of their shared solitude. Mera hoped this would be that day.

Mera stood, shook off sleep and stretched, dropping the wool cloak wrapped about his body, looking over at Reyne as he did.

Reyne's eyes followed Mera for half a tick. Mera watched and understood the young man remained too wounded to be approached. In hushed reverence for his campmate's malaise, Mera silently prepared breakfast. Reyne glanced up at Mera with deep-set eyes and slowly turned away.

Another meal of cold, dry sausage and alphen nuts comprised all Mera thought safe. He chose not to leave behind signs of a campfire for others to find. He even collected the empty shells of the discarded, energy-packed alphen nuts. The careful precautions gave whoever tracked them as little as possible to go on.

He expected the false story of Reyne's death to give the pair time to get far away. Evidar's assassins would discover the ruse, eventually. A detail Mera held back from Reyne or those left behind in Hensdale. Hunters would come looking for Reyne, most likely sooner than later. Whether it would be the same crew or another didn't make any difference. *They will be coming.*

Reyne looked worn, eating nothing since leaving Hensdale. The grieving man rejected all offers of food Mera put before him. His rundown appearance was to be expected, given the emotional stress his mind had put his body through. The lingering effects of his last convulsion and the many miles they'd traveled contributed in their own way to Reyne's haggard appearance.

Without sustenance, Reyne wouldn't have the energy to go much further. Cutting off a small piece from a short, fat sausage link, Mera leaned over without saying a word and held out the sliver of meat on the end of his pocketknife.

Reyne glared at the offering.

A moment moored in time, after what seemed like hours, Reyne slid the proffer from Mera's blade. Holding the small bite-sized slice between fingers, Reyne looked down at his first real nourishment in days. Seemingly mindless of his actions, his hand guided the nourishment into his mouth. After swallowing, Reyne surprised Mera when he said, "Thank you," in a hushed, somber tone. Melancholy dripped from his meek, tattered voice.

Mera didn't reply; he simply cut off another slice of sausage, stabbed the point of his knife into its center, and held it out. Without looking up, Reyne slipped the bounty off the end of the blade. As Reyne chewed the second morsel of the morning, Mera sliced the rest of the beefy link. With the pieces collected in his palm, Mera turned his hand over and delivered them into Reyne's.

It's a start.

The tidbits of meat settling in Reyne's stomach seemed to bring just the tiniest spark of life back to him. He became more aware of the damp, cold fog invading every level of his being. Finishing the last of the sausage slices, Reyne cupped his hands to his mouth, expelling his own warm breath. The effort brought a small measure of relief from the damp chill. It didn't last long. He crossed his arms and rubbed his upper limbs for warmth.

Without speaking, Mera held out the calorie-rich meat of several alphen nuts and dropped them into Reyne's reluctant palm. Reyne looked down at the fruit of the orchard that had once belonged to him and Daedyn. It belonged only to Reyne now.

Memories of Daedyn tugged at his heart. Daedyn had always liked the flavor of alphens more than Reyne. With each bite, remembrances of Daedyn washed over him, forcing him to contemplate being only half a man without his brother. He welcomed the pain his tastebuds delivered. Yet, the nuts revolted him. More than anything, he yearned for his brother with every bite.

Motionless, holding the remaining fragments in his palm, he stared into the pieces as though he might find his brother hiding among them. Not finding what he so desperately craved, he turned his hand over, letting drop the imagined bits-of-Daedyn to the ground.

Scents of the forest hung over the campsite and crept into Reyne's awareness. Wet leaves, dampened trees, and even the low-hanging fog smelled like morning at the homestead he shared with Daedyn and Mithany. Perhaps it was the sight of the alphens, or it was the forest aroma all around him? Or possibly it was all of it, all at once, but whatever the cause, Reyne became aware he had to stand up to face another painful day.

Mera hadn't disclosed his planned destination with Reyne. Most likely out of fear he would share the information with Mithany. Not looking back at Mera, a single thought broke free of the anger, the rage inside him threatening to be unleashed. "Where're we goin'?" he spit out.

"How's your head? That's a nasty gash," Mera said with little emotion. "Do you remember falling?"

"No."

Reyne searched his forehead for the pain he'd just realized. With a light touch he probed around the cut halfway between his right eye and his hairline. Fingers told him the blood had dried over, birthing a thin scab.

"I'm not worried about the bump on your head. Nothing serious, although it might scar. We'll have to keep an eye out for signs of the poison, too. Some of it is still in your system. You've been asleep since we hit camp yesterday." Mera didn't bother to recount any of the prior day's other events. Reyne didn't care to hear them, either.

"When I first became aware Evidar hunters knew about the others like you, my first reaction was to race back to Hensdale to protect you. To get you out of there as quickly as possible."

The words filled the air but held little of Reyne's attention.

"I'm the only one who knew who your actual father was, or that he had any living offspring. I didn't share that information with anyone, not even your mother or father, Gwerther and Pachelle."

Reyne didn't react to the comment about his parents. However, their mention ripped open a scab on his soul. Seeds of anger aimed at Mera sprouted in the exchange.

"So how did agents of Evidar know about you? I missed something and need to go back to where it began. I've got to find out who knew, and who did they report the info to? We've got to start at the beginning and trace each step from there until I figure this out."

Mera's voice grated on Reyne. "All I asked was where're we goin'."

"Teth," Mera said in reply to Reyne's challenge for brevity, then added, "That's where you were born. That's where it all began."

Being told of his birth—not in Hensdale but in Teth—stirred the growing angst coiling around his heart. He started the day despondent, and every word Mera spoke wound him that much tighter.

As morning forged on, the white shroud enveloping the camp began burning off, droplet by droplet. The strength of the sun's rays attacked the overcast cover surrounding them. Molecule by molecule, layer by layer, the gray-white veil of the engulfing mist peeled away.

Reyne reflected on the moment he discovered Daedyn slumped over the porch railing—dead. Mithany's screams echoed in his mind. His thoughts drifted. Memory of the moment stole him away from the here and now as though Reyne's mind floated above the horrific scene, bearing witness to Daedyn lying motionless before him.

Unlike any other out-of-body events he'd experienced while he slept, causing his body to lock down motionless, Reyne stood immobilized but wide awake. It clutched at him like the night terrors he experienced while asleep a dozen or so times each year, ever since he was a young boy.

Fear washed over him, thinking of the dread he always experienced inside his own mind when it floated free above his body. Fully awake, yet gripped in a dream-like sleep terror, not able to move or make a sound, he needed Mithany to pull him out of it—like she always did. He craved for Mithany to be by his side, now, more than ever, as his savior from this wide-awake astral projection.

Hovering above in mind only, while his body remained rooted to the ground, somehow, his awareness was being pulled towards Daedyn's death scene as his consciousness floated over the campsite.

He watched from above, outside his body, as Mera mulled about, paying no attention to his statue-like pose. Reyne struggled to regain control of his muscles, lacking the ability to move a single one.

Every other time he experienced an out-of-body event, he was asleep. And like every one of those times, he struggled to return his consciousness to his body. To move a foot, a hand, a finger. But he couldn't.

Reyne tried to speak, yet, not a sound escaped his throat.

He attempted to force out a single grunt, which sometimes worked, alerting Mithany to wake him. He looked down at himself from above as his physical body fought to move or to speak. Sounds, was making sounds, or was it only in his mind?

Then a single low, guttural noise escaped his gut. Awareness came to him slowly. Mera had him by the shoulders, shaking him. "Reyne, Reyne. You okay?"

In that moment, like a drowning man breaking through to the surface, sucking in his first gasp of air, his consciousness fled the ether to find its way back into the safety of his body.

He wiggled his fingers.

Reyne turned his head, forming a thought he pushed it out through his voice, and said, "Yeah. Sorry." He didn't share anything of his waking-dream with Mera. He'd never experienced an astral-projection event while awake. Neither had he shared his mind-body detachments with anyone except Mithany, and he wasn't about to start now.

Melancholy ripped thoughts of his dreamworld sleep terrors from his mind and returned him to his present miserable existence—a reality worse than all the nightmares he'd ever experienced.

But Reyne accepted that his own inaction played a part in Daedyn's death. It was his fault for not taking Mera's advice. He was part of the conflagration of events that led up to it. He would have to find a way to live with it.

Reyne wouldn't let that happen again—not to Mithany. As much as he hated leaving her, as much as he hated being without her, and as much as he hated the uncertainty of their future, he had to move forward for her sake, without her.

Mera pledged to get revenge for Daedyn and that he'd return to Mothany. How and when any of that would ever happen, remained uncertain. Resentment towards his self-proclaimed protector joined the cacophony of negative emotions building by the second.

Hate rattled around in its cage looking for a way out—aimed at Mera.

What's the purpose of this? We're going to Teth. Then what?

Reyne needed more.

Mera was holding back.

He was fed up with Mera's bullshit.

Wrath, like a trapped beast lurking inside his soul, exploded from its prison, and he lunged at Mera.

Hidden Truths

Hensdale: 29th Day of the Salmon Moon

Mithany

Mithany, with Arek at her side, stood at the Big Alphen where they'd buried Daedyn. Girded against the impending effects of the big lie on her soul, Mithany prepared herself for the onslaught of mourners who would be told Reyne's body lay beneath. Late morning, a day and a half after the murder, vigil rites for Reyne began and brought the first sign of trouble.

Not far away, perched on the top step of the porch, Brenal played his part, telling anyone asking to see Daedyn that the young man was too broken up to accept visitors, regardless of their good intentions. Brenal told each and every one who approached the house he would pass along their condolences.

With the turn of her head, Mithany noted a discussion between Brenal and the village's Judjurex: its sole law enforcement agent, sole investigator, and sole judge-type magistrate and the only village official tasked with carrying out whatever justice demanded. Judge, jury, and theoretical executioner but for the Covenant's obligation to do no harm, all rolled into one.

It took little imagination to accept Brenal's official cause of death. Hell hounds had been spotted in the area recently, and a few years past, a single hell hound had ferociously attacked two locals. Even though it had been several years since the last incident, for the good people of Hensdale, Doc Brenal's account proved easy enough to believe. On the other hand, Judjurex Tetrip's official acceptance of Reyne's death remained open.

Tetrip, a tall, thin man past his prime, hair fading to gray, did his job well. A direct-spoken man whose personality led him astray of the niceties of politeness long ago. Hensdale selected him Judjurex so many times, few in the small community recalled who'd served before him. Throughout the years, he remained the straightforward, matter-of-fact man he had been since his first day on the job.

Mithany called to mind Mera's words, "People will believe what they expect to believe." Mera also had reminded them all before departing with Reyne, "Keep it simple. It's more believable that way."

Judjurex Tetrip left Brenal alone on the porch. He made his way to Mithany and Arek, who were joined by the orchard's general manager, Santander, to pay his respects. Tetrip proffered an acknowledging bow to Mithany; the vigil rite's ceremonial leader as tradition allowed the deceased fiancée to stand in as next of kin. "I'm sorry for your loss."

A man of few words, his limited offering met all Mithany's expectations given the solemnity of the circumstance. "Thank you, sir."

He leaned in. "I mean no disrespect when I tell you I'm concerned. I'll accept the account based on Doc Brenal's word, but it is highly unusual burying someone in the dark of night. I don't like it one bit. I'll want to speak with Daedyn when he's feeling up to it. And I'll need some of your time as well." He nodded, stepped back and added, "Again, sorry for your loss."

Surprisingly, Judjurex Tetrip's unfeeling, unsympathetic words at the supposed gravesite of her beloved, Mithany thought refreshing. His words were direct, harsh, yet more than anything, honest with no pretense of feigned emotions.

If only the rest of them... Mithany's thoughts trailed off, interrupted at the sight of oncoming mourners making their way along the dirt road leading up to the Brenton family's Big Alphen.

News of Reyne's death had a full day the germinate amongst the small village of Hensdale. Hordes of individuals, couples, and families all came out to console Mithany, Arek, Brenal, and Santander, all standing vigil for Reyne's fictitious passing. Unable to hold back the depth of grief invading her soul, Mithany broke down with each consoling interaction.

She wept for Daedyn.

She wept for Reyne.

She wept for them both, gone from her life.

She cried, and she cried, and she cried throughout the day. As far as the townsfolk of Hensdale were concerned, they had returned Reyne to the Cycle of Life in body and soul. Mithany's devastation was proof of it all, despite what Hensdale's very active rumor mill speculated about the unusual midnight internment.

Arek never left her side through it all. Stroking her back for comfort, he said, "Hey, Sis. I'm here with you."

Hangus, the dry-goods shoppe owner, and his fun-loving daughter, Y'vay, were among the mourners. Mithany overheard Y'vay observe to her father, "Look how brave Arek is, how Mithany relies on him. He's her rock. He's more of a man than Daedyn. Hiding in his house from his responsibility to Reyne. How awful. To think I—" She stopped mid-sentence, remembering she was with her father.

Hangus asked innocently, "To think what, dear?"

"Nothing, Dad. Not sure what I was thinking. Let's go pay our respects."

Mithany unintentionally listened in on so many comments, many loving and heartfelt, while others were inconsiderate and downright offensive. She'd heard that people said the stupidest things at such times, never understanding the truth of it until today. When her mother died, she remembered the same thing happened at her vigil rite ceremony, but then she agreed with all the awful words spoken of the woman.

This was different. She wanted to shout the truth. She wanted to tell them Daedyn was dead, and he was a good man, not the coward they spoke about. She wanted to call out to them how they were destroying her soul with each ill-considered slap at Daedyn. In her moment of pain, she wanted to admonish them all.

Even more, she desired to proclaim to every villager how proud she was of Arek. Surely, the people of Hensdale observed for themselves something in him she always knew he possessed, inner strength. Arek, her rock, had always been her anchor; townsfolk had to realize that now. She loved him more than any of them would ever understand; she knew he loved her as well.

Mithany whispered to Arek, "I can't imagine what I would've done without you."

"Sis. There isn't anything in the world I wouldn't do for you. He's my friend too. I got two good reasons to be here."

Mithany knew Arek would do anything for her. He already had. Their mother always blamed Mithany for doing something wrong. Neither Mithany nor Arek ever understood what caused their mother to go off on Mithany so often. She was just a little girl. Time after time, Arek would say to their mother, "It's me, Ma. I did it," whatever "it" was. Whenever possible, he took the physical fury of their mother's abuse in her stead. Just a child, but even then, he stood as tall as any man.

Mithany tried to stop him every time he stood up to their mother in her place, but never with any success. How Arek still took joy in the affections of so many women after such a childhood, Mithany didn't understand. How fortunate she was that Reyne understood her. He and Arek were the only ones. At least she still had Arek.

Pride swelled in Mithany believing the rest of the village would see Arek for the strong, caring man he had become. She always knew he wasn't the misogynist good-time boy they erroneously pegged him to be. *There's so much more.*

With her head resting on his shoulder, she told him, "I know."

As the day moved forward, she held onto Arek throughout the vigil; she wouldn't have been able to stand the long day, the unintentional awful comments, or even the many caring gestures without Arek at her side. Santander stood vigil with them, but he wasn't Arek. Of course, she wanted Reyne there, too, who was sadly out of reach. She needed to trust Mera when he told her Reyne would return. They would have been married in a few days.

Spetzer, the leader of the often-drunk group who frequented the Forest Maiden Inn, came out to pay his respects with his crew in tow. "Ya know, between Doc Brenal's account and Mithany's raw emotions, I guess it's real. Reyne's dead." Turning his face away from Mithany as he approached, he said to his boys,

"Daedyn's a pussy. Should be here for his brother. What a dick. Guess that's par for the course."

She reeled, hearing his anger, though obviously not intended for her ears, withdrawing back a step as Spetzer strode up to offer his condolences. "Mithany, I'm so very sorry for your loss. You too, Arek." He nodded to Santander before turning back to Mithany. "I might stop over in a couple of days to help with anything you might need, Mithany." Spetzer inched forward to offer her a hug.

Mithany hesitated.

Spetzer moved in, swinging his arms around her.

Although diminutive, she extracted herself from Spetzer's embrace, long before he apparently wanted the physical contact to end. Mithany stepped back, leaving Spetzer standing alone.

Arek pulled Spetzer into a hug of his own. Spetzer tried to wiggle free, but Arek held him tight. The protection he provided his sister didn't end with their mother.

"Listen, fucker," Arek said, intending his words for no one but Spetzer, yet Mithany heard every word. "Don't be a perv. You never had a chance. You never will. Do us all a favor. Stay away from her. For your own safety. Got that, Spetzer Bilseck? Or is it Ballsack?" Arek released him and glared hard at Spetzer's stunned face, who turned and walked away.

Hensdale's rumor mill maintained a common thread of discussion over many years; Spetzer believed Mithany should have been his. Spetzer, walking away, muttered under his breath but loud enough for Mithany and Arek to hear, "We'll see, fucker. We'll see."

It proved one of the few exchanges under the Big Alphen that did not bring Mithany to tears. The vigil rite continued through the morning and into mid-day as Mithany, Arek, Santander, and Brenal thanked each who attended.

Neladith arrived in early afternoon to offer Arek and Mithany her sympathies. "I hope you don't mind that I am so late. I wanted to allow you both some time here together without me being too distracting." She finished with a warm smile aimed at Arek.

Mithany responded for them both before Arek said something stupid, "Thank you so much for coming. You didn't have to. It's very thoughtful of you."

Arek grasped onto Mithany's arm and replied, "Thanks, Nel." Clear to Mithany, he missed having his new friend at his side, but he wanted to be strong, without distraction, for her. Mithany needed every ounce of energy, every ounce of strength, and every scintilla of emotional support from Arek. She'd never have been able to make it this far without the total dedication Arek provided.

As polite as her words to Neladith appeared, Mithany's internal reaction was more staid. Gripping Arek's arm tight, she leaned in close to him. The two of them watched Neladith turn towards the dedication plaque over the family plot where Reyne's body supposedly rested. Mithany implored her brother, "Don't leave me."

"Come on, Sis, you don't need to ask. I'll always be here for you."

Patting his hand, Mithany readied herself for the rest of the encounter with Neladith. She didn't care for the red-eyed woman because she didn't trust her. Something about Neladith set off alarms in Mithany's head. Neladith activated something altogether different in Arek's head—just not the right head.

Because she loved her brother as much as she did, Mithany offered Neladith a polite compliment. "You look lovely."

"Thank you," Neladith coyly responded. "To be totally honest, I'm also a little later than I wanted to be, but I had to wait for the store to open. I didn't bring anything nice enough to wear."

Mithany stepped forward, still holding onto Arek. "Again, thank you so much for paying your respects."

Neladith leaned in, kissing Mithany on the right cheek, and then the left. "Again, I am so sorry for your loss. Reyne has given back to Mother Earth, and his life force will be shared with all in the Circle of Life." Neladith's words hit all the expected offerings to the loved one's standing for the vigil rite.

"Reyne's life force has rejoined the Community of Life. Our loss is slight compared to what h—he—" Mithany tried to say, but failed mid-sentence. Able to get out only a few words of the traditional response before emotions overwhelmed her, tears rolled down her cheeks as she released her arm from Arek's, bringing both hands to hide her face. She shook like a boat tethered to a dock in a violent storm.

Arek stepped in front of his sister. He guided her head to rest on his chest. He wrapped his arms around her. He comforted Mithany, gently stroking her back as she poured out grief, dropping her hands momentarily before wrapping them around Arek's waist.

With a kiss to the top of her head, Arek leaned in again and said to his sister, "You'll be with him again."

Her chest tightened. *Keep crying, keep shaking. Don't stop.* She told herself, *No one heard that.*

"Oh Arek, I love you so much, but why would you say such a thing?" She wanted to plead those words at him but didn't. *Not here. Not now.*

Her mind scrambled to find the proper response. Mithany wanted to look at Neladith, to evaluate her reaction. But if she did, she'd confirm for Neladith the importance of the words Arek let slip. The only action she could take was to pretend Arek said nothing of importance. She needed to show Neladith nothing wrong was said. She stole a quick glance Neladith's way. She wished she hadn't.

Tears and snotty sniffles flowed as Mithany stepped back. With a glance at Arek, she confirmed his lack of awareness of the breach he just committed. She gave him the same look she had when they were children. The secret language they used between them to avoid their mother's intrusions into their communications.

He reached down to hold her face in his hands, wiping her tears away. His mouth opened to speak when Mithany raised one finger to his lips. Her shaking had stopped. She offered him another sniffle, pulling in the loosened mucus dripping from her nose. It appeared as a gentle and special moment between brother and sister, but Mithany feared what he might say next.

With the same finger released from his lips, she moved it up to her own. "Shhh. My sweet brother. Thank you for being here for me. I *will* miss Reyne with all my heart. And I hope that somehow, in the vast Circle of Life, I find him again."

Mithany wanted to reassure her audience that Reyne was buried here. "I don't know how I am going to go on without Reyne, but I have you." Stepping up on her tiptoes, with both hands on his shoulders, she kissed him on the lips. "I love you, brother."

Let her think about that, Mithany considered, hoping to create an immediate distraction to give Neladith something different to ponder.

Afraid to even look toward Neladith again, Mithany settled back, wrapping her arms once again around his waist, resting her head in his chest. She could only imagine the smile on his face. She pictured in her mind's eye him looking over her head towards Neladith. She let the moment pass in silence.

As she stepped back, with her hand in his, Mithany entangled their fingers. Patting their intertwined hands, she said, "We have a special man, don't we, Neladith?" Offering Neladith a friendly smile as cover, Mithany watched for a reaction. *It's always in the eyes.*

There, written on Neladith's face, she spied it again. Mithany read more in the one second the two women locked eyes than Arek ever would in all his time with Neladith. An ever so slight tell. Unnoticeable to almost anyone else, Mithany found the quick, tiny, angry nostril flair with the concomitant tightening at the corners of the eyes. The same tell she observed at the stolen glance moments ago. It all happened quicker than a wink, but not quick enough to go unnoticed by Mithany. She beheld it all, and she knew it for what it was: disgust leaking off Neladith.

Mithany couldn't be sure she noted anything else. She was certain of what she detected, but its cause was the real question. *Was it in response to me? Was it the kiss? Is she jealous? Or did she make out Arek's slipup? And if she understood him to say I would see Reyne again, would it mean anything to Neladith beyond a simple comfort? Would it mean anything of consequence to her? Why should she care?*

Neladith didn't provide confirmation she heard Arek's misstep, or even if she did, that it held any meaning when she replied to Mithany, "Arek is a special guy. I'm glad that he's here for you, and I'm so lucky I met you both in Owls Neck."

Mithany replied, "Thank you so much. It means a lot to us both."

With her heart pounding, Mithany wondered, *Did she buy it?*

Concealed Beneath Acceptance

The Woolands: 29th Day of the Salmon Moon

Mera | Reyne

Reyne apparently had enough. With both hands, he lunged for Mera's throat. Mera took a small step back, but Reyne snatched him by the collar. He yanked Mera towards him, who offered no resistance. Nose to nose, Reyne exploded.

"Enough. Tell me what we're doin', or I'm done! And why can't you go to this fantasy world of yours? Why me?" Spittle flew as Reyne shouted.

Mera didn't blink. He stared back at Reyne. "Because I can't. Okay? I can't."

Mera had waited patiently the past day-and-a-half for this very moment. Reyne was either going to commit to the cause, or Mera was going to lose him for good—the moment of decision. Getting him to this point was one thing; getting him to make the right decision was an entirely different matter.

One by one, Mera pried Reyne's fingers from his collar, freeing himself from anger's grip.

The older man placed both hands on the younger man's shoulders and asked, "So what do you figure your options are?"

It wasn't a taunt but a challenge to help the younger man see he had limited choices and to nudge him towards the one option that led to Mithany's safety and a journey into another world. Capitalizing on Reyne's internal driving force, which he placed above all others, got Mera to the threshold of what he needed: Reyne on the path to Evidar. Free will, a necessity in the complicated process of transfiguration between realities, required Reyne's participation of his own volition. Whether manipulation thrust Reyne towards the perforce conclusion mattered little to either Mera or to the transitioning event that would move Reyne into Evidar.

"Either you explain everything to me," Reyne began, "or I'm going on my own, alone, without you, right now. I'll go back and face these hunters, or maybe I'll just steal Mithany away and go hide in some remote forest away from everyone."

Mera read Reyne's raised eyebrows at the end of his demand and determined he meant what he said. He would leave. But Mera didn't accept Reyne's threat. He understood, hidden in the threat to move on, Reyne was also making a round-about statement that he was willing to stay if he could make Reyne appreciate one thing: Why?

"My young friend, you need to accept you can't go back. What do you assume will happen when you show up in Hensdale? Don't answer. It's rhetorical. You may've guessed that there're people planted in and around Hensdale to gather intel. You show up tomorrow or next month, they will get to you."

"How can they get me if they can't find me?"

"Consider what will happen to Mithany if you do that. She'll become fodder for drawing you out. Chances are, Mithany won't live too long once they realize you're alive. You can try to fight back, but with what? Who're you fighting against? The white-haired man? The red-eyed woman? Both are trained killers. And they're not the only ones. Do you know who the other Evidar hunters are, what to look for to find them? You think you stand a chance with the skills you have?"

Reyne listened.

Not finished, Mera went on, "If hunters have an inkling you're alive, they'll keep tabs on her until you show up. Baiting the trap. If you never show and hide somewhere, they'll snatch her away and force you to search her out. They'll make it easy for you. They'll even tell you where they've taken her, but you'll never get to her. Ambush. You can't save her if you go back. One nut farmer against a handful of hardened, trained killers. You go back, you're a dead man. A lamb to the slaughter. Mithany most likely too. So, tell me, where're you going to go?"

It wasn't a question but a statement. This time, it was a taunt. True enough, but it didn't mean Reyne took the option off the table. Mera understood if Reyne didn't have the choice to go back to Hensdale, it didn't mean he had to go to Evidar.

"Either way, I'm not goin' anywhere until you tell me. Make me understand."

"Alright. I owe you as much, and I couldn't tell you sooner. Frankly, I worried you might have shared it back in Hensdale. And now I see you're ready. You're at the point of making a decision. So, it's time I guess you heard it all. Sit down. This is going to take a while. First of all, I can't transition to Evidar. It's that simple. Stop me along the way if you have questions."

"I have one before you start. How do I know if anything you're about to tell me is true?"

"I'll get you there. Just listen."

"Don't take too long. My patience with this fairytale is at its limits."

"It all starts with reality or what you and everyone assume reality to be—what the world seems to be. Give you an example: Temple of Life. People have faith, and it is embedded deep in our worldview. But what is faith? It's only a belief. People act, they behave, they conform to their shared belief in gods they define in their minds. As a pervasive, shared idea that the gods have real power, an actual ability to affect people, to govern people, to change people. It becomes real because individuals believe it's real. Belief equals reality. For the non-believers who don't accept the Temple of Life faith, the gods hold no power over them. Reality is what the mind believes it is."

"Sounds silly."

"The power of belief is as real as a tangible physical being living in the sky, silly or not. It is as real as if there were a living Sun God. God probably exists, in what form I don't know, but my point is, whether there is a physical being, god, or only the belief in one, doesn't alter the power it holds over our reality. It's our thoughts that give it authority over us. We hand over control of our actions to an idea. That's what gives form to reality. Stop believing in the Sun God, and he simply goes away. Humanity can kill a god with just a thought."

"What's this got to do with me?"

"All the world would change overnight if everyone stopped following the Temple of Life faith. Consider those words. Thoughts create reality. Every single achievement in the history of humanity began with a thought. If we never conceived it, it would never have happened. If some person, somewhere, never thought to do it, whatever 'it' is, it would never have happened. All borne of a simple notion inside someone's head. Proof that thinking of a thing can lead down the path to the reality of a thing."

"I get your point, but it changes nothin' for me. I haven't 'thought' about going to Evidar. I have no reality in Evidar."

"Reality has momentum, just like anything else. Consider this: what does it take to stop a marble rolling downhill? It takes a force greater than the energy of the rolling marble."

"What are you talkin' about?"

"How much energy is that? It depends on how much mass the marble has and how much momentum it has. A simple formula for momentum. Well, it all depends on how much force you apply to that rolling marble, whether you stop it or just alter its trajectory. A little bit of force, and you might change its path a little. A lot of force, and you can change its path a lot. With more energy applied to it than it's using to roll downhill, you can stop it altogether."

Mera stopped. His vision fixed on Reyne, gaging the young man's reaction.

"That's how it applies to you. That's what we're doing. We're the force that's going to apply to the marble we call Evidar. You're going there to alter the path Evidar is on. You go to Evidar not as a savior, not as a hero, but as a disrupter. There are key players over there that need to be removed. To die. How successful you are at that will change the path Evidar is on, a lot or a little. But if we do nothing, that dark reality will come crashing into ours. All of Tartica is at stake."

Reyne looked back at Mera. Confusion mixed with anger painted his face. "I gotta say it again. What are you talkin' about?"

Mera said, "Let me explain. The status of collective reality shackles human potential. It limits what you conceive as possible because you've been told what is impossible. Again, reality begins with a single thought. You don't think about it, and it will never come to be. Can you communicate a thought from the streets of Teth to the palace in Tandure in an instant? No. Because you can't conceive of a way it's possible, but the people of the Second Age did. Can you fly? No. Because you've been told humans can't fly, but the people of the Second Age did. Do you presume you can raise a mountain hundreds of feet tall from any spot on Earth? No, but the people of the Second Age did."

Reyne asked, "How can you know these things? And even if you do, so what? How does it affect me?"

Mera said, "I know these things because I've been around a long time and I understand the laws of physics. I can do the things I showed you, like talking to fire, calling up the past. You saw the red-haired girl because I understand physics. Magic is just another way to say, 'I don't understand' for all those who can't."

"I don't care what you call it, magic or physics, just teach me how to do it."

"It would take more than a lifetime for you to learn what I know, to do what I do."

"You did it. If it takes more than a lifetime, how d'you do it?"

"It took me more than one lifetime," Mera said. "But that's for another time."

"How am I supposed to believe any of this gibberish?"

"I'm not your mentor, and I'm not your teacher. I've tried to be your protector."

"You've done a shit job at that."

"Have I? You're the only Tweener still alive, and Mithany's alive as well."

"But Daedyn's not. Is he?"

Mera knew better than to respond to Reyne's challenge. Mera saw it on Reyne's face; a crushing weight landed on Reyne with the memory of Daedyn.

"Tell me somethin' of this physics of yours that I can trust in and accept. Make me get it, and I'll consider doin' what you ask."

Mera sat contemplative and unmoving for a minute, searching for just the right words.

"The things I've shown you are a part of reality we normally don't see or access. I've opened the way to it through that part of you, the Eye of Heaven, your Third Eye. That part of the brain people never consciously access. Thoughts are the tip of the arrow that points the way to reality. Thoughts connect the soul to the physical world. The soul is nothing more than the awareness of quantum energy clusters, never dying. And consider this, quantum particles reside in everything because they make up everything; therefore, life is in everything."

"Not that crap about the eyeballs of heaven again."

Mera ignored the slight and continued, "We created reality in our minds, our consciousness. Souls want to experience what can't be experienced as a single string of quantum energy. Souls need our physical bodies, our thoughts to experience love, hate, pain, feelings that can't be accessed otherwise. Quantum energy doesn't seek to change our world but strives only to experience it."

"Ah, yes. There you go with the quantum whatacles again," Reyne snickered.

"That's how I showed you the specter of the red-eyed woman. I simply asked all the quantum energy clusters I could reach out to in the trees, the grasses, the ground, and everything around that clearing to show me, to show us, what they've sensed, what information they'd amassed over time. In the entire universe, information can never be destroyed. It's stored in those tiny quantum particles. With my ability to communicate with my own soul, to ask it to reach out to the other quantum energies clustered in the living things all around us, to show us that single awful event."

"So now you talk to trees?"

"My mind pulled together the fragments they shared. Individually, quantum strings can't organize all the sensory input they collect. Our brains can, though. They collect snippets of input and organize them. There're energy waves, pieces of information, of untold, almost infinite quantities passing by us every second. Our bodies have a few input collectors, like eyes and ears, and we have a brain to interpret all of it, to piece it all together, to make sense of it. The brain is a beautiful device that can process and organize the information it collects. It's one reason souls love the human experience. But there is so much more because we don't have all the sensory inputs to all the information that's created and floating about out there. There's so much more, but that's the root of it. Reyne—"

"That's not possible. Trees don't see, and rocks don't talk. It can't be all put together in our minds."

"It sorta is."

"That's bullshit."

"Not at all. Smart men, very smart women in the Second Age learned through a Double Slit Experiment that the act of observing influenced the outcome. In the experiment, they proved thoughts affect reality. I digress, not important for now."

"Then why don't things change? Why don't we get different results when people like me see things differently?"

"One person's consciousness doesn't change the collective reality of a civilization. Not enough energy from one person's perception to affect the entire mass. Shared reality governs with a collective amount of energy. It takes a great measure of some force, a critical mass, to impact that level of change. It's what the Temple does, what governments do, what merchandizing is all about. Those are simply efforts to control what everyone is supposed to think, laying the foundation of a shared reality of a concept on small and large scales. That's our world, piece by piece. We don't all share one hundred percent the same ideas, yet there is enough overlap across the spectrum of beliefs to coalesce into a communal, cohesive reality."

"So, this idea about collective reality isn't just your idea?" Reyne asked.

"In limited application. But in a much larger sense, it's what's at stake between us and the world of Evidar. It's what Evidar is. Someone, something, has created an alternate reality, an alternate outcome from some point in Earth's history; it split off from ours into two distinct planets in separate dimensions. Evidar could be the tiniest of a fraction of an inch away from us right here and right now in another dimension, or it could be billions of billions of miles away. I don't know. But I do know it's real in every way. And whoever—he, she, it, God, gods—created this alternate reality, called Evidar, means to overtake ours.

To apply forces to our reality to change it. Change it into what, I can't say, but I suspect Evidar means to impose its paradigm on us. I don't know if it's evil or just wants something we have that it doesn't. To merge their Probability Wave, their timeline, into ours. But I do know that time after time, Evidar's efforts to change our world have been thwarted."

"How can I swallow any of this?"

"In the Temple Archives, there is a book. It's called the Bible. It tells us the First Age ended with a great flood that wiped out all of humankind except a few moral, decent people: stock to rebuild. And rebuild they did into the Second Age. The Second Age was a wondrous time but with many problems, culminating in the fiery near-destruction of our entire planet. Again, except for the few Teth gathered up and brought here, breeding stock to rebuild humanity anew, once more, under different, moral conditions. Could be the guiding hand of a superior being, like God looking out for humanity, saving a few to rebuild both times."

"That's quite a story. I've never heard of this Bible. Again, more facts only you have knowledge of?"

"The Temple lords have kept a lot from humanity to keep the masses on a path most desired by the Temple's leaders. Like I said, they've kept the marble rolling along the path they've chosen," Mera explained.

He went on, "Teth laid the foundation of the reality we know in the Third Age. What the Book of Teth doesn't tell you is the story about the epochs-long battle for souls. The battle for souls here on Earth. Evidar is close to getting the change they want, and whoever is Evidar's creators or creator wants to wipe Tartica's slate clean and start over. But in the past when evil looked like they might win, our side blew it all up so the bad people couldn't have it. Like the universe saying 'fuck you.' So, whether it's God, Mother Earth, or whatever entity you conceive of, it will not grant us many more chances to get it right. At some point, we're going to be a write-off. Evidar is a monumental risk to everything. Does that explain things clearly to you? If we don't stop them, everything here is going to be forever fucked."

Reyne remained silent for a few moments. "Let's say I accept your talk about reality and whatever. You want to send me off to kill people? People I don't know. Just because you say so?"

"As I said, you're to be a disruptor. If I'm right, and I almost always am, things over here are about to be thrown into chaos. Anarchy is a feeding ground for change. Evidar, in effect, is applying some force against our rolling marble of reality. Pandemonium is about to be unleashed on Tartica with enough force to impact civilization and change everything."

"Huh?"

"Chaos is like a capacitor. It stores up energy. Pressure on society will build and build and then explode across Tartica with some unknowable outcome being the result. Think of the marble. A lot of energy is about to be unleashed against our way of life. How far off the path our marble will roll, impossible to predict. Is Evidar just laying down a foundation for change to build upon, or is this the big one?"

"And you think little ole me can stick my finger in the bad guy's eye?"

"Those little quantum particles make up everything in the universe. They're like fairy dust. They can be anything you can conceive of. You just have to know the right physics to make it happen. To point them in the direction you want them to go. One probable outcome amongst trillions of all possible outcomes. There are a million, billion, trillion possibilities from one moment to the next. Momentum keeps the universe, and all its interconnected parts, moving forward in the direction it's currently pointed, so a new path out of the trillions of possible alternative paths doesn't have to be decided upon from one moment to the next. Our reality exists as one outcome amongst an infinite number of alternatives. If something applies enough force, enough energy at the right spot, momentum changes and reality shifts."

"You can't know all this."

"Something, let's call it a god, conceived of and set in motion the universe we know today. I doubt there is enough energy out there to alter the total momentum of the entire universe. But I can conceive of enough force applied to this place, right here and right now, to change the small part of reality we call Tartica."

Reyne looked at him like a lost puppy.

Mera followed with an answer he didn't want to hear. "You, my friend, are the only Tweener I know of that this world has left, and you're the only one who can transfigure into Evidar. This world needs you to get to Evidar, where it is my hope that you can fuck things up from that side of the equation."

"Just me. All alone. The heck with that. I'd be toast."

"You want to save Mithany? Have the life you want with her? Not if Evidar has its way. You might just be the only way to save Mithany's future. Chaos is coming to Tartica. No one can change that. Discord on Tartica will build up like a pressure cooker ready to explode. When it does, a new reality will emerge. I can't say if anyone, including Mithany, will be spared. Your presence in Evidar might just be the energy we need to apply to their marble to take their eye away from us and focus it on themselves. That's what Edruk did. Your father. He mustered enough disruption in Evidar to keep them focused inward, and that's what you can do."

"Sound like you're lookin' for a hero. I'm not remotely prepared and got no clue how to do this Tweener stuff. Sounds pretty dangerous. Was Edruk your hero? Your champion? What did that get him? Killed. I'm guessin' that could happen to me too," Reyne said in a calm voice.

"Evidar ain't no place for no hero. You asked me if you can trust anything I tell you. Here is something I hope helps you with that. I'm going to tell you the naked truth. You might die in the effort. I've sent others over since your father died. I haven't been silent these past twenty years. He came and went between Evidar and Earth frequently until the day he died. Even if you go, you're right. It's risky. Others have failed in his place, and you might too. I'll arrange for you to be well prepared, but there aren't any guarantees. Now here's another harsh truth: if you fail and die, hunters will stop looking for you. They'll have no reason to leverage Mithany as bait to find you. You'll buy Mithany's safety with your death. I don't want you to fail. To die. But you help Mithany either way. That's me being honest with you."

Reyne didn't speak for several minutes. He reconsidered his position, just not in the way Mera was pushing for. Reyne imagined a different path. It didn't involve Mera, but he would need Mera's help to achieve it. Mera made a mistake reminding him of his father, Edruk. A realization hit Reyne hard. Hidden in Mera's message was a way out.

Reyne said, "Fuck me. I'm not sure about any of this."

A plan began to coalesce. *If Edruk went to that place and got back, I should be able to come and go as well. If Mera can't get to Evidar, he can't see me leave from Evidar. I might be able to get back here whenever I want and get back to Mithany.*

Mera took the opening. "You're not ready for any of this. It takes a lot of effort to transfigure into a different reality. We'll get you there once you're prepared."

"So, what you're sayin' is that Mithany is fucked if I don't go, and if I do, even if I get killed, she'll be safe?"

"Essentially, that's the long and short of it."

"I go; she lives."

"Yes."

"I don't really have any choice then."

"No. You don't. If you want to protect her."

"Why didn't you just cut to the chase? All the rest of your bullshit doesn't matter. Only Mithany does."

"It does matter. You said you needed to hear it, to understand why you have to do what I'm asking of you in Evidar."

"I'll do this for her. Not for you."

Reyne agreed to put himself in Evidar, but unknown to Mera, not as his agent of change. He'd go to Evidar, but he would turn around and come right back to protect Mithany himself.

Mera said, "I'll have to prep you for what you're going to face in that dark world. There is someone here who will train you. Her name is Gina. You'll meet her once we get to Teth. Your training will begin there, and in Teth, I hope to find out how hunters discovered your existence."

Mera looked pleased with himself. He put both hands behind his head and leaned back. He told Reyne, "Change is imminent. I don't know how, but something big is going to happen soon. The presence of that girl's red eyes tells me they couldn't wait. Needed you out of the way immediately. But, if you can sow a little turmoil in Evidar, we just might stand a chance."

Reyne replied, "I guess I'm going to Evidar."

Mera said, "It's important that we get you ready as quickly as possible. Chaos is coming."

It's on You

Owls Neck: 29th day of the Salmon Moon

Quith

Soon after leaving Mithany and Arek at the place Reyne was supposed to have been buried, Neladith reported Arek's slipup to her leader, Selundra Quith.

Neladith's news set off a chain of events. If what she reported to Quith was true, there was a chance Reyne was still alive, and his wasn't the body interred in the family plot.

Quith had to bring this to Dylla's attention. He feared her reaction, and he had a good reason. Dylla didn't treat those who failed her with compassion or understanding.

Only hours after Neladith conveyed her intel to Quith, he'd arrived back in Owls Neck, where Dylla waited for him to deliver his status report. Meeting once again at the inn nestled in the tiny village of Owls Neck, he pushed down his fears and walked up the steps of the outdoor café where Dylla sat waiting.

After Quith took his seat at the same table where they'd met previously, both bypassed any pleasantries, getting right to the meat of his report. Quith passed on breakfast. He didn't have the stomach for it.

He told Dylla, "Neladith just caught an off-hand comment from the brother of Reyne's girlfriend. The same guy Neladith's been using as her beard."

Dylla tilted her head back, closed her eyes, took in the morning air permeating their surroundings. Its sweetness appeared to offend her and soured her mood even more. Both had grown familiar with the way things were in this world.

Morning. Sunlight. Birds. Quith hated them all, and he was certain Dylla did as well. It made the news from Quith cut deeper into her darkening frown.

"That poses a potential problem for us. And with the brother in seclusion, those two morsels of information, considered together, point to the possibility of an unfavorable outcome. I don't like what I'm hearing."

"It's most likely nothing. But I wanted to fill you in and to let you know I've given Neladith a new objective: Find out. She has one day, two tops, to either prove a confirmation of delivery or to determine where the package's been shipped."

A single bead of sweat rolled down the side of Quith's face, and his foot tapped wildly under the table. He slid his hand over his knee, clenched his thigh, digging deep into the muscle, hoping to interrupt his out-of-control foot.

His statement hung there for a moment while she sipped her coffee. Her pause, her silence, her scowl, it rattled him. A crow cawed, cutting through the silence between them, setting off a series of aviary replies. She let the birds finish their conversation. Quith squirmed through the emptiness engulfing them.

"Tell me again what Neladith reported. Her exact words."

"Again, let me say, it's what she *thought* she heard. Nothing certain. Just being cautious here. Like I reported before, we had Tylus confirm the deed was done. Admittedly, with Meratoruc nearby, he couldn't get in there for an up-close, but everything else matched the package." Hoping to shift blame if his team had failed to kill Reyne, he identified Tylus as the source of confirmation.

"Enough of the equivocating. You made the call for her to take the shot. You're the op's leader. It's on you."

A gulp escaped his efforts to hide it. He thought back on one of his many missions for Dylla. On that particular job, he ended the life of the last team leader who failed her. His predecessor.

"The guy said to his sister, the fiancée, 'You'll see him again.' The girl didn't react and made some remarks about meeting up in the Circle of Life or some such nonsense they believe in."

Quith opened his mouth to add something, but the middle-aged, red-haired woman raised one lone finger, shutting him down. In his experience, Dylla used dead air as a tool to instill fear. It was working.

In his role as operations leader, working for Dylla these past few years, quietude was her way of telling him he was in deep shit. There was nowhere to hide from it.

A crow cawed again, "Oh, those fucking birds. I hate those things," he said, trying to build on their other-worldly bond.

"Forget the birds. Look at me."

His eyes went wide, and adrenaline flooded through him as he looked directly at her.

She spoke in quiet, measured tones, carrying a message more menacing than if she screeched her demands. "You'll do whatever it takes—dig up the body if you have to, put more bodies back in the same hole when you're done if you have to. You're going to get me answers. Meet me here at midnight tomorrow. I've had enough of all this sunlight."

"I won't let you down," he was about to say before realizing he had already breached that threshold. Instead, Quith stated flatly, "It will be done."

Dylla sipped her coffee, then put the cup down on the table. Wrapping both hands around the mug, the woman in charge looked hard and threatening at Quith.

Continuing in her deceptively gentle manner, she said, "I'm going to assume you know I expect to see you here tomorrow, good news or bad. Sometimes people think of avoiding delivering me the bad news. That's your worst possible option."

Chaos Unleashed

Teth: 29th Day of the Salmon Moon

Tomelai | Jerithan

The Council of Nations began its annual meeting in the traditional manner, replete with pomp and circumstance appropriate for a gathering of world leaders. The Feast of Teth, now two days past, took a back seat in importance to the summit that brought together Tartica's four heads of state as equal voices in the ruling body responsible for implementing the Covenant of Absolute Human Obligations. The topic of electrics and whatever surprises it promised titillated everyone in the chamber as they eagerly awaited its turn for debate as pinned to the published agenda—none more than Madrotti Tomelai.

Adelle's Chancellor sat stoically, with First Lady Kaythlin seated directly behind him. In attendance, Prime Minister Hrotitem Larsed represented the Peoples Republic of Kantos. Also present to open the meeting were F'Saad Dimenk, President of Greenlin, and First Lord Jerithan Cree as Teth's head of government.

Dignitaries and commoners from all over the continent filled the chamber. Although the Council of Nations held sessions throughout the year, ambassadors relinquished their top-dog status in favor of their respective leaders for the special gathering.

Jerithan Cree, Tomelai, Dimenk, and Larsed occupied center stage as Tartica's ruling quadrumvirate. Each, in turn addressed the crowd with opening statements filled with ingratiating words, glorifying each of their respective homelands. As the first to speak, Tomelai held back a single mention of his contentious proposal for electrics, heightening the anticipation for its introduction and when focus of attention would be his alone.

The chamber was an exquisite amphitheater constructed from richly-colored redwood. The designers spaciously positioned twenty of the largest baobab trees along the perimeter of the chamber. The leaves of their branches formed an abundant covering that loomed overhead, creating a dome of greenery. The Sun's rays streamed gently between the leaves of the opened canopy to flood the enormous area with ample lighting.

The four leaders sat at a semicircular conference table set in the center of the room, facing the amphitheater. A fifth leader, Provost Kwuinan of Teth, served as the gathering's Chair and facilitator. Traditionally, the facilitator position was rotated year by year between the four independent governments. On the last day of the Salmon Moon in the year 1543 of the Third Age, the government of Teth held the honor.

Delegates from each nation were positioned along the first row of the amphitheaters immediately facing their respective leaders. Seating for other dignitaries filled the many subsequent forward rows. Their closeness to the center of the room reflected their status, with the remaining twenty tiered rows opened to anyone hoping to attend. Public seating was claimed on a first-come, first-served basis. As the meeting began, more than a thousand people filled the chamber.

A melee of sounds from nameless voices filled the ornate hall. Words carried in every direction, coming together as one monotone, unending cacophony. Provost Kwuinan brought down the gavel over and over demanding silence. After achieving his goal following several dozen swipes, Provost Kwuinan proclaimed, "Opening statements from our esteemed leaders concluded; the Chair would like to move to the first item on our agenda."

It sounded like a simple statement. Extensive negotiations between the delegations leading up to the annual gathering paved the way for their mutually agreed agenda.

Tomelai stood. All eyes turned to the Chancellor. The attendees did not expect him to speak at this point in the choreographed itinerary. He'd completely broken from decorum.

Chancellor Tomelai spoke up, "Before this august group takes up the first item on this important agenda, I ask permission to address the Chair."

First Lord Jerithan didn't move. Prime Minister Larsed was the first to impose. "Point of order," he declared, facing the facilitator.

Tomelai didn't give the Chair an opportunity to reply, "I ask your indulgence, Prime Minister Larsed. I agree it is unusual to make this request, but I'm permitted this privilege in the charter. If only at the annual meeting."

The provost was a competent man and familiar with the little-used privilege Tomelai spoke of. "It's permitted for any of the four leaders to ask for the privilege to speak at any time. Please feel free to proceed, Chancellor Tomelai." Provost Kwuinan, the pro tempore facilitator, cut off all discussion on Tomelai's request to address the Council and sat back down.

"Thank you, Provost. The Kingdom of Adelle and all Tartica's inhabitants, thank you. What I would ask the Council to consider is of great concern to our very existence." Tomelai gave his words time to have effect.

The meeting observers broke into hundreds of separate conversations. Tomelai did nothing to settle them down. He remained standing. He looked up and scanned the crowd. A piercing sound penetrated the din of voices when the facilitator struck the same gavel used to call the meeting to order.

Yelling above the melee, the Prime Minister from Kantos called out, just as sounds from the pounding gavel and from the tumultuous shouting faded away, "This item I presume the Chancellor will speak of is on the agenda to be taken up later this afternoon. We've all agreed to this agenda. I respectfully ask that the Chair take up this matter in its proper time."

Before the facilitator could reply, the Chancellor injected, "My respected colleague, I again ask for your gracious indulgence. You are correct in your observations of our agenda and of your presumption. I believe the item is of such great importance that a proper discussion will consume more than the limited time our afternoon can accommodate. Unless, of course, if you would like to move to approve the proposal without debate, I will then gladly withdraw my already granted privilege to speak."

The gavel rang out again. After a few moments passed, allowing the sound to dissipate, the acting facilitator stated, "The privilege has already been granted. This body cannot withdraw it without the good Chancellor's consent. The privilege grants the leader the right to speak on any topic he or she so desires. It does not preclude speaking on an agenda item. Chancellor Tomelai, do you wish to withdraw the privilege?"

"I do not," Chancellor Tomelai said defiantly as he stole a glance from his First Lady. First Lady Kaythlin offered her husband a reassuring nod. Jerithan and President Dimenk sat stone faced. The Prime Minister couldn't hide his displeasure at Tomelai's maneuver to commandeer the Council's agenda.

"Then proceed," Provost Kwuinan proclaimed to all.

Tomelai spoke in a loud, commanding voice. He turned from the provost, with his arms raised in a gesture to address the chamber. "Electrics! It is time we move our civilization forward. It's time to approve electrics. The benefits would accrue across the—"

The entire chamber roared. Tomelai couldn't be heard. People were yelling for and against the idea of infusing electricity into civilization and their way of life. Virtually everyone knew electricity existed and even flourished in remote black-market locations, yet humanity, in its current incarnation of the Third Age, was committed to the Gift of Nature. The Council had always branded electricity as a force outside of Nature. Electricity, in the Third Age, had been rejected by the Council repeatedly, believing it to be antithetical to the "all natural" way of life demanded by the Covenant: adherence to Nature, the guiding principles of the document they all swore to live by.

The gavel came down again and again. Provost Kwuinan tried to wrestle control over the engulfing chaos. After several minutes of constant pounding, the facilitator pried back control.

Almost yelling to be heard above the collective sounds bouncing about the amphitheater, President Dimenk called out, "Facilitator, I ask that we put formalities aside to permit us to explore the good Chancellor's proposal."

Jerithan secretively nodded his approval for Provost Kwuinan. While Provost Kwuinan was the official facilitator, the First Lord was the real authority controlling the meeting. Jerithan had prepared to deal with this issue, and he was certain the proposal would fail. He didn't see the harm in setting aside the official rules to get to Tomelai's disgrace sooner rather than later.

Kwuinan looked about at the faces of the four leaders. "Can we all agree then with President Dimenk?"

One by one, the four leaders nodded their approval to the facilitator, who responded, "Then let it be so."

"Thank you," Tomelai began before being cut off by the Prime Minister from Kantos.

"We've dealt with this issue before. I'm sure we will again. Let's put all this to rest with a vote. Now. If that meets with your approval, good Chancellor Tomelai," Larsed said, looking pleased with himself.

They'd widely discussed the issue between the delegations since electrics had been first proposed as an agenda item months ago. The real battle over electrics had already occurred. Whatever might be said in the faux debate over many hours inside the Council meeting would be for public posturing. First Lord Jerithan Cree was certain it would fail.

"Got you, Tomelai," Larsed said under his breath, yet loud enough for the others to hear.

To everyone's surprise, Tomelai called out, "I have no objection."

The Voice broke into Jerithan. *"Be careful here. Are you sure you know what's going on? Tomelai seems too sure of himself. Are you certain you've secured the votes?"*

Responding only to the Voice in his head, he offered his thoughts, *This is dead on arrival. No surprises. Dimenk is firm. We have her vote. Tomelai has no allies in this. You heard what Larsed said. He is a hard no. Nothing to worry about.*

The Chair took the vote. Three opposed permitting electrics, and only Chancellor Tomelai voted to support the proposal. Provost Kwuinan, Chair of the meeting, stood and proclaimed to all in attendance, "The proposal to permit electricity has been defeated."

Cheers and jeers overwhelmed the room. Fights broke out in the upper tiers. Kwuinan let it go on for several minutes before waving his arms up and down in a gesture to settle everyone.

Jerithan was pleased with the results. It came as no surprise. *See, we did not need to kill him. He has been dealt with. The threat from Tomelai is over,* he said to the Voice.

"Good Chancellor Tomelai, the proposal has been defeated. Do you relinquish the privilege and permit us to proceed to our agreed-upon agenda?" Provost Kwuinan asked.

To everyone's surprise, Chancellor Tomelai, still standing, proclaimed, "I do not."

The unruly crowd continued to sound off at the Chancellor's proclamation.

Now yelling to the crowd, "It is time," Chancellor Madrotti Tomelai shouted. The attendees all fell silent in anticipation of what he would say next.

What Jerithan could not have known beforehand and what only now became obvious was that Tomelai's demand for a vote on electrics was only a feint, a misdirection to rouse the passions of the attendees. As Chancellor Tomelai drove towards his ultimate objective, fear began to churn in Jerithan's gut.

With a hushed quiet settled over the amphitheater, Tomelai opened his arms, "We have come to a place where the survival of humanity has been secured. We have come to a place where all people, regardless of orientation, should be free to pursue their own lives as they see fit. We have come to a place where the priority of reproduction no longer needs to be required of every living adult. We have come to a place, and we have come to a time that demands of itself…" He paused.

Waited. And slammed his fist hard against the podium as he called out, "... that we dissolve the Covenant!"

He couldn't continue. Passions erupted. Everyone in the great hall was shouting, some in condemnation, others in jubilation. Every person in the chamber was screaming at the top of their lungs. The overwhelming sound was deafening. The gavel came down over and over and over, but its intended impact escaped little beyond where the provost stood.

Jerithan looked over to his provost. They needed to regroup.

The First Lord heard the Voice mocking him, *"Everything is under control, huh? Didn't need to kill him, huh? Nothing to worry about, huh?"*

Jerithan didn't know what to do. He was a plodder, not a man who governed by the seat of his pants. Worst of all, he didn't see this coming.

No one saw it coming.

Unthinkable.

Sacrilege.

Abomination.

An anathema to the Third Age.

Jerithan was defensive in his response to the Voice. *You say you glimpse at things to come. Did you foresee this?* There was no reply from the Voice. *I didn't think so,* First Lord Jerithan mocked.

Provost Kwuinan approached each of the leaders and barked into their ears. One by one, he got approval to end the session with the caveat to reconvene at a later time yet to be determined.

The Voice broke through Jerithan's reeling thoughts. Jerithan would have his answer from the Voice. *"I think I can see a different future now. This man, Chancellor Tomelai, may have given me an alternative path. This can work, but I'm uncertain of your part in it any longer."*

What are you talking about? Jerithan demanded of the Voice.

Jerithan received nothing from the Voice who'd been his companion for so long. The Voice went quiet, and something inside Jerithan felt different, empty.

Proud, standing, watching the chamber explode, Chancellor Tomelai had set First Lady Kaythlin's plan into motion. Tomelai nodded to his wife. His nod told her, *Fuck them all.*

The plan Derr, First Lady Kaythlin, and Tomelai settled on just the evening before throwing Tartica into chaos. It would transform Tomelai's piece on the board into one minor problem measured against the bigger threat facing everyone now: the proposal to dissolve the Covenant of Absolute Human Obligations. The proposal would create havoc in every corner of the continent. People's passions would line up for and against dismantling the Covenant. Chaos was implicit in both the all-consuming debate forced on society and in the aftermath of ending a way of life governing the behaviors of all of humanity. The trio had set the foundation of the Third Age on fire. Not just a simple fire, but a conflagration.

The proposal, if implemented, would unshackle humanity to reach beyond its current reality. The traditionalists would fight to maintain the status quo. Others would demand the promise of freedom the dissolution of the Covenant would bring. Whatever the outcome, neither side would accept the other's victory. Whichever side prevailed, severe damage would accrue to the other. Chaos was assured from this moment forward.

The proposal was out there and couldn't be taken back. This wasn't the ramblings of some drunk in a tavern decrying the failings of the Covenant. This came from one of only four people in the known world to govern a nation. It couldn't be dismissed or ignored.

Word would spread like wildfire throughout Tartica.

Leaders would have their hands full dealing with their own populations to keep them under control.

Large groups, entire nations with opposing demands on their leaders, would be enjoined in a battle to prevail over the other.

Governments would strain at every seam to keep their respective citizenry under control.

It would demand every ounce of Dimenk's, Larsed's, and Jerithan Cree's attention. Tomelai's piece on the board put in check the other three symbolic kings with just one move.

Tomelai stood at the center of the coming storm. Many would hate him. Others would hail him as a visionary. Same-sex partners would demand their freedom to live their lives as they chose without the indignity of waivers or the penalty of facing forced breeding farms. It would set innovation free. Education would explore taboo ideas. Nature would take its place in support of humanity, not as its ruler.

New beginnings and a new direction for humanity. That was the promise.

Tomelai unleashed the energy of revolution. There would be too many willing to throw off the shackles of the Covenant to hold back the winds of change.

The proposal was now in the ether.

There would be no stopping it.

But the traditionalist would try.

Chancellor Tomelai didn't do it for any of those reasons. He did it to save himself. The day went exactly as Chancellor Tomelai, First Lady Kaythlin, and Captain Druin Derr had planned.

Humanity stood at the precipice of all-consuming chaos.

APPENDIX 1: THE COVENANT

DECLARATION OF THE COVENANT OF ABSOLUTE UNIVERSAL OBLIGATIONS

In the course of history, when profound circumstances threaten the very existence of every man, woman, and child, we, the one thousand seven hundred forty-two souls that remain of Humanity, must rise up and endeavor to take extraordinary and necessary actions to secure the survival of humankind. Foremost amongst these actions is to unequivocally set forth this Declaration of a Covenant, establishing the Absolute Universal nature of certain Obligations that each person owes to all others, without exception and in perpetuity, until such time the long-term survival of humankind is, without question, able to secure itself a future without concern for extinction as a species. We, therefore, set forth this Declaration, a Covenant of Absolute Universal Obligations, to be unencumbered by any law, be it Man's or God's in any form, by any government or by any religious authority, made by any man or any woman or on behalf of any community, until such time as a prognosis of the unconditional survival of our kind is secured.

First and principally among these is the Universal Obligation to Procreation, to spread the seed and nurture in the womb the future generations of humankind. It shall be the Absolute Universal Obligation, above all other laws, for all men and women between the ages of sixteen years and forty-five years to bring forward into this world at least three children attaining the age of fifteen years. Without exception, we recognize this Absolute Universal Obligation upon all but for those medically determined infertile by way of natural cause; for those that surpass the age of forty-five; and without regard for any individual's carnal desire to know another of one's own gender, each must endeavor to Procreate for the General Welfare inherent in the perforce propagation of our species. Recognizing the sacrifices that may be visited upon loving and caring souls, a general waiver may be granted to allow for the individual pursuit of same gender couplings, upon recognition in law of one's fulfillment of the Absolute Universal Obligation to Procreations having been attained. This waiver cannot be denied for any reason to any individual having fulfilled their Obligation of Procreation.

Second, and as well Absolute, we recognize the Universal Obligation to Preserve Human Life; to do no harm nor to place any human life at risk; to take no human life either by direct action or indirect action or by inaction, by any man, by any woman, by any child, or by any community or governing body at any level; to require intervention on behalf of any person having knowledge of another being at risk of imminent death, and to do so without regard for one's own safety, save death itself.

Third, and as well Absolute, we recognize the Universal Obligation to Promote the General Welfare. Incumbent upon all to effort a positive contribution to the wellbeing of the community of humanity through actions that may be recognized in a myriad of diverse services, products, or other unconventional efforts that Promote the General Welfare. Promotion of the General Welfare being Universal upon all humankind may take sway in and be all-consuming at all-time in some, while limited in others but rare moments in life yet Absolute and Universal, nonetheless is the Obligation to Promote the General Welfare. Reward nor recognition is the desired payment for the fulfillment of the Universal Obligation to Promotion of the General Welfare yet may be so without encumbrance by the will of man, woman, or by the force of community as expressed in laws or religious strictures.

Fourth, and as well Absolute, we recognize the Universal Obligation to the Natural Path. The Obligation to pursue life by way of the natural gifts of Earth's offerings to the exclusion of all else that is not firmly rooted in the natural world. We recognize the purported circumstances contributing to the Great Destruction and seek to begin a new path for humanity that enjoins us all towards a different, more enlightened course rooted in the Gifts of Nature.

These Declared and Absolute Universal Obligations are demanding of action by each and every person for each and every Obligation. We recognize that we cannot leave Humanity's future to the fortuitous whims of events or the inevitable consequences of humankind's collective or individual actions and therefore establish the Council of D'CAUO to speak as one voice for all humankind concerning the interpretation and implementation of this Declaration of the Absolute Covenant of Universal Obligations. In so agreeing, we bind us all; we remaining few souls, now and forever, along with all future progeny including any and all future governing bodies, persons, leaders, or religions, until such time as the future of the human race is secure and as such is so recognized by the Council or D'CAUO. So say we all declared this first day of the Summer Moon in the year eighty-six of the Third Age.

APPENDIX 2: GLOSSARY

Acolyte: Rank of an initiate in the Temple of Life religious order.

Anatese: (Anna-tess-ee) People-like inhabitants of The Stand's canopy and defenders of Teth. Human-like, deformed, and enhanced by the unknown length of time they've lived atop The Stand.

Aquila: (Ah-quil-ah) Prudent serving on the Council of Prudents.

Arek: (Air-ek) The older brother of Mithany and a charming young fellow who is a favorite amongst the eligible women of Hensdale.

Brenal, Hollid: (Breen-al) Hensdale's village doctor serving the community for decades.

Celebratorium: A place where people go to celebrate each of the Six Gifts. Celebratoria, plural.

Covenant of Absolute Universal Obligations: The founding document created by the survivors of the Great Destruction to bind all of humanity, the few who remained, and all in perpetuity until such time as a self-sustaining population can be achieved. Its dictates apply to all governments, all religious orders, and all human beings as an absolute obligation that must be followed without exception. Its principles are revered throughout Tartican civilization, and it serves as the basis of the Temple of Life religion. See Appendix 1.

Crip: Young man, native to Hensdale, and a member of Spetzer's inner circle who frequents the Forest Maiden Inn.

Daedyn Brenton: (Day-din) Reyne's brother. He lives with Reyne and they run the alphen orchard together as business partners.

Damus: A mathematical genius of Evidar, capable of applying complicated equations to predict the flow of events through time.

Derr, Druin: (Dur, Drew-in) Captain and leader of the KCG. Childhood friend of Chancellor Madrotti Tomelai. A harsh, serious, single-minded man dedicated to his sole purpose in life, keeping Tomelai safe.

Devil's Blacksmith: Also known as the Architect. An Evidarian leading the effort to alter the version of Earth from which he hails.

Dillip: (Dill-up) Member of the KCG.

Dimenk, F'Saad: (Dem-ink, Fah-sod) President of Greenlin. She has no children and was elected by its citizens to a life term as President.

Dimenk, Tague: (Dem-ink, Tay-g) Married to F'Saad Dimenk for ten years.

Dorana: (Door-ann-ah) Older woman living in Hensdale. Wife to Valillia.

Dylla Weisner: (Dil-ah) Regional leader from Evidar overseeing all operations on Tartica to eliminate anyone thought capable of transitioning between the dimension of Earth to her home world.

Edruk: (Ed-ruc) Reyne's birth father. Died before Reyne was born.

Efros: (Ef-frose) Moon god and son of Father Sun and Mother Earth.

Emosh, Synja: (Ee-moe-sh, Sin-jah) An Evidarian of exceptional abilities in mathematics and physics. Declared a Damus by the Devil's Blacksmith.

Enlist, Fegmin: (En-list, Fig-minn) Tithe master for the Temple of Life serving in Hensdale and Owls Neck.

Eurithian: (Your-eh-thigh-in) Father Sun. The one god that all others are subordinate to.

Ferpratt, Wilem: (Fur-prat) A senior Lieutenant in the KCG. Trusted ally and right-hand man of Druin Derr.

Gifts of Teth: Six Gifts bestowed upon humanity by the Goddess Teth: the Gift of Love, the Gift of Knowledge, the Gift of Flesh, the Gift of Life, the Gift of Renewal, and the Gift of Nature.

Grafph: (Graff) An assassin from Evidar and member of Dylla's unit.

Great Destruction: Event in Earth's history, approximately fifteen hundred years ago, that brought an end to the Second Age of humanity and nearly wiped out all life on the planet.

Gwerther Brenton: (Ga-were-the-er) Reyne's adoptive father. Died a few years before his wife Pachelle when Reyne was young.

Hangus: (Hang-us) Owner of a dry goods shop in Hensdale. Father of Y'Vay.

Hansel: (Han-sell) A prudent serving on the Council of Prudents.

Jadle Capkate: (Jay-dul Cap-kate) Communal Temple leader with the title of Mistress, in the small village of Hensdale.

Jamine: (Jah-mean) Member of the KCG.

Jerith: (Jur-ith) Member of the KCG.

Jerithan Cree: (Jer-eh-than Cree) First Lord of the Temple of Life. He believes he is doing God's work in his own way.

Jirek: (Jer-eek) Husband of Lorique.

Judjurex: An elected civil servant tasked with the responsibility to investigate, arrest, and determine guilt or innocence of anyone accused of an offense or criminal act.

Kaythlin Tomelai: (Kay-th-lyn Tom-eh-lay) First Lady of Tandure and wife of Madrotti Tomelai. Maiden name F'Shiyn. She is loved by the citizens of Adelle and is smart, charming, and attractive.

Kingdom's Chancellor's Gurad (KCG): The KCG is the secret service, quasi-spy agency, and intelligence gathering security organization tasked with maintaining the safety of Adelle's Chancellor, Madrotti Tomelai. Under Capitan Druin Derr, the KCG has the authority to explore any avenue of inquiry, detention, or interrogation in fulfillment of its mission.

Kiple: (Kip-al) General and leader of the Kingdom of Adelle's national police force.

Kwuinan: (Coo-in-anne) He is the de facto leader of the secular government of Teth with the title of Provost. Appointed by First Lord of the Temple of Life and answers to him or her in all matters.

Larsed, Hrotitem: (Lar-said, Hor-o-teat-um) The Prime Minister of the Peoples Republic of Kantos. Leader of the democracy and elected Prime Minister by a majority of Chamber of Delegates.

Lilly Marvo: (Lil-ee Mar-voe) Prudent Marvo's granddaughter. Lilly is eighteen years old and selected as Teth Incarnate for the Feast of Teth celebration.

Lorique: (Lore-eek) She is suspected Tweener living in the coastal town of Jarouhar and married to Jirek.

Loseff Tomelai: (Low-sef) Son of Madrotti and Kaythlin Tomelai. Second in the line of succession to the position of Chancellor for the Kingdom of Adelle.

Lume: Crystal that glows green light after being exposed to sunlight.

Madrotti Tomelai: (Ma-drot-tee Tom-ah-lay) Chancellor for life of the Kingdom of Adelle. Physically fit and dedicated to power. He is sometimes called Rotti by only one man, Druin Derr.

Malthis: (Mall-this) God of the heavens and the stars. Son of Father Sun and Mother Earth.

Marvo, Prudent: (Mar-voe) A well respected and senior Prudent. He is also grandfather to Lilly Marvo.

Mera: (Meh-ra) Full name in Meratoruc. He is Reyne's mysterious protector. Little is known of his background.

Mithany: (Mith-an-nee) Reyne's fiancée. She grew up in Hensdale. She is petite, competitive, and the sister of her older brother, Arek.

Milvoe: (Mill-voe) Member of the KCG.

Muroy: (Murh-oi) Memeber of the KCG.

Nardel: (N-are-del) Specialist and newest member of the KCG.

Neladith Karlis: (Nel-eh-dith) Young Evidarian assassin, capable of moving between earthly dimension, sent to Tartica to kill Reyne.

O'Hurn: (Oh-hern) A prudent serving on the Council of Prudents.

Pachelle Brenton: (Pah-shell) Reyne's adoptive mother and Daedyn's birth mother. She died when both boys were in their teens.

Prudent: Highest rank in the Temple of Life religious order but for the positions of First Lord and Second Lord.

Quith, Selundra: (Kw-ith, Sa-lun-dra) Mister Whitetop. He reports to Dylla and is the on-site field leader of the Evidar ops team tasked with eliminating Reyne and all other known or suspected Tweeners.

Razoal Baswun: (Ras-ole) He is a Prudent and ally of Jerithan serving as Second Lord.

Reiger: (Ree-ger) Young man, native to Hensdale, and a member of Spetzer's inner circle who frequent the Forest Maiden Inn.

Reyne Brenton: (Rain) A young man, almost twenty-two years old and the owner, along with his brother Daedyn, of an alphen nut orchard on the outskirts of Hensdale. He is polite and well-liked by the community. Currently engaged to be married to his childhood sweetheart, Mithany.

Richelle: (Rish-el) Member of the KCG.

S'Leen: (Sah-lyn) Prudent serving of the Council of Prudents. She is an ally of First Lord Jerithan Cree.

Santander: (San-tan-der) General Manger of the Brenton alphen orchard. He has the reputation of being a gruff and demanding boss.

Satrin: (Sah-trin) God of water, air and fire. Son of Father Sun and Mother Earth.

Serco, Garragent: (Sir-coe, Ger-ah-gent)) Prudent assigned to the Kingdom of Adelle and who sits on the Coucil of Prudents.

Signum Circulus: A religious gesture made with the thumb moving in a circle around the heart and the hand coming to rest over the heart. It is a ritual to invoke internal peace through divine reverence.

Simurmure: (Sim-er-mure) Mother Earth. Mother to Teth, Satrin, Efros, and Malthis.

Spetzer Bilseck: (Spet-zher Bill-sek) Lives in Hensdale, same age as Reyne, and since childhood, had a thing for Mithany.

Sura Brenal: (Sue-rah) The wife of Hollid Brenal. Died long ago.

Tane Tomelai: Daughter of Madrotti and Kaythlin Tomelai. As the oldest child, age twenty-one, she is the heir apparent Chancellor of the Kingdom of Adelle.

Teth: Patron goddess of the children of Earth in the realm of Tartica. Daughter of Father Sun and Mother Earth. Born before the Great Destruction and savior of Tartica. She gathered up and led the survivors of the Second Age to settle in Tartica at the start of the Third Age.

Tetrip: (Tet-trip) An older man serving as Judjurex of Hensdale.

Thuggery: Loose association of criminals in Teth.

Ting: Member of the KCG.

Treestone: Wood product that tranforms into stone once treated in a special brine.

Trell: Young man, native to Hensdale, and a member of Spetzer's inner circle who frequents the Forest Maiden Inn.

Tweener: A person with the ability to move between the two known alternate dimensions of Earth, Evidar and Tartica.

Tylus: (Tie-lus) Assassin from Evidar and a member of Dylla's team.

Valillia: (Vah-lil-lee-ah) Older woman living in Hensdale and wife to Dorana.

Y'vay: (Yah-vay) The young, fun-loving adult daughter of the shopkeeper Hangus, living in Hensdale.

Connect With The Author

Thank you for reading *Utopia Falling: A Darkness Rises*. Building a relationship with readers is very important to me. Please let me know what you think of the book by leaving a review on the retailer's website where you purchased your copy or another you prefer. It would mean a lot to me and is easy to do.

Join my newsletter to receive advance notices on upcoming books in *The Utopia Falling Saga,* as well as progress reports, blog posts, and the occasional "extra" for those in my reader's group.

https://www.rcvielee.com/newsletter

You can also follow me on social media.

https://www.instagram.com/rcvielee
https://www.facebook.com/bob.vielee
https://www.twitter.com/rcvielee
https://www.goodreads.com

Books by R.C. Vielee

The Utopia Falling Saga

Utopia Falling: A Darkness Rises
Chaos Ascending: A Feast of Betrayal
Salvation Bleeding: Forge of the Soul Stone

To explore more visit https://www.RCVielee.com

About the Author

Robert Vielee

Robert grew up in a small town in northern New Jersey. He is married with four children and now lives with his family in Pennsylvania. Before turning his attention to writing, Robert's creative drive took him across North America as a freelance nature photographer—while holding down a day job. He loves nature, reading epic fantasy, and most of all, his family.

Connect online with Robert on his author website

RCVielee.com

ACKNOWLEDGMENTS

I would like to thank the many people I've encountered on this adventure who have been mentors, educators, and supporters. To the readers of the early draft, whose input helped improve the story, including Roger, Mark, and Gretchen, thank you.

To the editors Ciara, Lucy, and Kim, whose expertise contributed immensely, I could not have gotten this far without you. My heartfelt thanks.

To my loving wife Louise, thank you for your understanding and patience. To my wonderful children, whose creativity knowingly and unknowingly contributed here and there.